I0788587

A Crown of Deceit & Ruin

A Crown of Deceit & Ruin

JESSACA WILLIS

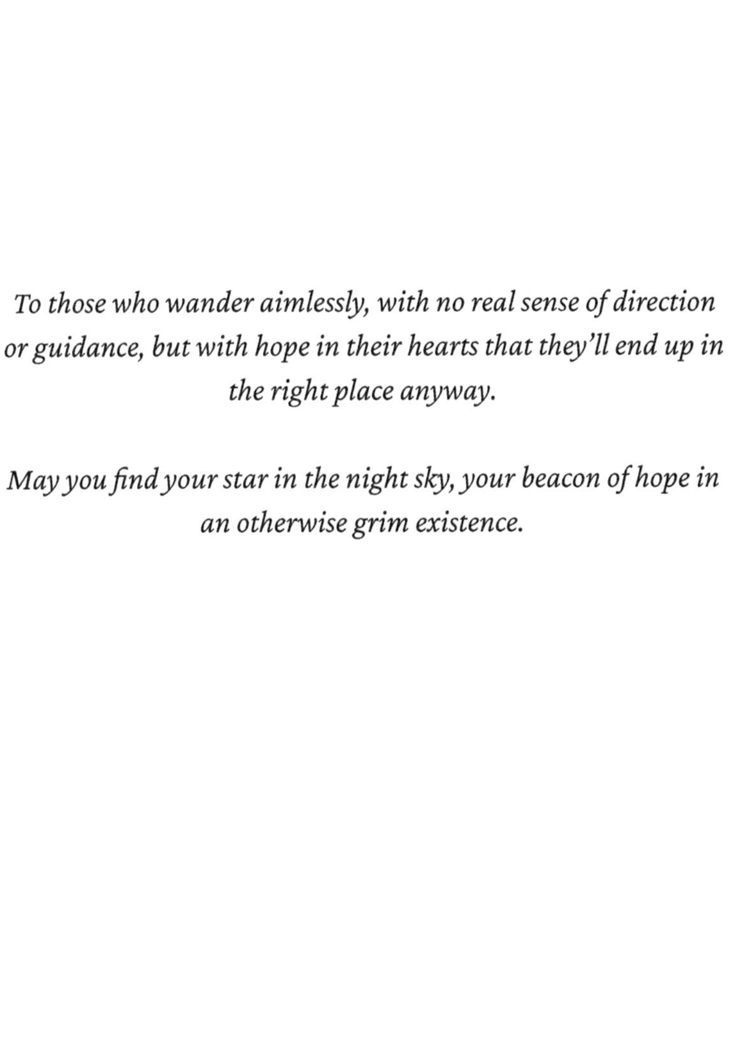

To those who wander aimlessly, with no real sense of direction or guidance, but with hope in their hearts that they'll end up in the right place anyway.

May you find your star in the night sky, your beacon of hope in an otherwise grim existence.

Grimtol
Arrin, City in the Clouds
Forneller the Frozen
Revular the Lamentating
NEGLECTED BAY
THE CLOUDED MOUNTAINS
TEMPTATION SPRINGS
Skydust Farms
Greenwitch
GHOSTLIGHT GULF
The Floating Isles
THE PASSA
Cynallore
SERENITY LAKE
Wingham
LOST LAKE
SELKIE LAGOON
Arebal Farms
Grant
MAELLYHONA OCEAN
WOODLAND OF THE SPRITES
Galorfin, City on Fire
Varlow
MORTAL
Ba
Blackmeadow
SEA OF THE MOLTEN SERPENT
Whispering Wasteland
INNISET SEA
UNFATHOMED WATERS
Alvernia
The Cursed Bridges of Aenwyn
The Ruins of Caelora
UNFATHOMED WATERS
LOURK BAY
CURSED CRAGS OF CAELORA
DORMINE OCEAN

ISAZ OCEAN
ISAZ OCEAN
NOFASKE SEA
Fortress of Fang the Bold
SANGAR MOUNTAINS
SphsFogar (North)
OsFogar (East)
SFogar
HAILSTONE SEA
Kingdom of Irongate
HINGSOL LAKE
Silent Crossing
RepsFogar (South)
Dornwood
The Hollows
LAKE OF SHADOWS
The Secret Barrow of Zensly Grimshane
DORMINE OCEAN
Shademoor
Rayong
MISTMOOR LAKE
Nanvor
DESOLATE PLAINS OF SADRE
Fortress of Thirst
The Great City of Vallonve
BAY OF LOST SOULS
Vallonve Temple
The Lost Isle
Vallonve Ruins
The Spears of Barga
MAINS
The Cursed Prison
DORMINE OCEAN
MAW OF DEATH
Hidden Oasis
Mutiny Bay
CARMAERN BAY

MORE BOOKS BY JESSACA WILLIS

THE CURSED KINGDOMS OF GRIMTOL

A Delicate Betrayal, Book 0

A Crown of Deceit & Ruin, Book 1

A Crown of Ashes & Death, Book 2

TBA

REAPERS OF VELTUUR

Assassin Reaper, Book 0

Soul of the Crow, Book 1

Heart of the Sungem, Book 2

Fate of the Vulture, Book 3

PRIMORDIALS OF SHADOWTHORN

Shadow Crusade, Book 1

Blighted Heart, Book 2

Immortal Return, Book 3

BLOOD & MAGIC ETERNAL

Hunger & Cursed Shadows, Book 0

Blood & Magic Eternal, Book 1

TBA

CONTENTS

Content Warning ... xi

1. A Bargain Struck in Iron ... 1
2. Into the Wilds ... 14
3. A Traitor ... 23
4. The Maw of Death ... 34
5. Cute & Nefarious ... 46
6. A Strange New World ... 57
7. What Happens in the Alleyway... ... 68
8. The Sting of Betrayal ... 86
9. To Trust a Prince ... 104
10. Adventuring Starts Here ... 131
11. A Gift ... 141
12. The Monster Inside ... 148
13. No Way Out ... 160
14. Family Ties ... 179
15. A Kingdom of Iron Spires ... 193
16. The Prince Returns ... 205
17. A Royal Reunion ... 210
18. Lost Family ... 223
19. A Queen's Command ... 239
20. The Bargains We Make ... 250
21. An Awkward Dinner ... 264
22. The Library ... 271
23. A Brief Lesson in History ... 276
24. By Week's End ... 304
25. The Queen's Magic ... 308
26. What Happens by the Fountain... ... 327
27. Songs, Dances, and Visions of the Dead ... 349

28. A Lesson in the Ballroom   362

29. The Dance of Two Princesses   373

30. A Vision, A Cure   383

31. A Decree from the Oracle Princess   391

32. The Dungeon   405

33. Forgiveness is a Tearing of the Heart   423

34. An Army   430

35. Into the Hollows   438

36. The Touch of Death   466

37. Daughter of Daybreak   475

38. The Cursed Beast   478

39. Awakened   485

40. The Road Ahead   492

Leave a Review   502

More Books by Jessaca   503

More Books by Jessaca   505

About the Author   507

CONTENT WARNING

A Crown of Deceit & Ruin is an adult book that features mature content. Below are some of the possible triggers found in this book; this is not an exhaustive list, as triggers will vary by reader, but the heaviest ones are listed below:

- Captivity/imprisonment
- Animal abuse/sacrifice (related to a system of magic)
- Torture (past, referred to, not on page)
- Uncertain parentage/lineage
- Maiming
- Deception

Please proceed with caution if any of the aforementioned themes will cause you emotional distress.

A Crown of Deceit & Ruin

JESSACA WILLIS

CHAPTER 1

A BARGAIN STRUCK IN IRON

ELORA

Elora leaned against the hailstone bars, grateful for the faint blue glow they provided in the otherwise dark and grim dungeon. Her mind was veering from one thought to the next like it usually did on the long, cold nights she was imprisoned here. It wasn't like there was much else to do but sit. Exist. To stew on her own persistent survival.

The saddest part was: this was perhaps the most peaceful moment she had experienced in years. And *that* realization soured her. Made her feel ashamed. Because how much had Elora given up that she was actually finding herself grateful in this moment—and for what? Simply because the torture had ceased? That she'd found herself in new captors' clutches, uncertain of what they were going to do with her?

She *should* be worried. Fearful that they were going to do something spectacularly awful with her, just waiting for her guard to finally drop.

And tonight it had.

Down the torch-lit corridor, Elora heard the heavy screech of the dungeon door opening. She listened to the footsteps that echoed, marching closer, as she tried to deduce if it was one set or two among them—if a guard was simply doing their rounds or if they were bringing another prisoner to their new home.

Elora only noted one set of footsteps though. And it wasn't until they halted before her cell door that true dread started to churn in her chest.

Keys jingled in the man's hand. Elora's back stiffened, alertness crashing down on her like a tree.

"You're coming with me," the guard said, cracking the door open enough to toss a pair of manacles inside. "Put these on."

The light blue shackles glowed faintly at her feet. More hailstone. So that even while she would be taken out of one prison, she would still be contained by another.

Elora did as she was told, slipping her frail wrists through the holes and latching them tightly. She held her bound hands out for him to inspect. He eyed them warily from every angle before opening the door farther and gesturing for her to come out.

No longer did Elora have it in her to ask questions or argue. She had learned years ago that it served no purpose. So she did as she was commanded, stopping just outside the hailstone cell as the guard instructed so that he could make a final examination of her restraints.

He reached out with a shaking hand, and clutched in his fist was a single, white flower—they always chose the white ones. As if those were the only buds that could be tested against her *impurity*.

The guard pressed the delicate petals against her grey skin and flinched, preparing for the worst.

Nothing happened. It never did and never would. Not as long as they had their hailstone in place and had her too scared to do anything as reckless as trying to break away from its magic.

Relaxing a bit, the guard threw the flower to the ground and grabbed Elora by the underarm. Distantly she wondered where he was taking her, what he would do to her once they arrived, but part of her didn't care. Everything had already been done. Asphyxiation, drowning, branding, breaking. There was no new torment they could inflict upon her that her previous Caeloran captors hadn't already forced her to endure.

Elora allowed the guard to drag her out of the dungeon and into the cool night air.

She nearly cried at the first inhale. Flowers and the rainfall from a recent storm; it was the first whiff of fresh air she'd had in who knew how many years and she could've stood there forever, trying to discern the different aromas and which species of flora they belonged to, if the guard hadn't tugged her along.

It shattered her heart to think that this could be the last time she ever smelled something so beautiful and vibrant ever again—that was until he marched her through the garden itself. It was large enough that Elora could've spent a dozen afternoons in it, wandering the winding paths as her thoughts drifted in and around every corner. She lost count of the number of blooms they passed by, but knew there were enough to fulfill every color of the rainbow tenfold.

She wanted to linger like she would've back at home. But that was a different life. A different Elora.

They emerged on the other side of the hedges before she could blink, and then she was being led into the cold, stone castle of Irongate.

Now the worried beating of her heart became erratic.

She had never met the royals of Irongate before, but had heard the rumors of their fierceness, the cold iron that seemed to flow through their veins and that of which their kingdom was named for. Their castle was much the same. Cold, dark, and unmoving. Previously, when she had been a prisoner of Caelora, Elora had only been brought into their castle once to face a hasty and biased judgement from their king before being thrown into the dungeon and left to his torturers. She had never been shown proof of her wrongdoings, or read her rights, or anything. Mostly because the citizens of Caelora didn't view her as human and worthy of rights at all. They didn't view the Ashen that way. Especially not ones from the royal family who were villainized and blamed for the resurrection of dragons and the chaos they had once reigned upon the kingdoms. Some claimed they'd even seen her and her brethren riding atop the massive beasts as they stormed through the southern regions, incinerating everything and everyone. But how in the Hollows would the Ashen ride dragons when their touch alone would've killed them? Just like it did with every other living thing.

The Caeloran people had never wanted reason though. Only someone to blame.

And she had been one of the poor souls to have carried that weight.

So when Elora had been transferred to Irongate, she wasn't surprised to face no trial there either. She'd simply been bagged and dragged into the dingy dungeon, left there to rot for years.

The guard holding her now nodded to one of his brethren standing post outside two large double doors. The other man opened them, and Elora and her jailor entered. The room was so dark inside that it took Elora's eyes a moment to adjust—despite years of captivity—as they walked down the lengthy path and came upon a dais with a throne and a queen perched inside.

To be completely honest, Elora had forgotten Irongate had procured another queen. Yet there she was, cradled in a throne of slate spires as sharp as the cold look in her obsidian eyes.

The queen was leaning on one of the armrests with her night-black gown draped over her slender, crossed legs. Beside her, Elora noted a blond-haired, blue-eyed young man. His golden, gleaming armor made him seem out of place in such a dark and dreary room, but he held himself with an air of authority, as if he belonged there more than any of them.

"I don't believe we've ever had the pleasure of meeting." The queen's saccharine voice echoed around the hall. She cocked her head to one side as she took in the sight of Elora. "I'm Queen Signe, and this is Prince Leighton, heir to the Irongate throne."

The queen paused long enough that Elora realized she was expecting something from her in return. A response. A gesture. It had been so long since Elora had found herself back in a royal court, that it took her a moment to dust off the cobwebs to remember the expected decorum.

Stiffly, she bowed. "Pleased to meet you, your highnesses." Her voice was so raspy, she almost didn't recognize it.

"The pleasure is ours." When Elora came back up, there was a hint of pride etched in the queen's cracked porcelain smile. "Thank you to both of you for joining me this day—"

"I wasn't aware we had a choice," is what Elora thought she heard the prince grumble, but from this distance, and with the crackling of torches beside her, it was difficult to say for certain.

If the queen was offended, she didn't let it show.

"I've summoned you both to propose a truce. As you're well aware, our lands have been...at odds for a number of years now. When Caelora fell, we inherited the title of enemy to the Ashen by default. They had been our allies, and we intended to aid and support them until King Everard could return to his throne. But I fear that has become increasingly unlikely."

Something about the queen's actions, the exaggerated shift of her tone and expressions, seemed fake to Elora. Perhaps it was just the dim lighting, or the fact that she wasn't used to the mannerisms of Signe's people, but whatever it was put Elora on edge. Made it difficult to focus on what she the queen was saying, let alone to anticipate what she was leading up to—which certainly would be something dreadful if they had brought Elora all the way out of her dungeon.

A muscle ticked in the prince's jaw. *"Increasingly unlikely* how?"

Queen Signe inhaled deeply, as if it brought her immense pain to relay whatever information she was about to share with them. "I'm afraid the Sky-Blessed have sent me a vision. King Everard will—he will fall by the year's end. Our own King Ulfaskr as well."

Elora tried to keep the equal amounts of shock and elation from her face. King Everard was the man who'd sentenced her in Caelora, while King Ulfaskr was once the reigning ruler of Irongate, and although Elora had no personal encounters with him, his reputation for cruelty preceded him.

If both of them fell, they would become the first of the cursed queens and kings to succumb to the dark magic that had spread across the kingdoms, as far as Elora knew.

She had a million questions but didn't muster a single one. Silence had been trained into her.

"How will they fall?" Leighton growled, a vein in his forehead throbbing. This was his father they were talking about, King Ulfaskr, a man who'd been cursed into a beast and sequestered from his people ever since. Or at least, that was what Elora had overheard during her years of captivity here. "How will my father die?"

"It was unclear," Queen Signe answered. "I only saw his corpse. It was dreadful. He was so broken and—"

With hands firmly planted on his hips, Prince Leighton began pacing the dais. "But we can stop this. You said in your vision it would happen within the year, so we still have time."

The queen looked upon him pityingly. "I'm afraid not.

King Everard has a year. Ulfaskr's death came much sooner. Before the first hints of winter, I believe."

When he reached the wall, Prince Leighton slammed a fist upon the stones. The curtains covering the floor-to-ceiling windows shook, a few slivers of moonlight seeping into the dark throne room.

The queen flinched out of the way of them, hissing at Leighton to be more careful.

Elora had heard about Queen Signe's plight from some of the other prisoners as well, that she refused to leave the castle and step into the light of day for fear of the transformation it would wrought upon her. But Elora hadn't believed them until just now. After all, that was unheard of with the curse that had befallen the kingdoms. All the other monarchs were true beasts with no human form, not something in between like Signe was.

Once the curtains resettled, the queen straightened her gown with the flat of her hands, sitting taller again.

"As I was saying, you have both been summoned here today because our people are in need of a truce. Two of the most powerful kingdoms of Grimtol will soon lose their reigning rulers, and that would leave us vulnerable to any attacks from Eynallore."

In another life, Elora would've protested. The people of Eynallore—*her* people—weren't malicious fighters and brutes. If anything, they'd been begging for peace for decades while the rest of Grimtol kept capturing and torturing them.

But Elora had been locked away for the last couple decades. There was no telling how much had changed, especially after the Cursed Night. Perhaps the people of Eynallore had grown desperate.

Leighton spun around from the wall, his flaxen locks springing around his pinched face. "What are you proposing then?"

"A unification through marriage," the queen said simply.

Elora almost fell over.

She didn't understand. Had clearly heard the queen incorrectly. Because there was no way the queen could possibly be suggesting that Elora marry the gleaming prince of Irongate while she herself was standing before them in rags, covered in her own filth and grime.

"Are you mad?" Leighton bellowed, storming across the dais to the side of the throne. He gripped the armrest so tightly, his knuckles whitened as he towered over the queen and bellowed. "I can't marry her! She's tainted—an Ashen. One touch would kill me!"

Queen Signe didn't flinch, but gave a half-hearted flick of her wrist. "We have hailstone for that."

Elora's hand caressed one side of the hailstone bracers she'd put on earlier. What would that mean exactly? That she'd have to wear them always? That she'd become a prisoner bride, shackled for the rest of her life?

The queen continued, addressing Leighton. "I have held the throne for your father long enough, and your name-day has come and gone too many times to count. The people are ready for you to ascend to the throne."

"I won't do it," he argued. "I won't marry her."

Queen Signe rose like shadows incarnate. "You shall

marry her because that is what a king would do. He marries to forge alliances to protect his people."

"We'll find a different bride then."

"There is no other bride who will forge a peace between the Ironbloods and the Ashen."

Leighton's mouth was unhinged, a bewildered expression freezing his features in horror. It looked as though he wanted to say a million things, but ultimately settled upon one word, one quiet, sad word that even made Elora's chest ache. "Why?"

The queen exhaled sadly. "As I've said, the people need a king, and it is time for—"

"No, I mean why this!" He gestured toward Elora with disgust, and just like that, the sympathy she'd felt for him evaporated. "Why *her* and a truce with her foul people? If we simply need a king, we already have one. We don't need a wedding to form an alliance. That's why my father was meant to marry you."

"Yes, well..." Queen Signe's gaze dropped to the floor. It was the first genuine look Elora thought she had seen from her. "A lot of good that alliance has done us. The people do not care for it. They do not care for me. They demand an Ironblood on the throne, and we require a solution to the threat posed by the Ashen."

Prince Leighton scoffed. He began pacing again.

Both Elora and the queen just watched him. Waiting. Letting him decide as if his choice was the only one that mattered. But any time Elora tried thinking about what *she* wanted, she couldn't. Couldn't allow herself to so much as hope for a voice in the matter.

"No," Leighton finally declared. "If we need a king, I'll give them one. I'll save my father. I'll bring him back."

The queen rolled her dark eyes. "There is no saving him. We've tried searching for the Corrupt Queen. We've tried beseeching the Sky-Blessed for an answer. No one knows how to lift the curse. You're insisting upon a fool's errand—"

But if she was hoping to reach the prince with some semblance of logic, it was of no use. His mind was already made up and Leighton stormed out of the throne room without another word.

When it was just Elora and the queen, Signe sighed and plopped back onto her throne. "Well, what say you?"

Once again, it took a moment to realize the queen was expecting an answer. "Me?"

"Of course, you. You are the other party in this matter."

"Oh. Well, I..."

The queen heaved another sigh. Every breathe of air that blew out of her sounded more irritated than the last. "Would you prefer to rot in a dungeon, or would you like to be the Queen of Irongate someday?"

Elora twisted, looking back the way the prince had just fled. "But Prince Leighton said—"

"I am aware of what he said. But the vision I had was clear: King Ulfaskr will die. Leighton will return in ruin. And when he does, he'll see no other path forward but the one I am suggesting. So, I will ask just one last time: what is your answer?"

Elora stood there, stunned.

It had been so many years since she had been offered a

choice about anything. Let alone something like *this*. To become a queen? Of an enemy kingdom that had held her prisoner for years? It all felt like a trick. Like it was too good to be true—or rather, the worst sort of nightmare she could've imagined. What was she missing?

"Where would I reside?" she asked hesitantly.

A trill of laughter fluttered from the queen. "Why, in the castle, of course. I've already prepared a bedchamber for you."

Elora's legs wobbled. "I'd...be given a bedchamber?"

"Of course. We can't have our queen living in filth and squalor."

Elora's brows furrowed, so much so that she felt the metal crown embedded in her forehead pinching the skin there. Some days, she forgot it existed. Forgot her own royal bloodline and lineage. That felt like another lifetime ago. But perhaps it would be a life she would soon get to revisit.

But there was that crushing ache of hope again, twisting and writhing inside her like poison. She shoved it down.

"I...don't understand."

The queen leaned forward. "This is no trick. It really is quite simple: would you like to return to the dungeons or would you prefer to be crowned a queen—in every sense of the word?"

If it truly wasn't a trick, if there was no catch, then Signe was right. It really was that simple. Elora could remain in a dungeon or ascend to a throne—either way, she would still be a prisoner. But didn't one of those options sound slightly less terrible than the other?

"Yes." Elora's voice cracked—not the way she wanted to start her reign as a queen. She straightened her back, the chains around her wrists clanking. "It would be my honor to end the feud between the Ashen and the Ironbloods. I will be your queen if Prince Leighton will have me."

Outside the castle walls, Elora swore she heard the solemn rumble of thunder.

CHAPTER 2

INTO THE WILDS
KESTREL

Drumming her fingers on the stone windowsill, Kestrel stared across the sea at the dragon bones half-buried in the sand.

From where she was perched in the highest window in a tower on an opposite shore, the sun-bleached carcass was a small thing that she could pinch between her fingertips—and she had. Hundreds, if not thousands of times over the nineteen years she had lived in that dreadful tower.

Dreadful? Thom's scoff rattled in her mind now. *It's a far cry from dreadful, if we're comparing it to the Wilds.*

Kestrel caught herself smirking and rolling her eyes at him, even though Thom wasn't there to say any of it. In fact, he hadn't been there for quite some time now.

Thom was late. *Very* late. The kind of late that left Kestrel tormented with worry.

When Thom had left for one of his routine supply runs, he told her he would be back within a fortnight.

But a fortnight had come and gone. Then another.

For weeks now, Kestrel had been waiting for her father's return, yet there had been no sign of him anywhere. And there was no possible explanation for such a delay other than the obvious...

Something was terribly wrong.

Kestrel sensed it in her bones the way she could sense a storm coming just by the scent of the sea breeze wafting in through the window. Something was wrong but she didn't know what to do other than to sit there and worry and hope that she was mistaken.

An overactive imagination, Thom would've chided. *No doubt thanks to those books you consume like wildfire.*

In his defense, he was right. She *did* have an extraordinary imagination. Spending years in isolation and having nothing but one's own company would do that to a person.

In her best moments, her diligent mind helped get her through the long and lonesome days when Thom was gone scouring the realm for supplies, food, and information about the curse. While he was away, Kestrel was enthralled by her daydreaming: pretending she was a battle-hardened warrior protecting all the lands, or falling in love with a charming prince or princess, or even simple things like strolling through a bustling town and chatting with people in the market—since those things were no longer possible.

In her worst moments, her thoughts wandered all-too frequently to any number of the vile creatures that had conquered the realm, and the brutal deaths they might be inflicting upon the only person she had ever known.

Kestrel couldn't stop imagining—in vivid detail—all the possible ways that the cursed beasts of the Wilds could've harmed Thom. Maybe he'd been caught in the plague of locusts and scorpions that would sometimes flood the desert in the dead of night. Or worse, perhaps he had encountered the cinders like she had, all those years ago, and they had clambered for him with their scorched hands until he'd had nowhere left to run, and no one around to save him.

Kestrel shuddered at the thought.

If Thom hadn't been there that day, if he hadn't slain that cinder and dragged her out of the oasis where she had been sinking like a pitiful stone, there would be no more Kestrel. Without him to save her, she would've died. But who was out there to save Thom?

Her rampant imaginings were getting harder to keep at bay the longer he was delayed, which was precisely why she had been staring longingly out her window at a dragon corpse—she needed a distraction. It was the only thing keeping her sane.

However, right at that moment the fog that typically clouded the nearby island resettled, and the dragon bones along with the distant shoreline disappeared behind it.

Kestrel sighed. At least the erratic sun was sticking around today. It had been up in the sky for a number of hours now, with little sign of retreating anytime soon. She always appreciated its longer visits; being stuck in a tower alone during the dark hours was unpleasant to say the least, but even more so when Thom was gone.

Even with the sun shining down upon her tower though, she was restless.

Kestrel tossed the orange length of her braid over her shoulder and sprang from the stone windowsill. She paced the small confines of their home.

"Come on, Thom," she pleaded to the empty chair where he usually sat after a long journey to take off his boots. "Where are you?"

The chair, of course, gave no reply.

Unease was brewing inside her; like a kettle put over a roaring fire, it could not be contained.

"What am I supposed to do?" she grumbled to no one. When she came face to face with the bare shelves on the kitchen side of the room, Kestrel threw her arms up. "Just look at this. Almost every jar of pickled or salted anything is empty. Every burlap sack deflated." She stormed over to the fireplace and peered inside the pot of soup she had left hanging there, only one serving remaining. "That won't even last me through the night."

"*It's called rationing,*" she answered for Thom, mimicking his gruff voice to near perfection. After spending so much time on her own, speaking for him was a habit she had developed to make herself feel less alone. And now more than ever, she needed it. Needed *him* to help soothe her.

Kestrel spun around to square off with Thom's chair. "I *have* been rationing. For weeks. The whole reason you left was because we were running out of supplies—there wasn't much left to work with before then, let alone now. I'm—" Noticing that the end of her braid was starting to get damp, and that this part of the conversation was one she would rather face with dignity, Kestrel spat out her hair, and straightened her spine— "I think

I'm reaching the point where I need to make a decision..."

The stagnant air in their tower turned to ice.

Thom wasn't even there, and yet she could feel his ire like she was standing atop hot coals.

Leaving wasn't an option. It was one of Thom's most adamant rules: remain inside the tower where it was safe, and do not leave no matter what.

The one time she had disobeyed him, she had almost gotten herself killed.

Thom still teased her about that incident. Last time her father had left, he'd jokingly said to her, "Don't go making yourself cinder-food this time, alright, Little Fury?"

At the time, she had only dragged her eyes away from her book long enough to glower and assure him that she had no intentions of leaving the book she was reading unfinished, let alone the safe confines of their tower.

Thom had chuckled and hoisted his pack over his shoulder before descending the stairs, neither of them knowing it would be the last time they would see each other for a long, long while.

Nibbling on the curled tip of her braid, Kestrel reached the top of the dimly lit stairwell. It spiraled downward, and for weeks she had kept the candles along the stairs lit for him, just in case he returned when it was dark out. All the candles had burned out by now though. She was rationing what was left of those too.

"How long am I supposed to wait?"

Even with the few small windows peppered along the outer walls, Kestrel couldn't see much farther than the first few steps. Still, she peered down the dark stairwell, foolishly expectant. As if any second now Thom might hobble up those steps and—

A horrible screech pierced her solitude. Distant but unnerving.

Kestrel's wide eyes jerked to the nearest slit of a window. All she could see was the blue sky, but she knew something—or someone—was off in the distance, shrieking in agony.

"Thom!"

Kestrel didn't hesitate.

She lunged for the walls and began scaling the uneven stones. It wasn't the first time she had climbed the interior of their tower—after all, what else was there for her to do when she was bored and antsy for entertainment? As a child, she had spent countless hours scaling the uneven bricks until she could boulder all the way down the winding staircase and back up again. Over and over, she would climb until her fingers were blistered and her feet were scuffed and bruised.

So it took her no time at all to reach the first window.

She pressed her skull against the stone cutout, her head too big to fit through now that she was older, and she tried to peer through the small gap.

Nothing but sand and a lone tumbleweed were visible.

Kestrel shimmied to the next window.

This time, she spotted a commotion. Off in the distance, beyond the smattering of cacti and desert flora between her and a far away treeline, she thought she saw movement. Something darting in between the trees. She could hear someone shouting as well, but from this distance, Kestrel couldn't tell if they were the one doing the chasing, or if they were being chased.

It sent her back to when she was younger. How frightened and doomed she had been, trying to evade a cinder with no one around to help her.

Her heart thundered fiercely against her chest. The palms of her hands had become so slick with sweat, she was starting to lose her grip.

Before she could fall, Kestrel took note of the direction the commotion was heading, and deftly made her way back down to the stone steps.

If ever there had been a reason to leave her tower, this was it.

Thom could be in trouble—no, he *was* in trouble. She'd known that for a while now, even before the screeching. But that horrifying sound *could* belong to him. He might need her help.

But trepidation gnawed at her insides, the same way she started gnawing on her hair again.

She hadn't wanted it to come to *this*. If Kestrel could've had it her way, she would've stayed locked away in this tower for the rest of her life, perfectly content to be buried in a book or gazing out across the sea every now and then, wondering about how the dragon had fallen, let alone the entire continent. She would've spent the rest of her days safe. Content.

If she left the tower, she could die.

But if she didn't, Thom might die. The only person she had ever known.

He was out there, possibly running for his life, maybe even injured or maimed—Kestrel didn't know. But she did know that right now the prospect of his life meant more to her than her own.

Kestrel stormed back up the stairs. She changed to clothes that seemed better suited for travel, things Thom typically wore: an airy tunic that she tucked into a pair of baggy trousers with patches sewn throughout. She tied a belt around her waist to make sure they wouldn't fall. It consequently gave her somewhere to stuff one of the sharpest knives they owned, just in case. The only thing she couldn't find was a pair of extra goggles—Thom always wore some whenever he left the tower, to protect his eyes from the frequent and unpredictable sandstorms that could blow through the barren desert. All she could find was a long, brown scarf, that she tied loosely around her neck, in case she needed to shield her face.

For a moment, she considered taking off her ring. It had belonged to her mother, and so the last thing she wanted to do was risk losing it. Then again, she had never taken the thing off, not once since Thom had given it to her.

Deciding against it, Kestrel turned her attention to the last of her tasks and grabbed a tattered pack from underneath Thom's cot. She hastily shoved a few supplies into it, things she had seen Thom cram into his bags for his excursions over the years—a waterskin, dried fruits, and the last of the bread.

Then, Kestrel turned to the dimly lit stairwell and sighed into the darkness.

"I can do this."

For Thom, she would have to. She would save him, and hopefully not die trying.

And so, for the first time in twelve years, since Kestrel had snuck out of their tower and been chased into an oasis by a cinder where she had nearly drowned, Kestrel would leave the safe confines of her tower and once again venture into the Wilds.

CHAPTER 3

A TRAITOR

ELORA

The shackle around Elora's neck made her skin itch. When she had agreed to the queen's proposal, she hadn't realized wearing such an overt sign of her captivity would be part of the deal. Then again, like the good little hostage she was, she hadn't exactly asked to review the fine print of the arrangement either. She had simply heard the word *bedchamber* and that had been all the convincing she had needed.

When Elora left her room in the earliest of the first-hours today, she had tried tucking the neckline of her silver gown under the hailstone collar, but even that wasn't protecting her sensitive skin enough. The anti-magic properties of the shackle seemed to be pervasive; hopefully in time, she'd become used to the *necklace*—that was what they wanted her to call it, a necklace. And Elora supposed if she hadn't known it for what it was, she might've found it to be a beautiful statement piece, the solid band of light blue stone a complimentary contrast to her slate-grey pigment.

But a collar was a collar.

A chain: a chain.

And although Queen Signe had released Elora from the dungeon and was now granting her permission to roam the castle grounds more freely, Elora knew she was still a prisoner.

But she tried not thinking about that as she enjoyed the modicum of freedom she had been granted to stroll the Irongate gardens.

They were the most beautiful sight her sorry eyes had beheld in decades. The white-pebbled paths wound in and around hundreds of species of flora, every size and shape imaginable. And Elora admired every one of them—the bright pink, cup-shaped petals that were still filled of dew from the last rainstorm; the bundles of clustered goldenrod flowers with a swarm of hungry honeybees surrounding them; the white and ruby roses that seemed to glow like gems wherever the sunlight touched them.

Elora marveled at the beauty of each and every display, even if flora here still paled in comparison to the breathtaking and wild beauty of the plants and flowers that thrived in Eynallore.

This was home now. She would need to get used to it. And truthfully, she *could* get used to daily strolls through this garden—there were far grimmer places to reign.

Every time she inhaled the richly floral scent though, her eyes closing gently in serenity, she feared that when she opened them again, she would find herself back inside the Irongate dungeon. Or worse, that the Caeloran Guard would be marching toward her, ready to drag her back to her former abusers. Suddenly, the sunshine beaming down felt like the burn of a hot iron. The gentle breeze wafting against her skin felt like the stinging lacerations of whips and knives and every other pain-inducing torture device the Caelorans had taken to her skin.

Elora cradled her arms over herself, her fingers rubbing all the places where they had harmed her. Only there was no proof of their cruelty—she had no scars to show for all that she had endured. That was part of the unbearable curse of being an Ashen: immortality and rejuvenation of the flesh. It made her the perfect prisoner of war. The perfect torture victim. Immune to death, but fully susceptible to pain.

Elora breathed in another waft of flowers, pulling herself out of those dark memories and back to the present. To the garden that represented her home now. But a home different than Eynallore.

She wondered what her family was doing at that very moment, if her sibling Dinian had found someone knew to pester, and what had come of their father, Aethic—presumably, he'd succumbed to the Corrupt Queen's curse as well, but in what ways and with how much severity, Elora didn't know. However, the thought of them ached just as much as it brought her joy, because now she knew she was never going back to Eynallore. Never returning to her people. She was to marry the prince of Irongate and become their queen so as to secure peace and assuage any historical grievances between their two lands.

Even if she wasn't, it wasn't like the Ashen had wanted her.

No one had come for her.

Without Queen Signe's bargain, Elora would still be stuck in that dungeon.

So she shook thoughts of Eynallore and her family away, and focused on her future instead.

If she was to live in Irongate, if she was to be their queen, she would need to play by their courtly rules—starting with the queen.

Reluctantly, Elora pulled herself out of the gardens and made her way back into the castle. The rest of the castle had finally awoken, the servants scurrying through the halls to start their day. They gave Elora a wide berth, even with the hailstone *necklace* rendering her Ashen powers utterly useless. Elora tried not to take it personally, and she didn't want to make anyone uncomfortable, so she tried giving them space.

But as someone marched by with a heaping tray of fresh pastries, she had to stop them.

"Excuse me, are you taking those to the dining hall?"

"Y-yes, my lady," the young woman squeaked. She glanced down the torch-lit hallway as if she was worried someone was about to yell at her. "I was told the royal family is expected to dine any minute now. Has there been a change of plans?"

Elora faltered. She was no longer accustomed to people looking to her for answers, let alone that the people of Irongate would willingly seek the word of an Ashen. But she supposed by now the queen had already informed the entire castle about her presence and the role she would soon inherit, otherwise every guard would've been upon her the minute she stepped foot out of her bedchamber.

"No, no change of plans, but I am in need of your assistance. I am still learning the layout of the castle and don't know where our meals are to be held."

The servant gave a curt nod, not a hair of her tightly wrapped, blonde bun falling out of place. "Of course, Princess Elora. Right this way."

Elora held her breath as she followed the woman through the castle, wondering who else might be joining the meal. No matter who it was, it would be awkward nonetheless. There were centuries of distrust between the Ironbloods and the Ashen; that wouldn't just disappear overnight. But hopefully the more they came to know Elora, the more trust they could help foster between their people.

Elora was surprised to find the dining hall nearly empty, only the queen waiting inside.

"Blessed day, Princess Elora," the queen said in greeting, a golden goblet of wine swirling in her hand.

Elora gave her a stiff bow, still getting used to the respect and decorum she had long-since forgotten. "Blessed day, Queen Signe."

"Please, sit. Join me for breakfast."

Smoothing her silk gown beneath her, Elora did as was requested and took a seat near the queen at the end of the table, but with a respectable number of chairs between them.

"Will it just be the two of us?" Elora asked.

The queen finished a sip. "I'm afraid so. The twins left

with Prince Leighton yesterday, and Barnabus and Niculas rarely take breakfast this early in the day."

All the while the queen spoke, Elora couldn't stop staring at the crimson stain on her teeth. It seemed thicker than wine, and it made Elora question whether she had been wrong about the contents of that goblet. With the curse in effect, she wasn't even sure the queen could eat regular food. She would soon find out, she supposed.

The queen set her empty goblet down with a quiet thud. "Are you settling in well?"

Servants clustered around them, dishing fruits and meats and pastries onto their respective plates.

"Yes, I believe so," Elora answered around the drool pooling on her tongue. It had been ages since she'd eaten anything other than moldy cheese and stale bread. It took every ounce of strength within her to keep her hands clasped politely in her lap while she waited for the cue to eat. Patience was her greatest strength though, and nothing would ruin this opportunity for her—if there was anyone in the castle worth impressing, it was the queen.

"Good. If there is anything you need, don't hesitate to let one of the servants know."

And with a wave of her hand, Queen Signe dismissed the flurry of service surrounding them, the servants retreating to the shadows and giving the two of them space to eat. Elora waited for the queen to take her first bite, but once she had, Elora delayed herself no longer. She picked up her fork and pierced a slice of cooked peach into her mouth. The combination of butter and sugar melted on her tongue, and Elora had to refrain from moaning.

If she had been alone, she would've cleared her plate

in one inhale and regretted it afterward. Instead, she timed her bites with the queen's, pausing in between to dab her mouth or take a sip of water. She was almost certain she caught the queen watching her on more than one occasion, which only served to bolster Elora's steadiness more.

Elora hadn't even eaten a third of the contents on her plate when a guard stormed into the room, disturbing their silence.

"My queen—" he bowed to Signe before hastily and warily addressing Elora. "My...lady."

"We are in the middle of a meal," the queen replied through a tight smile. "Surely this can wait until our daily check-in."

"My apologies for the interruption, Queen Signe, but this is news you've requested to receive immediately."

She perked up at that, and dabbed the corners of her mouth. "Go on then."

He cast an anxious glance toward Elora. "Should we maybe speak in private?"

"Nonsense. She is your future queen. It is imperative that she be informed of the ongoings of Irongate henceforth. So, what is it? What couldn't wait?"

"It's the traitor, Darius Graeme. He—"

Elora choked on the bite of her peaches, cutting the guard off before he could finish. Darius Graeme, King Everard's most trusted knight. Oh, how that name alone had haunted her every waking moment. Although many of the knights of Caelora had a hand in her torment while she was their prisoner, he was the one who oversaw most of her torture, as if by request.

Her hacking continued, echoing around the room as both the guard and Queen Signe watched her curiously.

She was drawing too much attention to herself.

Elora reached for her goblet, downed half the water inside, and forced a smile. "Sorry. It's been awhile since I've eaten food that required chewing. Please, continue."

The guard nodded, easily convinced. But Signe's inquisitive gaze lingered.

"Right. Well, I am pleased to inform you, my queen, that after all these years, Darius Graeme has finally been spotted."

The queen finally pulled her dark eyes away from Elora. "He's been spotted countless times. What makes this any different?"

"Our sources are credible; I can assure you. Besides, he's been seen in Mutiny Bay numerous times over the years. But each time we've investigated, he's nowhere to be found, likely keeping on the move or going back into hiding. But reports of his whereabouts are becoming more frequent. We believe he's growing comfortable, getting sloppy with his hiding."

"Letting his guard down," the queen added.

"Indeed."

"Well, this is fortuitous news." The queen grinned wickedly, and the sight of those blood-red teeth made Elora's full belly roil. "Prince Leighton left with a small convoy of the Thundersworn headed to Vallonde to fetch his father, just yesterday."

"Fetch him...?" The guard stiffened.

Queen Signe waved off his nervousness. "He will return empty-handed and heartbroken, no doubt. But that's not our concern. Send word for him to stop in Mutiny Bay while he's down there."

"Are you sure? If the prince is busy, my troop and I could easily—"

"That won't be necessary. Strangely enough, this aligns quite nicely with his fool's errand anyway. If you tell him he might find the key to the curse there, he'll willingly divert his attention to Mutiny Bay for a few days. And with any luck, your reports will reign true, he'll apprehend the traitor Darius Graeme, and we'll all be that much closer to learning how to end this forsaken curse."

The guard dismissed himself with a bow before hurrying out of the room.

The queen summoned a servant forward to refill her goblet. She held it high toward Elora, a toast to a victory they hadn't yet won.

But Elora was still frozen, her entire body numb.

That name, Darius Graeme, it had her in a spell.

When she dreamed, it was his face that ravaged her nightmares. His voice that taunted her thoughts. His hands that strangled her neck.

She wasn't sure what Queen Signe had meant by claiming that Darius would know how to end the curse, but, if Darius Graeme had played a role in the curse, that meant Elora and Queen Signe had a common enemy.

This could be Elora's chance at justice.

Her one shot at *true* freedom—at healing from the cruelties that had been thrust upon her.

"Does this news trouble you?" the queen asked, her goblet still in the air. "I would've thought a former prisoner of Caelora would be overjoyed to learn that we may soon have a former Caeloran Guard in our custody."

"I—I am," Elora stammered, a frightening yet exciting idea emerging in her mind. "More than you know. Darius Graeme was one of my...he was one of the guards who..." The words caught in Elora's throat, because how could she explain all the ways in which he had harmed her, broken her, without it becoming a never-ending monologue of experiences that were too painful to recount aloud, especially in the midst of a queen she was still assessing.

But she needed this. Needed the queen to trust her enough to grant her this one request.

Clearing her throat, Elora summoned the grace she once effortlessly carried herself with. "Forgive my boldness, my queen, but my hesitation did not stem from a lack of joy, but from scheming."

"Oh? What scheming were you pondering, princess?"

Elora swallowed the lump growing in her throat. "Only that of which you would hopefully be agreeable to."

It was a fool's game to make a demand of a queen. Yet here she was, doing just that. Jeopardizing her freedom that was still only in its infancy.

The queen's pitch-black eyes dazzled with intrigue though. "Speak plainly."

There was no turning back now. Elora sucked in a deep breath and turned toward the queen.

"If they return with Darius Graeme, I would like to be the one to deliver his sentencing."

The queen watched her silently for a long while. The flames from the candles on the table stood still in time with Elora's bated breaths.

Finally, the queen raised her goblet higher, a sliver of a smile inching up her pale cheeks. "I could think of no better indoctrination for you, Princess Elora. You shall make a fine queen for Irongate someday."

Hastily, Elora raised her own glass, and the two of them drank to a strange and budding camaraderie.

And for the first time in years, Elora felt a spark of hope. It would be Elora, a former prisoner, a princess of death, and the future Queen of Irongate to deliver his punishment. And she would ensure that Darius Graeme rued the day he ever laid hands upon her.

CHAPTER 4

THE MAW OF DEATH

KESTREL

From the outside, their tower seemed smaller than Kestrel remembered. She supposed she had grown a lot since the last time she saw it from this view. Still, it looked too narrow and too short to have contained her entire life inside it.

Not that she was going to dwell on that for long though.

The screeching had stopped by the time she came barreling out the front door, her heavy braid thwacking against her back.

The silence hollowed a pit in her stomach. Kestrel scanned the horizon where she thought she had heard the sound coming from, but there was no movement. No rustling of underbrush. Nothing.

"They've just run farther inland," Kestrel tried reassuring herself. "That's all."

But her reassurances were empty. Not being able to hear anything—no shouting or crying, even off in the distance—it made her worry what that would mean for Thom.

Cinching the bag on her shoulder tighter, Kestrel broke out into a run across the open desert, chasing after the unknown.

The Wilds were different than she remembered. Quieter. Untouched in ways that felt impossible. There was no sign of life to speak of. On this side of the trees that were off in the distance, everything was flat and barren. Not so much as a bird in the sky or a cactus in the earth. It made her all the jumpier—every moaning cry of the wind or the sands sent skittering made her neck crane and snap to see if danger was approaching. But every time she looked, there was nothing but the desolate flatlands and the foreboding treeline ahead of her.

No monsters to speak of either though. Anywhere. She'd count that as a blessing.

But Kestrel knew from experience that there could be some just beyond those trees ahead. She also knew that Thom had set up traps all over the area just to ensure none of the creatures would ever venture too near their tower to threaten her safety. Hopefully, she wouldn't be unlucky enough to stumble into one.

Within a matter of moments, Kestrel's pace was already beginning to slow.

She wasn't used to such exertion. Every muscle seemed to protest an insatiable need for rest already. The desert heat had her thirsting for water as well and she pulled the scarf over her head to provide some protection, though it didn't do much. *Now* she longed for the unpredictable moon, or for the sun to drop down toward the horizon. Anything to relinquish the heat.

Determined not to waste any precious time, Kestrel ignored her inner protests for thirst and rest, and pressed onward.

In just an hour, she reached the treeline only to collapse under the sparse shade it provided. Ignoring her body's cries was no longer an option. Kestrel fumbled for the waterskin in her sack and gorged herself.

"How do you do this all the time?" she asked Imaginary Thom between gulps.

"*It was a necessity.*"

With the back of her hand, Kestrel wiped the residue from her lips before securing the cap back into place. She shoved the waterskin into her pack, aware that at least half of its contents were gone now.

"Sure, but it's unnerving being out here. Like it's just you and nothing."

"*Not just nothing. There are monsters and death out here, and don't you forget it.*"

Like usual, she hadn't consciously decided to carry on a conversation with a man who wasn't even there, but sometimes hearing Thom's responses—even if they were only from her own head or occasionally spewed from her own lips—it made her feel safer. Like he was right there beside her, ready to protect her if she needed it, like he had all those years ago.

It made her feel as if she wasn't so alone.

"I'll be smart about this. I'll keep my eyes out for the beasts, and I'll find you," Kestrel insisted, and she peered around the tree trunk in search of the proof she needed to bolster her spirits.

An oasis rippled just a few paces ahead. Likely the same one she had nearly drowned in all those years ago. Kestrel's throat shriveled at the thought. Suddenly all of her nerves were active and alert. She scanned the area for the charred, bumbling creatures known as the cinders, searching for their blackened bodies as well as the wretched stench of burned flesh filling the air. All she smelled though was the salty heat of sun-warmed water, and the slight honeyed sweetness of whatever tree was offering her shade.

Maybe there were no cinders nearby, and for that she was grateful. But Imaginary Thom was right. There were other monsters in the Wilds, and she would need to keep her guard up, to keep herself safe and hidden if she ever hoped to find Thom.

He was all she had. She could not fail him.

"Where in the Hollows are you?" she whispered to no one.

Imaginary Thom's reply came anyway. "*Who knows, Little Fury. The Wilds are a big place; you could wander from coast to coast and never find me.*"

"Don't say things like that! They're not helpful."

"*I'm just saying what we're both thinking: it's about time you turned back, yeah? Before you get too lost again like last time.*"

It wasn't the first time the thought had crossed her mind.

But, oh, how she was tiring of having to convince herself otherwise.

"I'm not lost. And I'm not turning back. Not until I've found you. So you can either pipe down or, better yet, tell me something useful for once. Like which direction I should be going, or how far away you are, or—or anything that might help me find you!"

The voice in her head went as quiet as a windless sky.

Kestrel rolled her eyes. But maybe it would be better this way, with Thom quiet in her skull. She didn't need the distraction, especially if he was just going to feed into her own inklings of doubt. She needed fortitude. And that, Kestrel was learning, would have to be wrenched out of her, dragged along the scorched sands beside her, kicking and screaming the entire way.

So that's just what she would do.

Kestrel pulled the knife out of her pack, gripped the wooden hilt firmly in her fist, and carried onward. She passed the oasis without a second glance and weaved through the sparse trees with canopies like molted feathers. They couldn't provide much cover, but the small streaks of shade they could were a welcomed reprieve, one that her pale-but-stinging forehead was grateful for. Her freckled skin was not used to so much sunlight, so Kestrel did her best to keep to the shade as much as possible.

Hours dragged by.

The moon finally rose high overhead and Kestrel tucked herself into the crevice of two boulders to get some rest and hide from whatever terrors the night might bring. Fortunately, there were none, but she still didn't sleep with ease. All night her dreams ravaged her. She kept waking toward the sound of that gut-wrenching screech only to find that it was just her imagination.

The moon's visit was short-lived, and when the sun greeted her again, Kestrel was still bone-weary, but eager to get moving again.

The farther she trekked, the deeper her doubts dug into her.

Once again, Kestrel found herself out in the Wilds with no idea where she was going. She didn't have a map, nor the familiarity with the terrain like Thom had. She was following a trail without actually following anything—there were no footprints leading her way. The worrying truth was that Kestrel was traversing the Wilds blindly and with nothing but hope to guide her. And if Thom had taught her anything, it was that hope was perhaps the most dangerous thing to bring out here.

When Kestrel emerged from the trees and found open desert once more, she wasn't sure if she had made it to the other side or if she had just gone in one big circle and would wind up back at her tower if she kept pressing onward.

With a frustrated shriek, Kestrel chucked her knife at the sands. "I swear to the blessed moon, Thom, when I find you, I'm never letting you live down what I had to go through just to—"

But as she screamed, a hoarse voice called out to her from across the parched horizon.

"Kestrel?" At first, she wasn't sure if it was real or another figment of her imagination. But then he shouted louder. "Kestrel! Is that you?"

She would recognize the sound of him anywhere.

His was the only voice she had ever heard. The same voice that had hushed her to sleep when the storms were so fierce they rattled the stones in their walls. The same voice that had laughed with her. Cried with her. Reassured her that everything would be okay even when it seemed like nothing ever could be again.

Kestrel whipped around, her braid smacking the center of her chest.

"Thom!" she forced her dry throat to yell. "Thom! Where are you?"

"I'm here!" he shouted back to her, coughing through each word. "I need your help."

"I'm coming! Just—just stay there!" Following the sound of him, Kestrel broke into a sprint. The sand was harder here, the earth a dry and withered thing that made it easier to bound across, unlike the soft sands surrounding her tower that wanted to swallow each stride. "Just keep talking to me. Where are you?"

"*Are you sure about this, Little Fury?*" asked the voice inside her head.

It sounded so much like Thom that for a moment it jostled her. Made her doubt herself, yet again. Kestrel was used to Thom's imaginary voice creeping in unannounced. Oftentimes she would be mid-conversation with the real Thom when the imaginary one would try joining in. And she knew him so well that the voices almost always echoed one another.

But that was what made this feel so alarming.

It was rare that the two ever differed...

"Yes, I'm sure," Kestrel grumbled, sounding nothing of the sort. "This is the whole reason I'm out here, to find you. Isn't it?"

He didn't respond immediately, and so Kestrel kept

running. Nothing could stop her from reuniting with the only other person in this realm she had ever loved.

Then something dark began to bloom on the horizon.

Kestrel heard the faintest whisper in her mind: *Think about it. Better to be safe than stupid.*

She might've slowed down if Thom's real voice hadn't egged her onward at that exact moment.

"You're getting closer," he yelled, voice cracking with relief. "That's it. You're almost here!"

Desperation and delirium had her racing as fast as her feet would allow.

The dark smudge on the horizon grew into something massive. A crater that left the earth hollowed and black. Kestrel didn't know much about the lands beyond her tower, but she knew *that* dreadful place. It had been marked prominently on one of the maps Thom had left lying around after one of his travels:

The Maw of Death.

A foreboding and forsaken place.

The meager contents in Kestrel's stomach churned.

A small voice inside her told her not to take another step. But by the time she was even remotely suspicious, it was already too late. It was like someone else was controlling her legs now. They dragged each foot out from under her. One step after another, the space between her and that gaping chasm growing smaller and smaller by the second.

She ambled until she stood at the Maw's yawning edge.

"Thom?" she called out, peering into the abyss below. "Are you down there?"

No more of Thom's replies came.

Hot, dense air wafted up from the chasm. It reminded her of what the carcasses rotting in the sun smelled like when Thom wasn't able to discard of them quickly enough. Kestrel gagged on the acrid stench that rose from the Maw. She shielded her nose with her knifed hand—only to realize her weapon was gone. In her haste to reach Thom, she had left her knife buried in the sands and was now defenseless—not that a knife could stop this stench. It rose and fell around her like a dying breath, but Kestrel was certain it belonged to something living, something even more horrifying than a cinder.

Something was down there.

Something dark and malevolent, Kestrel could feel it.

A quiet voice in the corner of her mind told her to back away. Told her to run. To never *ever* come to this place again.

Kestrel knew she should heed its warnings. Every inch of her wanted to. After all, there was a reason Thom—a man who battled monsters every day—was wary of it.

She tried backing up a step but could not budge.

Something held her in place. Not like the strong hands of the vagrants Thom had warned her about who sometimes wandered the Wilds, the ruffians who would beat her, rob her, and leave her for dead.

No, this was something softer, gentler. A coaxing caress of the mind, drawing her nearer.

"Look down," the voice said.

The allure of the place was too powerful. Its mysteries too grand.

No one had ever ventured down into the Maw before.

They had all been too scared. She could do it though; Kestrel could be the one to find out what was down below. After all, she was an excellent climber. Flawless, even. She could easily make the descent—if not for that blasted heat. It blew through the small tendrils of fiery hair that framed her face, wrapped around her neck, and threatened to squeeze the life out of her if she dared to get any closer.

Part of her knew she wouldn't survive going deeper than a few feet. Knew that her freckled, porcelain skin would crack and singe.

But another part of her...

Another part of her was overcome with wanderlust. A sense of fate tugging on her.

"If not you, then who?" the voice called out to her again, only this time it no longer sounded like Thom. It was as smooth and dark as molasses; a baritone beat that lulled her to succumb to its sweet promises. "You are right in your wonderings, lost daughter. There is a reason you have found your way here."

If Kestrel had any amount of awareness left in her, she would have noticed the hairs on her arms rising, felt her spine becoming as rigid as a sword.

In her daze, she felt none of it. All Kestrel knew was that she was alone in the world. Alone and in need of a friend. And that was exactly what this decidedly male voice sounded like, a friend. Someone kind and inviting, and willing to soothe Kestrel's doubts and fears.

"This is why you left your home: to find me. It is why you and—" he paused a moment, as if thinking, searching. "—why you and your Thom lived so close all those years.

It was fate intervening. Setting you into motion to embark on your path, leading you here."

Kestrel nodded. Yes, that would make sense. Why else would she and Thom have lived at the edge of the realm in such a barren place?

"I have waited a long time for you, lost daughter." The saccharine voice purred, a sound that made Kestrel feel as if someone were stroking her head. "But now you are here, ready to uncover my secrets. Ready to unearth my truths. To be the hero the realm needs."

He was right. Kestrel hadn't known it before, but she *was* ready. All that time spent waiting in isolation. All those years with her life on hold, while she just sat in her tower reading. Now it was time for a new chapter in her life. Now she was about to be someone. To do something —to become a hero like in all the books she had read.

To be like Thom.

"All you have to do is come closer."

Every bone in her body was moved to oblige.

Kestrel lifted her foot.

It dangled over the chasm, and she prepared to step into the nothingness.

Until something screeched. It was the same sound she had heard from her tower window. The same agonizing howl that had led her on her charge.

The grating cries were so harsh and jarring that they dissipated the fugue that had shrouded her. Kestrel blinked, awareness flooding back. And she suddenly realized what she'd been about to do, the dire fate she would've met if she had taken one more step...

Kestrel threw herself backward.

Not a moment too soon either, for at that exact moment, an oily tentacle slithered up from the darkness, reaching for the place where her ankle had been hovering.

Her eyes bulged in fear as she tried desperately to inch farther away. Something told her that she was already doomed. That those tendrils of inky demise could reach much farther than she would be able to run. But she feared moving too suddenly as well. Even now, the tentacle was still fixated on the last place it thought she had been, as if it hadn't seen her move away yet, as if it had been relying on the sight of her, or perhaps the sound of her movements.

Kestrel continued inching away as slow as her shaking limbs would allow.

Once the black tentacle had coiled around where her foot had been, it squeezed with all its might. But it grasped nothing. And a shriek split the air like thunder.

CHAPTER 5
CUTE & NEFARIOUS
KESTREL

Its bellows shook the earth and Kestrel's senses. Blind, hot pain lanced through her. She gripped her ears, trying to protect herself from the talons that sliced into her skull, but no amount of pressure could block out the monster's frenzied cries.

Kestrel's knees buckled. Her vision quivered. And soon the ground was flipping upside down, with her crashing atop it.

Dust billowed from the cracked earth. Kestrel squeezed her eyes and mouth shut, but she was unable to stop herself from inhaling the harsh dryness through her nose.

A cough wrenched out of her.

A sound that she knew would mean her doom.

Kestrel needed to flee, just like when she had encountered that cinder all those years ago. Only this time, Thom wouldn't be there to rescue her. How foolish she had been to stumble into a monster's trap—again. But there would be time to chastise herself and hear Thom's voice echoing reprimands in her head later.

Kestrel clawed at the ground and began hauling herself away. Clay piled underneath her nails. Jagged rocks sliced her forearms and cut through her trousers. She gritted her teeth through the sting of it and kept moving. Kept dragging her body as far as she could, begging for the screeching to lessen so that she might regain some sense of coherence and be able to run.

"Where are you going, lost daughter!" With each word the Maw bellowed, its façade cracked more. Gone was his soothing lull, and all signs of the acceptance and warmth he had promised. In its place was a sound so raw and guttural, it made Kestrel feel as if she had been swallowed by death. "Come back to me!" the monster roared, the earth shaking beneath Kestrel's fingertips. "Let us enter the darkness together!"

Tears leaked down her face at the putrid rage erupting from the crater. That voice wanted nothing more than to devour her, to tear her to shreds and relish in her agony.

And she had been the naïve idiot who had almost willingly delivered herself to it.

Even after all these years, she had still learned nothing from Thom's warnings.

Kestrel heard and felt the heavy thud behind her before she saw it. Checking over her shoulder, she gaped at the source of the tremor. One thick, writhing tentacle slithered across the wasteland, a predator set to strike, and she was the helpless prey.

But in the midst of the rumbling and Kestrel's quiet

sobs, she heard it again. A rasping, high-pitched cry was growing louder, sounding more and more like a growl.

Kestrel had almost forgotten about it.

But there it was again.

That cry for help that she was beginning to realize wasn't a cry for help at all, but a declaration of battle.

A blur of orange leapt over her head. Something small thudded by her face, but her eyes were trained on the furry creature bounding over her as it landed in a skittering of rocks next to her prone body. Kestrel recognized the animal by its bushy tail and pointed ears, although the foxes she was used to spying from her tower windows were usually more sand-colored.

This one, however, was as orange as her own hair.

The fox stood its ground, hackles raised as a low growl emanated from its throat. It might've been menacing if it hadn't been aimed at a monster tenfold its size. But Kestrel was grateful for its comradery all the same.

She pulled her gaze away long enough to see what had fallen from the fox as it jumped over her and was surprised to find her own knife glistening in the sunlight in front of her. Surely, the heat was making her imagine things, otherwise she would be inclined to believe that this small creature had seen her in trouble, retrieved her blade, and was now coming to help her fight.

Kestrel didn't have a second longer to think about it though, for scouring the lands behind her, she heard the tentacle gaining haste. It felt around the dried cracks of the earth for her. Hungry and undeterred.

Soon it would reach them, and then all hope would be lost.

Kestrel palmed the knife and twisted back around, but her time was already up.

The slimy tendril of darkness was gliding over her foot and up her calf. It was already coiling around her thigh before she had a chance to think about what she might do. If she struck it, the knife might pierce her own flesh. If she tried wriggling free—well, there was no room to wriggle free now. The monster had her. All it had to do was squeeze.

Before Kestrel could conjure a viable third option, the fox lunged. Its sharp fangs dug into the oily flesh. A black, tar-like liquid oozed from the wound.

The bellow that shook from the depths was more enraged than it was in pain.

With a deft flick, the tentacle knocked the fox onto its haunches, right into the grasp of another tentacle.

Kestrel could've sworn she felt the primal attention of the Maw shifting then, releasing her. No longer was she the easy mark it desired. It had ensnared a new creature.

The tentacle that had been mere moments away from dragging Kestrel to her death below unfurled itself and began charging toward the fox instead.

The fox's orange body twisted and flailed, only making its situation worse. The tentacle constricted around its chest, turning its cries into ear-piercing screams. Too many times to count, Kestrel had heard similar shrieks of terror from her tower, when coyotes or worse would corner some frightened creature below, and Kestrel could do nothing but listen to their shrieks for mercy while they were given none.

The fox was helpless. Immobilized. It wouldn't be able to break free on its own.

It needed a hero.

Like one of the many brave warriors Kestrel had read about.

The Maw was distracted. This was her chance to do something courageous.

Thom would tell her to run. To leave the fox behind to defend for itself while she used the distraction to get as far away from the Maw as possible. He wouldn't even hesitate. Even now, she heard him shouting in her mind to— *run. Go. Flee. What are you doing? Get out of there!*

"Leave it," the Maw hissed, shattering her thoughts. "The creature is mine."

And if she hadn't been convinced already, Kestrel certainly was now.

She would not leave the poor fox to its death. Especially not after it had just saved her life.

The fox bit into the tentacle over and over again, as Kestrel shoved herself onto shaking feet. Black oil stained the fox's jaw and chest; it matted its fur. It was a fighter, and Kestrel knew both from her books and from Thom's own adventures, that fighters always prevailed.

Before anyone could talk her out of it, Kestrel bolted for the fox.

The earth crunched beneath her pounding strides, rocks and dust spewing behind her like ocean mist. Beneath her, the ground rumbled. A slow and steady growl that seemed to creep right behind her, darting with her every move. As if something were chasing her.

Kestrel didn't look back.

Blade held high, she leapt into the air and struck the monstrous tentacle with all her might. The knife pierced into the oily flesh up to the hilt. She pulled the knife back out, ready to strike again but the tentacle writhed. It uncoiled on impact, and deep within the Maw, the monster roared as it jerked its limb back toward safety.

The fox tumbled to the ground in a heap. Its eyes were open, gazing up at Kestrel with something between despair and hope as the poor creature crumpled limply, its body unmoving aside from its heaving breaths.

Kestrel shoved the knife back into her belt, gathered the fox into her arms, and ran.

Somewhere, distantly, she could hear Thom calling out for her again, hear him begging her to come back and save him. But now she knew he had never been real. A trick that the Maw had played on her to lure her toward her death.

Even as her tears blurred her vision, Kestrel kept running. She ran long after Thom's voice shifted back into the Maw's. Long after the monster's rage and cries went silent.

Only once she was certain the Maw was no more than a black speck on the horizon behind them, only once they reached a spire of rocks thick enough that even the Maw's girthy tentacles couldn't break through, did Kestrel finally stop.

She skidded to the ground, knees burning where rock tore through the fabric of her trousers. Kestrel tossed her pack down and used the soft backside as a pillow to lay the fox atop it. Its eyes were closed now. Its breathing shallow.

On more than one occasion, Kestrel had needed to tend to some of Thom's wounds. He'd taught her how to clean and stitch skin back together. How to treat a mild burn. He'd even instructed her on how to reset a dislocated shoulder.

But that had all been done on a human body.

Kestrel was unfamiliar with the anatomy of a fox, but she supposed they likely shared similar elements. So, she ran her fingers over the fox's unconscious body anyway, searching the shoulders, ribcage, and hips for any bones that might be out of place. It was a thin creature, its ribs protruding more than she expected, but none of them seemed to be bent at odd angles, and when she pulled her hand away, she was relieved to find no blood anywhere.

Maybe the fox just needed some rest and a meal.

Luckily, both her waterskin and a container of dried figs were easily accessible in a side pouch without disturbing the creature's rest.

Using the place where her trousers had torn at the knee, Kestrel ripped the bottom half of her pantleg off. She dribbled some water over the fabric and began cleaning the Maw's black blood from the fox's chest and mouth. It was too thick and sticky to remove all of it, but she did her best to clean as much as she could, so that it wouldn't have to taste that vile monster upon awakening.

When she figured it was as good as it was going to get, Kestrel held the waterskin up to the fox's lips.

Have we learned nothing today about the dangers of trusting things out in the Wilds?

Kestrel winced at Imaginary Thom's harsh reprimand.

I've told you once, I've told you a thousand times, there is nothing good out here. Not monsters. Not people. Not even animals.

It was something he told her quite often. Anytime a curious bird would flit onto their windowsill, Thom was swift to squash her innocent curiosity and excitement by shooing it away. According to him, animals could be just as nefarious as anything out here. They were built to survive and that was it. And Kestrel knew it too. She'd heard the way that some of the predators would corner a frightened rabbit and rip it to shreds while it was still alive. They weren't doing it to be mean, they just needed to eat. To survive.

But this fox hadn't just been surviving.

It had gone out of its way to save her.

Leave the creature and be on your way back home.

"No," Kestrel's words were quiet, but firm. They silenced the voice in her head long enough for her to see the fox's eyes twitching open. "Oh, hello there. It's alright. I have some water for you if you're thirsty."

Kestrel tilted the waterskin back, the sky-blue stone of her mother's signet ring sparkling in the sun. Trapped inside their dark tower, it had never shined so bright as it did now.

The fox seemed to notice it too, for as it lapped at the water, it squinted its eyes shut.

After a few licks, Kestrel set the waterskin down, not wanting to drown the poor creature. She retrieved the figs.

"Are you hungry? I'm not sure what you eat, but I have some figs."

Tearing off a small piece, she set the dried fruit atop the pack and let the fox decide. It sniffed it once before licking it into its mouth as well. Kestrel chuckled to herself; maybe Thom had forgotten the meaning of the word nefarious, but this creature wasn't anything of the sort.

Gently, she dragged her ringed hand through the fox's fur and—

The fox yipped and leapt out of her grasp. Cowering, it growled at her, much the way it had growled at the Maw.

"I'm so sorry. I didn't mean to—are you hurt? I—I didn't know."

The fox's black eyes glared at her outstretched hands and slowly started backing away.

"No, please don't go." Kestrel bolted upright, foolishly startling the animal even more.

Already, the fox was turning on its heels and bounding across the desert once more. Kestrel snatched her pack, instinctually wanting to chase after it. She got a few strides in before she realized how futile that would be. It was a wild animal, not her friend. No matter how grateful she was to it, she would never be able to convince it to trust her; she wasn't even sure she should want to. It would mean one more mouth to feed, one more being to keep alive when she was clearly struggling with the two lives she'd been charged with already.

With an acquiescent sigh, Kestrel stopped pursuing her savior. She supposed she should just be glad that the fox had made a full recovery and could still run. If it wanted to be on its own, that was probably for the better.

Just as Kestrel was about to turn around and try to figure out what she was going to do next, something large caught her eye in the distance. It rippled in the heat, a long, brick-shaped lump on the horizon. It reminded her of her tower, only if the tower had been knocked onto its side and painted the color of burnt sand.

Curiosity got the better of her. Kestrel grabbed her pack, and soon found herself was walking, jogging, then sprinting to get a closer look. An abandoned fortress erupted into view.

Thom had told her about places like this. Towns and cities where people had once lived together in harmony, now lay utterly vacant and decimated because of the curse that plagued their realm with monsters. They were often the same places where Thom would sometimes seek shelter, if he ever needed to wait out a horde of cursed beasts that roamed the Wilds.

Thom could be hiding somewhere inside.

Maybe he was hurt and needed her help.

With the fortress growing in view, Kestrel slowed to a cautionary gait. If there were monsters inside, she didn't want to alert them of her arrival by accidentally kicking a loose rock. As she slowed, Kestrel eyed the surrounding area, searching for any signs of trouble—and this time vowing to keep her wits about her.

The closer she got, the more her ears perked.

There was noise coming from beyond the walls. A quiet whirring that grew as she approached. It was unlike anything she had ever heard before, and it wasn't long before it battled even the familiar roaring of the ocean on a stormy night.

When she was so close she could press a hand onto the clay wall, Kestrel recognized what she was listening to.

An unending tidal wave of conversation.

A cacophony of laughter.

Shouting.

Crying.

Singing.

Kestrel shook her head, mouth hanging limply. There were people inside. Survivors, just like she and Thom.

But that was impossible. Everyone was supposed to be dead.

CHAPTER 6
A STRANGE NEW WORLD
KESTREL

O kay, maybe not *everyone* was supposed to be dead. But most of the population who hadn't been wiped out by the curse had supposedly become monster food shortly thereafter. That's what Thom had said. It's what Kestrel had been led to believe.

Maybe Thom had been wrong.

Maybe, in all his travels and scouring of the lands, he had somehow missed this little corner of the realm, and so he hadn't known that there were other survivors out there like them.

Or maybe these were the types of survivors he had warned her about. The kind of ruthless, horrible villains that she couldn't even imagine in her worst nightmares. The kind who possessed even less humanity within them than the monsters themselves.

Kestrel staggered away from the wall. She clung her ringed hand close to her chest as if to protect her heart from the wickedness before her.

She considered running before anyone could notice she was there. But what if Thom really was inside? What if he had been captured and the only way he could get out was if Kestrel found a way to break him free?

Clearly, Kestrel needed a new plan.

The walls were short enough, the uneven stones providing ample handholds—she could easily climb her way inside. But then what? There was no way of knowing what was on the other side. She could wind up climbing right into a prison cell herself.

All Kestrel knew right now was that she couldn't stay out here in the open while she sorted through all of her options. She needed to find cover before—

"You there!"

Kestrel jolted. A voice—another person.

Footsteps thudded as someone marched toward her. Excitement had Kestrel spinning around on the heels of her feet, eager to meet the first person she had ever met out in the Wilds. Then she remembered Thom's stories, the ones about how the people who remained out here were untrustworthy, bandits and vagrants who only wanted to hurt each other for their own gains.

All her excitement disappeared when she came face-to-face with the pointed tip of a spear.

Kestrel reached for the knife in her belt.

"Leave it, or die," the feminine voice hissed.

Kestrel knew the spear would be through her throat before she could even swipe with her knife, so she did as she was commanded and left it in her belt.

Her empty hands drifted toward the sky as she took the woman in. Her armor and robes all but blended in with the desert behind her, but her skin? Every visible inch of the woman's bronze skin shimmered with iridescent scales. Kestrel had never seen anything like it—never even heard Thom speak of such a thing. And her eyes? Two black slits amidst amber fillings. They reminded Kestrel more of the cobras that liked to hide around their tower.

The snakelike woman's reptilian eyes looked down the length of her, snagging on Kestrel's missing pant leg for only a moment.

"*Sss*tate your purpos*sse*, girl."

She didn't quite jab her with the tip of her spear, but she did make sure to press it into Kestrel's neck, indenting the skin in warning.

No, no, no. Kestrel didn't know what to do. She searched her thoughts for Thom's counsel, but he was silent as well. She was in this alone.

Kestrel could tell in one glance that this woman was easily double her size. All it would take was one tackle, or grasp, and the woman would have her. More than that, Kestrel couldn't stop thinking about what her snakelike flesh and eyes meant. Thom never talked much about the Wilds and what was out here. Occasionally he'd let slip the name of a monster—like the cinders—or off-handedly mention a trade that had gone wrong with one of the few swindlers left roaming the lands. And when he did, Kestrel tucked that information away for safekeeping, clutching onto it as if it were the only lifeline she had.

Most of what she knew and understood about the Wilds, she had learned accidentally.

But in all those years, Thom had never once mentioned something like...like this.

Was it a side effect of the curse? That seemed to be the only thing that made sense. Maybe the curse changed people, turned them into the very monsters he had to fight.

Coming from somewhere behind the woman, someone else shouted. "You gonna need my help with this one?"

A man from the sounds of it, though Kestrel couldn't see him. The cursed woman had her gaze entirely blocked, and she didn't dare move to try to view him better. Kestrel didn't doubt for a second how quickly this woman would impale her if she needed to.

The cursed woman shook her head. "Doubtful. She'*sss* trembling life a leaf."

Kestrel felt her shoulders slump. The last thing she wanted was to be deemed an easy target—*again*. It was like everything out here could smell the inexperience on her. Like they knew she was out of place, that she was lost and frightened and easy to devour.

But Kestrel was learning.

The fox had taught her something, a lesson that seemed integral out here.

Survival wasn't always handed to the bigger and stronger. Sometimes all it took was determination, cleverness—and perhaps a little bit of luck.

If there was an opportunity of survival here, Kestrel just needed to find it.

The cursed woman poked her again with the spear. "Do you *ssspeak*?"

"Yes," Kestrel managed to blurt finally. "Sorry, I just...I thought this place was abandoned. I didn't expect you."

"Abandoned?" the woman scoffed, a raspy sound full of distrust. But for whatever reason, the longer she scrutinized Kestrel, the more the squint in her eyes waned. She took in Kestrel's soft hands, her almost entirely pale skin —aside from the sunburn that was starting to blister on her forehead and cheeks. The cursed woman lowered her spear and gave a nod toward the perimeter. "Mutiny Bay lie*sss* beyond that wall. You've heard of it?"

Kestrel shook her head.

Mutiny Bay.

The name sounded exactly like the sort of place she should steer clear of, but instead, she found herself marveling and even more drawn to it. Kestrel's gaze wandered up the stonework, wishing she could see beyond those fortified walls. A place with a name, as well as people. A home for who knew how many survivors. Somewhere Thom had likely never been but would've been so excited to learn about. Because, although Kestrel had been worried about the possible wickedness of those who dwelled inside, she wasn't sensing anything evil from the woman before her—other than a curse that wasn't her fault. When she had approached Kestrel though, it had been to protect the people inside, she was sure of it. And now that she deemed Kestrel unthreatening, she was already showing her small acts of trust by lowering her weapon.

"Where do you come from?" the cursed woman asked.

Kestrel opened her mouth to answer, but realized she didn't know the name of where they lived. What town or region or beach it resided on. "I don't know. I lived with my father, but it was just us."

"And before that?"

Kestrel's brow wrinkled. "Before...what?"

"Before it wa*sss* only the two of you. Where did you live then?"

The question made the underside of her skin itch. Like there *should've* been a before, even though there wasn't. At least, not that she was aware of. Kestrel didn't want to lie, but she was worried the truth might disappoint her interrogator. Ultimately, she had no other option though, for Kestrel didn't even know a name of another place to give.

"It's always just been the two of us. We've never been anywhere like—like in there." When she nodded to the wall, the woman's reptilian eyes didn't follow. They were fixed upon her, calculating, analyzing. Kestrel continued. "So, I didn't mean to ignore you, I just...I thought everyone was dead."

Apparently, such a notion seemed absurd to the woman because those creases returned to the edges of the woman's eyes.

It made Kestrel's head hurt, but she couldn't figure out why yet.

"And where i*sss* he now?" the cursed woman asked after a long moment. "Your father?"

"I don't know," Kestrel answered honestly, and could've left it at that. But she was running out of options. Out of clues to follow. Kestrel could use someone to trust, and so she decided to tell the woman more. "Thom went on a supply run and never returned. He said he'd be back within a few weeks, and I waited for him, and waited. But...I know he always says I should never leave the tower, that it's too dangerous. But he never came back. And I got worried. So...I left our home to come find him."

By the time she finished, Kestrel's eyes were burning, the desperation so immense it overcame her. She had been running for so long, it had been a while since she had let all her worries and fears sink in. Thom was all she had. He was her rock. Her safe haven since the day she was born.

If she couldn't find him—or worse, if he was dead—she didn't know what she would do.

The last shred of the cursed woman's stony exterior finally dropped. "Did you *sss*ay Thom?"

Kestrel straightened, wiping her eyes. "Yes! Do you know him?"

"Perhap*sss*." The cursed woman stepped aside and gestured for Kestrel to walk with her. "De*sss*scribe him to me."

"Oh, of course. Umm—" Hope burned in Kestrel's throat, making her speech come frantic and quick. "Well, he has a beard. It's a little grey, but not fully yet. I keep telling him to shave it, but he says that he likes it like that, says that it shows how much he's been through. Between you and me though, I think it just makes him look ancient."

The cursed woman smiled. "Men and their beard*sss*."

Kestrel smiled back, even though she knew nothing about the men of the Wilds and the beards they apparently loved to grow.

"He also has a scar over his eye—oh, but he usually wears these ridiculous leather goggles when he goes out into the Wilds, so you might not have seen the scar. Umm, he also—"

"Does*sss* he walk with a limp?"

"Yes!"

They reached the cursed woman's male friend and she nodded to him. "She *isss* with Thom."

The man—who stood a good two heads taller than either of them and had a thick beard that fell down past his chest—looked stunned by the news. He gave Kestrel a quick up and down as he assessed her. "This little beansprout's with the Broken Wanderer?"

"According to her," replied the cursed woman.

He folded arms as thick as tree trunks over his chest. "What's a girl like you doing with a guy like him?"

Kestrel opened her mouth to stutter out a poor response, when the cursed woman gave his bicep a thwack.

"Say*sss* he'*sss* her father." The two of them looked at each other in a way that told Kestrel they didn't believe her at all. She started to worry about what that would mean for her, if they knew him but didn't trust her story. Then the cursed woman returned her attention to Kestrel. "It *isss* your lucky day."

"It is?"

"Thom *isss* inside. He arrived maybe two or three day*sss* ago."

"Two or three days?" Something heavy plummeted inside Kestrel. She knew how quickly he liked to move during his travels; it was safer that way, he always said. Staying somewhere for more than a day was almost unheard of. "Has he already gone then?"

The man shrugged. "Haven't seen him leave."

"You are more than welcome to see if he'*sss* still around. A friend of Thom*'sss* is a friend of Mutiny Bay'*sss*."

Together, they stepped aside to let Kestrel enter the place they were calling Mutiny Bay. From the name alone, it didn't sound like a place she shouldn't willingly enter. But before her was something Kestrel had only ever dreamed of seeing: an actual, functioning town—or maybe it was a village? Whatever the correct verbiage was, Kestrel didn't care. All she knew was that she was standing at the entrance of a community, with a stable and a market and any number of buildings that *weren't* her tower.

More exhilarating than anything though, was that this was a community *full* of people.

And Thom was somewhere inside.

As Kestrel thanked the two guards and headed through the gate, she ogled every person bustling about. There were throngs of them—each one vastly different from the last.

Kestrel hadn't known people could vary so drastically. Her experience with faces extended to Thom and herself— and even her own reflection had been limited to sightings in pots of water or found in the steel of a polished knife. Before, Kestrel had always believed she and Thom to be quite different. They had different hair, age, weight, frame —his face was scarred and hairy, whereas hers was pale and freckled. His eyes shone like liquid night, whereas hers were a dull shade of green that she likened to algae.

But as Kestrel gazed beyond the front gate, she realized they were more alike than many of the people around her.

Some of the people here had animal features—much like the snakelike guard—and they strode through the streets with their tails and furry ears held high as if they were completely unbothered by the curse—or maybe that wasn't the curse at all. There were others with skin so radiant and burning that they looked like they had been made from sunlight, melted it down, and forged into human shapes.

Others were like her, or at least had all the same features she and Thom did, but they wore different clothes. Some adorned their heads with wolf skulls, or armor that looked like it was made from dragon scales, or gauzy robes that left almost every inch of their bodies on display.

The people of Mutiny Bay came in every size, shape, and color she could think of, and they flooded the streets. It left Kestrel dizzy trying to take note of everyone, to drink them all in the way she might gorge herself on the next watering hole she came across.

When she was only a mere few steps past the gates, Kestrel stopped.

This place was sprawling. And she knew nothing about it.

It could take her days to explore every nook and cranny, and she still might never find Thom.

She called back over her shoulder. "Do you have any idea where he might be? Any suggestions on where I should go first?"

The cursed woman was already in conversation with her male counterpart, but she stopped mid-sentence to meet Kestrel where she stood. She pointed down a narrow, sand-strewn street that looked nearly identical to all the others.

"Try the *Ssstinging* Drip. That'*sss* where the Veiled Bane like to conduct their bus*ss*iness."

Kestrel wasn't sure what the Veiled Bane was, and she considered asking the woman to elaborate, but she was already sauntering back to her post and making small talk with her partner.

Instead, Kestrel took a deep breath. She had made it this far and could figure out the rest.

With an invigorating inhale, Kestrel faced the town that seemed to be swirling with possibilities.

CHAPTER 7

WHAT HAPPENS IN THE ALLEYWAY...

KESTREL

"The Stinging Drip," she repeated, not having a clue what that meant. But it was the best lead she had.

What had started as pure wonder and reverence had quickly soured. The deeper into the town Kestrel ventured, the more overwhelming it became. There were people everywhere. More than she had ever imagined.

To be surrounded by so many others—to be bumped and banged into, to have someone shout across the street, for children to be crying and screaming—it was an assault on Kestrel's untrained eardrums.

Noise was a foreign concept to her.

After a lifetime of solitude, to hear anything other than her own breathing and the sound of the crashing waves was like thunder cracking inside her skull. Despite the pain jostling her head, part of her still appreciated it though. Appreciated knowing that despite all odds, others had survived. They had endured, like she and Thom. And

68

now here they were, smiling, walking hand-in-hand with their loved ones, and buying herbs and trinkets from the market, without so much as a cautious glance over their shoulders or any mention of the monsters that should've been lurking behind every corner.

Kestrel didn't understand how they could be so relaxed. How they could feel so safe.

Then again, she supposed she always felt safe behind her stone walls as well.

The deeper she went, the thicker the bustle became. The pounding between her temples deepened. And she didn't know if she was any closer to finding this *Stinging Drip* place.

"Excuse me?" Kestrel tried saying over the commotion. She tapped people on their shoulders, she raised her voice. "Do you know where I can find the—" but no one seemed to notice her. What was one more assault on their bodies when they were in a tidal wave of sensory overload.

The city had a mind of its own. The people moved as one, the way that the seagulls would swarm and maneuver together over the ocean, a rhythm inherently known by all of them, but foreign to any outsider, any imposter.

That's what Kestrel was.

An imposter.

Not only to this bustling town, but to the idea of society in general.

She didn't know how to move about them. Didn't know how to maintain her balance as the others collided into her. She didn't have years of experience learning how to anticipate their strides to get out of their way in time, nor how to assert herself to squeeze between the cracks like she saw some of the children doing.

In only a matter of moments, Kestrel was swept away by the current.

"Please, I—I just need to get through," she spluttered, her voice hitching as the bodies pressed tighter around her. They slammed and crashed—the sharp edges of elbows and shoulders digging into her. They left ghost-like marks all over her body.

It made her skin crawl.

Touch, it would seem, was also foreign to her. At least the kind that was pressing in on her, threatening to squeeze her until she couldn't breathe.

Disorientation swallowed her, gobbled her up like she'd been flung into the Maw and now she was tumbling. Falling. Sinking.

As the people thickened around her, she lost all sense of direction. Kestrel couldn't tell which way was which—where she had come from or where she was going. Strange faces crowded her. She couldn't see around them. Over them. Through them.

A dizzying spiral of flesh and heat folded around her.

"I can't—breathe." She clutched her chest. "Help?"

The world was spinning like a desert twister, and she was caught in its churning forces.

Kestrel couldn't get any air. Her chest was a tight knot, her ribcage collapsing with each strained breath. And the bodies—the bodies, they just kept bumping and slamming and crashing into her, tossing her around like a fragile seashell swept up by the tide.

A grey, swirling cloud engulfed her vision.

Kestrel's nails dug into flesh, threatening to tear into her chest if it meant creating a hole for her to just breathe.

She needed air.

Needed space.

Then something warm wrapped around her bicep. An arm slipped around her waist and Kestrel was dragged out of the crowd the way Thom had dragged her out of that oasis all those years ago.

It took her a moment to realize what was happening—her lungs still gasping, her head still spinning—but once she realized someone was saving her, she put every ounce of energy she had into helping them succeed. Kestrel kicked at the ground, using the heels of her feet to scoot her body along as much as she could until she was out of the chaos.

The person didn't stop dragging her once she was safe though. They kept going, her body being lugged into an empty alleyway nestled between two sandstone buildings.

Every cautionary tale Thom had ever told her screamed into her mind.

The people of the Wilds can't be trusted.

They're all thieves.

Kidnappers.

Murderers.

Slavers.

Cannibals.

Once they were well inside the alleyway, the formerly-deemed *savior* propped Kestrel up against a wall in the shade.

Bleary-eyed, she craned her neck to get a look at the person. She prepared herself to find a hideous, monstruous man, with a face smashed-in from one too many brawls and covered in fresh blood from a recent kill.

Instead, heat rose to her cheeks, her stomach fluttering.

The young man before her looked as if he could've been conjured from a dream—she honestly wasn't sure he hadn't been. Maybe she had been knocked unconscious by the crowd and now she was drifting into one of her many fantasies. It wasn't rare for her to dream about handsome men and beautiful women. After all, the books she read had their fair share of romance in them, and Kestrel often found herself longing to experience what entangling with some of the morally grey characters she had read about would be like.

But this man wasn't one of those characters.

He wasn't the tall, dark, and handsome type featured in her latest read. In fact, there wasn't a single shadow or crevice upon the dashing face that hovered over her.

Even despite his drab robe and raggedy trousers, he was shining. Luminescent, really.

The sun haloed behind his head, its radiance casting his short, blond locks in a gilded glow that made him gleam like gold and treasure. Not that Kestrel had seen many faces, but as this young man smiled down at her, she could've sworn that every inch of him was flawless, bordering divine perfection. If the Sky-Blessed still bestowed their magic upon humans, he had surely been a recipient.

He was radiant and regal.

Gleaming and gallant.

And for a moment, Kestrel forgot that he had just

hoisted her by the waist and taken her into an alleyway… away from everyone.

She tried putting herself on guard, though his smile was disarming.

"It looked like you were about to drown in that crowd," he said in voice just as charming as he looked. That gleaming, half-cocked smile of his barely faltering as he knelt down next to her and examined her missing trouser leg. "Are you alright?"

Their gazes locked, and she noticed his eyes were the same sky-blue color as the ring she wore. Staring into them made her feel as if she were falling through the clouds, her stomach twisting and tumbling after her.

He had saved her.

This gallant knight-of-a-man had rescued *her*.

Just like in one of her stories.

And like in those stories, whenever the brave hero would stare death in the face just to protect his maiden, an ache built deep in the pit of Kestrel's belly.

Now her breaths were hitching for different reasons.

"I'm…much better now. Thanks." Kestrel flashed him a smile of her own, and when he brightened even more at the sight of it, she became warm and buttery inside. This Gallant Hero could stick a knife in her, and she would simply spread.

But that was crazy, wasn't it? Strangers didn't just meet in a crowded marketplace and then fall over themselves for each other.

Did they?

Kestrel wasn't sure. She didn't know much about how people interacted with one another, let alone strangers who felt an attraction. Thom made it seem like people hardly even spoke to each other in the Wilds anymore, but in her books the characters were often friendly toward everyone—at least until they had reason not to be. Although even in those stories, the interactions between the love interests varied. Sometimes it might take them months of courting, while others were betrothed before they even met. Sometimes they would be at each other's throats one second and then in bed the next. It made it difficult to gauge what would be acceptable in these circumstances.

The only thing Kestrel knew for certain was that his closeness was stoking a fire inside her. One she had never dreamed of being able to actually feed considering she had thought everyone else was dead up until a few moments ago.

All those years spent daydreaming, alone in her tower, just aching for any sort of human connection had built into a crescendo. She was filled to the brim with longing. And here he was, someone she could direct it at. Someone drawing it out of her like a magnet.

Maybe this *was* what strangers did. Maybe this was the very reason he had pulled her out of that crowd and took her somewhere where they could be alone. The clay building was cool against her sweat-drenched back and she felt herself lifting away from it, drifting closer to the heat smoldering between them.

"It seems I came just in time then—" the Gallant Hero started to say, but Kestrel could hold herself back no longer.

"Is this the part where you kiss me?"

For a moment, he pulled back, but that charming smile of his remained, even if it did skew a bit more toward confusion.

"I'm sorry. I think I misheard you," he said, a dozen other emotions sifting behind those sky-blue eyes. "What was that?"

Kestrel bit her lip. Repeating herself meant asking again, and asking again felt too much like begging, like desperation—even though she was *very* desperate for that first kiss. She wanted to taste him. To know what it felt like to have her jaw grasped as her lips locked onto another's. And she might've been mistaken, but something about the way his eyes kept drifting down to her mouth made her think that, perhaps, he wanted the same.

But she would not beg him. Not ask again for fear that she had already performed a social faux pas that she hadn't fully understood. She would apologize and say she didn't mean it. But she *had* meant. Had wanted it. And lying felt more wrong than the alternative.

Only then, in the silence of her agonizing contemplation, did his smile finally begin to slip. The confusion and hesitation went along with it, leaving behind only a curious sort of hunger that Kestrel wanted to satiate.

Whether what she had asked was normal or not, she was pretty sure he liked it.

Gallant Hero licked his lips, and a spiral of heat coiled around Kestrel's core, tightening. She had never been watched more intently. Never knew that having someone's full attention bearing into her could make her feel so exposed, so ravenous. It made her hands tremble, sent her thoughts scattering to the most gluttonous crevices of her mind.

Need erupted inside her.

Begging didn't seem so bad after all anymore.

"Please," she whispered softly.

Kestrel didn't know this person, this side of herself that was emerging now that she was as free as the bird for which she was named. But after wasting years of her life trapped in isolation, it seemed she owed it to herself to chase every whim, to race toward every dream and opportunity that presented itself.

This might be her only chance. She didn't want to waste another second.

Gallant Hero hitched an eyebrow the same color as the sand. "Do you know who I am?"

The way he asked it made it seem like there was both a right and wrong answer, and Kestrel didn't know which was which. But she wanted so desperately to be right.

Honesty had already gotten her this far, so Kestrel sucked in a breath and barreled forward with the truth.

"We've never met."

"That's not what I asked you." His smirk returned in full force. "I know we haven't met. I would've remembered you," he crooned, and Kestrel's heart raced faster. "But *you* know who I am. You recognized me. That's why you asked for a kiss, correct?"

Now it was Kestrel's turn to look confused. "Should I recognize you?"

The longer the two of them stared at each other, the more worrying his question became. Why did he expect her to recognize him? Was he an infamous criminal in the area, someone who regularly pillaged this town, known and feared by everyone? Was his face plastered on *Wanted* posters?

That's what Thom's cautionary tales would have her believing. But this young man didn't *look* like a criminal to her. It wasn't just that he was beautiful, there was a heroic strength in the way he carried himself—his shoulders back, his broad chest lifted. And when he had first pulled her from the crowd, behind his gleaming smile, she'd seen the worry in his eyes. He had wanted to make sure she was alright.

Maybe he wasn't the town villain then, but the town hero.

He was *her* hero, anyway.

Still, the longer she thought about it, the more it gnawed at her. "Why should I know who you are if we've never met?"

He didn't answer her, but his gaze dropped down to the rags of clothes he donned as if the answer was right there. He shook his head, met her gaze again, and his scrutiny of her deepened, those sky-blue eyes becoming even more suspicious and critical as he assessed every contour of her face. He still didn't believe her.

Or maybe it wasn't that he didn't believe her.

Maybe he was disappointed that she didn't know him.

Maybe that had been the wrong answer.

The heat of his gaze had her squirming where she sat. "Is that...a problem? That we don't know each other?"

Gallant Hero's laugh was airy and light. But as it blew past his lips, the last hint of his smile faded, his voice shaking a little. "No. It might be quite the opposite."

Kestrel didn't understand, but when the apple of his throat bobbed, she didn't need to.

Without his charming smile, it was like she was seeing him for the first time. The mask of confidence had been stripped away, leaving behind something older, something heavy, like he had the weight of the world upon his shoulders but couldn't bear the thought of anyone seeing it. The longer she gazed upon this new version of him, the more she was drawn to it. No longer was he a flawless manifestation of her wildest dreams, but a genuine person. Someone authentic. Someone vulnerable.

And it made her want him all the more.

Cautiously, Gallant Hero turned his attention over his shoulder, searching back the way they had come. Kestrel leaned forward, trying to peer around him to see what he was looking for, but he twisted back around before she could see anything.

Their faces were closer now, the heat of his breath warm where it caressed her nose and cheeks. She breathed him in—iron and salt and cedar.

He was everything she had imagined.

Everything the books had said he would be, and more.

His gaze fell upon her mouth and her lips parted for him on instinct. Heat pooled low in her belly.

When he leaned forward Kestrel felt the world tipping beneath her until their noses touched. It was the only thing holding her steady, that singular point of contact, the only thing keeping her grounded. His touch. His warmth. His nearness.

Solitude was something Kestrel knew intimately. But the opposite? Having someone so close to her, so intertwined with the very air she was breathing—it was dizzying.

As his hand reached up, cradling the back of her head, Kestrel sucked in a breath.

"One kiss," he said, almost sounding as if he needed to give himself permission.

Kestrel nodded, but already she could tell she was going to want more than just one. The headiness in his voice alone told her he already did too.

He leaned in. She closed her eyes.

His lips were a soft graze against hers, like the petal of a flower, but smoother. Gentler. Like a whisper. And for a moment, she feared that it wasn't real. That if she opened her eyes, she would be dreaming this whole thing, and he would be gone.

So she pressed against him harder, hungry not to let that connection break.

It seemed to surprise him at first, every muscle in his body tensing as he inhaled sharply. But then he relaxed into the kiss. His fingers tightened in her hair, and he opened his lips to her. Having read about these moments and how they could unfold, Kestrel opened hers too. For a moment, she feared she wouldn't know what to do. Something about tongues colliding, but in what maneuvers and to what rhythm? It would be her luck that this would be yet another behavior or experience that she didn't understand, that she couldn't replicate, just like at the market.

But to her surprise, the rhythm came easily. As natural as breathing.

His tongue coaxed hers in delicious, gentle strokes, sending tiny shivers across her skin. He tasted of parchment, but it wasn't an unpleasant thing. For her, it was perhaps the most familiar. All those years she spent devouring book after book, and now she was devouring him.

The pounding in her chest moved lower. Kestrel shoved herself the rest of the way off the wall and pressed into him harder, desperate to feel the heat of his body against hers. To deepen the kiss. To fill herself with him in mind, body, and soul.

"Leighton!" a man shouted from the other end of the alleyway.

Kestrel had been determined to ignore them—she wasn't about to let anything come between her and this perfect, long-awaited moment.

If it hadn't been for the way Gallant Hero's mouth clamped shut, forcing her tongue out, the name might've been lost to her, swept up by the cacophony of voices bustling about the marketplace.

But because his body had turned as rigid as stone, the name struck her.

Leighton.

So elegant. So enchanting. So—

Gallant Hero—or *Leighton*, she supposed—thrust himself away from her. He staggered to his feet, and when she saw the look of horror on his face, it made her feel as if she had just been sucker-punched in the gut.

Kestrel had been left on the ground, gaping and wounded.

Something had changed between them, but she didn't yet know what, couldn't possibly comprehend how the magic had been entirely snuffed out in an instant. But as the man jogged up to them, she could tell by Leighton's paling skin that now wasn't the time to ask.

So Kestrel stilled. She tried becoming invisible and blending in with the clay walls behind her as the man reached Leighton's shoulder. This one had coppery, shoulder-length hair, and though Kestrel was still dumbfounded and blinking, trying and failing to make sense out of what was unfolding around her, it was through that haze that she noticed how notably similar they looked. The two of them could've been brothers, although this new one was a duller version, at least to her. They had the same strong jawline though, the same disarming smile. But her *Gallant Hero* was a little more hardened around the edges, and his striking sky-blue gaze was unmatched by this new man's steely blue one.

"Leighton, there you are. I've been looking all over for you," the man with coppery hair said. He folded over and braced his hands on his knees as he caught his breath. "Efrem will go mad when he sees your face isn't covered —"

He stopped mid-sentence when he caught sight of Kestrel on the ground just a few paces away. She pressed her back harder into the wall, as if that would help conceal her now.

"Oh," said the man, his eyes widening with some perceived, mischievous understanding. "Oh!" Spinning around, he thwacked Leighton on the chest. "You ran off to rendezvous with girls in alleyways and you didn't think to invite me?"

"Ow," Leighton grumbled, rubbing the sore spot on his chest. "Don't be crass, Micah. I wasn't—"

Another man appeared from the end of the alleyway, this one identical to the one apparently called Micah, although this one was followed by a black cloud that shadowed his disposition. He saw Kestrel immediately.

"What's this then?" Black Cloud asked, folding his arms.

Micah shouted over his shoulder. "Leighton's kissing locals and didn't have the decency of inviting us." He folded his arms as well, although with less judgement and more amusement.

"Nothing happened!" Leighton insisted, glancing between the two of them.

Sharpness pierced Kestrel's chest, but none of the boys seemed to notice.

"Oh right. Sure," Micah said, dragging his gaze up and down the length of Kestrel where she sat. "And nothing happens between me and any of the ladies I rendezvous with on these outings either. Isn't that right, Efrem?"

Efrem just rolled his eyes. "We need to get going. And cover your faces—we're supposed to be laying low while we're here."

"Ah, let him have his fun. He can't smooch lovely girls with his face covered now, can he?"

Efrem just grumbled and turned his attention back out toward the marketplace. It was as if he was standing guard for some reason, but Kestrel didn't know why. Not that she was even certain that's what he was doing, for she was too distracted by the lie that had just spilled off Leighton's tongue so effortlessly.

Nothing happened.

But kissing *was* exactly what they had been doing. And

it had been a beautiful, heartfelt moment that had meant so much to her, had felt like a once-lost and now-found treasure that she would hold dear to her heart for the rest of her life, and he was denying it. Destroying it.

He made it seem like even the idea that he could've been kissing her was unfathomable.

What Kestrel couldn't figure out was why? Why was he hiding the truth? Clearly Micah didn't care; he seemed more than excited about the prospect of romantic entanglements, whether he was involved in them or not. And Efrem seemed more irritated by having to deal with the two of them than he was by the prospect of Leighton being involved in the kiss itself.

The only reason Kestrel could think of was that Leighton was ashamed, and that thought made her belly feel like it was a decaying nest of weeds.

Micah waved Leighton off and turned to Kestrel, this time donning a charismatic smile that could've melted the sun. "It's awfully rude of him to keep such a rare beauty all to himself. Then again, my brother has always been a bit stingy."

When he winked, Kestrel's stomach dipped against her will. It was probably just leftover excitement from earlier; she hadn't had this much attention since...well, ever. And certainly no one had ever called her *such a rare beauty* before. It was enough to make her head drift into the clouds.

Then his hand reached up to tuck a lock of hair behind her ear.

"Leave her alone, Micah."

Leighton's tone had become as cold and deadly as a

curse. He caught Micah by the wrist and shoved his hand away.

His protectiveness only made the tumbling in Kestrel's stomach grow wilder.

If Leighton's actions had been meant as a warning toward Micah, he didn't seem to notice. Instead, Micah's face lit up, his jaw unhinging. "You scoundrel! You really *were* necking!"

"Quiet!" Efrem warned over his shoulder.

Leighton pinched the tension on the bridge of his nose. "I told you, it's not like that. She was just—"

"She was just what?" Micah continued, thoroughly amused now. He pretended to pull up a chair, take a seat, and rest his head on perched hands. "Wandering around, all alone, just begging for some tall, strapping gentleman to whisk her away for a romantic romp in this pitiful passageway?"

When Leighton's sorrowful glance met Kestrel's, Micah's sarcastic, knowing grin faded.

"No, wait, really?" Micah asked in disbelief.

"No, not really! She needed help and I provided it." Exasperated by the conversation, Leighton started to explain how he had seen Kestrel struggling in the crowd and had to pull her to safety.

But in his retelling, the kiss remained omitted. A dark and shameful secret he wanted no one to know about.

Kestrel wanted to shrink out of existence. Was it her that he was ashamed of, or the kiss itself? Had it meant so little to him that he was willing to pretend it had never happened—or worse, was he regretting it? Had it been a mistake?

Kestrel hadn't regretted any of it. Until now.

She didn't want to be here. Didn't want to be the fuel that emboldened Micah's laughter, nor the shame that lingered on Leighton's face.

While the two of them were still distracted, Kestrel picked herself up off the ground. She felt cold rush in around her, so she tucked her arms around herself.

Leighton's sharp, arctic gaze finally noticed her then.

"Wait, don't go yet. I didn't mean—"

There was no point in hearing him out. She had heard enough already.

Kestrel ran as fast as she could out of the alleyway and didn't bother looking back. Didn't stop. Not even as her shoulder bumped into Efrem's as she made her escape.

They would not see the tears streaming down her face.

Thom's predictions were proving right; maybe the people out here were truly terrible. The only thought that brought her any comfort was the hope that she would soon be reunited with his familiar face.

CHAPTER 8
THE STING OF BETRAYAL
KESTREL

The next few encounters Kestrel had with the locals went decidedly better.

Once she made her way past the marketplace, the crowds thinned, and most of the lively noise along with it.

Kestrel was able to hear herself think again. The people around her could hear her too, so she started asking folks if they could point her in the direction of the Stinging Drip. These interactions involved *no* kissing, but Kestrel was okay with that. She needed to stay focused on what mattered: finding Thom, not gallivanting around with the first pretty face she met.

With only the kindness of strangers and the draw of the city to guide her, Kestrel meandered through Mutiny Bay.

Its vivacity was quickly healing the dull ache of her mortified heart. Kestrel had always known the desert to be a drab and barren place, but Mutiny Bay managed to breathe life into it that she hadn't expected. It was far from the picture of desolation Thom had painted of the Wilds. The buildings here were made from plain, cream-colored bricks, but what really brought them to life were the colorfully patchworked awnings that hung above every doorway. They swept across the sky like rainbows, and Kestrel craned her neck to take in every one. If the awnings weren't captivating enough, the painted vases that sat outside homes captured her as well—and then sometimes the homes and buildings themselves were also bejeweled in color. Nearly every street Kestrel walked down had a different mosaic on the walls or even the ground itself, entire scenes of desert flora and sunsets pieced together by tiny shards of broken, painted ceramics that sent her heart fluttering.

Everything was so vivid and beautiful.

And seeing it all, all this color and vibrancy, it made her even more excited to find Thom and share this experience with him.

By now, Kestrel had reasoned that he had probably stumbled upon this place after enduring some troubles on the road, and what a sight for sore eyes it must've been. Kestrel imagined they'd taken him somewhere to treat his wounds, a place called the Stinging Drip—a name that conjured for her both the danger of a viper, and the medicinal uses of its venom.

Once she found the Stinging Drip—and with any luck Thom inside it—everything would be right again. Then she could put all memory of this dreadful journey, as well as Leighton and his intruding brothers, out of her head for good.

Finding this place was proving more difficult than she imagined though.

Every time Kestrel stopped to ask for directions, the people giving them seemed more reluctant to do so. They were skeptical. Not *of* her, but *for* her, she realized. It made her worry about just how serious Thom's injuries must've been.

Kestrel steeled herself for the worst, just as she rounded a dark corner.

Everything was dimmer down this street. At first, Kestrel thought it was because there were fewer awnings and mosaics to brighten the place up. But the darkness kept thickening.

Kestrel tilted her head to the clouds and watched as the black curtain of night was drawn over the sky.

Dread settled in her gut like a brick. She knew all too well what plagued the desert cities at nightfall.

The scourge.

That's what she and Thom called it, the horde of enlarged and bloodthirsty locusts, beetles, and various other horrendous insects that would ravage an entire town in seconds.

Every now and then, the scourge would wander as far as her coastline, and Kestrel would spend the entirety of the dark hours huddled under her bed as the large insects rammed themselves against the tower, skittered up the exterior walls, the buzzing of their wings a call of death.

The first time they came while Thom was away. At the next glimpse of sunlight, Thom had barged through the front door, eyes wide as he frantically searched for her.

That was the day he told her about them. How they

were the deadliest monstrosity in the Wilds, due to their sheer numbers alone. They migrated from one corner of the desert to the next, in no real discernible pattern, so he never knew where they would venture next. And anyone unlucky enough to be caught in their swarm would be nothing but bones by the time the scourge was done with them.

Kestrel had come too far to be turned to bones now.

Just because it was dark though, didn't mean the scourge would come here. There was still a small chance they were preoccupied somewhere else. Still, the people of Mutiny Bay weren't willing to take the chance. On the streets behind her, Kestrel listened as everyone shuffled back inside to the safety of their homes or whatever buildings were closest. Doors were barred and windows bolted.

If the drab road had been uninviting before, now that she stood on it alone it looked downright haunted.

No one remained outside but her.

In the distance, Kestrel thought she detected the faintest buzzing.

Her pale skin pebbled. Fear shook her to her core as she began racing down the street, searching for some place to hide. The dark gaps between the buildings were gaping, ravenous maws ready to swallow her whole should she stumble inside them.

She banged on every closed door, but none opened.

She called out for help, but no one replied.

Still, Kestrel kept running. Kept searching. Surely, there had to be some place where she would be safe.

She eyed an empty barrel, but worried the cracks would be too easy for giant pincers to break. There was a half-full trough of who-knew-what that she could plunge into as well, but there was no telling how long she'd have to hold her breath, let alone if any of the scourge might be desperate enough to devour the contents inside just to find her submerged underneath like a tasty treat.

Kestrel came to dead end, with only a dark and broken building at the end of the street. The wooden sign out front was barely hanging on, and as she approached, she saw the only letters visible in dulled black ink read: *The S-ing D-ip.*

Her heart sang. She'd found it.

Kestrel was about to knock, when the door cracked open, and a stout man peered outside.

"Well don't just stand there. Get in! Get in!"

Kestrel did as she was told. The man closed the door behind her, and together they stared, waiting.

The moments ticked by, but no scourge came.

Eventually, the man heaved a sigh and shouted to the room, "Looks as though we live to see another day, fellas!"

Cheers erupted behind her, and Kestrel had to shield her ears as she turned around to see the type of place she'd just stumbled into.

From the outside, it had appeared abandoned, ready to crumble. But now that she was inside and the threat of the scourge had passed, a boisterous energy rose from every corner of the open room, one alive with tomfoolery and merriment. Of the dozen tables Kestrel saw spread out across the space, every single one of them was packed with patrons. Some were deeply immersed in an arm-wrestling match or card game. Others clanked their mugs, a frothy substance spilling over the tops like hoppy waterfalls. A few more clung to the women on their laps or argued about who amongst them would've been able to take the entire scourge.

This wasn't an infirmary, Kestrel realized.

It was a tavern.

Already, her chest was starting to tighten again, much like it had in the marketplace. It wasn't nearly as packed in here as it was there though, so Kestrel did her best to veer around the clustered groups, keeping her distance, not letting anyone bump into her or crowd too near.

A brawl broke out at the table closest to her, and the claws of panic squeezed her chest. Kestrel had to dodge out of the way as two men fought, scrambling over each other and sending one another staggering back, as they made their way outside.

Yet again, Kestrel found herself at odds with what she was seeing versus what she had expected.

It didn't make sense for Thom to be here, especially when he was meant to be home weeks ago. No one here was injured or sick. In fact, everyone seemed to be enjoying themselves rather thoroughly. Kestrel kept a keen eye out for the pick-pockets and poisoners, for the thieves and murderers Thom had said were all that was left of the humans of the Wilds, but Kestrel found none. Only friends. Even the fellows who had been punching each other eventually ambled back inside, their arms thrown around one another's shoulders, smiles wide as they shouted at the barkeep for another round of ale.

This was nothing like the world she had been preparing for. The world that Thom had told her about. And if he was here? Kestrel was starting to worry what that would mean for the two of them—for her and every-thing she had been led to believe...

Someone collided into Kestrel then, a gruff man with a ragged beard that fell down to his belly.

It was only then that anyone seemed to notice how out of place she was. The man watched her the entire way back to his seat. He kept watching her as his ale arrived, and he downed half of it in one gulp. Kestrel was uneasy under his scrutiny, and she realized she wasn't doing herself any favors by just standing around and gawking.

Even if Thom was a liar, even if he had a lifetime of truths to make up to her, she still wanted to find him—*needed* to see for herself what state he was in.

She took a deep breath and immersed herself further.

Each table hushed at Kestrel's passing.

The farther into the tavern she ventured, the more it felt like she had just willingly walked into a den of wolves. Or at least, that's how her body was responding. Her heart had only ever beaten this fast when she was running from the cinder or the Maw. She swore as she passed by the tables, she could hear every single person in the tavern breathing. It was both wonderous and grating. All the shouts. All the hearty laughs. The scuffing of wooden chairs on wooden floors. The clinking of mugs.

Once she found Thom, things would feel right again, she reassured herself.

Thom would help alleviate the pressures building inside her. He'd reassure her that the worst of her fears were wrong, and he'd tell her all about how he'd needed to stop here to recover after his grueling journey. How he had planned on returning the minute he was able to.

All would be well. She would have a friend in this loud and busy place.

Thom would be right there beside her, making her feel safe and grounded, the way he always had. And maybe, now that they'd found this place, they could even move here and become a part of something good. Something bigger than just surviving in their tower. Maybe that's why he was still here, scoping the place out to see how safe it really was for them.

A smile started to bloom across her face.

Then Kestrel would never know boredom again.

Never be alone.

From the middle of the tavern, Kestrel finally spotted him—or rather, heard him. Laughing somewhere near the back. It didn't matter if every person in the tavern suddenly stood up to block her path, nothing could've stopped her from plowing through them to see *him*. To see Thom. The only person who mattered to her in the entire realm.

Kestrel barreled around patrons and tables, and in a few short strides, there he was, sitting with his back turned toward her with five other men and women at the table around him. Kestrel didn't need to see his face to recognize him—although the goggles resting atop his head helped. But even without them, Thom was the most familiar thing in the world to her—the way he slouched, the way he mindlessly rubbed the thigh of his bum leg, the way he periodically dragged a hand through the slicked-back greasiness of his tree-root hair.

She would recognize him anywhere.

But it was the bellowing sound of his laughter as it

carried into the dusty rafters that removed any question of doubt. It was *him*.

But mixed in with the relief, something darker gnawed at her insides now. Something more akin to betrayal.

There he was, practically falling over himself, having the time of his life. The way he bumped elbows with the man next to him as their heads dunked backward with laughter was too familiar for this to be a first encounter. In fact, the way his guard was down at all, showed how much he trusted these people and this place.

He was so thoroughly at peace here that he hadn't even noticed the tavern quieting at her passing.

Everything crashed into her then. The liveliness of the town. The prosperous market. The kindness of the few strangers she had already encountered.

This was not Thom's first time here.

Nor his second or third.

Thom had been lying to her. Perhaps her entire life. This wasn't the dangerous world he had warned her about. It was messy and chaotic, sure. But not once had she ever been in true peril like he had told her she would be. No one had robbed her. No one had snatched her off the streets—except to save her. No one had caused her any physical harm, and even the brothers who had wounded her pride, she was fairly certain they hadn't meant to.

Other than the Maw, she had been perfectly safe out here.

Kestrel had spent a lifetime locked away in a tower out of fear. And for what? So that Thom could have this secret refuge to himself? So that he could drink and be merry with friends, while she worried herself to death wondering if he would ever make it back to her alive?

The hot sting of tears swelled in her eyes.

The other people at Thom's table took notice of her and their laughter stopped.

Thom was mid-drink, so it took him a moment longer to catch on. But as the rest of the bar fell into a curious silence, Thom's spine finally went taut.

Slowly, he turned around to see what everyone else was staring at.

He blanched at the sight of her.

"K-Kestrel!" Thom shot to his feet, his thighs crashing against the table so suddenly he almost knocked over every mug of ale atop it. He winced at the jolt of pain it sent through his bum leg, and Kestrel felt a small modicum of satisfaction. It was the least he deserved. Thom scrambled to his feet and faced her. "What are you doing here..." He was breathless at first. But the initial shock of seeing her wore off quickly, and Kestrel watched a wave of ire flood his face. "You shouldn't be here. I told you to stay inside—"

A humorless laugh as sharp as glass cut through her. "Yeah, well, I'm glad I didn't."

The audacity of him. To act as if *she* were the one in the wrong here? He had imprisoned her with lies. He owed her a lifetime of apologies, and instead he was scolding her like a child.

Thom hobbled around his chair and reached for her as if he was ready to drag her all the way back to their tower and lock her away again.

She wouldn't allow it.

Not now.

Not ever.

Kestrel jumped back and put one of the other populated tables between them.

"You lied to me," she said through gritted teeth. She didn't want to look at him, but looking out at the room full of people—of so many more living souls than what he led her to believe were still out there—it only made her outrage louder. Made it burn brighter. Kestrel clenched her fists. "You said everyone was dead. You said there was nothing out here except monsters and madness!"

"There *are* monsters out here," he countered. Using the back of a chair to support himself, Thom grunted and pushed himself to stand taller. His leg wobbled, but he forced it to steady. As if he couldn't dream of being cowed by her. "I never lied to you. People *have* died. Hundreds of thousands of them, and that number grows every day."

All around the tavern, heads bobbed and mugs rose in agreement. It seemed to be what made Thom realize just how much attention they had drawn.

He lowered his voice and extended a hand toward her. "I know you're upset, but let's talk about this outside, alright?"

Kestrel folded her arms. "I'm fine talking here."

As much as the vise on her chest was tightening and she would've loved to be back in the open air, Kestrel wanted the audience. They were the only way she could gauge the truth of his words now.

Thom went to drag a hand through his greasy hair, but the goggles stopped him. He sighed and stretched out his hands instead, appearing conflicted and frustrated, but more so the latter. "I can't give you the answers you want here."

"As if you'd give them to me anyway," she bit back.

He looked at her pleadingly and Kestrel had half a mind to grab the nearest pint and chuck it in his face. For almost two decades he'd been lying to her. *Two decades!* It would take a lot more than his big sad eyes to earn back her trust now.

"Why?" The word broke free from her before she even knew she was asking it. "Why did you lie to me? And don't tell me you didn't—because you did! You made me believe there was nothing out here. That the realm was all but gone. That there was no one left. And I want to know why —I *deserve* to know why."

Thom's hand still remained extended toward her. Those night-sky eyes of his flicked to the door. "Please just come outside, and I promise I will tell you everything."

"Tell me here."

"Some of what I have to tell you isn't safe to be told here," he growled, glancing suspiciously around the room.

But Kestrel would not be budged. She clutched onto her rage tighter. Let it bolster her. "According to you, it's not safe anywhere. How am I supposed to believe you when all you do is lie to me?"

"Kestrel, I—"

"You kept me away from everyone and everything, for nineteen years! I was locked away in some tower, foolishly believing that—"

"That's enough!" The veins at his temples bulged with each syllable of his booming voice.

Never had Kestrel seen him angrier. She had said too

much; their tower had been a secret that only the two of them had known about. Another one of his senseless rules.

Kestrel was done hiding. Let the world know everything there was to know about them and the life they had led.

"Tell me why." Kestrel enunciated each word, her voice surprisingly firm despite the way every bone in her body trembled. "Why did you lie to me?"

Thom heaved a heavy sigh. "Everything I did, I did to protect you."

"Protect me from what? I made it here just fine. All on my own. No bumps, bruises, or scrapes." For the first time, he seemed to truly look at her. His careful gaze ran over every inch of her, noting the torn knee of her trousers, her parched lips, and the raw, burnt skin on her forehead. "Alright, fine. So I'm not completely unscathed. But I feel like that's to be expected from someone who was never taught to survive out here, so I did the best I could."

And already, she was learning. Adapting. Next time she ventured into the desert, she would do better. She would prove it to him.

Thom smiled sadly. But the pride Kestrel thought he would have for her withered beneath the wrinkles of his brow, under the scar over his eye.

"You did well, Little Fury," Thom said. "But I'm afraid it's more complicated than surviving a few days on your own in the middle of nowhere. There are things you don't know yet about the Wild—" He stopped himself then, reconsidering his choice of words as if he actually did want to be honest with her. "There are things you don't know yet about *Grimtol*, about why we live the way we do. Things you're not ready to hear yet."

There was a sharp pinch where Kestrel's heart belonged.

How could he still think her unworthy of the truth? Here she was, practically begging him for answers, to let her in on all the secrets he'd been keeping from her, and he was telling her she wasn't ready.

Kestrel opened her mouth, prepared to insist that he couldn't continue keeping her in the dark, when a commanding voice rumbled from behind her.

"Maybe you need to clean out your ears, Old Man. The lady already told you: she's quite ready to hear these *things* you're alluding to."

The tavern muttered, their confusion at this new person to enter the conversation apparent. But Kestrel recognized his voice instantly.

She spun around to find Leighton standing in the tavern doorway flanked on either side by a hooded figure —likely Micah and Efrem, though it was difficult to tell since both of their faces were shrouded behind fabric that left only their eyes showing.

Leighton, however, had already lowered his face covering and hood. And as the tavern collectively drew in a breath, those crystal blue eyes of his bored into her own and seemed to say, *I've got you.*

Once again, his impeccable timing had saved her.

"It seems to me—" he continued, striding across the tavern with his cloaked friends falling in line behind him "—that you're the one not ready to admit the truth."

When Leighton stopped and stood beside her, Kestrel

swore she had never felt safer in her whole life.

But something in Thom snapped. "What are you doing here? Get away from her!" There was a panic in his tone that frightened her. Something primal and unbound. Thom glared between Leighton, the hooded figures, and then his wrathful gaze finally settled upon her. "What did you do?"

She couldn't believe he was still blaming her for everything.

Just to piss him off, she said, "I ignored your advice for once, and I made some friends."

"Friends?" Thom snorted. "Oh, that young man there is *not* your friend. Do you even know who he is?" Something cold frosted over her, making it difficult to breathe. Her non-response was all he needed. "Didn't think so. Might I introduce you to the son of the tyrannical King Ulfaskr Erickson, the misguided and cruel Prince Leighton Erickson of the corrupt crown of Irongate. And you've seemingly allied yourself with him."

Kestrel's mind was reeling. The truths, the lies, the omissions—they were all amassing into some giant tidal wave and threatening to crash down on her.

She didn't know who King Ulfaskr was. Had never heard of Irongate. And Leighton, a prince? She had kissed a prince? It didn't make sense—none of it did. Princes came from noble families and were betrothed to noble ladies, she knew that much from her books. They didn't just wander into alleyways and kiss any girl that asked them to.

This had to be another one of Thom's lies. A way to manipulate her.

Kestrel glanced over at Leighton, searching for any signs of reassurance, apology, or even denial.

But he gave her none.

In fact, he wasn't even looking at her. His focus had fully shifted to Thom.

"You're going to pretend like I'm the one she should be worried about allying with?" He smirked, but there was a sharpness to the curve of his lips. "I supposed you'd rather have her trust a man like you, Darius Graeme?"

The name jostled awkwardly in Kestrel's thoughts. It was so unexpected, so unknown and foreign, that at first, she thought she might have heard him wrong. But the conviction with which Leighton had spoken left no room for doubt. He had said that name intentionally.

Kestrel had never heard that name before.

But apparently Thom had.

All the blood had drained from his face. It had drained from all the other patrons he had been with as well.

That chill that had settled over her chest earlier was beginning to crack, sending icy torrents of betrayal through her in surges.

"Thom?" Kestrel said softly. Amidst the murmurs spreading across the tavern, she wasn't sure if he was able to hear her. But it was all the volume she could muster. All the effort she had left to give. "What is he talking about?"

Thom shook his head, a pained expression twisting his features. "It's...not an easy answer, and one I can't give here—"

"No," she said, cutting him off before he could stall any longer. "I need to hear it from you. It's better than hearing it from—" she turned to Leighton, tempted to call him a stranger, but still wanting to call him something more. But according to Thom, she hardly knew him either. Kestrel clutched her braid, staring down at the end of it. "It's better than hearing it from anyone else."

Out of her periphery, she saw Thom hold out his hand again. "Then let me tell you outside where *prying ears* aren't listening."

If he hadn't sneered at Leighton when he said it, she might have taken him up on the offer. But their mutual disdain for each other had her on edge. It made her feel as if neither of them could be trusted, as if she shouldn't be left alone with either of them.

Kestrel shook her head.

"So what?" Thom said—or Darius, or whatever his name was. He threw up his hands in frustration. "You've been out here a few days and now you think you're ready to take on the world? You think you know who to trust? How to make your own choices?"

"Clearly, I do."

Thom looked upon her with pity. "I hate to be the one to keep telling you this, but clearly you don't. I mean look at you. What's the one thing I've told you to be wary of your whole life? People out here are not as trustworthy as they would have you believe. Ask yourself, why are these young men hiding their faces? And what are they doing out here so far away from their own homelands?"

Kestrel frowned. "I—"

She tried speaking, but what would her argument be anyway?

Thom was right. She had only known them for the blink of an eye compared to how long she had known him.

But if the day had taught her anything it was that knowing someone for a long time wasn't a reliable way to gauge whether or not they could be trusted either.

Besides, they were getting off topic.

"I'm not here to talk about them!" Kestrel shouted so loudly her ribs ached. Or perhaps that was just her heart finally shattering for good because she was finally starting to understand.

Thom had never intended on telling her the truth.

Even now, when she was confronting him directly, he was doing everything in his power to avoid answering her very simple questions.

"I only came here to make sure you were alright. And you are. And..." Tears obscured her vision, but she kept her attention trained on the blurriness that was his silhouette. "I thought that when I found you, you'd be proud. To see that I had survived out here, just like you. But you'll never see me as more than that frightened, stupid little girl who nearly got herself killed by cinders, will you?"

Thom's mouth worked before his gaze dropped to the sand-strewn floor.

He didn't answer her. He didn't need to.

It was all the heartbreak Kestrel could take. The room was collapsing around her. The dusty air filling her throat. The heat pressing against her flesh.

He saw it in her eyes before she spun on her heels.

"Wait!" Thom cried out, attempting to hobble after her.

But the room was a labyrinth of tables and chairs that would take him forever to maneuver around. And Kestrel was already gone.

CHAPTER 9

TO TRUST A PRINCE

KESTREL

There was only one place Kestrel thought to go, the only place she had ever known. But she couldn't go back to their tower now. Not that she even knew where it was.

Kestrel was lost.

Stranded.

Alone in a world that she knew nothing about.

So she ran as fast as her feet would carry her, without a destination in mind. She ran until her legs were throbbing, until the heels of her feet felt as if they had split down the centers. And then she ran some more. Through the tight alleyways and heaps of goods that shop owners had left behind. She ran until she lost track of that irksome tavern somewhere long, long behind her.

All that mattered was putting distance between her and Thom—or *Darius* or whoever he was.

So Kestrel kept running.

It wasn't until she whipped past the town gates and

into the dark desert that she finally succumbed to the sobs clawing at her lungs. Kestrel collapsed to her hands and knees beside a sparse cluster of wildflowers and cacti. And once the tears came, it seemed like they might never stop. Like the acidic pain around her broken heart would burn through her before she ever saw the sun again.

She didn't know what hurt more: Thom's lies about the state of humanity, the false identity he'd upheld in her presence, or his complete an utter lack of respect for her and their relationship.

Kestrel's life had been a tightly spun spool of deception and now it had completely unraveled—*she* was unraveled.

And the worst part was that now that she was out here in the quiet, in the dark, with no one around for as far as the eye could see, all she wanted was *him*. To throw her arms around Thom's neck and have him tell her that everything would be alright. That it had all been a big misunderstanding. That he would tell her everything.

Her heartache seemed endless. Her tears bitter with misery.

The sobs were just starting to crescendo again, when something rustled in the flowers before her. Kestrel jolted onto her knees, reaching for her knife. She had forgotten about what dangers could lurk out in the open desert until just now. If it was the scourge, one knife wouldn't do much against their hundreds, but it seemed better to face them armed than completely vulnerable.

When the thing behind the flowers whimpered though, Kestrel knew it wasn't anything so frightening.

She parted the tall flowers. An orange, fluffy bundle of

fur leapt out at her.

"Fox?" Kestrel yelped as the creature curled into her arms. "What in the Hollows are you doing out here? How did you even find me?"

The contented fox licked her face in reply and Kestrel let it nuzzle into her lap.

"Oh, it doesn't even matter. I'm just happy to see you. You have no idea how much I..."

The heartbreak almost pushed itself back up again, but Kestrel fought through it with a new realization. She wasn't alone after all—not that a fox would be much company for most people, but she had survived off far less.

"Thank you for finding me." She scratched the top of the fox's head. "It's just you and me now."

The fox tilted its head, as if in question. So Kestrel told it everything. She told it about the prince. About their private, shameful kiss. About the tavern, and finding Thom there amongst all his friends. About the name he'd been called that bore with it a lifetime that Kestrel had never known.

But mostly, Kestrel just lamented.

"I couldn't have been a bigger fool," she went on, mindlessly stroking the fox's fur, an act that seemed just as comforting for her companion as it was for her. "How could I have not known? Every time he came home, he was so sour. I always thought it must just be miserable out there. Harrowing, even. But all this time, what if he just regretted having to come back? Sometimes I would see him on the horizon and watch him walk all the way to our doorstep, and I swear he grew heavier with every step."

Kestrel swallowed against the sting in her chest. "I never knew—I never even suspected…"

If she had, she wondered if things might've been different. If she would've confronted him, asked him to take her with him. To show her the world and how to survive in it. After all, her books had made her curious about such adventures. In most of the stories, seemingly ordinary people would do extraordinary things. They would fight dragons, take on tyrannical governments, explore unchartered lands.

The Wilds had always seemed far too dangerous for her to even dream of such a thing. But maybe that was just the fear that Thom had instilled in her talking. Maybe this was the start of her own adventure. The day she would seize her own destiny. Make a life all her own.

The only problem was: Kestrel didn't have a clue what that life would entail.

When she had left their tower, her only goal had been to find Thom and return home safely. But now?

"I don't know what to do," she confessed, her hand stilling on the fox's back. A poisonous concoction of shame and remorse twisted in her belly. "I don't even know where to begin because I don't even know where is safe. Thom never told me the places that could be trusted—I didn't even know there were places that could be trusted. And now, the only place I've found, I can't return to. Not if Thom's there."

The fox made a grumbling noise again, nudging her hand with its dry nose.

Kestrel mustered a weak grin. "Don't worry, we'll figure something out."

It wasn't an empty promise, but one she intended to keep. Not that she had a choice, really. It was her life on the line and Kestrel intended on figuring out how to survive, even if she had to do it without Thom.

So she thought back to all the books she had read, especially the ones where the heroines found themselves wandering foreign lands with no clue how to survive on their feet. If she put her mind to it, she could do the same.

Kestrel's stomach grumbled. Food, she supposed, was a good first place to start. Then probably lodging so that she could rest awhile. Although she didn't want to run into Thom again, the guards she'd encountered earlier were still at the front gates. Maybe they could point her to a place where she was unlikely to run into him for the night.

Before she could nudge the fox out of her lap and start making her way back toward Mutiny Bay though, the fox's ear twitched in the moonlight.

"What is it?"

The fox sprang from her lap, teeth bared.

It was then that Kestrel heard the sound of footfalls in the sand behind her. She jumped up too, snapping around to face whatever was approaching.

Through the darkness, she could discern the silhouettes of two people walking toward her.

Kestrel snatched the knife from her belt again and thrust it outward. "S-stay back! I'm warning you. I know how to fight."

That was a lie, but she hoped between the gleam of the blade and the fox's vicious growls it would be enough to deter anyone who meant her harm.

The one in the middle threw their arms up. "It's okay. It's just us."

Hearing Leighton's voice was like curling up next to a warm fire in the middle of winter. Her blade arm dropped. Kestrel stepped toward him, desperate to leap into his arms and soak in as much of his reassurance as she could. But she stopped herself. As much as she wanted to be comforted, she hadn't yet forgotten that he had kept secrets from her as well.

Kestrel squared her shoulders instead. "What do you want?"

"I wanted to—"

Leighton was interrupted by the cursed sun shooting back into the sky. Everyone winced, the sudden burst of light leaving them all temporarily blinded and disoriented. But Kestrel tried keeping her attention on the two of them—not *three*, she noticed. For the first time, she wondered where Efrem was.

"Ah, you never do get used to that blasted thing, do you?" Micah groaned, hands shielding his steel blue eyes.

If he was waiting for a reaction, Kestrel wasn't giving him one. She didn't want them to feel welcome in her presence. She wanted them gone.

"Sorry to interrupt," Leighton said, also readjusting to the light. "It didn't feel right letting you run off without checking in on you after...after all of that." He dared a step closer. Then another. When she flinched as if she would bolt, he held up his hands. "I just wanted to see if you were okay?"

How could she lie? Her face was still covered in tears.

But she didn't want to admit her vulnerability to him

either. He hadn't earned her trust earlier, she'd just given it willingly. And that had been a mistake. One she wouldn't repeat so readily.

Kestrel folded her arms instead, and the fox at her heels yipped a bark.

"Thoughtless question," Leighton admitted. Then, noticing the creature for the first time, he added, "Is this a friend of yours?"

"I...I think so. It saved me before I came across Mutiny Bay. And then it was out here waiting for me when I came back out." Kestrel smiled down at her furry companion.

Micah inched closer, an eagerness in his tone she hadn't heard before. "Is it a fox or Animali?"

"Ani-what?" Kestrel asked.

Leighton and his brother exchanged a curious look, one she couldn't quite decipher. It frustrated her all the more. One more secret to add to the mix.

As if sensing her impatience, Leighton looked at her apologetically.

"Let me try this again—" Carefully, he reached up to the fabric covering the lower half of his face and untied it, revealing the alabaster sheen of his face. "I don't know exactly what that argument was about, but I've had my fair share of family quarrels, and none have ever ended with one of us fleeing an entire town just to get away from the other."

"Speak for yourself," Micah interjected.

Leighton ignored him, continuing. "What I mean to say is, I can only imagine how *not* okay you are, so we wanted to check on you."

It was perhaps the most genuine thing anyone had

said to her in hours. And even if she didn't know these young men very well, she appreciated the comforting words, and more so the idea that she wasn't so alone, nonetheless.

"Thank you."

Leighton nodded. "I...also owe you an apology. And an explanation, if you'll hear it."

It was all she needed. That was all she had been asking of Thom as well. Even now, if he were to come up to her and confess everything, she knew that she could find it in her heart to forgive him.

The problem was, he wasn't willing to give her the truth.

But maybe the strangers would.

Kestrel gestured to the ground near the flowers. "Have a seat."

"After the day we've had? Gladly." Micah plopped down to the dusty ground with a huff. The fox immediately scurried to his side, eager to sniff him. He chuckled as he held out his hand to the creature's twitching nose. "I'm Micah, by the way. And that's—"

"Leighton," Kestrel finished for him. Seeing the way his eyebrows shot to his hairline brought a tinge of pink to her cheeks, and she felt the need to elaborate. "I overheard you use each other's names in the alleyway."

"Right. Then that's all the introductions except one." Micah watched her expectantly, waiting. She didn't have it in her to keep her name a secret, or to fabricate one on the spot.

"Kestrel. My name is Kestrel."

"Like the bird?" asked Micah.

"So I've been told." She had never actually seen one before, but it was nice to know that this wasn't another one of Thom's lies.

Leighton approached her slowly, one hand extended outward. "A pleasure to meet you, Kestrel."

She was reluctant to take it. Accepting his hand felt too much like wiping the slate clean. But in the end, she was compelled to, if not only because she hoped beyond all hopes that they could somehow mend the broken trust between them, but also to curb that insatiable desire to feel him again, despite everything.

With their hands clasped together, Leighton guided her under the insufficient shade of one of the cacti and helped her to sit. Would all human contact make her heart skip and her vision swirl? Or was there something about his touch specifically?

"Where's the other one you were traveling with?" she asked, trying to change the subject before her cheeks could flush any harder.

"Efrem?" Leighton squatted down beside her and gave a nonchalant shrug. "Ah, he's probably standing guard somewhere."

"My twin takes his duties very seriously," Micah added, a bit sarcastically.

"Unlike someone I know," Leighton teased his brother.

Kestrel found their playful banter comforting, but still she wanted to know them more. "So, are you all..."

"Princes of Irongate?" Micah finished for her. "Can't you tell by our dashing good looks and charm?"

Leighton shot a glower at his brother before returning his attention to Kestrel. "He means, yes. We are. And I'm sorry I didn't come forward with that information sooner but, we were meant to travel through Vallonde unrecognized. And then once you saw me without my face covered, I originally thought you'd know who I was. When you said you didn't recognize me, it felt like a blessing, and spoiling our disguises to out our titles seemed too risky."

"She probably only remembers the most handsome of the Erickson brothers, so don't let it hurt your ego too much," Micah teased, giving the fox a rough scratch on the top of its head.

A relentless smile worked its way onto Kestrel's expression. And upon seeing it, Micah fist bumped the air in victory. But Kestrel was already remembering something else Thom had said. Something about them belonging to a corrupt crown.

"Why were you trying to stay unrecognized in—did you call it Vallonde?"

Micah's silent cheering stopped. He gaped at her, dumbfounded. "Cursed sky! You really don't know much about anything do you—hey! Ow!" When Leighton flicked a pebble at him, Micah rolled his eyes. "Fine, fine. You can tell her everything and I'll just be over here, keeping my mouth shut like a good prince." He turned his attention instead to the sand, where he started to draw patterns with his finger.

Leighton cleared his throat and tossed his golden hair out of his eyes. "We're not exactly welcomed this far south. Irongate and Vallonde have had many...disagreements throughout Grimtol's history."

There it was again. That name—both of them, she'd

heard for the first time ever today. "Vallonde? Grimtol? I feel like I'm supposed to know these names, but I don't."

Micah's head jerked up, eyes bulging again, but his brother silenced him with a scowl and returned his attention to her.

"That's alright. I'll tell you everything you want to know." His crystalline eyes locked with hers, sending an arctic shudder up her spine.

"T-thank you. You have no idea how much I appreciate the honesty."

He nodded. As he considered his next words, Leighton wet his lips. It was an innocuous act, and one that very likely had nothing to do with her and everything to do with the sweltering heat beating down from above, but Kestrel found her body responding in strange ways. His proximity reminded her of when they were in the alleyway, and how she could feel the heat pouring off him, feel the static charge between their two bodies.

In her books, the scenes Kestrel loved reading almost as much as the heroic ones were the romantic ones. The ones where the tension would build and build before finally bursting into a crescendo that would send delicious pulses of excitement to her core.

But those were stories.

What happened in the alleyway...it had been a mistake. She needed to remember that.

Kestrel jerked her gaze away and stared down at the fox instead, anywhere but at Leighton.

After thinking about his next words, Leighton finally found them. With his chin held high, he pounded a fist to his chest. "Allow me to formally introduce myself. I am

Prince Leighton Erickson, eldest son of King Ulfaskr, and heir to the throne of Irongate."

So it really was true. Thom hadn't been lying about that part at least.

Mortification heated Kestrel's face. Not only was he a prince, but he was also the *crown prince?*

"Heir to the throne? Does that mean someday you'll be the—"

"King of Irongate?" Micah supplied, finishing the final touches on what looked like a shield with lightning bolts on it drawn in the sand. "That's my big brother for you, always the impressive one."

A king.

The boy she had kissed in an alleyway would one day be king!

She wondered if she should get up and bow, but it seemed a little late for that.

"Someday, yes," Leighton agreed, but there was a darkness to his tone that didn't belong there. Not for someone who shone so brilliantly. Someone who was destined to become a king. "Are you familiar with the Cursed Night?"

This one, she did know.

"Actually, yes—" she said, perking up with confidence at first. Then she remembered that everything she thought she knew had come from Thom, and that so far most of what he'd told her had turned out to be false. "Or at least, I've heard a version of the story. But I don't know if it's the truth..."

The crown prince nodded, his sky-blue eyes drifting somewhere distant. "I was only five when it happened, but I still remember it like it was yesterday. The day the Corrupt Queen of Caelora placed a dark curse upon Grimtol. Were you alive then to see it?"

"Only just barely. Thom tells me..." she swallowed the lump around his name and thought about correcting herself. It seemed wrong though and she couldn't bring herself to do it. Not yet anyway. "He tells me I was just a babe; I had been born that very day."

As if her birth had brought nothing but heartache.

She wasn't even sure Leighton had heard her. His expression had already turned haunted, as if he was somewhere far, far away, snagged by the dark brambles of his memories.

"Our mother disappeared when were very young," Leighton continued. "Efrem had nightmares every night for years about the bad things that might've befallen her. He would wake up in fits of terror, screaming so loudly that I and anyone in the castle who heard him could've sworn someone was torturing him."

"That's awful," Kestrel said, thinking about her own mother and how maybe she had been fortunate not to remember her.

"It was awful," agreed Leighton. "Not even the nurse maids could settle him. Only I could soothe his woes and calm him down long enough to get him back to sleep." A shadow blanketed his princely features. "That's what I was doing on the Cursed Night. I was tucking Efrem back into bed, assuring him that everything was alright. That he was safe. And then I saw it. The dark rise of magic that blasted into the sky.

"It looked like a blackened waterfall pouring upward

into the clouds. It was beyond unnatural. Beyond foreboding. But I saw it, that power shot into the sky and then branched out like black bolts of lightning. I watched the dark tendrils of power slither their way across the lands like massive veins pumping evil into every corner of the realm. Into every kingdom. I felt the rumble of their impact as they met their targets."

If it weren't for the powerful sun overhead, Kestrel might've felt the chill threatening to seep into her bones. This was part of a story that she knew, but only bits and pieces of. It was a time in Thom's life that he didn't like speaking about, the day Kestrel's mother had died in his arms. It was also the day Kestrel had been born. The only thing Thom had ever said about it was that the sky had gone black and the curse was upon them, and it had been his sole purpose to get Kestrel somewhere safe.

But the Cursed Night, as Leighton called it, happened a long time ago. What did it have to do with the princes and their secret excursion to Vallonde?

Micah had found a canteen and was finishing a refreshing drink of water when he pulled it from his lips. "Let it be remembered that it was my scaredy-cat brother, Efrem, who suffered from the nightmares. Not I."

"I'll remember." Kestrel chuckled, relieved for a reprieve from the gloomy topic for now.

The fox was pawing at the canteen. Micah poured a mouthful's worth into the cap and let it drink.

"Good," he said. "As long as you know that I'm the brave one. So if you ever need any saving, you can count on me to be there." Micah winked, but she didn't think it was meant to be flirtatious, just the way he was.

"Thank you. I'll keep that in mind."

Leighton reached for the canteen and between gulps started again. "As I was saying—"

"Oh excuse me for interrupting and trying to save our dear friend here from what everyone already knows about Grimtol's very recent history," Micah said, casting a knowing smile Kestrel's way. But she lowered her head, tucked the braid behind her ear before she started fidgeting with the tip. His voice drew serious. "Surely, you know the rest of it. Right?"

Kestrel worried her lip, embarrassment threatening to claim her. Even though it wasn't her fault that she didn't know any of it. It was Thom's.

She tried mustering some pride and shook her head. "I don't think I know anything."

"About the curse? All the damage it did? Everyone it harmed?"

The fox sauntered back into Kestrel's lap, as if it knew how much she needed the distraction and comfort its soft fur would provide.

"Like I said, I don't think I know much about anything. The way Thom told it, the curse is what brought the monsters upon us, and it killed everyone in the realm. But Mutiny Bay over there proves that wasn't true."

"It wasn't entirely false though, either," Leighton countered, gently. "Some monsters did rise with the curse. And many people were slain in its wake—like the dragons and other beasts. The knights who had been trying to stop the Corrupt Queen, they were caught in her rageful inferno as well. They are who you see roaming the lands of

Vallonde now, the charred, vengeful husks of the people they once were."

Kestrel stopped petting the fox's head. "Do you mean the cinders? They were knights?"

Leighton nodded.

Her thoughts went to the woman with snake-like skin. Was that what was going to happen to her? Or was that the cause of something else? Were all the monstrosities of the realm former people?

Leighton continued, "Perhaps the most horrific impact of the curse, however, was how it devastated the king-doms, especially their leaders."

Dread was pooling in her gut. She almost didn't even want to ask, but she didn't want to be left in the dark either. "How do you mean?"

"Every king, queen, and other ruler of Grimtol was turned into some cursed creature, unleashed upon their people. Our father was among them, the Great King Ulfaskr Erickson of Irongate."

The muscles in Leighton's jaw tightened. He glanced to his brother who was already watching him with mournful eyes. Ceremoniously, the two brothers clenched both hands into fists, punching their arms out in front of them, as straight as boards. They bent them inward then, bracketing one arm over the other to create a square or perhaps a sort of shield. Kestrel imagined it was a cultural custom, something meant to symbolize the strength and fortitude of their Irongate kingdom.

"Storm and steel, never broken," Leighton said.

"Never broken," repeated Micah.

Unsure if she should copy them or if that would be an

intrusion on this shared moment, Kestrel opted to lower her head in respect instead.

She had never heard about any of this. Hadn't even known there were kingdoms. Not really, anyway. Thom never wanted to talk about anything before the curse. He talked about wanting to find a cure, but she hadn't realized to what extent that would've impacted the entire realm. Hadn't realized how many countless people, like Leighton and his brother, were relying on it. And now she also wondered why Thom had wanted it anyway. He had Kestrel locked up safe in a tower, he had his life in Mutiny Bay. What did he have to do with the kings and queens of Grimtol?

Lowering his arms, Leighton continued his tale.

"The curse turned our father into a crazed thing. Glutinous and insatiable. He rampaged our halls, slew dozens of our guards before breaking out of our castle and tearing through the streets where he...he ate countless of our citizens."

Kestrel's hand floated to her mouth. "That's awful." And then, trying to fill in the rest of the story, she asked, "And only you survived?"

Micah's laugh was hollow compared to his formerly robust joy. "Flattered, truly, that you think the three of us defended our kingdom alone, as small children, nonetheless. But no. Others survived, thank the sun."

Leighton nodded. "What remained of our guard managed to capture our father and put him somewhere safe, somewhere he wouldn't be able to hurt anyone anymore."

Her first thought was *where*? But that seemed like an

insensitive thing to say to the sons who had lost their father in such a horrific way.

"No child should have to know the pain of living without their parent," Kestrel said, eyes fixed on where her fingers threaded through the fox's soft fur. She was trying desperately not to think of her own losses, for how could they even compare? Her mother had not been transformed into a monster; she had not been forced to witness as her mother attacked the homeland she loved.

And they were just two of the victims. If this had happened to all the kingdoms—the number of which she had yet to uncover—Kestrel imagined many innocents had been harmed in the making of this dreadful curse. Families ripped apart. Civilians slain.

It didn't seem fair.

"Why would the Corrupt Queen have done such a thing?" she asked at last.

Micah shrugged, a tuft of his long, auburn locks shifting out of his eye. "To punish them?"

"But—" Kestrel frowned. "Those kings and queens weren't the only ones who suffered. She punished you and countless of innocents as well."

Kestrel and the fox both startled as Leighton jumped to his feet, fists clenched.

"That was the point though, wasn't it? The Cursed Night was a calculated attack on not only her enemies, but their children—on the entire realm. She didn't care how many innocents were harmed along the way. She didn't care about dooming every kingdom into a time of darkness and misery. She only cared about destruction. About asserting power."

Kestrel clutched the fox tighter. She hadn't seen him like this yet. Hadn't seen what it was like to watch the last glimpse of his light be snuffed out. Not that she could blame him though. He had every right to be livid at such an injustice.

"Hey, Leigh, maybe take a breath. You're scaring this fine young lady, yeah?" Micah winked at her, an attempt to lighten the mood, but his tone was anything but light. There was warning and worry behind those words. It made Kestrel wonder how many times he'd had to calm the crown prince when he'd become fixated on this matter before.

For all his outrage though, the words reached Leighton easily.

He sucked in a breath and tilted his head up to the clear sky.

"Right..." he said, a calm washing over him. "As I was saying, eight kingdoms lost nine leaders that day. All of us have spent the years since searching for the Corrupt Queen, trying to break her spell, trying to figure out how to rescue our rulers. But Irongate cannot wait any longer. Our kingdom needs their king. And if it can't be our father, then it is my duty to take his place and lead our kingdom."

Leighton's gaze came back down from the clouds, and some of the light had returned behind those dazzling eyes of his, as if they had absorbed part of the sky itself. He returned to his spot beside her, his features softening with each step. Only once he was seated again, his ire cooled, did he finally meet her gaze and begin again.

"So, to answer your very reasonable question in the most long-winded way that I can—" Leighton smirked, looking a bit embarrassed— "Now that I am of age, I will be crowned king. But it's a custom in Irongate for the next prince in line to prove himself worthy of the title first."

"Oh," she said, surprised and remembering that her original question hadn't been about the history of Grimtol at all, but about what the princes had been doing here. And true to his word, Leighton was answering her. "And how do you prove yourself worthy of the title?"

"By doing the only thing that matters these days: slaying a monster."

Heat swirled in Kestrel's belly. He was the Gallant Hero she'd pegged him for, after all. More than that, this was sounding more and more like the adventures she had read about. An unsuspecting young woman meets a heroic, handsome prince, and together they set out to rid the realm of darkness—

But that overactive imagination of hers was getting ahead of herself.

This was *his* adventure. Not hers.

Besides, Kestrel didn't know the first thing about slaying a monster. In fact, both times she'd encountered one—the cinder and then whatever horrid thing was at the bottom of the Maw—they had both nearly killed her.

She was letting a silly daydream get the better of her.

Still, she was curious. She had always loved a book with a good hero. An adventure.

"What kind of monster?" she asked.

She was surprised to find Leighton deflating at the question. As if this wasn't the greatest honor that it sounded like. The realm was teeming with cursed beasts, at least according to Thom. They had terrorized people since the Cursed Night. What reason did Leighton have for such trepidation?

The crown prince rubbed his face, seeming to avoid eye contact with his brother. "It doesn't matter now. We're back to square one anyway."

"Cursed sky! We weren't even that late!" groaned Micah. In a show of frustration, he made his best attempt at kicking the sand, but from his seated position with his knees bent, all he managed to do was jostle his own body and kick a cloud of dust in the wind that blew back in his face.

"We were *two days* late," Leighton corrected him.

Micah blew sand out of his mouth. "That's nothing. You once waited a whole month for Efrem and I to return from Greenwitch. And that's just across the sea, not across entire kingdoms."

"That's different."

"Yeah, a few weeks different! That's my point!"

"No, I mean—" Leighton shook his head, the blond tuft of hair swaying and catching the light. "I know the kind of trouble the two of you can get yourselves into, and the kind you can pull yourselves out of. I knew you'd make it back. Our contact at Mutiny Bay, however? He doesn't know us. What was he supposed to do when we didn't show? Wait forever?"

"People are always late when they travel. A couple days is hardly asking much. You'd think a businessman would know that," grumbled Micah.

"A businessman also knows that time is money," Leighton shot back. "And if he spent all his days waiting on people who might've died in their journeys, let alone changed their minds, then he'd go out of business."

As they bickered, Kestrel's head jerked between the two of them, struggling to keep up. When there was a lull, she managed to butt in, "What sort of business brought you to Mutiny Bay then? And what does it have to do with proving you're ready for your crown?"

Micah's arms shot up. "Look, it's not all my fault is all I'm saying."

Leighton gave him a look that said he disagreed, but rather than arguing anymore he answered Kestrel. "Rumor has it there is a mighty beast that dwells in one of the abandon fortresses in Vallonde. The Fortress of Thirst, they call it. Have you heard of it?"

Kestrel shook her head, and the way he nodded made her feel like it was okay not to know things, like he under-stood her and would help her learn.

"Our plan was to meet a man in Mutiny Bay to inquire about buying some boars off him because we heard the beast has a proclivity for hunting them."

"So much for that plan." Micah sighed.

The fox whined, one eye twitching open.

"Surely they didn't mean to feed them to the monster —" Kestrel said to the fox, giving its head a reassuring scratch. And then she added to Leighton— "Right? Animals are a sacred thing. At least that's what Thom..."

The brothers exchanged another look, only this time she thought she understood it. That would be a topic for another time. For now, Leighton continued his story.

"If we could've helped it, the hogs would've survived. But I'd be lying if I said we weren't bringing them with us to use as bait. And as I mentioned before, my intention is to keep no more lies between us; I get the sense that you've had enough of those to last you a lifetime."

Kestrel's chest tightened, her gratitude immense.

Micah averted his gaze, perhaps to give the two of them a modicum of privacy, for which she was also grateful for. Leighton's words had churned a warmth inside her that she hadn't felt since they'd first laid eyes upon each other. Only this was more intimate. More personal. They were just strangers then, using each other to meet whatever the need was in the moment. But now they were learning about one another, discovering each other's vulnerabilities, their fears, their strengths.

Leighton's lips twitched in a cautious smile, one that begged for forgiveness.

The truth was, the longer they spoke, the less certain Kestrel was that he had owed the truth to her back then anyway. They'd only spent a handful of moments together in that alleyway. He hardly had the time to divulge his life story to her. But maybe that wasn't what he was apologizing for now.

She had sensed it the moment she fled the alleyway and left him behind with his brothers. Saw the remorse in his eyes as he watched her go. He had regretted his words to her, even then. Perhaps if she had waited, he would've been able to explain, would've tried making things right.

Kestrel was too short on friends to hold a grudge now.

With a soft smile of her own, she granted him the forgiveness he sought.

Relief and appreciation washed over him. But it was short-lived when Micah, who apparently had been growing uncomfortable in the silence, clapped his hands suddenly. "Alright, so, now that the old plan is out, we need a new one. If we don't have bait, we'll need another advantage."

"Lookouts, I guess," Leighton suggested, although neither of them seemed too confident about the idea. "There are those window arches, high up on the fortress walls. If you and Efrem could climb up to them, perch from the ledge, you'd be out of harm's way and could maybe throw some rocks across the room below as a distraction while I sneak inside?"

"What do we look to you, little desert lizards? Efrem's so clumsy, he'd slip before he was even a foot off the ground. And me—" Micah shoved his hands in both of their directions— "You think these hands have ever seen a callous a day in their lives?"

Kestrel scrutinized them and thought they might be the smoothest hands she'd ever seen. "Unlikely."

"Exactly."

Leighton blew his lips. "Oh, I'm sure a callous or two wouldn't hurt you. The ladies may even like seeing you a bit rougher around the edges."

"Please, they love me for my charming delicateness." Micah flashed Kestrel a smile before turning a glare back onto his brother. "I will not be climbing up a stone wall. We'll have to think of something else. Flanking the fortress and entering from all sides, or something?"

Leighton grunted his disapproval. The two brothers burst into another argument where they considered about a half dozen insufficient plans, each more desperate and hole-ridden than the last.

But while they argued, Kestrel couldn't help but wonder...

She was an avid climber.

Even without having seen the fortress they were speaking about, she knew with certainty that she would have no trouble scaling its walls and being the distraction they needed.

Maybe this was the purpose she had been waiting for. The start of her life. She could help the prince earn his crown, become a hero of sorts in her own right.

Leighton was up and pacing again, a thumb pressed to his chin. "I suppose we could ask around. See if anyone knows how to—"

Kestrel bounced to her feet, the fox flopping to the dirt. "I could do it! I could be your distraction!"

Both brothers cocked their heads. Leighton looked worried, while Micah seemed caught somewhere between shocked and impressed that she would suggest something so reckless.

Slowly, Micah rose too. "Don't get me wrong, little bird, you are beautiful. But that's not the sort of thing that will distract this creature."

The nickname threw her. It sounded so similar to what Thom had called her all her life, that at first she thought Micah had said Little *Fury* and it took her a moment to collect herself.

"I'm not talking about me walking into the monster's lair with a smile on my face. I'm saying I could be the one to climb those walls. I could reach those windows."

Leighton still looked skeptical. "How do you know? You haven't even seen the place."

As the two brothers continued arguing, desperation bloomed inside Kestrel's chest. It felt as if her entire future was hinging on this moment. A fork in the road she had never considered. They could leave her there, and she could set out into the realm, alone, with no destination or goal in mind...

Or...

Or her life could change forever. She could make friends with people other than Thom. She could leave this small corner of the realm for the first time in her life. Travel somewhere new. Do something daring and heroic, and for once in her endlessly mundane and meaningless existence actually experience *something*.

No more fantasizing about stories.

No more daydreaming.

This would be a real adventure.

"You don't know how high it is, or what—" Leighton was saying, when Kestrel bolted.

"Come on, follow me!"

Before either of the brothers could decline, she was running the short distance back toward Mutiny Bay. The fox and the two princes had no choice but to follow.

When she reached the wall, she tossed her pack in the sand and began untying her boots.

"What are you doing now?" Micah asked.

"Just watch. You'll see."

Kestrel reached her hands up to the sienna-colored stones. They were smoother than the ones used to construct her tower; those had likely been worn down by the salt in the ocean air. But these were still rough enough that she could find a nice, firm grip. She began to climb.

"Wait!" Leighton shouted. "You don't have to do this. We'll find another..."

Although his words had been booming at first, as Kestrel made her ascension with alarming celerity, he quieted. Even from where she was, already halfway up the chalky wall, Kestrel could hear the enthrallment in his voice. It made her feel all fluttery with pride and it was all the incentive she needed to climb higher. Because this proved that she wasn't as useless as she thought. Even someone like her, someone who had no real experience out here, even she had a valuable skillset to offer—and maybe she had others too. She just had to believe in herself and find the right opportunities—and the right people to appreciate them.

When Kestrel reached the top of the wall, she spun around to give Leighton and Micah a satisfied wave, but they weren't the only ones watching. She had accrued a small audience that now included both of the guards she'd spoken to earlier on her way into Mutiny Bay.

Micah's arms were folded as he smirked up at her, more than impressed. The cursed woman and her male guard counterpart, too, watched her with a reverent tilt to their smiles.

But it was Leighton's beaming grin that sent Kestrel's head floating into the clouds.

"Alright, you've proven your point, you show-off!" Micah shouted out. "Now come back down here so we can get you to the real thing."

CHAPTER 10

ADVENTURING STARTS HERE

KESTREL

The two princes led Kestrel and the fox back into the open desert.

As Mutiny Bay was becoming hardly more than a ripple of heat behind them, she asked, "What about your other brother? Is he staying behind?"

"*Other brother?*" Micah said, frowning playfully. "Hmm. Sorry, not ringing any bells."

A small smirk tugged on Leighton's mouth, but he kept his focus on the desert before them. "He's probably already with the rest of our convoy up ahead."

"You have a convoy?"

Micah angled an eyebrow at her. "Oh, little bird, you didn't think the most handsome princes in all the lands would travel alone, did you?"

"I guess I'll let you know when I meet them," Kestrel quipped back, starting to get the hang of Micah's inflated ego and sense of humor. The nickname he had so easily given her was growing on her as well. There was something so familiar and endearing about it that it made warmth bloom across her chest.

Leighton burst into a barking fit of laughter, a robust and joyous sound that Kestrel would cherish for the rest of her days.

"Ooo, she's got teeth," sang Micah. And then wriggling his brow at her again, he added, "It's a good thing I don't mind a little bite."

Kestrel rolled her eyes, but that was about as much of a retort as she could think of in the moment. Her stamina for witty banter still needed some exercising, but she was pretty sure that the more time she spent with Micah, the stronger it would become.

Fortunately, she didn't need to think of a response though, for beyond the princes' heads, she could just start to make out a collection of objects in the distance.

"Your convoy?"

Leighton nodded. "Not much farther now."

And he wasn't wrong.

Within no time at all, the four of them were close enough that she could count seventeen vessels in total, a variety of strange-looking contraptions of thrown together wooden planks, pipes, and in some cases, sails. It seemed there were a few different types of caravans awaiting them. Some were small enough that only one or two people could fit inside, and there were pedals that appeared to be connected to the wheels underneath it. Others were massive, like they held enough cargo and supplies to feed the entire entourage—of which, she had seen at least a few dozen in the distance. They meandered between the contraptions, checking the nuts and bolts, securing different wires and unfastening them.

Kestrel's eye caught on one contraption in particular. It was dingier than all the others, but somehow more fortified as well. Whereas most of the vessels were open-aired or had ample windows, this one was bolted tight without a single way to view inside. Unlike the others, it was so large that it didn't look like the wind or humans would be able to drag the weight of it across the sand. That was when she noticed the beast at the front end of it, a giant scorpion harnessed at the helm.

Kestrel gasped, her steps faltering.

"The scourge," she breathed.

Leighton, who had been walking a few paces ahead, doubled back for her. He placed a hand on her lower back, jolting her back to her senses. "Don't worry about them. They're harmless now. Once their stingers and pincers were dealt with, they became relatively docile and obedient."

Kestrel noticed now that the creature's pincers were, in fact, bound in iron cages. The sharp tip of its tail was missing too, as if it had been shorn off. Something about the sight of it made her stomach queasy, but she supposed at least the creature would no longer be a threat to them or to anyone.

They continued walking, getting close enough that the vessels now surrounded them. But Kestrel remained focused on the one with the scorpion.

At the back of the giant caravan came a loud bang, like a heavy door slamming closed. Kestrel scanned the back for the source of the noise, surprised to find that she recognized the person exiting the other end. Efrem.

Micah dropped the sack that had been slung over his shoulder and bound for his twin brother. The two collided like they were drawn by an invisible force. Efrem released his brother, and with a wily grin, punched him in the shoulder. Micah jumped up, an arm wrapping over his slightly-taller brother's neck as he wrenched him downward. He gave Efrem's already disheveled, auburn hair a rough tousle before finally liberating him, and the two of them walked arm-over-shoulder, conversing enthusiastically as they went to the other side of the cargo where she could no longer see them.

There was a twang of jealousy pinching her insides, but mostly she just felt awestricken curiosity. And gratitude. So much gratitude that she was finally getting to meet people.

"Are you sure you want to do this?" Leighton asked, drawing her attention back to him. "You'd be putting your life in danger for a cause that you are not beholden to."

Turning around, Kestrel faced the young man she had first met in the marketplace, only to find he had shed the tattered cloths and robes that had kept him disguised in Vallonde.

As he shoved the final pieces of old fabric into the back of one of the single-person carts, she noticed the regal garb he'd been wearing underneath. Now he donned a tunic the same color of the deepest depths of the ocean. The golden accents embroidered down the center shimmered in the sunlight and burst into a plume of designs across his chest that she wanted to run her fingers over. He reached into the cart and pulled out a cape to match, one with golden tassels that rested on his broad shoulders and made him look equal parts ravishing and intimidating. His height didn't help. Now that he wasn't weighed down by his disguise, she realized for the first time just how tall he was, maybe a whole head taller than her.

It was easy to see the king he would soon become.

Kestrel had to resist the urge to bow. She focused instead on his question, though it wasn't an easy one.

"I've...lived a sheltered life. Thom raised me. And for all of that time, he led me to believe that the rest of the realm was too dangerous to venture into. Out of fear and obedience, I spent my entire life trapped in a tower, reading books and imagining what the realm could've been like if things had just been different, not knowing that what I dreamt of was already out there."

Feeling small in his now domineering presence, Kestrel peered down at her hands. Hands that hadn't done much in their time but could maybe do so much more. Her eyes drifted back toward Mutiny Bay, now hardly more than a blur on the horizon.

"As scared as I was to leave my tower, the whole time I was there, I longed for something more. I dreamt of adventure. Of freedom. Of seeing the kingdoms and being brave enough to defend them, as brave as Thom had been..." Kestrel had to pause to swallow the bubble ballooning in the back of her throat like a swarm of locusts. Finally, she met Leighton's kind and striking gaze. "When you found me again, I was thinking that I didn't know what to do with myself after all that. I knew I couldn't go back to the tower. But I didn't know anything about being out here; I didn't know where to go next.

"I might not be beholden to your mission, but it gives me purpose. Makes me feel useful for once in my life. So, as much as I appreciate you trying to give me an out, I should honestly be thanking you for allowing me to join you."

"Thanking me?" Leighton guffawed with a shake of his head. "I feel like I'm marching you into certain death."

"You're not though." She grabbed his hand, not even thinking about it, and forced him to meet her eyes. "Not to sound dramatic, but it feels like the opposite. For the first time in a long while, I actually feel like I'm alive."

He glanced down at their hands and his mouth twitched into a sad grin. "I think I know the feeling."

Finally, realizing what she had done, she released his hand. She may have forgiven him, but that didn't mean they could go back to being close like *that* so easily. She still didn't understand why he had lied to Micah about the kiss, why he had seemed so ashamed about it.

Glancing around them now, Kestrel noticed there were dozens of people—likely his men—bustling about, but that she and Leighton were still relatively alone, tucked away by one of the many contraptions out here.

Most importantly, there wasn't a single brother in sight.

If she was going to ask him, now might be the only chance she had to get an honest answer out of him.

"What happened back in Mutiny Bay? When your brothers arrived, you...you were different. You lied to them about what we did."

He kept his eyes downcast. "I'm sorry for that. I never meant to hurt you—"

"Well, you did," she bit back, not ready to let him off the hook so easily. "You made me feel like I was a mistake."

Leighton's hands twitched like they were going to reach out for her, but he stopped himself. His scanning eyes seemed to notice his regiment around them, and so instead he clenched his fists at his sides and kept his voice to a gentle whisper. "You could never be a mistake."

Kestrel's cheeks flushed, but it wasn't enough. It wasn't a full answer, and she wanted more.

"Then why did you lie to Micah about what we were doing?"

"I was caught off guard by their arrival, much like I was caught off guard by your forwardness—in a good way," he added hastily, seeing the look of embarrassment that was starting to emerge on her face. "Being next in line to the throne comes with many responsibilities and expectations. My brothers, they have rules as well, but they're much more malleable. For the most part, they can do what they want, when they want. Follow every whim and fancy. Whereas, I simply cannot. People look to me as their leader, and so I must act as one."

Worrying at her lip, Kestrel tried piecing the rest together. "I understand. And soon-to-be kings don't kiss lost commoners in alleyways."

Leighton winced, but he didn't correct her. It made heat prick her eyes again, only this time she wasn't able to fight it or flee. Instead, the sorrow consumed her. And not just because she wanted the first boy she ever kissed to be more than just a one-time kiss. It felt like so much more than just this one moment. For an entire lifetime, Kestrel had been left to her fantasies, to the stories she read and the happy ever after endings. When she had met Leighton, when they had kissed, all of those fantasies came piling into that one moment. They built it into something far greater than it was, and she should've known better. Perhaps any other nineteen-year-old would've. But she was new to this world, to the cruel twists of fate.

It was a ridiculous fantasy anyway. To think she might fall in love with someone so quickly—a prince, at that— and that he might love her in return.

Kestrel's vision was still blurry when a hand wrapped around hers.

She brought her shocked gaze up to meet Leighton's bright blue eyes. He was so much taller than her, she had to crane her neck back just to meet his eyes, but she was drawn to them like the tide was drawn to the coast.

"I'm sorry I made you feel like a mistake. You were not. You were...a reprieve. You gave me a chance to experience something I never thought I'd get to experience."

She felt herself leaning closer, a moth drawn to a flame. "And what's that?"

"Fancying a girl as beautiful as a sunset," he said, but then his smirk faded and an intensity swept through him that made her dizzy. His other hand came up to the side of her neck, a thumb brushing her chin. "That and following my heart to give said girl my first kiss."

A first kiss for him as well? Kestrel wasn't sure she believed her ears. Except he was looking down at her the way she felt like she was looking at him. With so much longing. So much desire. She was inclined to believe him. To believe that kiss meant as much to him as it did her. To believe that they both wanted another.

Slowly, Kestrel lifted herself onto her toes.

Their lips drew nearer, his breath hot on her mouth.

She could almost taste him already.

"Kestrel!"

It was as if that single shout was a great war hammer, cleaving the space between them. The two of them jumped backward, although Kestrel was fairly certain if anyone had been watching, they had already seen enough to guess what was about to happen.

"Kestrel! Come quick!"

She spun around to find Micah waving his arms and jumping up and down off in the distance, a plume of dust billowing around him. She glanced back to Leighton, questioning.

"Go," he said with a soft smile. "I need to check-in with my second-in-command and update them on our plan anyway."

As much as she would've rather stayed locked in Leighton's embrace, she also didn't want to stand between him and his duties.

It took everything in her to leave him, and with the fox weaving in and out of her feet, she ran to meet Micah.

"What is it? Is something wrong?" she asked, trying to minimize the irritation in her tone.

"Not wrong," he said, angling his body to the wooden contraption behind him. This one looked more like a boat instead of a cart, with a long, canoe-like board under either side that made it look perfect for gliding across the sands. Micah held out his arms dramatically. "Have you ever steered a sand-glider before?"

"No?" she said, the irritation already waning, replaced with excitement instead. "I can't say that I even knew what—"

Grabbing her hand, Micah jerked her up onto the deck. The sand-glider swayed a bit with each of their bounding strides, but the depressions of sand it was nestled into kept it sturdy enough that they were able to reach the helm.

Micah slapped her hands atop the great, wooden wheel, and Kestrel's jaw fell slack.

"Are you—are you sure you want me to steer?"

He gave her back a hearty slap. "Are you kidding me? You haven't lived until you've tried it!"

Kestrel bit her lip, feeling hesitant but also not wanting to discourage him. After all, wasn't this what she wanted? A chance to live? To be an adventurer?

Her fingers gripped the wheel tighter, a smile already emerging on her lips as she gazed across the desert ahead of them.

"What do I do?" she asked.

Micah hooted and jumped in celebration. The sand-glider wobbled, and they both cast each other worried glances, but once it righted itself again, they were both laughing.

"It's easy, little bird," he said. "And I'll be right here the whole time to guide you."

Kestrel suddenly felt like she had never been more ready for anything in her entire life. "Well then, I believe my adventuring starts here."

CHAPTER 11

A GIFT

ELORA

Unlike most of the other nobles and ladies, Elora had not been granted a handmaiden—but that was fine with her. She found it a strange custom, to have someone always tending to her daily needs so closely. It wasn't something the Ashen people ever did, so she had no problem brushing out the tangles in her long, white hair while she sat at her vanity. In fact, it felt like a luxury, still after all these weeks.

She stared at the reflection in her mirror, eyes drifting to the ornate, silver coronet embedded in her forehead. Leaning over the dressing table, she let a hand drift up to it and gently caressed the smooth, metal. Once she became Queen of Irongate, she wondered if she'd have to wear their crown atop this one, or if the one in her skin would be accepted among the Ironblood. Knowing these proud people, she doubted it.

Elora sighed, sinking back into her chair. A small price,

she reminded herself, words that had been echoing in her mind for days, if not weeks now.

It seemed that was all she did with her newfound freedom: dwell on the past and gripe about the future.

Things might've been different, if she ever had anything to preoccupy herself with. But there was never anything to do. None of the lords and ladies of the castle would engage with her, so pastimes such as carrying on conversations, let alone participating in games or outings, were well out of the question. Not even the servants would dare look at her, if they allowed themselves to cross paths at all.

Irongate Castle was proving to be a cold and lonesome place, not too dissimilar to the dungeons Elora had spent most of her second life in. At least in the dungeons, she had occasionally been surrounded by other miserable offenders—as well as innocents. Not all of them would ordain to conversing with an Ashen like her, but some would. Some of them would pass the long hours moaning over the woeful and unfortunate circumstances that had led them to where they were, the two of them commiserating over grievances and lost opportunities.

Those were the only times she ever felt seen down there. Ever felt real.

When the queen had released her, Elora hadn't realized that the unending boredom and loneliness would linger, leaving endless hours for her mind to wander. It seemed that was all she did these days, her thoughts drifting to all the things that haunted her, all the questions she had trained it not to ask.

Why had no one come for her?

That one, more than any of the others, cycled through her mind every chance it got.

Because, at least when she'd been locked away, part of her had been able to convince herself that they had at least tried to come and save her. They were the most powerful Ashen in Eynallore, her family. They had fought wars and navigated countless rescue missions before her, so she could assume they had been doing the same for her.

But the queen already publicly announced Elora's betrothal to the prince—certain that the prince was going to agree upon his return. She sent news of their engagement to every corner of the realm. And in the weeks that followed, they'd received congratulations from nearly every kingdom still standing.

All except for Eynallore.

Except her family.

Not that they were technically even *family*. Since the Ashen had lost their memories following their resurrections, none of them knew who they belonged to before they met their grim deaths. But there were bonds among them that could not be described by any other word than familial.

For her, that had been with Aethic and Dinian.

Aethic had been declared the Hand of Death almost immediately following their long and cold ascent up the Ghostlight Gulf, following their resurrections. But to her and her sibling Dinian, Aethic had been more than just a leader of their people; he had been a father. And still, she missed them both dearly. Missed the unsolicited but protective advice Aethic would give her about minding her touch whenever she planned to venture out into the forests surrounding their kingdom. She missed the way Dinian would tease her about her fascination with the plants and stars, telling her that she got along better with them than anyone living.

They had loved her. That much, she had been certain of.

So then why hadn't they come for her? If not when she was first captured and taken into the fortified bowels of the Caeloran kingdom, then what about after? Why had their faces not been among the first she'd seen when Caelora had fallen? Why did they let her slip into Irongate's clutches, and why had she been here ever since?

Most importantly, now that she was freed, why weren't they reaching out now?

They knew her better than most. Knew that she would not willingly choose to marry a prince of an enemy kingdom, or any man for that matter.

Elora slammed the hairbrush on the vanity. The mirror wobbled but righted itself. Part of her hoped it would tip and shatter into a thousand sharp pieces, because that was how she felt. Unstable and broken.

It didn't matter if they reached out, Elora told herself. Soon she would be living a new life. In some ways, she already was. According to the people here, being the daughter of the Hand of Death made her a princess. And soon she would become a queen.

Though she tried sitting up and wearing the title with bravery, the thought still soured her stomach.

Elora felt herself hunching back over when a knock came at the door. The person on the other side didn't wait for a reply before they barged in, and Elora wasn't surprised to see it was the queen.

As was expected of her, Elora stood quickly from where she sat.

"Oh please, don't rise on my account." Though Signe spoke with sweetness, there was still a bite of warning in her tone. A sense of power that Elora dared not challenge. Obliging the queen, Elora sat back down, but twisted in her chair so that she could give the woman her full attention.

She buried her surprise and fear, leaving space for only politeness and dignity. "I wasn't expecting visitors this late, my queen. Is everything alright?"

The queen had stopped across the room, a slender finger dragging along one of the broad-leafed plants in Elora's room.

"Better than alright," the queen said. "I come bearing great news and couldn't wait another day to share it." She paused for dramatic effect, awaiting her cue. So Elora gave it, inching closer in her seat as if she couldn't wait to hear. The queen's smile was vicious. "The traitor has been apprehended."

Suddenly, Elora was grateful for the chair beneath her, otherwise the realm surely would've bucked her right off the edge.

She couldn't believe her ears. He actually did it, that future husband of hers had actually found and captured her greatest abuser. Man or not, perhaps the prince wasn't so bad after all.

"That's...wonderful news, my queen. Thank you. Thank you for telling me." Elora was breathless, her mind skittering like mice in the larder at the first sight of the cooks. "Do we know when they'll be returning?"

"Shortly. Perhaps within a week, based on the last letter the prince sent."

Elora's insides were still tumbling, this time for different reasons. "And what of his mission regarding his father? The wedding?"

"There have been no updates on that front yet. But rest assured, the wedding will continue as planned. I am certain of it."

If the queen was correct—and she struck Elora as the sort of person who always was, even when they weren't—then that meant she would be future queen sooner than later. After all, Queen Signe had already told Elora that once the prince returned, they would begin planning immediately, with the goal of having them wed by the month's end, if not sooner.

Elora tried not worrying about that now though.

All that mattered was that her torturer had been caught. She would have her justice.

"And…" Elora tested her voice, the queen's overpowering presence making her waver with uncertainty, even though they had already discussed this part. But she needed to ask again. Needed to hear her say it. "You'll still leave his sentencing to me?"

"As the future queen of Irongate, I see no better opportunity for you to practice one of your royal obligations. Don't you?"

There was nothing she wanted more.

Elora bowed her head in acceptance.

"Well, that was all for now, Princess Elora. I'll leave

you to your nighttime routine." Queen Signe clasped her hands at the waist of her black gown, and spun toward the door. But then stopped. Over her slender shoulder, she added, "Quite the wedding gift from your betrothed, wouldn't you say?"

Bile, hot and rancid climbed up the back of Elora's throat. But she swallowed it down. Met the queen's poisonous grin with a grateful one of her own.

"Yes. He is proving himself to be a fine future husband."

One of the queen's eyebrows cocked, and Elora knew she had made a mistake. "How very amusing. I wasn't aware it was the prince who needed to prove himself and not the former prisoner."

The words pierced her like a spear. Elora spluttered to find the words, to apologize, to take back the insult she had accidentally given.

But before she could, the queen was gone.

It was only then, in the solitude and comfort of her room, that Elora's senses returned to her. She had done nothing wrong. This was just the queen's way of reminding her of her place, which she seemed to do upon exiting any conversation with anyone.

Elora wouldn't let it get under her grey, undead skin.

She would be Queen of Irongate soon enough, and then Queen Signe's subtle threats would mean nothing. Elora would reign.

CHAPTER 12

THE MONSTER INSIDE

KESTREL

They traveled across the desert for days—maybe weeks—over flat wastelands and through heaping dunes that the larger sand-gliders struggled to get up and over without additional men pushing and pulling on all the ropes. Kestrel learned they had to rely on the whims of the desert winds to guide them, as well as the crew's astute sailing.

With the feel of the wheel under her hands, she had never felt more alive.

But she couldn't stand at the helm the entire time. Micah and her took turns on their sand-glider, and although the rest should've been a welcome reprieve, she found herself dreading it every time.

Her thoughts kept drifting back to Thom. She felt guilty for how she'd left him, how he would have no idea where she was or how she was doing. He would worry endlessly about her. And as the days stretched, sometimes Kestrel wished she had gone back to him, at least to make sure he knew she would be alright. Then she remembered how irate he was seeing her in the princes' company and knew it had been better this way. He would've only tried to stop her.

When this was all said and done, Kestrel would return to Mutiny Bay, she decided. She would let him know she was alive and well. Maybe she could even tell him about her brave adventures, how she'd sailed a sand-glider and helped princes take down a monster. Maybe then he might see her as an equal, someone finally worthy of hearing the truth he'd been harboring for so long.

"Halt!" someone shouted from the front ship. "Time to disembark!"

Micah steered them to a stop before closing the sails. "I guess we're on foot from here, little bird."

After that, it wasn't long before the terrain started to shift. The soft sands turned to dirt, then to sharp, green blades of grass that she had never seen before. They reached a coastline, but this one was different from her own. Hers was nothing more than dangerous rocks that plummeted to an even more dangerous tide. This one was calm, surrounded by fields of small, yellow flowers, and with an actual beach to walk along!

Leighton dismissed most of their knights as him, Micah, and Kestrel would continue onward. Kestrel would've been surprised that Efrem wasn't joining them, but the more she observed of him, the more she realized he was much more connected with the soldiers than the other two, almost like he was one of them. Kestrel tried leaving the fox behind as well, but the creature didn't seem to want to leave her side, and honestly, she was okay with that. Wherever they were headed, whatever monsters they were about to face, Kestrel felt comfort in knowing the fox would be by her side her again, ready to defend her if needed.

"It's safer if we travel as a smaller group from here forward," he answered her questioning frown. "Too many people means too much noise, and this plan only works if the monster doesn't hear us coming."

The princes' faces had grown solemn, and Kestrel knew she should be worried too. But no matter how hard she tried to be, she couldn't quell the overwhelming excitement burgeoning inside her.

She was going to help them slay a monster.

She was going to be like all the heroes in her books.

As nightfall stretched above them, she finally saw the foreboding fortress ahead. Everyone fell silent as they approached, except the fox who growled its distaste. Kestrel hushed it with a glare, and hoped that their cover hadn't already been blown. But none of the princes seemed worried about that. They stood together, rigid with fear, as the four of them and the fox gazed up at the black stone walls.

The Fortress of Thirst was an ominous, crumbling place that reeked of death and sorrow, even from where Kestrel stood a good distance back. Even the ocean beyond it was menacing, a storm brewing on the horizon that seemed like it was meant just for this place.

No one had uttered a word since the fortress had come into view. The sense of evil was palpable here, much like it had been at the Maw.

Kestrel knew nothing about this place or the beast that

dwelled beyond its collapsing walls, and she was starting to wonder if she had bit off more than she could chew.

"Are you sure you want to do this?" Micah asked.

She assumed he was talking to her, and eager to assuage his doubts—as much as her own—she turned to respond, only to find him staring at his older brother.

Leighton's fists were clenched at his sides, his knuckles paler than the moon overhead.

There was a wrinkle in his brow that Kestrel hadn't seen before, and she realized just how worried he must be, for all of them. These were his brothers he was sending inside. Lives that mattered to him.

But there was something else. Something darker warring beyond his expression, but Kestrel couldn't quite decipher it.

"Storm and steel," he said at last, with the conviction of a future king.

"Storm and steel." Micah nodded, his auburn hair looking more disheveled than usual.

As they made their way closer to the Fortress of Thirst, Micah retreated inward. Gone was the relentless flirt with mischief in his eyes. This Micah was quiet, almost mournful, much more than Kestrel imagined he would be in this moment. This was what they'd been traveling for. For Leighton to prove himself worthy of his kingdom's crown. A way for the kingdom to heal and move on from the tragedy that the Corrupt Queen had wrought upon them.

Seeing all of them so scared fractured some of the resolve that had felt so firm in Kestrel's heart before.

Don't do this—came Thom's unwanted voice in her

head, paranoid and judging—*Better safe than stupid, remember?*

Kestrel shushed him out loud by accident, earning confused looks from everyone but Leighton. His gaze remained fixed ahead. Unwavering.

It was just fear talking, she reminded herself. Nothing was going to go wrong. Kestrel would climb to the window, create a distraction, and Leighton would have the opportunity he needed to slay the beast. Everything would go as planned. They would all see. Including Imaginary Thom.

Besides, I thought it was better safe than stupid, she said in her head.

Same thing, came his unhelpful reply.

"This way." Leighton motioned for Kestrel to follow, and she did without hesitation. If her friends and Thom lacked faith, then she would exude it in stride.

The fox leapt after her. And hearing the snapping of twigs under its foot, Leighton whipped around to shush it.

"Stay here," he growled at it as best as he could while still trying to keep his voice down.

The creature heeded him none and bounded forward anyway, desperate to reach Kestrel's heels.

"It can't come with us," Leighton whispered to her, a pleading look softening his brow. They had already had this conversation on the way here. A fox couldn't climb a stone wall, after all, and the poor thing seemed very attached to her. He worried that if they allowed it to wait at the bottom for her, it might start yipping and barking, impatient for her return.

Kestrel squatted down to give the fox's head a scratch. "You'll have to wait here with Micah."

The fox gave a dissatisfied whine, but after one more behind-the-ear rub, it sauntered over to the other brother.

Kestrel stood back up, giving the creature a farewell wave. Micah looked as if he was trying to tell her he'd take care of the fox, but the fear in his eyes was distorting the expression into more of a grimace. She had to turn away.

"Once you're inside, just remember," Leighton whispered again, continuing forward and taking his time with where he placed each and every step. "This is a creature of darkness. It relies on sound to hunt its prey. It will not know where you are as long as you are careful and quiet."

Kestrel nodded and mimicked his path, each placement of her foot an exact recreation of his.

Whenever they neared a thick tree or shrub, they crouched behind it and waited a few moments, listening for anything that might be moving about from beyond those dark, stone walls. All that answered was the low wail of wind that billowed out the gaping hole where the double doors had once stood. The shrapnel of wood lay scattered about the entrance, and Kestrel shuddered to think of how mighty something must've been to obliterate them like that, and how he was so certain the monster was still inside.

The sea breeze carried with it the acrid stench of decay, and more than once Kestrel had to shield her nose to prevent herself from gagging.

Leighton, however, seemed impervious to it. He didn't so much as flinch when they began walking out into the open again, the rotten air blowing so fiercely it jostled his hair. Stench or not, she wouldn't let him down. Especially not when no one had ever trusted her with such a dangerous feat before.

Thom would've never allowed her to risk her life like this.

And for good reason, he said in her mind again.

This time, Kestrel made sure not to utter anything aloud, but she growled back into her head, *Shut up!* and that seemed to do the trick.

With the gaping entrance swiftly approaching, Kestrel let her gaze wander up the front walls of the castle. The stones themselves were smoother than she expected, but there were still enough chinks and cracks that she knew she could handle it.

The only problem was, she saw no windows.

Kestrel tapped the golden epaulet on Leighton's broad shoulder. His head twisted to her, and she pointed up at the windowless walls. Now that they were this close, she didn't want to make a sound.

Leighton peered up and then back at her, confused.

"Windows?" she mouthed.

He tilted his head, indicating toward the side of the building, but he didn't move toward it.

Kestrel's brow pinched at first. She thought he'd be taking her to the windows to ensure her safe climb. But then she realized he was exactly where he needed to be: at the entrance, awaiting her distraction so that he could then run inside and finish the job.

Kestrel nodded her understanding. But when she started to step around him and make her way to the side of the building, he reached for her hand.

The gentle touch stopped her in her tracks. Her breath caught in her lungs as he pulled her hand up to his chest with the gentleness of a lover.

Kestrel looked up to him, expecting to meet his fiercely blue eyes and to fall desperately into the intoxicating allure of them again. But instead, she found his attention fixed on her hand, on the place where his thumb was twirling her ring.

"You can do this," he told her, and it sent her heart drumming. "Dig deep and you'll find the power you need to end this."

The drumming stopped, confusion settling in. "To end what?"

Without another word, Leighton ripped the ring off her finger and shoved Kestrel backward.

She stumbled, feet tripping and catching on the broken pieces of the door beneath her, until she lost her balance entirely. She was sent crashing into the darkness beyond the entrance of the fortress, landing on debris. A loud boom echoed down the derelict hall behind her.

Kestrel's mind was a cyclone. Her heart a thunderstorm. Both banging and churning and flooding her with alarm and confusion.

Her helpless eyes met Leighton's. "What's happening? What are you doing?"

Before he could answer, she was already running back for the opening.

Behind her, she heard a low, distant rumble, like something large was stirring from the depths of the fortress. She knew she didn't want to be there when it arrived.

She flung her body out the entrance, but when she reached it, something blocked her from exiting. Something unseen to her eyes. She slammed against a wall of nothing instead, and staggered back.

"What have you done?" she demanded, breathless. Leighton wouldn't meet her eyes, so she banged on the nothingness between them and shouted louder. "What have you done!"

The fox squealed outside.

"Deal with the Animali, Micah!" Leighton commanded, and in one fell swoop, Micah grabbed the fox by the scruff of its neck and disappeared from sight.

Kestrel screamed after them. She banged harder on the barrier, the edges of her hands smarting with each impact, but it seemed like nothing would break it. She was trapped. Caught between two monsters—the one she thought she knew, and the one lurking somewhere behind her.

"I know who you are," Leighton said to the ground. Gone was his gleaming façade. Had he always sounded so deadly? So sinister? "I know the magic that courses through your veins."

"Magic? I have no magic," Kestrel growled, giving the unseeable barrier another pounding of her fist.

Leighton held up the ring, as if that was proof enough. The clear blue turned almost opaque in the moonlight. "You do. It's why you wear this. Your mother's ring."

Kestrel was about to protest, but then she jerked back, brow furrowing. "How did you know that belonged to my mother?"

She racked her brain, trying to remember if she had

told Leighton about her ring yet, how it had belonged to her mother long ago before Thom had given it to her. Despite the dozens of conversations they'd had over the past few days though, she couldn't recall it ever coming up.

Perhaps even more unsettling was what he was claiming the ring did.

To stifle magic. Kestrel didn't have any magic though. She would know by now.

Then again, she always wore that ring. It had been a gift from Thom. A piece of her mother that he had told her to always keep close so that she might keep her mother's memory close as well.

Could that have been yet another one of his many lies?

"I know more about you than you might know about yourself, and for that, I am sorry," Leighton continued, his voice starting to shake. "We have spent many years searching for your mother so that she might remove the curse she placed upon my father. I was sent to Mutiny Bay because we heard rumors that Darius Graeme had been spotted there. I was meant to arrest and question him for intel on the Corrupt Queen. But then I found you as well. I noticed your ring in the alleyway, and I knew—I knew that meant you had not only her blood, but also her magic."

Booming strides thudded down the hall behind Kestrel, still a distance away but rapidly approaching. She couldn't think straight. Couldn't make sense of what the prince was telling her, especially with the impending danger creeping up behind her. There was no time to sort through the details—who her mother was, how she'd been played this whole time by both Thom and Leighton, and likely the other brothers as well.

"Let me go," she begged him. "Please."

"I'm afraid I can't. Only you can do that now."

Horrified, she stared at him. She wanted to scream. To cry. To beg for an alternative. But she would not give him the pleasure.

Besides, she could tell from the conviction in his tone that he wasn't going to let her go.

Kestrel was yet again trapped behind stone walls, and her only chance of escape fell onto her.

"Tell me what I need to do."

It was only then that he finally met her gaze. "It's simple, really. Your magic will save him. I know it will."

Kestrel realized then who else must've been trapped inside these walls.

The beast bounding toward her was Leighton's father. The King of Irongate. Which meant Leighton's entire story about needing to prove himself to his people had been a lie. He wasn't here to slay a monster. He was here to force Kestrel to cure a curse that she knew hardly anything about.

Her chest ached like it had been torn apart.

"I don't know how to end his curse," she told Leighton, choking on tears. "I didn't even know I had magic."

The thrashing beast was nearing now. Stones and rubble wobbled on the ground around her.

Leighton started to slowly inch away. "End his curse, and the boundary around this place will be lifted. You will be free."

"Wait!" Kestrel cried into the unseen barrier, pressing the entire weight of her body against it. "Don't leave me here!"

To his credit, his expression actually wilted with a hint of remorse, though he did not stay. Leighton's pace hastened as he continued to back away, abandoning her to the most miserable fate she could even imagine.

"Remember, silence is your greatest weapon in there. I believe in you, Princess Kestrel of Caelora."

And with that, Leighton spun around and ran, cape billowing behind him.

Kestrel was alone in the world again. Just her and the cursed monster.

CHAPTER 13
NO WAY OUT

KESTREL

By the time Kestrel turned around, the beast was already bounding into the grand but dilapidated foyer.

There was nothing human about it, let alone kingly. As the creature of her darkest nightmares leapt into the room, its pale skin shone in the moonlight beaming down from the broken windows, making it almost appear translucent. It was a miracle its sickly arms could hold up the massive weight of its rotund belly, and Kestrel was almost certain she could make out the shapes of faces and hooves and bones undigested that were protruding from within the taut skin.

The monster's jaw hung limply as his tongue lapped at the air. As if he could already taste her.

The creature stared at her, but did not move. After a moment she realized it was more like it was staring straight through her, waiting.

Kestrel wasn't sure if what Leighton had told her was

160

true, but it was all she had to go off of. Even though her hands were quaking, her cheeks slick with tears, she forced herself not to make a sound. Maybe if she stood as still as possible, the monster would give up and retreat back into the darkness.

But that wasn't a plan at all, it was wishful thinking.

She needed something concrete.

There's always the walls, Imaginary Thom said into her thoughts.

Without moving a muscle in her neck, Kestrel's eyes swiveled to the wall beside her. The stones were large and rough, most of them jutting out in ways that would make for great handholds.

You always told me climbing was dangerous, she said into her mind, grateful to have someone with her—even if he was just a figment of her imagination.

Yeah, well, aren't I glad you never listened.

Kestrel moved slowly as she reached for the nearby wall. The stones were dusty beneath her fingertips, but fortunately the inside of the fortress was even more destroyed than the outside. It looked as if something had slammed into every surface and wall, the stones cracking and crumbling in dozens of places. It made for even better handholds than she had previously deduced.

The monster panted and sniffed the air, masking what little sounds Kestrel made as she slowly began her ascent.

She gripped one stone, then the next, careful as ever. But that was the thing about climbing. It was an art. A slow and steady dance of the body as she climbed higher. Every foot placement was always delicate, every handhold precise.

When Kestrel was high enough up that she was certain the monster could not reach her even if it jumped, she scanned the room. On the wall opposite her, she noted the shattered windows. It looked like the only exit, aside from the door that she already knew was blocked by some magical, unseeable boundary. It was possible the windows were blocked too, but for the chance at freedom, it would be worth testing that theory.

Only, the monster stood snarling in the center of the room. To creep past it would require a level of stealth—and an abundance of luck—that Kestrel wasn't confident she possessed. Unless she had a distraction.

Tightening her grasp on the wall with one hand, she reached down her leg to remove one of her leather slippers. Then the other. It was easier to climb barefooted anyway.

Amidst the stress and fear though, her palms were starting to sweat, her grip slipping.

Before she could fall and risk making a clamor, Kestrel flung one of the shoes across the room, as far as she could make it fly. It smacked the wooden chandelier as it soared through the air. The monster's neck snapped upwards as he listened to the creaking of the wood as the chandelier swayed. A guttural snarl erupted from the creature's corpulent belly and he flung himself up high—higher than she expected him to be able to lunge.

Kestrel filed that bit of information away just as the slipper landed in a heap of rubble on the other side of the room.

The beast skittered into action, teeth gnashing as he bounded across the room toward the source of the noise.

As he tore through the pile of debris there, Kestrel made her way back down to solid ground.

Finding nothing of sustenance, the creature roared his defeat. His head swiveled this way and that, as if he was listening for his next clue, searching for his next mark.

Kestrel was already standing in the middle of the room. She couldn't allow it to be her.

She flung the other leather slipper. It collided into a vase that had surprisingly not been shattered yet, but the minute it crashed to the ground, Kestrel bolted for the other wall.

Behind her, she listened to the monster snarling and devouring broken glass, desperate for that first taste of flesh. She hoped the distraction would last long enough for her to reach the window, that his snarling would be loud enough to mask her movements the entire way.

He stopped too soon though.

Kestrel's foot slipped on a loose brick, and she could hear every bone in the monster's spine cracking as he stood up straighter to listen, to gauge its direction.

And then he was barreling toward her.

Kestrel climbed as fast as she could. Faster than she ever had. Completely giving up on doing so quietly.

What had she been thinking? Trusting complete strangers and volunteering herself for such a mission? It was ludicrous. The exact kind of bone-headed thinking that made Thom believe she couldn't make it out here. And what's worse: he had warned her. Told her that princes couldn't be trusted. And she had blindly chosen to believe them anyway.

She would be eaten alive now for her foolishness.

Focus, Thom's voice rang in her ears, the encouragement more than she deserved. *Make it out of here alive, and then you can beat yourself up about it.*

Nodding, Kestrel fortified her determination. She quieted her mind. There was no room for anything else but the strategic placement of her hands and the drooling, gnashing teeth below her. Her fingernails scraped against the stone. Her heavy, panting breaths only served to feed the monster's frenzy. His growling grew wilder, more feral with each of his leaping strides.

Just as she grasped the ledge of the windowsill, she felt the beast hurl itself against the wall beneath her. Stones quaked. One wobbled within her grasp, almost threatening to break free and send her crashing below with some of the others that had soared from the wall on impact.

But Kestrel held tight. She did not fall—Kestrel never fell.

She heaved the rest of her body onto the window ledge.

The king-beast wasted no time in trying to rip the fallen stones to shreds. He slammed against the wall one —two—three more times, but Kestrel was solid where she perched. She was safe.

When the monster didn't find the blood he was searching for, his milky-white eyes scaled up the wall to meet hers. Hunger dripped from his tongue and she shuddered. That had been close, but she wasn't free yet.

Kestrel turned her back to him and to the forsaken fortress, and gazed out the window, at her only option for escape.

With her heart in her throat, Kestrel tried to reach through the window, testing her theory. Her fingers collided on a shield of air.

Kestrel cursed under her breath, and plopped onto her rear, one leg dangling over the edge.

Below, the beast waited, almost as if he had already known she couldn't escape.

That's alright, it ain't over yet.

A bitter laugh escaped her. It sure felt like it was. Leighton had said the only way out of here was by breaking his father's curse and she was starting to believe him. The only problem was, she didn't know how to break a curse.

A new idea began to emerge.

The prince had said she had magic in her blood...

But that was ridiculous. In all her nineteen years, not once had anything remotely magical happened to her— and she would know the signs. After all, she had read plenty of books with girls in similar predicaments. And the first hints of magic always came during big, volatile moments of heightened emotion.

Kestrel had plenty of those. Thom didn't call her *Little Fury* for nothing. Then again, she had always worn her mother's ring. But it was gone now. And Kestrel had never been in a more heightened state of emotion, never been more desperate.

She examined the palms of her hands. She flipped them over, wiggled her fingers.

Nothing. She felt nothing. No tingling of dormant magic that had long-since been waiting to awaken.

And the beast below still lingered. Still watched her with that unsettling gaze.

Kestrel rolled her eyes at herself. Magic wasn't the answer. She needed to use her wits. It's what Thom would do. And despite hating him for all the lies he weaved around her, she knew if he were here right now, he'd know exactly what to do.

Another distraction, Thom said in unison with her own thoughts.

Kestrel felt the loose brick under her hand from earlier. It didn't take more than a few wiggles and shoves to break the loose brick, and when she did, she chucked it across the room. It hopped through the doorway the king-beast had originally bounded through before crashing into something solid beyond the door that she couldn't see.

It was enough to catch his attention.

The king-beast twisted on his spindly heels and scrambled out the antechamber back the way he'd came, leaving Kestrel to think in peace.

She gave the room another once-over, this time noting the rafters just above her head. Those could make for safer travel through the rooms, or at least from one side to another. But one of them was already split in two and lay shattered on the floor below. She wasn't sure how much weight the ones still standing could hold. Unless she was desperate, she didn't think she should try.

Her gaze traveled lower, to the now-bare walls that had dozens of ghostlike impressions on them. Paintings used to hang in those barren spots. More frames and décor than she could even imagine. They must've covered the walls nearly floor-to-ceiling for how many now lay in shambles on the ground.

This place was so unlike her simple tower, it made her wonder who used to live here and what might've happened to them. It was then that she noticed the bones littered among the debris. Seeing them now, it was a surprise she hadn't noticed them sooner. They covered nearly every corner of the room. Some larger, but most small, likely belonging to the innocent woodland animals that were unfortunate enough to stumble through here. There were larger skulls as well though, some that looked canine like the coyotes common in Vallonde, others more human-like.

A weapon, Thom said.

Kestrel silently shot back, *I don't know how to make a weapon out of bones. Who do you think I am?*

Thom's laughter, warm and rich, rippled through her, bringing tears to her eyes.

Besides, she would need twine or something to tie them all together, and even then, most of the bones were so small that they'd hardly create something strong enough like the kind of weapon she thought she would need to defeat this beast.

Not to mention, Prince Leighton's final words still echoed around her. The only way to drop the barrier trapping her inside was to end his father's curse, not kill him.

Do I have magic, Thom? Is that why you made me where that ring?

The question rang in her skull, and Kestrel wish desperately that the real Thom could answer.

Of course, not even the Imaginary-Thom gave a reply.

With a sigh, Kestrel turned her attention back to her hands. Without the ring, she didn't feel any different. Maybe there was a slight buzz beneath her skin, but that could also just be the adrenaline from having to narrowly escape whatever ravenous creature was in the other room now, hunting her.

But what if Leighton had been right? What if there really was magic in her blood, given to her by a mother who she had never known was the Corrupt Queen? And what if her magic was unknown to her, all because of a ring. If it had been a few days ago, the mere suggestion would've seemed farfetched to her. But now? Kestrel had already learnt that Thom was keeping secrets from her, keeping her hidden from communities of people she never knew existed. And what if magic was the reason? And if he knew about the magic, he knew about her mother.

Tears pricked her eyes, and Kestrel buried her face in hands that no longer felt like her own. Just for once, she wanted someone to be honest with her. To help her sift through all this impossible new information.

"Psst!" something hissed outside the window behind her. "Princess!"

Kestrel spun around, searching the dark woodland outside. She almost didn't see him at first, but then the traitorous Micah stepped into the moonlight beneath her. There was no fox within his grasp anymore, and Kestrel felt herself crack in two at all the possibilities that came rushing at her. She wanted to scream. Wanted to grab the loose brick from the windowsill and chuck it at Micah's skull for the part he played in all of this. But her own survival was more important.

Kestrel wiped the tears from her eyes the way a warrior would paint their face in red before battle.

"What do you want?" she hissed. "And don't call me that."

"Little bird it is then," he said meekly, trying to lighten to mood. "I came to help you. If—if I can."

He was keeping his voice low, either so the monster wouldn't hear him, or perhaps so someone else wouldn't.

"Does Leighton know you're here?"

Micah shook his head. "Nah, the plan was to meet back down the trail that led here once he had gotten you inside. He's either heading there now or just realizing I'm not there."

"Why are you here then?"

"Like I told you before, I'm the brave brother." A crooked smile tried inching up his face, but it promptly fell when he realized his charms weren't going to work this time. With a long sigh, he amended, "Look, Leighton thinks people discover their magic when they're forced to. But I don't think that's true. I want our father's curse lifted as much as he does, but I think there could've been a better way to go about all this."

How convenient that he felt this way now, after she had already been doomed.

Kestrel folded her arms. "Then why didn't you—"

Micah shushed her. His eyes were wide as he scanned the lower walls of the fortress, as if he could see through them.

Kestrel bit her lip, cursing herself for almost forgetting to be quiet while they conversed. Fortunately, the beast was still crashing around in the other room, so he hadn't heard them. Yet.

"Why didn't you stop him sooner?" her voice was barely more than a whisper as she hissed down at Micah.

He looked like a little boy, scratching his neck and staring down at the ground in shame.

"I...I don't have a good answer for that. He's my older brother, my future king. When it comes to the well-being of our people, I do as he says. But this was the wrong call. I realized that too late." His tone lifted a little, that signature jovialness returning to brighten his broken smile. "But I'm here now, trying to help. If you'll allow it."

Kestrel couldn't look at him, but he had piqued her curiosity, and she cursed herself for it. She shouldn't trust any of them. But Micah's boyish charm always seemed to put her at ease.

"Do you know how I get out of here?" she asked, finally turning toward him.

Micah nodded so vigorously; it sent his auburn locks tumbling. "The magic that keeps everything living trapped inside, it will break when his soul is cleansed."

"I can't *cleanse his soul*," Kestrel said with a sigh. Her head fell back, thumping on the stone windowsill behind her. "I don't even have magic—or if I did, I don't know how to use it."

"Have you tried?"

"Of course I tried!" she shrieked, the volume of her voice getting away from her again.

This time the beast roared in the next room. He had heard her mistake.

Claws scraped against glass and rock as the creature

came crashing into the antechamber with her once more. His head swiveled, tilting one ear to the ceiling, then the other. All the while that dripping tongue of his swayed from his hanging jaw, ready to devour anything.

"Dragon's fire!" Micah cursed from outside, making the monster's head twitch in their direction. "I'll run around to the far end of the building, draw him away from you so you can try again," he shouted up at her, already starting to dash away. "Stay there! I'll be right back."

And then, Micah was bolting down the length of the dilapidated fortress, hollering along the way. The king-beast gnashed his sharp teeth and followed the raucous Micah was causing as he banged on the exterior walls.

Soon, both the prince and the monster had faded out of view.

Kestrel didn't dare move for a long while, even after she could no longer make out the sounds of the creature's booming footsteps or Micah's taunting hollers.

Only once it was as quiet as a moonless night did she fix her attention upon her hands again.

If what Leighton had told her was true, these were the hands of the daughter of the Corrupt Queen. It meant Kestrel descended from a powerful bloodline—but a wicked one as well. If she tapped into that magic now, she wondered what it would do to her. Would it turn her corrupt, like it had her mother? Would it unleash a curse as equally wicked as the one they now faced?

Maybe that was why Thom had shielded her from the truth for all these years. If only he were there so she could ask him. If only anyone in this forsaken realm was reliable enough to tell her the truth.

But none of them had been, she reminded herself. The only person she could rely on was herself. And so, instead of listening to Micah and trying to draw upon magic she knew nothing about, Kestrel chose her own path.

Slowly, she lowered herself from the window, and made her descent back to the dusty foyer floor. Nearby, bones lay scattered. She grabbed a few of the longer ones and shoved them into her belt, in case she needed anything to throw later. Or to hit and stab, if it came to it.

Then Kestrel did something she really, *really* didn't want to do.

She descended farther into the dark fortress, searching for another way out.

Every window was shattered, allowing the moonlight to illuminate a safe path among the rubble. But every now and then her foot would inadvertently kick a small pebble she hadn't noticed, or her sock would catch on the edge of a splintered piece of framing, and her mistakes would echo in the rooms around her.

She would wait for the monster to come bounding after her again.

But he never came. And she was grateful that Micah's distraction was still working.

Kestrel plucked a splinter from her toe, a bead of blood pearling beneath the sock. Hopefully the monster wasn't drawn to the scent of it. Still, she pushed onward, meandering through the rundown rooms, one hallway leading into another. All the while she searched for another way out, hoping that maybe there was a weak spot in the unseen magical barrier, or a crumbled wall that she could slip through.

She found none.

The farther into the fortress she crept, the more she could discern Micah's commotion outside. She hadn't meant to follow him, but Kestrel had needed to stick to the rooms facing the outside of the building where the windows permitted moonlight inside, otherwise she wouldn't be able to see. But unfortunately, those seemed to be the same rooms Micah had led the beast down. She was following their trail.

From the entrance of the kitchen, she spotted the adjoined larder, and a door leading to the outside. The beast's mangled shape blocked most of the doorway, but through the crevices between its translucent skin and the brightening light of dawn outside, she saw Micah waving his arms wildly.

She cursed under her breath. If that door was a viable way out, she wouldn't be able to reach it with the monster standing in her way, and it seemed Micah had no intentions of easing up on his taunting anytime soon. Every time he did fall quiet for a moment, the creature would lose interest almost immediately, his head twitching as if in search of his next mark to hunt.

Kestrel shuffled along the edge of the room. Maybe if Micah kept the monster's attention long enough, she could get close to the door and run through it. But when she was about halfway along the wall, she stopped, realizing a fatal flaw in her plan.

If the beast could leave, he would.

He would barrel out that doorway right now and sink his teeth into Micah's heckling face.

Since he wasn't, since the creature was slamming his

body against the opening as if it were blocked by a door, it meant the spell blocked this exit as well.

Kestrel would need to find another way out.

She twisted on her toes, ready to leave the same way she had come in.

Unbeknownst to her though, one of the bones she had grabbed earlier was easing from her belt. It came crashing to the ground with a hollow thud.

The beast's head snapped around, his eyes flashing with hunger.

Micah spied Kestrel through the doorway for the first time, and his skin paled. He started kicking the doorframe, trying to regain the monster's attention. "Hey! Don't look over there. I'm what you really want, you hideous beast!"

But the monster wasn't listening. He had found his new mark.

The king-beast lunged for her. Kestrel screamed, a sound she'd been holding in since the moment she had been trapped. Only an island separated the two of them, but she used it to her advantage as best as she could. As the creature careened one way, she dodged the other. The monster landed behind the counter and crashed into a set of wooden cupboards that collapsed around him. It would've been a perfect opportunity to escape, to bolt for the doorway that was now wide open, but at the same time the monster crashed, Kestrel stumbled into a pile of pots, pans, and cutlery that had already been knocked out of their places.

There was a sharp sting as something slit into her heel. She wouldn't be able to run now, might not even be able to climb.

Even if she could, the ceiling in here was too low. The monster could reach her in one swipe.

Fueled by human desperation, Kestrel flung herself at the open doorway, forgetting it was a mockery of an exit.

Her face slammed against nothing, and she cried out.

She couldn't escape.

She would die in this torturous place if she couldn't think of something.

Micah was at the doorway, hands pressed against the frame, his face so close to hers she could feel his breath. "Use your magic."

"I can't," she whimpered.

"You have to! It's the only way!"

She shook her head. He didn't understand—he couldn't. Kestrel hadn't felt any hint of magic inside her. She didn't even know how to summon it if she could, let alone how to command it to do something like breaking whatever hold this monstrous magic had on his father.

What she did have was one final, last-ditch effort to save herself.

Remembering the bones she'd taken earlier, Kestrel yanked the ones that remained from her belt. She needed to throw them, to create another distraction that would hopefully draw the monster's attention away from her. But a stirring awakened somewhere deep within the cavern of her chest. Something dark that crackled like thunder.

The king-beast was already scrambling out of the rubble. She didn't have time to wait.

Kestrel sent the bones hurtling across the kitchen. The

sensation in her chest left instantly, the storm inside her gone.

The bones skittered among the wreckage as the last of the cupboards fell from the monster's backside. His head hardly even twitched in their direction. The king-beast roared, pinning her with his ravenous gaze.

She was out of options.

With her back pressed against the exit-that-was-not-an-exit, Kestrel slid down to the ground and reached for the first thing she could grab. Splinters and debris sliced and poked at her skin, until she pulled up a wooden plank that had previously belonged to the door that now lay broken around her.

She held it in front of her, the only weapon she had.

It likely wouldn't be enough to stop him, let alone kill him. But if she could knock him in the head, perhaps disorient or subdue him for a few moments, she could scurry away again. Find somewhere safe to hide. To nurse her wounds and collect herself.

The king-beast lunged.

Kestrel drew the plank back, prepared her attack, and hoped for the best. "Blessed moon, keep me safe."

And there it was again.

That unknown swirling, like something coming to life inside her.

This time it was lighter, like sunshine peeking through the clouds after a storm, and she wanted to bask in it. To throw herself overboard into its warmth.

But the fear in her chest pulled her back. The wooden board wobbled in her hands as the beast's bellow shook everything. Kestrel squeezed her eyes shut and swung.

And then the room fell silent.

The unseeable door she'd been leaning against disappeared. Kestrel tumbled backward out of the larder and into fresh air.

When she opened her eyes, she sat up and saw Micah standing inside the doorway. His arm was thrust out, a sword held in his trembling grasp.

The silver stretched all the way up to the creature's chest.

It disappeared behind a bloom of red.

The creature's tongue hung limply.

With a shuddering breath, Micah twisted the blade, the monster's lifeless body wrenching with it. Then he let the weight of it collapse, Micah going down as well. He sobbed.

Kestrel inched back from the forsaken fortress. This was her chance to run. She was free. No longer a prisoner trapped inside that cursed place, nor an unknowing prisoner to the princes any longer.

But Micah had gone in for her.

He had slain his own father, just to save her.

Despite everything, despite all the lies and deceit, she couldn't bring herself to leave him. The only friend she had ever really had.

So instead, Kestrel dragged her body over to Micah's side. She pressed a hand on his shoulder. At the first hint of contact, he twisted around and flung himself into her arms. The sobs racked through him like a storm. They made her cry too, for they reminded her of everything she had been through. For a third time in her life now, she had almost died because she still didn't know how to survive in this cruel and terrifying world. She had trusted the wrong people. Made the wrong choices. And been helpless in the end to defend herself.

Although this time, something *had* been different.

She had felt it. That pull. That awakening inside her.

And although at first it had seemed dark and cursed, there was a lightness to it as well. A calm and comforting side to it that she wanted to learn more about.

As the tears began to slow, Kestrel felt the exertion finally catching up to her. She needed a hot bath and a long night's rest. And for someone to tend to the gash that throbbed in her right foot.

But there was a crunching of footsteps outside, and both of their spines went rigid as they spun around to face the new threat.

Leighton stood in the doorway, appearing every bit as angry as a scorching sun. "What have you done?"

CHAPTER 14

FAMILY TIES

KESTREL

Kestrel and Micah helped each other to stand and face the wrath of the soon-to-be King of Irongate.

The sun had already risen behind him, casting Leighton's figure in a dark shadow in the doorway. He was so tall he had to hunch over just to fit inside, making him look all the more menacing. Kestrel wasn't ready for another threat yet. Her heart was still thrumming, her foot bleeding. And Leighton was far too cunning, too unpredictable for her rattled mind.

Judging from the unwavering way in which Micah stared down his brother though, she supposed he felt differently.

"I did what had to be done, Leigh," he said, wiping his nose with the back of his forearm. "What should've been done years ago, if we'd only—"

"You did what had to be done?" In two swift strides, Leighton was inside the kitchen, grabbing Micah by the collar of his blue tunic and hoisting him across the room. He slammed him up against the wall, the stones rattling. "I told you I had this handled! That our father's curse would be broken if you had just stayed back. But you couldn't help yourself, could you? You just had to meddle and do whatever Micah wanted to do, because Hollows forbid you ever just follow the rules!"

With a scowl that made even Kestrel recoil, Micah grabbed Leighton's hands from his collar and peeled back his fingers. She wasn't sure if he was stronger than his older brother, or if Leighton had simply relented, releasing Micah to fall down to his feet.

Regardless, the ire was not done burning within him. Leighton shot a hand back toward their father. "Look at what your interference cost us. Fatherless now, because of you!"

He shoved him again, Micah's back slamming into the wall so forcefully the wind gushed from his lungs.

"Don't you dare!" Kestrel shot back, face hot with rage. She stormed closer, her foot throbbing with each pounding step, and Leighton actually flinched at her proximity. "Because of Micah, I'm still alive. If he had listened to you, your father would be feasting on my bones now, and I'd be dead, so either way you'd still be fatherless."

She watched the sting of that word whip him across the face. But she didn't care. After everything he'd done, he deserved to feel an ounce of the pain he had caused her.

Leighton was shaking his head, eyes pleading. "I don't understand. Your magic, it should've saved him. It should be the cure—"

Kestrel threw her arms in the air. "And maybe it is. But

I've never used magic a day in my life. What makes you think that I'm just going to suddenly learn how to undo a decades-old curse when I'm having to run for my life?"

Behind him, Micah nursed the ache in his chest and gave her a nod of approval.

She ignored it. As grateful as she was that he had saved her, she still wasn't fully ready to forgive him for letting Leighton led her to her doom.

Kestrel glared up at the older brother, waiting for a reply. Part of her wanted him to argue back. To fight with her so she could continue screaming and unleashing all of her pain upon him. But instead, Leighton's bloodshot eyes were just staring at the heap of pale skin and tattered cloth that had once been their father.

Dejected and limp, Leighton shoved past her, ambling until the corpse was at his feet. A lifetime of hope that now lay shattered before him.

And despite herself—despite everything he had done to her, every lie he had whispered into her ear, every falsehood he had led her to believe—despite it all, she actually felt sorry for him. She was familiar with the pain of losing a parent. Even if she had never met her mother, there was still a hole in her heart that belonged exclusively to her. And she couldn't imagine how much deeper it would be if she had spent years awaiting her mother's return.

This man didn't deserve her pity though. He likely didn't even want it. So instead, she remained silent. Watchful.

Picking himself off the wall, Micah joined his brother's side. "I'm sorry it ended this way. But your plan wasn't working. Kestrel showed no signs of magic, and I couldn't just let her die. If she is who you think she is, then—"

"I know," Leighton cut him off, nothing but quiet surrender in his tone now. "I'm...I'm glad she's alright." He glanced over his shoulder to meet her gaze, eyes full of sorrow and regret. "I'm glad you survived. I'm—"

Kestrel recoiled, worried for a moment that the prince was about to utter a useless apology. Like that little word would mean anything to her now. He only felt sorry because his plan hadn't worked. He hadn't approved of the *interference* on her behalf, no matter how much he tried pretending otherwise now.

For whatever reason, Leighton swallowed the apology.

Tentatively, Micah put a hand on his brother's shoulder. "You'll be a great king. Irongate will be better with you on the throne now."

Kestrel might have scoffed if they weren't all still standing around their dead father. She didn't know much, if anything, about what it took to be a good king, but she was pretty sure Leighton's actions today suggested he would be anything but. Kings were supposed to be just. To protect the lives of innocence. He had done the opposite.

Kestrel noticed the open doorway and the sunlight shining through. She didn't want to be in his company anymore. Didn't want to witness the two brothers making up and planning for Leighton's ascension to the throne while she was still roiling with rage and injustice.

Spinning on her heels, Kestrel practically ran out of the gloomy fortress and into the light of day. Or at least she tried to. That blasted foot of hers was going to be a problem—and now she had no shoes either since she had thrown them at the beast to create a distraction. It didn't matter, she told herself. She would figure out how to bind her wounds and protect her feet later. For now, she just needed to get away from them. Needed to find Thom. She had so much to tell him, and so many questions she hoped he would finally answer.

"Hey," shouted Micah. He chased after her with those stupidly long legs of his, and caught up to her in no time. Grabbing her shoulder, he spun her around to face him. She had no energy in her to fight him "Where are you going?"

"Back to Mutiny Bay. To find Thom—or Darius, or whatever his name is. I don't care. I should've never left him and I should've never trusted *you*."

She aimed the last part like an arrow at Leighton who was ducking out of the larder behind them. But if the word was meant to strike, he appeared utterly unimpacted as he said, "You won't find him in Mutiny Bay."

Kestrel's breath quickened.

"What do you mean?" she asked, glancing between the two of them. Micah just avoided her gaze. "Where is he then?"

It was Leighton who replied, "He's been arrested for treason by the Thundersworn Brigade."

"Treason?" Kestrel exclaimed. But then she started piecing things together. Efrem's absence after their encounter with Thom in the tavern. Him slamming a loud, metallic door shut when they arrived to the sand-gliders. "What in the Hollows for?"

Beside her, Micah looked apologetic, and she could've punched him right in those big, bulging eyes. "He was helping the Corrupt Quee—your mother when she cursed the realm. He's been wanted for nearly two decades. It's why we were sent to Mutiny Bay, to retrieve him."

Kestrel had forgotten that part. It was one of the many world-shattering confessions Leighton had given her before shoving her to her death. But now that there wasn't a bloodthirsty beast rampaging after her, she was starting to think more clearly.

"Who sent you after Thom?"

Leighton answered. "By order of the Queen of Irongate, Queen Signe."

"But—but Thom wouldn't do anything like that. He's been trying to figure out how to undo the curse. He's told me!"

"Probably out of guilt," Leighton reasoned. Seeing how his words cut her like a knife, he softened his expression a little, tried taking a step closer as if to comfort her. But Kestrel backed away, wincing as her foot landed directly on the knife wound. Leighton acquiesced, and said softly, "We've been charged with apprehending him and bringing him to court, where Queen Signe will determine the sentencing for his crimes."

Kestrel's heart shattered.

Surely, there was a mistake. Thom clearly had his secrets, but she knew his heart was good. There was no way he would've willingly played a part in something as evil as what had happened to Leighton's father. And she didn't even want to think about what this meant about her own mother; she'd have time to grieve over her dark past later.

But she couldn't just let them have Thom. Couldn't let

them take him to a doomed fate as well. She had to do something. But what?

"She'll want to speak with you as well, actually," he said, pulling her from her spiraling thoughts and into something even more worrying. "After all, she is your mother's sister, your aunt."

Kestrel's thoughts halted.

At first, she wasn't sure she heard him correctly. But when she searched Micah for that signature smirk of his or any indication that this was a cruel and twisted joke, his flatness told her it wasn't.

But that couldn't be right. Kestrel had never heard about an aunt before, let alone an aunt who was a *queen*. Then again, she hadn't heard about her own mother being a queen either, and what that made her—

Kestrel growled outwardly. "Thom and his cursed secrets!" She wanted to stomp her foot, but this time thought better of it.

But something didn't make sense. Why would Thom have kept her hidden away in the remote desert if they could've been living in castles or palaces like royalty—*as* royalty. As a princess to one land and a niece to another?

Unless he hadn't wanted her to meet this Queen Signe. But then that begged the question: why?

Kestrel was beginning to lose track of all the questions she had hovering over her. And without Thom there to answer any of them, she'd have to make her own decisions with what little information she had been given.

If Queen Signe *was* her aunt, she didn't think she would mind meeting her. After all, she had so little family in this world already. It would be nice to...

A confusing thought slammed into her. Leighton and Micah had said that their mother had gone missing, so Kestrel had just assumed their kingdom had no queen. But perhaps that had just been another of their lies, one meant to garner her sympathy and trust. Now she was finding out there kingdom had a queen—not only a queen, but one that Kestrel was also related to.

And with that realization, a sickening dread pooled in her gut.

"Wouldn't that make us siblings!" Kestrel's eyes bulged, horror threatening to implode her stomach. She hobbled the few short steps over to Leighton just to shove her hands at his strong chest. "But we kissed!"

"I knew it!" shouted Micah, jutting an accusatory finger at his brother.

Leighton held up his arms in defense. "We're not related, just to be clear."

"What do you mean we're not related? If your mother is also my aunt, then—"

"She is not my mother," Leighton said firmly, his nose wrinkling as if the very notion repulsed him. And she supposed she was glad it did. He pointed between himself and Micah. "Our mother went missing years ago, shortly after the twins were born. That was the truth. And our father's betrothal to Signe hadn't even been completed by the time the curse came. It twisted them both though, so Signe remained, acting as the Queen of Irongate while we wait for..."

His voice trailed off, his eyes going distant. But she couldn't afford the darkness to consume him. She still had questions.

Kestrel snapped her fingers before his nose. "And what happened to Queen Signe? With the curse, I mean. How was she able to stay at the castle, when your father wasn't?"

Leighton blinked back to reality, but was non-responsive, so Micah stepped in.

"Each of the kingdoms' rulers were corrupted differently. Our father was turned into *that*—" he gestured toward the darkness of the fortress, but Kestrel was thankful they couldn't actually see him from where they stood now. "—while Signe's transformation was only... intermittent."

"Intermittent how?"

"Queen Signe is—"

"Her curse is different," Leighton said, the irritation in his voice making both Micah and her flinch. "Our father became an insatiable monster. The sultana of Vallonde was turned into an unending sandstorm. The chieftain of the Skogar Mountains transformed into a giant bear. The king of Caelora, a devastating water dragon."

At the mention of Caelora, Kestrel's heart stopped.

That was where Leighton said her mother had reigned, or at least it had been implied when he'd referred to Kestrel as the Princess of Caelora. But if the Corrupt Queen had been married to a king, what did that make of the man she presumed to be her father? Thom had raised her, and she had loved him, but what if he'd raised her without permission. What if the reason he'd kept her locked away from the realm was so that her real family could not find her?

Doubt clouded her mind like thick ink, but she tried

preventing it from flooding. There would be time to dwell on Thom's intentions later. For now, she wanted to hear more about the family that had been kept a secret from her.

By the time Kestrel tuned back in, Leighton was wrapping up the final curses that had befallen all nine rulers of Grimtol. His face was haunted.

"All of them turned into something terrible, monsters with the innate desire to crush their own kingdoms. All of them, except Queen Signe. At first, it seemed the curse had skipped her, for she was awoken like the rest of us when our father began tearing through the castle. But as she and the palace guards ran out after him, that was when she noticed the effects."

When it seemed like he was just going to stop there, Kestrel pressed him for more. "What sort of effects?"

He glanced to Micah before answering. "Her curse is... alarming. But it's just a visual side effect. Nothing more. Nothing nearly as sinister as any of the other rulers, perhaps because she wasn't officially queen yet."

Micah added, "And as long as she remains within the castle walls, there is no effect. She looks the same as she always has."

Leighton nodded.

They were hiding something though, Kestrel could feel it. But she didn't think she was going to be able to get them to say what. So instead she redirected her attention away from the curse and their now fallen father, and to the aunt she never knew she had.

"So she stayed and raised you?"

Micah shrugged, folding his hands behind his head. "Not really. We had servants for that, little bird."

"Okay," Kestrel said, worrying at her bottom lip. "But she stayed and ruled your kingdom?"

The brothers nodded.

Something warm like pride bloomed inside her. So her aunt was loyal and dutiful, a revered leader with a strong sense of justice. But if she was so revered, why had none of them spoken about her before? Even now, they were still being vague about her, as if talking about the woman was causing them discomfort.

Or maybe they just didn't want to talk about her to Kestrel, worried she might still be upset—and she was. But she was also curious. And cursed sky if she wasn't a little hopeful, even though she knew she shouldn't be. This woman had sent the princes after Thom, the only man she'd ever known as a father. But maybe Queen Signe didn't know that. Leighton had already said he'd been surprised when he'd found Kestrel first, so it was possible the queen didn't know about her either.

And now he was saying she would want to speak with her. Since the woman hadn't even raised them after the king's exile, Kestrel wasn't foolish enough to think it was just out of some strong sense of familial longing that she would want to meet her.

"You think she'll want me to lift her curse," Kestrel said, finally sorting through all the details.

"Perhaps," Leighton said, though he had never sounded more certain of anything.

Kestrel's gaze drifted downward. She raised her hands

into view, rubbing her fingers against her upturned palms. "But I can't break the curse. I don't know how."

This time, those words tasted bitter on her tongue. Even though they had felt so true before, now she was beginning to wonder. That sensation she'd felt earlier, there was power there, although dormant. It both terrified and intrigued her.

"She might be able to teach you."

Leighton's words made her head jerk up.

"What?"

She met his direct gaze for the first time since he'd abandoned her at the entrance of the fortress. And she hated it—hated the way the crystal blue of his irises comforted her. How familiar they felt. How the intense depth of them called to her and drew her in like the tide.

But she knew better now. Despite all her wanting and longing.

The tide was dangerous. She could not float in its waves and survive.

But they had Thom. Soon they would be taking him to some far away kingdom called Irongate, where he would face judgement for crimes that Kestrel wasn't even convinced he had committed. But her aunt was apparently. And Leighton, and Micah, and all the others in their company, could take Kestrel to this woman, to her aunt, so that maybe she could plea on Thom's behalf.

The tide could be learnt. Studied. Understood.

And Kestrel was beginning to understand she couldn't allow herself to believe everything the prince was telling her. He was still hiding things, she just didn't know what yet.

But she didn't see any other options either. She didn't know where she was, or how to get back to Mutiny Bay on her own. And even if she did, there was nothing left for her there. There was only Thom now and his fate.

"Fine, I'll go with you and speak to your queen. But I want to see Thom first."

Micah's head jerk back in surprise. He either hadn't expected her to agree, or hadn't expected that to be one of her demands.

Leighton, however, didn't flinch.

"Of course." He bowed his head, a gesture that might've been meant as a show of respect, but Kestrel knew better now. It was all part of a façade to him. A game. And he was all too good at playing his part. "But I must warn you, it will not be an easy sight to see him in chains. And you will not be permitted to speak to him, nor see him unsupervised."

Kestrel stood taller, even though something twisted deep in her gut. "I don't care, I just want to make sure you have him and that you're not lying to me again."

A crack of guilt fissured Leighton's regal façade, but in the blink of an eye it was gone again. "Of course. I would be glad to prove our honesty to you."

Kestrel barely stopped herself from rolling her eyes.

"I'll be the judge of that," Kestrel said before twisting on her toes and heading for the front side of the fortress.

And as the two princes followed after her, Kestrel felt that swirling in her chest again. That fluid energy that seemed to churn with more might than the ocean. With every step she took, it pounded through her. A force like the rising tide. But as unyielding as the stones of her tower.

With each step, her foot ached a little less.

She asked the brothers to lead the way, telling them she didn't know her way back. But once they were ahead of her, Kestrel snuck a peek at the bottom of her foot. Blood caked the side of her heel. But the cut was gone.

Suddenly, Kestrel felt even more confident about her plan. Because now she had leverage the queen would want.

Now she had magic.

And magic, as it turned out, was power.

CHAPTER 15

A KINGDOM OF IRON SPIRES

KESTREL

Before they left the fortress grounds, Leighton noticed Kestrel's bare feet. He ran back inside to retrieve her shoes for her, likely hoping that it would go a long way in mending some of the damage he had wrought, but it would take a lot more than a simple good deed.

While Kestrel waited with Micah outside, she realized she'd forgotten something else.

"Micah?" she asked. "What did you do with the fox?"

She dreaded hearing the answer but wanted it anyway. Better to get one more betrayal and heartbreak out of the way while she was still tender and healing.

Micah jumped, twisting away from where he'd been gazing out across the settling sea and huddling in closer.

"Leighton told me to get rid of it."

There was a twisting ache in her chest. "As in—"

"No! No, I would never do that, and he wouldn't ask me to. But where we come from, people don't necessarily trust animals. We couldn't bring it back with us, but I didn't want it following after you either, getting itself stuck in there, becoming endangered."

Kestrel stiffened. She hadn't even considered that. Given the way the fox had reacted when the Maw had almost taken her, there was no doubt in her mind that the fox wouldn't have come to her aid inside the fortress as well.

"What did you do then?"

"I tied it up," he said simply. Then, seeing her immediate outrage, held up his hands and added hastily. "Loosely! I tied it up loosely! It should be able to wiggle free in an hour or so."

Kestrel worried at her lip. She supposed it was a good thing that the creature had been subdued. But she didn't like the idea of just leaving it.

As if he could see the thought in her eyes, Micah said, "We can't bring it with us. It's better off out here. The people of Irongate...they don't treat animals well."

"Why not?" Kestrel demanded. Then she remembered a word Leighton had shouted just after shoving her inside the fortress. "Because of the Animali? Is that what it's called?"

Before he could reply, Leighton emerged from the fortress, shoes in hand.

Micah spun away from her, arms raised high in victory. "You found them! Well done, brother."

"It wasn't too difficult. They were right where she said they would be." Leighton tossed them to Micah, who caught one in each hand.

He hissed, and when he handed them over to Kestrel

she could see why. One of his fingers was protruding from the inside of the slipper. "Yikes, looks like he took a bite out of one of them."

"I'll be fine," said Kestrel as she grabbed the shoes from him. She was eager to get them back on and hide the bloodied but healed flesh on her feet.

"We will see to it that you are fitted with new ones," offered Leighton.

"That won't be necessary," she said.

Micah barked a laugh. "It absolutely will be. You think we plan on bringing some sand flea into our home and to muddy the place up?"

With one shoe still in hand, Kestrel thwacked him across the chest.

"Ow!"

"Come on you two," Leighton called over his shoulder, already marching back the way they'd came. "We should return to the others. I don't like keeping them waiting, especially with the moon cycle that just passed."

Micah shuddered, likely thinking about the scourge that could've crossed their paths in time with the night sky. "I for one will be grateful to never set foot in this barren desert ever again, if I can help it."

The smile he flashed Kestrel faltered when he realized who he was talking to. This place was her home, or at least the only home she'd ever known. As barren and as dangerous as it might be, her stomach still soured at the thought of leaving it and never returning.

That didn't need to be her plan, she reminded herself. Once she spoke with the queen and arranged Thom's release, they could come back. They could return home.

But as the three of them began their march back to the Thundersworn Brigade, something told Kestrel it would be a long while before she saw her home again.

Upon returning to where they'd left the rest of the Irongate entourage, Leighton summoned a small convoy of the Thundersworn Brigade and commanded them to collect the king's body from where he had been left in the fortress. And once the knights were on their dutiful way, he upheld his promise to Kestrel and took her to the prisoner carriage. As expected, it was the same sand-glider being piloted by the giant scorpion, the one Efrem had been near.

As they approached, Leighton cast a wary glance her way. "Remember, prisoners are not permitted to speak with anyone, not even those guarding them."

"I understand."

"He will be punished if you utter even a word to him —"

"Alright, I get it," she snapped, annoyed that he felt the need to remind her, but also somewhat appreciative that he was making it so clear. The last thing she wanted was to get Thom in more trouble.

But Leighton still wasn't finished.

"That includes if he talks to you."

This time when Kestrel opened her mouth to respond, she fell silent. There was no telling how Thom would react upon seeing her, especially seeing that she was still in the company of the very people he had warned her not to trust.

But she needed to see him.

So Kestrel bit her lip and nodded, hoping that would

be enough. Hoping she could stay quiet for the both of them.

When they arrived, Leighton nodded to the guard who opened the door for them.

A burst of light flooded the dark entryway, blinding the handful of prisoners who were sitting closest to the doors. There were others farther back who were left undisturbed, both by the light and the metallic clang of the door opening.

Kestrel spotted Thom among them. Eyes closed. Breathing heavy. He was sound asleep.

Perhaps that was for the best. This way he wouldn't be tempted to break any of the rules, and neither would she.

His shoes were gone, she noted. And even with what minimal light reached him, she could still see the dirt caked on his toes, noted the bruises around his ankles where the chains were rubbing his skin raw. Her eyes brimmed with tears as she turned her back and left him there.

Every instinct in her told her to run back to him, to rip off those chains and help him to his feet. But she knew better. The better plan was to wait.

For now, she tried finding solace in knowing where he was and knowing that the prince had at least been telling the truth about that.

Leaving Leighton where he stood, Kestrel found her own way back to Micah's sand-glider while she waited for the Thundersworn Brigade to return with their fallen king so that the fleet could embark on their return to Irongate.

Micah readied his sails and called out to her. "I know it's not exactly the circumstances you were hoping for, little bird, but I think you'll like it in Irongate. It's quite different from Vallonde. Much more temperate. Easier to breathe than always inhaling dust."

Kestrel tried to smile, but it wasn't in her. So instead she hunkered into her seat as they set sail across the sands.

As they navigated the upper outskirts of Vallonde, Kestrel did her best to appreciate what was left of her time here. These deserts were all she had ever known, and she wanted to store their memories somewhere safe inside her forever. The way the sweltering sun sometimes relented, feeling more like a warm embrace than a scalding pan pressed upon her flesh. The way the breeze smelled of toasted nuts and dry leaves. The way the horizon rippled as if it were waving goodbye or beckoning for her to stay.

In only a short few days, they were greeted by the slow changes of the northern terrain. The sand hardening beneath their sand-gliders. A smattering of trees reaching up from the earth like fingers. Animals with fur instead of scales—her heart tinged, thinking of the fox, but she took solace in knowing that it would be safer in Vallonde than it would be in Irongate.

When he wasn't navigating, Micah excitedly told her everything he knew about these lands. The difference between the elks and the does. The names of the lakes they passed by, and how many of them he'd been skinny dipping in or which one his twin brother could swim all the way to the bottom of.

"One of you will have to teach me someday," she replied, staring longingly at the calm waters of the lake.

"Teach you what?" Micah clarified. "To swim?"

Kestrel nodded and Micah's jaw nearly fell off.

"But didn't you say you grew up near the ocean? You can't tell me you don't know how to—" At the caustic glare she shot him, he quieted, before donning a more gentlemanly manner. "It would be my pleasure to teach you. Clothing optional, of course."

She elbowed him in the ribs, and Micah theatrically tumbled over, nursing his exaggerated wound.

As he prepared to launch some likely flirty, mischievous retort back at her, a low horn rumbled from the front of their ranks. The mischievous twinkle in his eyes vanished as Micah twisted around, both him and Kestrel craning for a better look.

The terrain ahead was changing again.

Darkness slithered across the lands like an infestation. The trees on the horizon didn't have bright green canopies like the ones they had passed through just hours before. This forest was every shade of grey and black, the branches mottled and mangled like charred bones. Kestrel didn't see a single sign of life. There were no deer frolicking. No birds singing their songs. Just an eerie, unmistakenly foul quiet.

Kestrel leaned over to whisper, "What is this place?"

Even the dull copper hue of Micah's hair seemed duller here, as he dragged a hand through it to clear his view. "The Hollows."

Around them, everyone else had fallen silent. But Kestrel had so many questions. She'd never seen such a place and wanted to better understand.

Huddling closer, she kept her voice down. "Is this

another of my mother's curses? Did she corrupt the lands here?"

Micah shook his head, and whispered, "No, the curse that took root here dates way back before the Corrupt Queen's magic. Maybe even before recorded history. This place used to be a burial ground, somewhere our people came to remember their loved ones. Now it's home to creatures that make my father look like a dream."

Kestrel's eyes snapped to meet his, searching for signs of jest.

Micah's merely widened as if to exaggerate his seriousness.

"And we have to go through there?" She shuddered at the thought. "To get back to Irongate?"

"Dragon's fire, no!" exclaimed Micah, a little too loudly. It earned him a hush from multiple knights in nearby sand-gliders. Leighton, too, glared over his shoulder at his younger brother with a look that threatened to lock him away if he wasn't more careful. Micah merely rolled his eyes and held his hands up in mock surrender before he continued explaining more quietly, "There's a small pass between the mountain range and the Lake of Shadows. That's how we got to Vallonde, and that's our way back home."

Kestrel nodded as if she understood, but something didn't feel right.

If they were safe to travel the route they were headed, why was everyone so on edge?

Every member of the Thundersworn Brigade had eyes as wide as the moon, their fearful glances darting to every corner of the forest, even though they were still a safe distance outside of it.

"The creatures you said were in the Hollows, can they get us out here?"

"No," Micah said at first. Then frowning, amended, "Maybe. I'm not really sure."

"What do you mean you're not sure?"

He shrugged with a near-apologetic grin. "Mostly it's superstition to be quiet when passing by the Hollows, but that's because this place has been expanding for centuries. It's the roots you gotta look out for. They're not just tree roots."

Not just tree roots?

Kestrel hugged herself tighter. She inched even closer to the center of their sand-glider, even though they were nowhere near any of those gnarled roots.

"If they aren't roots, what are they?"

"Gravemoors, mostly," he said. "They've been known to reach for travelers and drag them under."

Gravemoors, she repeated in her head. Something about that name sounded familiar. Maybe Thom had mentioned them by accident one of the times he over-shared about an adventure with her. If he had encountered them, she supposed she should be grateful they hadn't done to him what Micah was describing now. But something else he said snagged her attention.

"*Mostly* gravemoors? What else is in there?"

Now it was Micah's turn to shudder. "We call them the rootless, because unlike the gravemoors who are stuck at the bases of trees, the rootless meander about. Mostly they stay deeper inside the Hollows. But some people say they've seen them climb up from the earth, like they're being born from it. Call it myth or superstition, but most around here believe that the rootless are what becomes of the travelers captured by the gravemoors, that they turn them into these walking, tree-like monsters that haunt the Hollows."

Now her eyes scanned the root-line for nefarious signs of movements.

Part of her wanted to ask him why they hadn't placed their father here. It seemed like that would've been a better plan than keeping him somewhere so far away and where it would be difficult to monitor him.

Before she could though, the sand-gliders all came to halt.

"We're on foot from here," Micah informed her before he and the rest of the fleet made quick-but-quiet work of tidying the sails and gathering their belongings. Even the prisoners were brought out of their jail, though their heads were bagged so it was difficult to spot Thom among them at first. Not that she wanted to see him like that, so Kestrel averted her gaze, her head fixed forward.

The Thundersworn Brigade used hand signals from then on, and directed the group to travel by two's, steering clear of the ominous reach of the blackened woods to their right. Kestrel locked her arm with Micah, refusing to let go, while he followed closely behind his two brothers, both of whom kept glancing back to check on them. Every time Efrem did, Kestrel could've sworn he was doing so specifically to glare at her—though she wasn't sure why—while Leighton seemed worried that one of these times he'd glance back and his entire fleet would be gone.

She had read about mountains before, cold places with winds so powerful they could blow down trees and snow so deep it could swallow people up to their waists. This mountain pass was nothing but lush, green, rolling hills. It didn't make her shiver once the entire way through. And by the time they reached the other side, the ominous weight had lifted.

Every knight collectively sighed at the sight of Irongate's formidable walls. Kestrel, however, shivered.

The great, towering stonework was chilling. Everything grey and sharp. Even the slate blue banners that hung evenly around the perimeter were cold. But what really took her breath away was how gargantuan the place was. If Kestrel had thought Mutiny Bay was large, Irongate was easily three or four times the size. As far as she could tell, it was entirely surrounded by this towering wall.

"Allow me the pleasure of being the first to introduce you to the great kingdom of Irongate," Micah said with an air of boastfulness. He gestured to the right, "East of us is Hingsol Lake, which leads directly into the Skogar territories—that's where your mother was from. And to the west, a few more Irongate territories we adopted over the years, before you reach the lands of the Ashen and the Sky-Blessed."

Aside from the Sky-Blessed, it was more names and places and people that her ears had never had the pleasure of hearing before, but still she couldn't be more elated. Her heart fuller. It was as if she was standing at the precipice of a new life, and Kestrel was eager to leap into it.

Not too eager, she reminded herself.

Once she was inside these gates, she would need to

keep her wits about her. She was on a mission: speak to the queen and get her to release her father. Adventuring and exploring could come once she knew he was safe.

"And Queen Signe? Where is she?"

Micah smiled, though it didn't quite reach his eyes. "Patience. We're not even in the main kingdom yet."

As if on cue, someone atop the wall hollered from behind the parapet, "Prince Leighton, Prince Efrem, and Prince Micah have returned!"

The men standing guard at the portcullis had a crest with two crossed swords and jagged marks of lightning blazing around them. It was the same emblem Micah had been drawing in the sand outside Mutiny Bay. The same emblem stitched in the back of Leighton's cape.

The knights thrust out their arms, bending and stacking them inward to create a shield, just like Kestrel had seen Leighton and Micah do in the desert.

Leighton saluted them in return, and only then did they made hasty work of their wheels and chains to raise the gate and welcome the royal convoy inside.

CHAPTER 16

THE PRINCE RETURNS

KESTREL

Horns trumpeted in the distance. One singular, long blast, followed by a staccato of four more. Dropping the hideous piece of embroidery she'd been mangling, Elora sat upright.

Those horns could only mean one thing. The princes were home. And with them, a special prisoner whom she had been eager to see.

Elora tore the thin night robe from her body and tossed it to the floor. She scrambled in the wardrobe for the first and simplest gown she could find, something she could slip on with minimal effort and then race through to palace to greet them in the throne room like she and the queen had discussed.

She settled on a midnight blue gown almost as dark as her skin. The narrow neckline caught on her collar as she tugged it down and over her slender body. But Elora was surprised to find that she was already getting used to the way the hailstone collar and bracelets would snag on her clothes, so this time she didn't even grumble when she tucked the high neck underneath it and continued smoothing out the rest of the dress.

Thankfully, she had already dealt with her hair earlier. Half of it was pulled back and wrapped into a tightly spun bun, while the rest of it had been brushed a hundred times. The queen likely would've preferred her to wear it in a style more customary to the women of Irongate, especially upon greeting her betrothed again after his journey, but for now it would have to do.

Before making her way to the door, Elora paused to take a look at herself in the mirror.

A skeleton of her former self stared back at her, all ribs and bones from years of malnourishment and beatings. But some of the sharp angles of her face were beginning to fill in, making her seem more intimidating than starved.

She stood straighter. Pretended the sharpness of her boney body was an armor. An omen.

It would have to do for now.

Elora stormed across her bedchamber and headed for the door.

For the first time in twenty years, Elora would face her torturer, and this time she would be the one to claim justice.

But as she reached for the iron doorknob, her hand trembled. Behind her eyelids, she saw it, the moment she would see him there in the throne room. He'd be bound, perhaps gagged and on his knees, completely at her mercy—only, in her mind, he wasn't. The minute they locked eyes, Darius Graeme lunged for her. He grabbed whatever weapon he could find and speared her through the stomach. Burned her with a nearby torch. Choked her. Beat her.

Elora's breath quickened. But being the intelligent woman she was, she reminded herself how impossible that scenario was. It was just fear getting the better of her. The guards of Irongate would never allow such disobedience—as a former prisoner, she would know.

Shaking the irrational fear away, she reached out again, this time actually managing to grasp the cool iron in her hand. She took in a deep breath. Told herself to twist.

But her wrist wouldn't budge.

Because a new, even more frightening thought had entered the realm of possibilities now.

What if there *weren't* guards holding him down? What if when Elora entered the throne room, everyone was waiting for her to arrive as if *she* was the spectacle?

They could be down there waiting to unleash her greatest fear upon her. The guards would snatch her, pin down her arms as Darius cycled through every torture device at his disposal, and this time there would be an entire room full of people to watch. To laugh. To mock her anguish.

And when she was finally so bloodied and broken that she was fading out of consciousness, it would be Queen Signe who approached her. She'd have that sickeningly sweet but venomous slit of a grin as she stood over Elora and snickered.

"Silly girl, you didn't actually think someone as tainted as you would be marrying a prince? This is just the beginning of your suffering."

The room would echo her mocking laughter, and a tear would roll down Elora's face.

Horrified and shaking uncontrollably now, Elora snatched her hand back from the door. The rational side of her mind warred with the fear, making it impossible for her to tell what was real and what was just the exaggerated imaginings of someone who had suffered too much already.

She couldn't go down there. Not now.

Elora shuffled away from the door, clutching her hand to her chest as if the doorknob had seared into her. She backed away until she bumped into a small table, a decorative vase atop it. It wobbled and she spun around to steady it just before it could crash and shatter.

A light rapping came at the door not a moment later, making her jump and spin around again.

"C-come in," she said, though she wished she could've told them not to enter. But her room was not permitted to ever be locked, so it would've been futile anyway. If the queen wanted her, she would have her.

This time, it wasn't the queen to step inside though. It was a mousy servant who kept her head turned down, afraid of locking eyes with her.

"The prince has returned, my lady. Queen Signe requests you to join her in the throne room."

Eyes wide as the moon and likely shining just as brightly under so much duress, all Elora could do was nod. But the servant wasn't watching her. Elora couldn't force herself to budge and obey the command anyway. She couldn't go to the throne room. Couldn't face Darius Graeme or the others. She was a coward. A shell of the battle-hardened warrior who had led hundreds into war all those years ago.

It was another life.

This was who she was now.

Who they had made her to become.

"I'm unwell," Elora said hurriedly. "Please tell the queen not to wait for me, but that I will come when I am able."

Concern bloomed behind the servant's eyes, likely because no one wanted to relay a declined invitation to the queen, although part of Elora wondered if it was because she had been meant as the main entertainment.

"Very well, princess." The servant scuttled out of the room, closing the door behind her.

Already Elora felt the panic settling. The tightness of her breath loosening. Her hands stilling.

Because apparently after decades of imprisonment, the only place Elora felt safe anymore was behind a shut door, confined to a singular room, trapped and imprisoned.

CHAPTER 17

A ROYAL REUNION

KESTREL

Kestrel held her breath as she walked under the portcullis, entering Irongate for the first time.

It seemed a storm was rolling in with them, dark clouds forming in the sky overhead and casting a gloomy tone over the kingdom. Regardless, Kestrel still balked at the magnitude of the place. She wasn't sure what she had expected, but it hadn't been the sprawling city before her. Irongate seemed to be forged of steel spires and slate bannisters. Of formidable buildings and indestructible towers. The people walking the streets seemed to be hewn from the same sturdy materials their homeland was named after. Nothing but fierce resolve reflected in their eyes as Kestrel and their entourage marched by.

Every townsfolk they passed stopped what they were doing to pay their respect. As they passed the docks, fishermen dropped their entire catches just to salute their princes with the same stacked-arm gesture Kestrel had seen the princes and the knights use. Once they reached the trades district, blacksmiths stopped their clanging, wiped the sweat from their foreheads, and even with tools in their hands, they still mimicked the Irongate salute.

Thunder rumbled overhead, matching the kingdom's heavy and serious demeanor.

Kestrel couldn't decide if that was because everything was constructed out of the same grey stones and metal, or if it was because the people here lacked the kind of joviality she'd seen from the ones back in Mutiny Bay. They were all so…formal. So dutiful. Nothing at all like the rambunctious and wily folks who'd inhabited the Stinging Drip.

Kestrel felt herself shrinking inward, not wanting to stand out. Standing out, being too colorful, felt wrong here.

But shrinking inward didn't seem to help her hide. The same labor-worn eyes that followed the princes marked Kestrel not a second later, and she was beginning to understand why. Everyone here looked so similar. Unlike Mutiny Bay, which had been an explosion of human differences and uniqueness, the townspeople of Irongate were all pale of skin and had blonde or light brown hair.

Kestrel's bright orange locks made her standout like a mirage on the horizon.

Everyone stared. Everyone whispered. And it wasn't until then, when she heard the snippets of hushed voices, that she realized just how distinct her hair was to the people.

"Corrupt Queen—"

"Another traitor—"

"—hang her and put this darkness behind us."

The more she focused on the people, the harder it was to draw air.

So many faces surrounded them, and not a single one was kind.

Another roar of thunder overhead.

Kestrel's chest was tightening. Her skin becoming so itchy she wanted to rip it off.

Then Micah's hand brushed against hers. She turned her horrified eyes up to his and found him smiling with a sort of calmness that put her at ease. He nodded to the guards behind them, then to the ones surrounding them on all sides, as if to say she was safe. Nothing would happen to her.

As much as she appreciated his kindness—and she did —the reminder of how encircled by strangers she was only tightened the knot around her chest. It felt like some-one's hands were inside her, squeezing the life from her lungs, preventing any air from reaching the places it needed to reach.

Kestrel gripped Micah's hand and closed her eyes.

Maybe if she couldn't see them, it would be easier. She could pretend she was still alone in her tower, gazing out her window across the sea, hoping for the fog to lift so that she could wonder at the hidden island and the dragon bones atop it.

She imagined the sea breeze, and oh how grateful she would be to feel it graze across the nape of her neck now. To feel it tangle in her hair. Inhaling deeply, she could almost smell it, that fresh scent of water and salt that reminded her of home. Of safety. Of comfort.

There was no salt in the air here though.

Instead, she smelled something floral and velvety.

Kestrel opened her eyes to find the crowd had thinned. All but disappeared behind them. No more townsfolk speculating and gossiping. Even the guards had dispersed some, as the princes and Kestrel now approached a network of lush, pristinely kept gardens.

She was surrounded by flowers every shade of pastel, from purples to pinks to blues. Kestrel hadn't known that so many flowers could cluster together like that, didn't know that each bloom had its own petal shape and texture and smell. And oh, did she take the time to smell them all. With childlike wonder, Kestrel pressed each new bud to her nose and inhaled the variety of fresh, floral, creamy, and some even spicy aromas.

The garden was so beautiful, it almost seemed out of place compared to the cold and fortified kingdom at her backside.

Or maybe it was exactly what this kingdom had needed.

A touch of femininity.

A reminder of beauty in a realm that could oftentimes feel so harsh. So doomed.

Kestrel would've been content to spend the rest of her days in the garden alone. But the princes kept marching forward, winding through the garden paths, so Kestrel followed.

At the center erupted a massive estate, the stone walls covered in vines and moss.

Kestrel stopped in her tracks, marveling up at the three or four stories. But a commotion drew her attention off to the side, and she turned to find Efrem and a handful of other guards who were handling the prisoners. Kestrel had forgotten they were with them, too caught up in the newness of her arrival. Now, she watched them shuffle the prisoners around, and even though their heads were still shrouded in burlap sacks, she was able to spot Thom among them. The limp in his leg was worse than ever, and he hobbled to Efrem's side while the others were taken away to another stone building on the property.

When Efrem rejoined Kestrel and the princes, she wasn't sure if she should be relieved that he hadn't been taken away, or worried that his crimes were apparently so significant that he was being brought to the queen immediately. Ultimately, she decided this was a good thing. This meant they could deal with his charges sooner rather than later, maybe even earn his freedom immediately.

Efrem guided Thom up the front steps, Micah, Leighton, and Kestrel falling in line behind him. Two of the castle guards opened the large iron doors for them and they slipped inside.

With Kestrel's heart sloshing around in her stomach, she hardly noticed the chill that seemed to permeate these halls, despite the floor-to-ceiling windows that flooded the foyer with overcast sunlight. Even after the doors had been shut, a breeze trickled down the halls, rattling the metal adorning the room. But Kestrel could not rip her eyes from Efrem's back as he guided them into the throne room.

It was almost entirely pitch-black inside, a stark contrast to the illumination behind them.

The darkness only served to feed her dread. Kestrel's stomach squeezed tighter. It wasn't what she had expected, to find the throne room so thoroughly doused. None of the princes seemed surprised though, as if this was a place that never saw the light of day. She noted the thick curtains that hung over the places where she presumed windows were, but they were all closed tight, pressed against the walls as if to ensure that not a single sliver of light could enter.

With just a few sconces and tall candelabras to light their way, Kestrel stayed close to the princes, afraid of what might be lurking in the shadows.

She didn't even notice the throne until they were practically upon it, much less the queen perched inside.

In unison, the princes bowed at the waist, but Kestrel gawked a moment longer. She had never seen someone look so regal, as if the woman before her had been made for the throne. Despite her lithe frame and delicate features, the queen oozed power. Kestrel could tell by the way she sat languid in the throne, as if nothing could harm her, that there was nothing this woman couldn't do with a simple command or a snap of her fingers.

Efrem shoved Thom's shoulder to make him do the same.

Eventually, Kestrel dragged her gaze away long enough to follow suit, buckling at the waist and staring at her dusty shoes.

"I see you have returned," a velvety, feminine voice bled into the room like shadow itself. "And you've brought guests?"

Leighton was the first to straighten, his brothers doing the same after. "We traveled far and wide in search of the traitor, Queen Signe, and I am proud to report we found him."

With a nod to his brother, Efrem removed the burlap sack from Thom's head. His hair was more disheveled than usual, and when Kestrel realized his goggles weren't atop his skull, something panged in her chest. Thom glanced around the room, his eyes adjusting even though there wasn't much light.

When his gaze crossed hers, it snagged. Shattered. Unspoken fear and a thousand pleas reverberated in the space between them. Never before had she seen him more disappointed.

Before he could speak, Efrem jerked his attention forward.

"Ser Darius Graeme." The queen had been lounging in her throne, her legs as long as spiders where they had rested over the armrest. Now she straightened at the sight of him, her dark eyes blooming with something like hunger as she took him in. "My, my, it has been a lifetime."

"Signe," Thom said. He snorted something grotesque as if he was about to spit snot at her feet. "I see you're faring well after the mess you caused. Although those eyes of yours, they're much darker than I remember them being last time. How's that curse treating you?"

The slightest twitch wrinkled beneath Signe's left eye. Before it could fully form though, Efrem kicked the back of Thom's knees, sending him sprawling onto the floor.

Kestrel couldn't stop herself.

"Don't hurt him!" she screamed, her voice an ominous echo that reverberated throughout the room.

It drew the queen's gaze toward her. Kestrel felt like a fly that had just flown into a spider's web.

"Oh? And who do we have here? Is this one of your pets, Darius—" But before she could finish the thought, the queen's brow twitched, a hint of curiosity wriggling into her expression. It warred with the denial that reared up after, as if whatever possibility she had imagined couldn't be true. Signe stood, the black length of her gown spilling to the ground as she made her way across the room to them. With cold fingers, she grasped Kestrel's chin, tilting her this way and that way. "It cannot be."

Leighton stepped around them, angling himself into the queen's peripherals. "I believe so. We spotted her in Mutiny Bay, same place we found him. The similarities were uncanny, but it was *this* that put my suspicions to rest—"

He had to shift the gold-embroidered tails of his tunic out of the way to reach the pocket in the side of his trousers. From it, he pulled out Kestrel's ring.

Suddenly, she became all too aware of the barren spot on her finger where the ring belonged. After everything that had happened in the Fortress of Thirst, she hadn't even thought about demanding it back, and now that he was showing it to the queen, she feared she was too late.

Leighton presented the ring to the queen, and out of the corner of Kestrel's eyes, she saw Thom's head droop. Signe inspected it thoroughly, or as thoroughly as she could with just her eyes. Kestrel noted the way she seemed averse to touching it.

"So it's true then," the queen said at last, breathless. "You must be her daughter."

Leighton tucked the ring back into his pocket. "Queen Signe, allow me the pleasure of formally introducing you to whom I believe to be Kestrel Highmore, your niece and the lost princess of Caelora."

Highmore. The foreign surname echoed in Kestrel's skull.

It sounded so...so regal.

So poised.

So *not* her.

But Kestrel didn't want to appear offended or caught off guard, so she bowed her head, like she'd seen the princes do upon arrival, hoping that it would convey her good intentions toward the queen and their meeting.

The queen chuckled, bringing a torrent of flames to Kestrel's cheeks. But it was to Thom who she spoke, "My my, Darius. You have been quite devious indeed these past few years. Keeping my niece from me."

"The girl is innocent," he bit out, so fiercely that even Kestrel snapped her attention toward him. Efrem's hands were firmly pinning his shoulders down, keeping him in place, but it was clear from both of their struggles that Thom was pushing against him, trying to stand, maybe trying to lunge. "Let her go! It's me you want."

Efrem raised a fist, ready to slam it across Thom's jaw. Kestrel's heart lurched out for him, her mouth opening to scream her protest.

But it was the queen's command that saved him, a lazy wave of her delicate hand.

"Don't you worry, Ser Darius, you and I will have much to converse about later." Bringing her gaze up to Efrem, she added, "Take him to the dungeons with the rest of the traitors. I'll deal with him when I see fit. For now though—" she twisted back toward Kestrel, her voice honeyed and singsong in a way that made Kestrel's stomach churn. "For now, I'd like to get acquainted with my darling niece."

"Let her go!" Thom screamed as Efrem dragged him out of the throne room. A few other guards rushed in to help, securing his thrashing arms and legs and shoving the sack back over his head. None of it deterred his wails. "Don't believe a word she says! Signe is poison! She's the whole reason your mother—"

And then, he was gone.

Only Kestrel, Leighton, and Micah remained in a room that now felt more like a tomb than a throne room. Kestrel had already learned about Prince Leighton's inclination toward duplicity. She was already beginning to sense something sinister about Signe as well. Only Micah seemed innocent of heart, at least in the ways that mattered to Kestrel. As the queen made her way back to the throne in slow, languid strides, it was Micah's gaze that Kestrel searched for. But he looked just as worried as she felt, his eyes pinned on the queen, waiting for her next move.

As she sat in the throne, Queen Signe draped herself over the armrest once more. "What of your mother, Kestrel? Where is she?"

She felt her throat constrict. "Dead. Thom says—" at seeing the slight twitch of the queen's brow, Kestrel remembered that wasn't the name anyone else knew him by. It was yet another lie, however, in this moment, it felt more like a secret, like something special that only the two of them knew. Kestrel corrected herself. "I mean *Darius*, he says that the curse killed her."

Signe released a long, pained sigh. "That's what I was afraid of."

The room fell into an uncomfortable silence as everyone waited for the queen to say more. When she didn't, Leighton stepped forward.

"There is something else, my queen."

"Oh?" Signe lifted one eyebrow as she fussed with the slit of her gown.

"I'm afraid King Ulfaskr is dead. I wanted to be sure Kestrel was who I thought she was, so we brought her to the Fortress of Thirst to test her magic. But she showed no signs of any, and we had to—"

"Well of course she didn't, you fool. She's had no one to teach her." Queen Signe smiled down at Kestrel. "We'll fix that, as well, my darling." The smile remained fixed on her face as she returned her attention to Leighton. "I suppose that means your coronation is finally in order. And that your engagement will resume as planned."

Kestrel's heart stuttered on the word engagement, and it took her a moment to convince herself the queen was still talking to Leighton. Someone who had willingly kissed *her* not maybe a few weeks prior. She had to remind herself that all of that had been a lie though, a con, much like everything else that had come out of his mouth.

But the way he winced at her words, or perhaps at her announcing them in front of Kestrel, suggested that there was something else going on there. Not that Kestrel cared. The prince and her were done. They had to be. Not only because she could no longer trust him, but dragon's fire, he had been raised by her aunt! They were practically related—although ever since stepping into the throne room, Kestrel had noticed that there had been no sense of love or affection between the two of them. Toward any of the princes, really. Not the way Kestrel had imagined a mother would treat her sons. They'd been gone for weeks, if not months, and yet Signe had shown no signs of relief upon seeing them returned home safely. No pride in hearing that they had accomplished their task of bringing her the man they kept calling *Darius Graeme*.

If anything, the princes seemed cowed by her. Perhaps even afraid.

Kestrel was still wondering what that meant for her own safety, when the queen clapped her hands and a servant rushed to her side.

"Send someone else to ready the Princess Elora, would you? And when she's presentable, bring her down here to greet her husband and congratulate him on his coronation announcement."

"Betrothed," Leighton corrected under his breath, but the queen merely waved him off as the servant hurried out of the room.

"Yes, yes, *betrothed*. But now that you'll soon be king, the time to wed is fast-approaching." Leighton shifted on his feet, and Kestrel saw the worried way Micah watched him. "Why don't you both go freshen up a bit while we wait for the princess to join us. And my niece can tell me all about her upbringing with the fallen knight."

Leighton and Micah shot Kestrel a worried glance, as if to ask if she was alright to stay there alone. The truth was, she wasn't. This was all uncharted territory for her, quite literally. But getting close to the queen had been her goal. This was what she wanted, to speak with her privately about Thom. Besides, she already knew as well as them that none of them had a choice; what the queen demanded was what occurred.

So Kestrel nodded to both of them, and as they obliged the queen's dismissal, she prepared herself for the most important conversation of her life.

CHAPTER 18
LOST FAMILY
KESTREL

The doors closed before even a sliver of light could seep into the dark throne room, leaving Kestrel and Signe entirely alone.

There were only a handful of times in her lifetime that Kestrel could recall ever experiencing true fear. Most recently, when the prince shoved her into the fortress with no way out and the king-beast's galloping footsteps pounding after her. The cinders, the Maw, and the weeks when Thom hadn't returned home.

Being alone in a room with the Queen of Irongate felt an awful lot like any of those moments.

A shiver ran through her. Kestrel absently rubbed at the loose sleeves of her tunic. She glanced over to the curtains, wishing someone would open them and allow the warmth of the sun inside.

"I don't think I'm used to the temperatures outside of Vallonde yet," Kestrel said, attempting to make small talk. "Would it be alright if we opened the curtains?"

She moved toward them, but the queen lunged.

"No!" she hissed, something dark and sinister ravaging her voice. It was the first time Kestrel caught a glimpse of the curse upon her, she suspected. But the queen recovered quickly, plastering a thin smile over her porcelain skin as she resettled into her throne. "I mean, I'd rather you didn't."

The sheer darkness was no happenstance then, nor was it caused by a forgetful servant. This was the queen's doing. And the reason why was starting to make sense.

"Is it because of your curse?"

Signe gave a single, almost pained nod. "My hope is that you will come to love me the way that I already love you. However, if you bear witness to what the light does to my skin, I fear it would only serve to frighten you." Curiosity tugged at Kestrel, and she opened her mouth to reassure the queen that it wouldn't change her opinion, that she understood it wasn't her choice, but Signe snapped her fingers and set her servants to work instead. "But here, we can warm you up in other ways."

Servants swarmed from the shadows, from every corner of the room. They gathered the candelabras that had been lining the walkway up to the throne and brought them all nearer, until Kestrel was encircled by torch fire.

"There, how's that, my darling?"

"Better. Thank you," she said, a bit uncertain. Having the light so close to her eyes made it even harder to be aware of her darkened surroundings.

The queen's smile widened though, a thin crack of a line that looked like shattered glass. The woman had been nothing but kind to Kestrel so far though, and if what she was saying was true, if she really did want a loving relationship with her niece, then Kestrel wanted that as well. It wasn't like she had many contenders for family. Especially none that had the power to do what she needed them to do.

Kestrel hovered her hands by the torchlight. "Why have you imprisoned Thom—I mean, Darius?"

Through the flames, Kestrel thought she spotted the woman admiring her sharp, pointed nails. "Well, it's quite simple: he's a traitor."

"He's my father."

Queen Signe barked out a laugh. "Oh no, my darling. You have been entirely misinformed. Your mother was married to King Everard of the Caeloran kingdom. *He's* your father, I would presume, as well as one of the many victims of the curse that Darius Graeme is responsible for."

Kestrel tried wrapping her head around what Signe was suggesting.

When the prince had told her about her lineage, Kestrel hadn't wanted it to be true. She didn't want to even consider the possibility that she might have a father other than Thom. Thom had been there for her throughout her entire life. He was the one who comforted her during the storms and the scourge attacks. The one who provided for her. Kept her safe. Taught her how to cook and care for herself. The very notion that this could be yet another one of his lies made her stomach twist and knot itself.

But perhaps even more alarming than that was hearing someone claiming that Thom was responsible for the curse, not her mother.

"But I thought everyone blamed the *Corrupt Queen*," she said, the moniker burning like acid on her tongue.

"Most do, perhaps. But need I remind you that she was my sister long before she was a queen. I knew her better than anyone else, and she would never have done such a demented thing if she didn't have another choice. When the traitor absconded with Queen Aenwyn, I had always wondered how he'd convinced her to use her magic to curse all of Grimtol. Now that I'm meeting you, I think it's quite obvious."

Kestrel thought she was following. "You think he used me? To coerce her?"

"It's the only thing that makes any sense. Queen Aenwyn was a gentle and just queen. Even before her marriage, she had a kind heart and would've never performed such brutal magic upon her people—upon innocents—if she hadn't been forced to."

Kestrel was shaking her head. Not that she wanted her mother to be viewed as some demented witch, but Thom wasn't a manipulative mastermind either. Well, okay, maybe he had been in ways. But not like this. Besides, if he had wanted to curse the lands, then why had he spent her entire life trying to put an end to that curse? It was one of the reasons he insisted on going out on his missions, to find a way to end the dark magic.

Unless...that had been part of an act too. A way to ingratiate himself to her. To cement him as a hero in her eyes. As a leader worth heeding.

Knowing about the monsters had kept Kestrel locked away in that tower. And knowing he was out there looking for a way to stop them, had assuaged her wanderlust and made it easier to endure the long days and nights without him. It had given her no reason to insist he stay whenever he *needed* to go. After all, who was she to prevent the future savior of the lands from rescuing them all?

All the while, he'd kept her hidden away from the rest of the realm. From her real family. From a father she hadn't even realized she'd been missing.

The pieces were beginning to fall into place, only instead of making Kestrel feel complete, it made her feel like a boar addled with holes, slowly sinking into a lake.

Kestrel tried shaking her despair away. These questions didn't change anything. She still had one purpose.

"Can I speak to him? To Darius?"

The queen swiped her slender nails through the air. "Must we continue drudging up such dreadful memories when we have so much more important issues to discuss? You are a princess—an heir to the Caeloran throne. Your mother might not have survived, but you did, my darling. With proper training, you could be the savior our kingdoms need. The savior your father has been waiting for."

Doubt twisted inside her.

"I tried that already. With King..." Kestrel couldn't remember his name, but fortunately the queen understood what she was trying to say.

"King Ulfaskr. Yes well, between you and I, the realm is likely a better place without him."

Kestrel blanched at Signe's boldness. She didn't know much about royal politics, but she was fairly certain speaking ill of a king, even a late king, was not generally advisable. The queen waved off her concern.

"Oh honestly, Kestrel, there is so much for you to learn about the innerworkings of this realm. Perhaps when you are betrothed yourself, one day you will understand." Signe's black eyes fell to a ring on her hand. She rolled the band this way and that, the gaudy gemstone catching the refracted lights from the flames and making it dazzle like a determined star on a cloudy night. "Of course, it is a tragedy that King Ulfaskr could not be returned to us as his former self, and we shall mourn for him and the loss of our kingdom in due time. However, make no mistake, my darling. You did not fail because you are incapable. You failed because you do not yet understand your magic."

"And—" Kestrel squinted through the fire, daring to feel a flicker of hope "—you can help me?"

"To save your father? To save all our kingdoms? My darling, it would be my greatest honor."

For the first time since entering the throne room, the icy pressure that had surrounded Kestrel was starting to thaw. She smiled up at the queen, who returned her own beatific display of affection.

Queen Signe was just opening her mouth, perhaps to tell Kestrel when their training would begin and what it would entail, when someone new entered the room from a door beyond the queen's throne. A woman. One Kestrel almost couldn't see at first because her slate-grey skin nearly concealed her within the darkness. If it wasn't for her moon-white hair, half of it pulled back into a bun, the other half draped over her shoulders, she might've been completely invisible before stepping into the candlelight.

As she approached Queen Signe's side, Kestrel noted how graceful the young woman's movements were. Like a stream gliding over hundreds of pebbles and rocks, she moved with the mesmerizing fluidity of water.

She kept her gaze cast downward as she approached them, and Kestrel saw markings on her forehead and temples that reminded her of a crown, one made of stars. Like the young woman was a midnight sky turned to flesh.

Reaching the throne, the woman bowed. "You summoned me, Queen Signe?"

Kestrel realized then that this was the Princess Elora the queen had referred to earlier, the one betrothed to Prince Leighton. Of course she was. The crown, the grace, the regal aura that emanated from her the moment she entered the room.

She was adorned in lavish jewelry, a crystalline blue necklace cuffed around her neck and shoulders, a beautiful accent to the midnight blue gown that fell down her curves like liquid metal.

Kestrel didn't know how either of them could stand the constriction of wearing dresses, but they both wore them beautifully. But Elora especially—she was ethereal grace. And a prince—or rather, a soon-to-be *king*—deserved nothing less.

"Princess Elora, what a vision you are." The queen slid an approving smile toward the princess, but none of the admiration quite reached her icy tone. "I am sure you have heard by now about the return of your betrothed."

"Yes, the servants informed me. They requested I join you all here, but I see he has left us again already?"

"Not for long. I merely sent him to wash up before

greeting you. He's been on the road so long, he smelled like a dog, and I care too much about your delicate senses to force you to endure such company."

"To a love as true as ours, I'm sure neither of us would've minded." There was an edge to Elora's tone, an unmistakable bite that made it seem like everything she said held a different meaning.

The closer Kestrel watched her, the more she realized the woman wasn't just elegant, she was deadly. There was an alertness to her gaze, an intentionality of her movements that reminded Kestrel of a predator. Not the mangy coyotes of Vallonde who stalked their prey and overpowered them as a herd. More like the unseen dangers that lurked in the dark, the ones you knew were there, but would never see until it was too late.

There was an air about Elora that suggested she knew how to wield a sword. Deadlier still, that she had killed before. Kestrel couldn't help but wonder if it had been Elora's blood that was the answer to the curse, if she could've been able to handle the king-beast all on her own.

As Kestrel scrutinized her up on the dais, thoroughly entranced and intrigued, Elora slid her magenta eyes toward her. "And who do we have here?"

Every muscle in Kestrel's body constricted.

"Ah, Princess Elora, I would like you to meet Princess Kestrel—" then Signe amended with some pleasure— "The secret princess of Caelora. Or perhaps stolen might be a better word for it."

Elora's eyes widened, her magenta irises flashing with an impossible glow. "Caelora? But I didn't know they—"

"Neither did I," the queen agreed, one of her sharp nails dragging up and down the neckline of her gown. Her gaze was fixed upon Kestrel, like she was a puzzle to be solved. "Who knew we'd have so much royalty under one house."

Kestrel thought she saw Elora almost roll her eyes, but instead her lips quirked up in a forced smile. "A pleasure to meet you, Princess Kestrel."

In some of the books Kestrel had read, when commoners or people of similar stations in life met, they would grab each other's hands and shake them up and down as a way to show trust and friendliness. Considering that she had already crossed a line with her by kissing her betrothed—albeit unknowingly—Kestrel wanted nothing more than to show the woman that she meant her no ill will.

So, marching toward the princess, Kestrel eagerly thrust her hand out.

Queen Signe gasped, and Elora recoiled—*actually* recoiled. As if Kestrel's touch would've singed her skin. Only, it wasn't *her* touch that was the problem.

The queen shrieked, "By the Hollows! What has overcome you, girl?"

Kestrel froze. "I...I don't know. I thought that—I was just trying to be nice and say hello."

Queen Signe's look of disgust did not vanish immediately. She stared at her, horrified and then confused for a long, awful moment. Finally, she tried fixing her voice with a modicum of understanding. "Right. You must've noticed the hailstone then." Kestrel would've shaken her head if the queen had given her any time to, but she didn't know what hailstone was. "Don't let those shackles fool you, my darling. You must never willingly touch an Ashen. Not ever."

Kestrel's mind stuttered on the word shackles before returning her focus to Princess Elora's jewelry. On closer inspection, she realized the necklace was a familiar shade of light blue, one she hadn't recognized at first. Now that she was looking again, she thought it might be hewn from the same stone as her mother's ring. Her eyes trailed lower then, to the cuffs around Elora's wrists that she had first mistaken for bracelets. They, too, were the same color. The same stone meant to block a person's magic.

She glanced up to Princess Elora. Her jaw was a taut line, but she forced herself to relax again into that neutral, regal expression.

No one was treating Kestrel this way. They weren't afraid to touch her. They hadn't called her an *Ashen*, whatever that was.

Attempting to bring some levity to the conversation, Kestrel laughed. "I don't even know what an Ashen is, let alone why it would be so unthinkable to shake one's hand."

The queen balked, looking as if she might faint.

Elora's expression was harder to read. It almost reminded her of the way Leighton had looked at her when they first met, when he asked her if she'd recognized him. There had been a sort of disbelief mirrored in his eyes, but also hope. Relief. A weight lifted.

"My, how little the traitor has taught you." Queen

Signe sighed, her slender fingers rubbing along her temples.

The double doors behind Kestrel burst open.

"Give her a break," Micah said, catching the tail end of their conversation. A ray of sunshine beamed into the room momentarily, making the queen shrink toward the back of her throne, even though the light could never reach that far into the room. "She's been locked away from the realm for her entire life. She might need a devout tutor before she can be expected to understand the basics of Grimtol's history and its people."

Through the doorway emerged three young men whom, despite having brushed the tangles out of their hair, Kestrel recognized as the princes she'd been traveling with. Neither Efrem nor Leighton appeared to have changed their clothes, although Leighton's armor did have a sharper glint to it, as if he'd at least rubbed polish on it and attempted to make it shine. Micah, however, had discarded his old, dusty clothes in favor of a new crimson tunic that complimented his hair and complexion.

Signe made her contempt for Micah's interruption known. Or perhaps it was seeing Leighton returned so utterly unchanged, as if he'd hardly heeded her instructions at all.

Despite what seemed like a very overt slight, he bowed at the waist again upon his return, deeper toward the queen before giving a swift nod to Princess Elora. "My lady."

The princess grabbed her gown at the hip, and bowed in return. And that was that. No demure smiles or flirtatious glances. The two beheld each other for as long as was required before Leighton returned his attention to the topic at hand.

"We shared a broad overview of Grimtol's histories with Kestrel while we were traveling, but I agree with Micah. If Kestrel is to sit on the throne of Caelora someday, she would benefit from further teachings."

Kestrel's mouth hung agape. No one had spoken to her about having her own throne and kingdom to rule over. She didn't even want that! She just wanted Thom to be released and for them to return home, to return to some semblance of normalcy.

"I simply don't have the time to teach her," the queen growled through a fixed smile.

"Let Barnabus handle it," Leighton offered in a way that felt more like he was interjecting before she could put her foot down. "No one knows our histories or our libraries better. He is an excellent scholar, and could aid with her cultural and historical studies while the two of you focus on heightening her magic skills."

"Yes, your brother is quite adept with his books..." Queen Signe tapped her nails on the throne armrest, considering.

It was only then that Kestrel realized she didn't know there had been another brother. That would make four now. How many of them were there?

"Five," Micah whispered beside her, apparently reading the confusion on her face. "All boys. Leighton, us twins, Barnabus, and then baby Nic."

"He's nineteen now," Leighton corrected under his

breath, apparently not trying to disrupt the queen from her pondering.

A grin split Micah's face. "He'll always be a baby to me."

A frown had crinkled the queen's otherwise flawless complexion. "Princesses are trained over a lifetime; we don't have time to catch her up on all of her lost teachings. There are people suffering now, myself included. She needs to focus on harnessing her magic so that she can put an end to this curse—"

"She didn't even know what hailstone was," argued Leighton. He pulled out her mother's ring again for emphasis. Every time Kestrel saw it, her chest ached as if he were shoving her back into the fortress and breaking her heart all over again. "When we first met, she had been wearing this ring and didn't even know she had magic, let alone that the ring was inhibiting her from using it. She didn't know what Animali were either. And I'm guessing she had never met an Ashen before today."

By way of confirmation, the queen downcast her eyes. Princess Elora averted her gaze as well.

Satisfied with his point being made, Leighton continued. "There are things about the realm that will be useful for her to understand. If you send her out to stop a curse but she doesn't know about the dangers of the realm, the historical tensions among the kingdoms, and which territories she will be treated as a prisoner, then she will be of no use to anyone. She'll be an easy target...like she was for us."

Shame heated her cheeks. Kestrel wanted to snuff out all the torchlights and hide. But there was a gentleness in the way Leighton said it that made her feel like it wasn't her fault. And she knew it wasn't. All of this, being out in the realm, it was all new to her, and she was doing the best she could to deepen her understanding of it all.

But the more they discussed her role as the realm's savior, the more Kestrel questioned whether they had the right woman.

Leighton was right, after all. She knew little to nothing about Grimtol and its dangers. And according to Signe, it would take years to learn them—*a lifetime*, she had said.

As if in protest to her doubt, that flicker of darkness rippled inside her. Then again, maybe there was more for her to uncover about herself yet. That sense of intrigue couldn't quell the full extent of her doubts though. They had been ingrained in her since childhood. Thom always said this world was too dangerous for someone like her. And so far, her experiences had mostly proven him right.

Her chest was doing that thing again, where it felt like it was caving in on itself.

The darkness seemed to be thickening around her. The walls pressing in.

"You make some valid points," the queen said. "A basic understanding of Grimtol and its histories will only serve to strengthen her, and therefore our kingdoms. You may instruct Barnabus to head her non-magical studies at once. She and I..."

Kestrel's ears were starting to ring, and she could no longer hear what the queen was saying.

This was all too much.

Thom was a traitor, possibly not even a father.

Her mother had cursed the lands. She had ruined so many lives.

And they wanted Kestrel to fix them.

But she hadn't even been able to fix the king. She hadn't been able to save herself from him, from the Maw, from the cinders. The fate of the realm was resting upon unskilled hands, and it terrified her.

Kestrel felt as if she were tipping over. And maybe she was because Micah's hands gripped her shoulders not a moment too late, steadying her.

"Are you alright?" he whispered so only she could hear, but the sudden movement of his arm wrapping around her had drawn the attention of everyone in the room.

She searched for the right words, for the decorum that she had never been taught but knew was now expected of her as a *princess*—as the *savior* they were all relying on.

"Yes, I—I think I just..."

"It's been a rather arduous journey, my queen," Leighton cut in for her. "Princess Kestrel has wandered far, through the desolate deserts of Vallonde, and narrowly escaped the bloodlust of my father; this has all been a lot to take in, I'm sure." He paused a moment, watching her with those knowing eyes, almost as if he was asking for her permission to continue. Kestrel's chest was still so tight, she could hardly think, let alone say yes. Thankfully, when she didn't interject, nor did her pained expression change, he continued. "She wanted to meet you first upon our arrival, but I believe the princess could use some rest after everything she has endured. Perhaps she can begin her studies with a fresh mind come first-hours."

Kestrel had never been more grateful to have someone at her side. Two someone's.

"Very well," the queen said with a flick of her wrist. "Inform Barnabus that his pupil will join him in the library at rooster's first crow. Kestrel, you and I will meet after lunch. And don't be late. Your magic training starts now."

CHAPTER 19

A QUEEN'S COMMAND

ELORA

When Queen Signe had sent for Elora again, she'd had no choice but to come down. Fortunately, by then she had calmed her nerves enough that she was able to think rationally again. To remind herself that although she had been kept prisoner in Irongate for the last couple of decades, they had never subjected her to torture the way the Caelorans had. It was unlikely they'd start now with the most elaborate and cruel tactics yet.

Still, after Elora made her way downstairs, she had lingered outside the throne room, listening for Darius to make sure he had been taken away. She still hadn't been ready to face him yet. She wasn't sure when she would be.

But as she'd stood there, she heard something else that actually made her want to go inside. She had expected to hear the queen, but not the second female voice that trilled from the other side of the door. A younger woman. And she sounded...scared? No, that wasn't quite it. But she definitely sounded out of place. Uncertain.

It had been curiosity that finally forced Elora into the throne room. She wanted to see the mysterious woman her future husband had unexpectedly returned home with, ready to get the unpleasantness done and over with. If he wanted to engage with other women, Elora couldn't be happier. That was precisely the sort of arrangement she wanted from him, one where he was utterly disinterested, and they were only betrothed to the public's eyes, not behind closed doors where they could both go about their lives as they pleased. That would be the perfect arrangement. So if he had returned home with a mistress, it wouldn't offend her, though it might be awkward to start with. At least until the wedding was final, and Elora's crown—and more importantly, her freedom—was secured.

But what she hadn't expected was for this mystery woman to be another princess.

That could change everything.

Especially given the tender glances he shot her way.

It wasn't jealousy, exactly, that twisted inside her. More like fear. Defensiveness. A clawing sense of survivorship that made her irrationally irate to have competition threatening her standing with the prince. Because Elora might not love Leighton, but dragon's fire if she was going to let him marry someone else and ruin her only chance at freedom.

The longer Elora listened to the conversation however, the more at ease she became.

Leighton only brought Kestrel here—that was her

name, apparently—because she was Queen Signe's niece. A lost family member that none of them had even known about.

Elora tried not to outwardly show her signs of relief, but she felt them.

The wedding would go on as planned.

The only difference now was that there was a vile Caeloran who would also be in attendance.

Her fingernails dug little moons into her palms, but no one seemed to notice.

As the conversation ended, the queen permitted Kestrel her leave so that she could rest after her long journey up from Vallonde. No one else dared move though, as if they could all sense the queen wasn't yet done with any of them. Even from where Elora stood, a short distance behind Queen Signe's throne and therefore not within view of the subtle shift in her expression, Elora knew the queen was saving the worst of it for her.

With her hands still clasped together, Elora waited for Kestrel to leave. Her gaze pinned to the back of the princess' head of untamed braids the entire time. Another Caeloran, at least by blood if she was the daughter of King Everard and the Corrupt Queen. Which meant she was just another person who likely viewed Elora's people as less than human, worthy of punishment and pain for a crime they didn't even commit.

Good riddance, she thought as the door closed behind the other princess.

And in that moment, Elora vowed to do everything in her power to stay far away from the girl. From any Caeloran, really.

"Wonderful for you to finally join us," the queen said into the cavernous hall. "We were waiting for you."

Knowing her place and what was expected of her, Elora bowed her head. "My apologies, my queen. I was feeling...ill." It sounded like a lie even to her own ears, and though Elora couldn't see the queen's face, and Efrem's remained stoic as ever, she could tell from Micah's and Leighton's expressions that they didn't believe her either. When no one immediately responded, Elora ventured cautiously, "Did you pass his sentence then?"

Another long silence.

"No," the queen said. "I decided to leave that to you. That is, if you're still up for the responsibilities of being a queen?"

A test.

A threat.

"Of course, Queen Signe. It won't happen again."

The queen nodded. Then she looked to Micah. "Find your brother, Barnabus. Tell him he has been tasked with educating our new guest on the history of Grimtol. But make sure he understands that part of his role is to illumi-nate this poor, naïve girl of the horrors that her mother and that traitorous knight caused all of the kingdoms. They are not the heroes in her story, no matter what that deserter has led her to believe."

"I'll tell him," Micah said with a shrug, and he was already making his way to the door, seemingly grateful to leave the throne room. Elora couldn't blame him.

But Leighton put a hand on Micah's chest, stopping him mid-step. "No, I'll do it."

Elora heard steam billow from Queen Signe's nostrils.

"I did not ask you to do it. I asked your brother. Your role is to remain here. Having dinner with your betrothed."

"And I will return to fulfill my duties. However, we can't leave this up to Micah—"

"Hey!" Micah blurted, looking wounded.

"No offense."

"*All* the offense," countered Micah, swatting Leighton's hand away before folding his arms over his chest. "I can relay a simple task to our brother, just as well as you can, Leigh."

The nickname seemed to be an attempt to undermine him, to shift the power in the room. But Leighton was unfazed by it.

"Really?" The elder prince angled a brow at his brother in a condescending way that only a future king could. "You and Barnabus don't exactly get along. What happened the last time you told him to do something? Do you remember?"

Micah's shoulders slouched a bit, conceding already. But Leighton wasn't done yet. If there was a point to be made, he was going to make it.

"Go on. Tell us, brother. What was it you asked Barnabus to do?"

Micah's voice was low and grumbly, like a child being made to pick up a mess he didn't want to. "I asked him not to bring his books to the dining hall so that we could actually see his face and talk to him occasionally."

"And what did he do instead?"

With a roll of his eyes, Micah answered, "He stacked a wall of books at one end of the table and then sat behind it. He refused to talk the entire meal."

Gesturing to his brother as if to say *see, I'm right*, Leighton addressed the queen. "If we let Micah deliver this task to Barnabus, he'll almost certainly do the exact opposite, just to spite him."

"Then tell him the order is coming from the queen—" Queen Signe growled, each word coming out tight and hot.

But if either prince sensed danger in the air, they didn't show it. Instead, they winced at her suggestion, a look that seemed to mock her plan and call her a fool. It wasn't like the queen to be swayed, especially not by such a brazen show of disrespect.

But even Elora knew based on what little interactions she'd had with Barnabus that Leighton was right; he trusted no one. More than that, he was controlled by no one. And not out of malice or petulance in the way that some princes were. He simply did what he wanted because it was what made sense to him. He did, however, seem to have a modicum of respect for Leighton, which everyone, including the queen apparently, understood.

With a long sigh, Queen Signe finally conceded. "Fine. Go deal with your brother, then hurry straight back. Dinner will be served shortly. We'll meet you in the dining hall."

Both princes bowed their leave, Micah swatting Leighton in the chest before they bound down the hall and out the throne room. It didn't escape Elora that Leighton had chosen to leave the same way Kestrel had, even though another exit would've been closer to the library and therefore Barnabus.

If Queen Signe noticed, she didn't show it. Instead, she dismissed Efrem as well, asking him to ensure that the

Thundersworn knights on watch over the dungeon knew to keep a keen eye on Darius. It seemed an odd directive, considering the jailors always kept their prisoners under a tight watch—Elora would know—but then she realized that the queen likely just wanted to get the two of them alone.

Once the room was cleared, Queen Signe rose from the throne. Hair as pale as silk fell down her back as she twisted around to face Elora.

Elora steeled herself for the private chastisement that was headed her way. It had been risky to deny the queen's summons earlier, she had known that. But she was here now. Surely, that would count for something?

"About the girl," Queen Signe said at last, and Elora had to force her expression to remain neutral. What about the girl? She thought for sure this would've been about Darius or Leighton or not following the queen's commands. But the new princess? What did she care about her? "I want you to befriend her."

"Befriend her?" The suggestion caught Elora so off guard that she couldn't hide the confusion, let alone the distaste from her tone. "But she's...she's Caeloran." As if that was explanation enough.

"I don't care if she's Vallondean or Sky-Blessed, or even a Molten who somehow floated their way across the sea from Galorfin. She is my sister's daughter and therefore she has her magic. She could break the curse."

Of course, that was what this was about. Not that she could blame the queen for wanting a cure. If it had been Elora caught within the Corrupt Queen's spell, she supposed breaking it would be all she could think of too.

But that didn't mean Elora had to be the one involved in manipulating the princess to do such a thing. Besides, from the conversation she had overhead, Princess Kestrel seemed more than willing, if not way in over her head.

"I understand that, but what does me befriending her have to do with her undoing the curse? You're her aunt. She'll want to help you. She won't need me to convince her."

"Perhaps." The queen waved her hand and started pacing. "But there's no telling what poisonous thoughts Darius has filled her head with. It's clear she trusts him. She was worried about his imprisonment—which, by the way, his sentencing will need to be postponed."

Something hot gripped Elora's chest. "Postponed? Why?"

"Rest assured, he will get the punishment he deserves. But for now, we have to treat his imprisonment delicately. At least until the girl is on our side."

Elora wasn't sure what the queen meant by *on our side*, considering it seemed everyone in Grimtol was against the curse and supportive of breaking it. No matter how many prisoners they had brought in and out of the dungeons, every single one of them had spoken about the Corrupt Queen and her derelict knight with disdain.

But most of them also felt similarly about the Ashen.

"And you think she'll want to be friends with someone like me?"

The queen flashed her a vicious, mocking grin. "I would be surprised as well, but I honestly don't know. She clearly was not afraid of you, and perhaps that can be used to our advantage. We'll need everyone working their charm on her to ensure that she feels welcome. Protected. Valued, even. I want her to feel like she's a part of this court, and that her magic is an asset to us all."

Something was tightening in the bottom of Elora's stomach, but she couldn't quite place why. Ending the curse had been a priority for a number of people, for a variety of reasons. But knowing the order was coming from Queen Signe gave Elora pause. She couldn't help but wonder if this was part of some grander scheme, a power-play that she had yet to fully understand.

"So you want her to end your curse?"

"Not just mine. Everyone's." Power glinted in the queen's eyes, or perhaps that was just the dark curse churning within her, begging to be let out. "Don't you?"

Elora nodded, but a hollowness was taking over her.

Curing the curse for *everyone* meant curing King Ever-ard, the man who had given the command to capture her. The man who had approved of her torture. If he was set free, what did that mean for Elora? Was she to be his captive again? She wasn't foolish enough to think that this was why the queen was wedding her to Prince Leighton, as a way to protect her for once King Everard was free. No one cared about Elora that much. But she also wasn't foolish to believe this was some random happenstance.

There was something she was missing, but she didn't know what, and knew the queen wasn't going to tell her anyway. For now, Elora had only one goal.

"And what does this mean for the wedding?"

The queen raised a slender eyebrow. "In a hurry to start your married life so soon?"

This time, the mockery didn't cut as deep. It felt more

like she was attempting to relate to her. But it also felt like a trap. Another test to gauge her commitment. This time, Elora wouldn't fail it.

"I've been waiting to start the rest of my life for decades. So yes, I am ready. Is the wedding still happening as planned or does this change things?"

The queen seemed to appreciate her response, but she still kept her waiting for a reply. As if this were a game to her. A cat toying with the dying bird in its paws, seeing how long she could stretch her suffering.

"Yes, the wedding is still happening as planned—although, I suppose it will have to be a joint affair now. A coronation as well as a wedding, since King Ulfaskr is officially dead."

"Oh." Elora had missed that part of the conversation. She wasn't sure what to say, so she said the only thing that people did in those circumstances. "I'm sorry."

"Ha! Don't be foolish, girl. You know as well as I do that arranged marriages are never what a woman wants, but we accept them out of necessity."

Elora swallowed. This was new territory for them. This type of bonding over shared experiences that felt...fake. Dangerous in the way that every conversation with Queen Signe felt like she was dangling over the edge one minute and tucked safely in the plush covers of her bed in another.

But the queen was being genuine and honest in a way that Elora rarely ever saw, so now more than ever she didn't want to ruin this. A nod seemed like the safest bet, but she kept it not too enthusiastic, in case this was a trap meant to prove that Elora wasn't worthy of marrying the prince.

The queen seemed pleased enough with her response, for she motioned Elora to follow her.

"Come, let us continue this conversation of weddings and coronations with Leighton in the dining hall."

"Of course," Elora said, following after her, relieved to know that at least she would still have the protection of their bargain.

"Oh, but one more thing." The queen spun around, one finger raised. Elora barely had enough time to stop before running into her, which she was certain would be seen as an act of attempted murder, considering her Ashen nature. "The girl, my niece, we need her to *want* to practice magic. I need you to encourage her to do so. However, she is still my sister's daughter, which means her magic might be too corrupt. And if that is the case, I will need you to kill her."

Elora wasn't sure what she was expecting, but it wasn't that.

"Deal?"

Then again, she didn't even know the girl. All she knew about her was that she was Caeloran. And if Kestrel was all that stood in Elora's way between the crown and the freedom she deserved, she supposed killing her would be a small price to pay.

"Of course, my queen. Whatever you command."

The wicked smile that crept up Queen Signe's face made Elora's stomach writhe like a nest of slippery snakes.

CHAPTER 20

THE BARGAINS WE MAKE

KESTREL

The further Kestrel was from the throne room, the more the tension eased in her chest. Not completely, but enough that she was starting to feel as if she could breathe again. The more she felt like she was back in control of her own body, aware of her surroundings.

She realized then that a servant was guiding her through the halls. She was short and stout, with her hair pulled into a taut bun at the nape of her neck. She carried a candlestick in one hand, as some of the rooms and hallways out here had their curtains drawn as well, likely to keep the queen's curse at bay.

"Where are we going?" Kestrel asked the woman, not really remembering anything that had been said in the throne room leading up to her departure.

"I'll be taking you to your room, miss. This way."

Kestrel was surprised to hear that she even had a room, considering no one in the castle had been expecting her. She supposed that in a place as grand as this they simply had extra rooms for unexpected visitors.

So Kestrel followed close behind the servant, not wanting to let herself fall too far into the darkness the candlestick left in its wake. Weaponry of all kinds decorated the hallway walls. From swords to shields, and a dozen other sharp or bulbous items that Kestrel didn't even know the names of. They glistened like embers as they passed by, and Kestrel wondered how many of them had seen battle.

After entering and exiting a number of dimly-lit labyrinthian passageways and stairwells, they finally entered a hallway with sunlight. The blue velvet curtains were drawn open on all six of the large windows, and through the windowpanes, Kestrel could now see that they were two or three stories up.

She raced toward one of the windows, pressing her face upon the sun-warmed glass. From this vantage point, she could see the full spread of the kingdom, all the shops and townspeople they'd passed by earlier. The wall surrounding Irongate seemed even more expansive now that she could behold all of it, a formidable perimeter that likely kept every type of monster from entering the city.

They were safe here.

She was safe.

At least from the monsters.

Just beyond the Irongate walls, Kestrel spotted the lake Micah said separated them from the mountain pass and her mother's original homeland. She wondered what it had been like living there. Maybe it would be something she could ask her aunt about tomorrow during their training.

"Come along now, miss," the servant said, gently grabbing hold of her elbows and ushering her along.

They didn't have much farther to go, and in just a few short strides, they reached a door.

"Here you are," the servant said with a quick bow. Kestrel noticed for the first time how warm her tone was, especially compared to how the townspeople had been speaking about her.

"Oh. Th—thank you," Kestrel said, wishing she knew how to express her gratitude better.

The servant turned the iron knob and creaked the wooden door ajar.

Kestrel started to walk inside when she realized she had no idea where she was. They had taken so many turns and covered so much ground in the castle that she wasn't sure she would be able to find her way back to the throne room, let alone to a library she'd never been to when it was time to begin her studies with Barnabus.

"Before you go," she called out to the servant who was already hurrying back down the hallway. The woman spun back around, waiting. "I need to meet someone in the library at the *rooster's first crow*—" she said, unintentionally mimicking the queen's voice. It was out of habit, something she did with Thom, and apparently now the queen, as well. Kestrel cleared her throat, embarrassed and not wanting to offend. "What I mean is, how will I find the library? And will I be able to hear the rooster's first crow from my room?"

The servant smiled at her as if she were a child. "I will return for you when it is time."

"Oh, okay. Thank you again."

The servant nodded, and then hurried away to resume the dozens of other tasks Kestrel expected a servant like her had to do around here.

And then, it was just Kestrel, alone again in a cold, stone building.

There was something both comforting and unsettling about it. At least when she had been left at home, she had all of her things—her books, her stove, her sewing. She wondered what might be waiting for her in a room that wasn't meant for her.

Twisting around and letting the door close behind her, Kestrel entered the cold room. Not cold in the sense of temperature, for it seemed some of the servants had already been around to start a fire in the hearth and light some of the candlesticks within the bedchamber. But this was a space that had no life to it. There was none of the lived-in clutter she was accustomed to—not that she and Thom had many things, but they had their pile of sandals and boots clustered by the door, a tall stack of clothes that needed repairing and was almost about to topple over, all their jars of spices and dried legumes.

This room felt barren by comparison, even though it was double the size of their entire living space.

Everything here felt too far away. The reading chair between the window and the fireplace had so much space between them that Kestrel could've danced in a circle around the chair, neither risking breaking the window nor touching the fire.

There was a large armoire opposite the windows, and a vanity with a mirror atop it. But the armoire was empty, the vanity void of so much as a hairbrush.

The room made her feel hollow.

Empty.

So severely alone in ways that Kestrel never felt at home.

But as her eyes found their way over to the magnificent bed, excitement began to fill the void. The bed was bigger than her and Thom's beds combined. Maybe double the size. At each corner was an ornately carved wooden bedpost. Squealing with delight, Kestrel drew nearer, examining the craftsmanship and marveling at the depictions carved into the wood. Entire gruesome scenes of battle, the culminating triumph of peace that followed. It was a work of art, not something Kestrel had ever beheld before.

With a hoot and a holler, Kestrel jumped onto the bed, sinking into the thick, feather-down blanket atop it.

Looking up at the stone ceiling, guilt began to settle into her belly. Her thoughts drifted to Thom. He was likely staring at a stone ceiling as well, only in a room far colder and devoid of all comfort than her own. Did jail cells even have beds to lay on at night? The sand-glider he'd been detained in while he was transported up here didn't.

I'll be fine, Little Fury, Imaginary Thom said into her thoughts. *I've endured far worse.*

The comment made her scoff. She had no doubt he hadn't endured far worse, but not that she would know anything about it, considering all the secrets he had kept from her. Which reminded Kestrel that Thom's comfort should be the furthest thing from her mind. The more she learned about him, about the vastness of his lies, the more she realized she didn't know him nearly as well as she always thought she had.

But she couldn't bring herself to believe the queen and just condemn him either.

Thom had proven himself to be a liar, but being the mastermind behind the curse? Kidnapping Kestrel from her own family? It didn't seem like him—or at least not like the Thom she had known and loved and had always idolized.

"You wouldn't do that, right, Thom?"

Of course not. This is what I was trying to warn you about. You can't trust them. They'll try to turn you against me—

Kestrel rolled onto her side and grabbed one of the pillows. She crammed it against her ear, trying to shut him up. There was no use talking to the imaginary voice of his in her head. She needed to speak with the *real* Thom. But how? Kestrel didn't even know when his sentencing would be. The conversation in the throne room had gone so distinctly awry, she had forgotten to make her own demands. Or rather, had forgotten to bring them back up again before she left. Tomorrow though. She would speak to the queen again tomorrow and set everything in motion.

Feeling good about her plan, Kestrel was just beginning to doze when there was a knock at the door.

Begrudgingly, she climbed out of the lavish bed and made her way across the room. Rubbing her eyes, she opened the door, not expecting to find Leighton towering on the other side.

A complicated flood of want and fear rushed over her.

The prince was alone.

There had been a time quite recently when Kestrel had wanted nothing more than to have more alone time with him, the way they had when they'd first met in the alleyway.

But now being in his looming presence made her spine turn ice cold.

"If I could just—"

Without a word, Kestrel slammed the heavy door in his face.

"I deserve that." His regal voice came muffled through the cracks, and she cursed herself for the way her belly fluttered at the familiar sound of him. "And I know you have every right not to want to speak to me. But please, allow me to say I am sorry. Truly."

Kestrel folded her arms over herself, refusing to give him the forgiveness he was so clearly seeking. Whenever she and Thom would argue, he'd say she could hold a grudge like no one he'd ever known before. It's why he so lovingly bestowed the nickname Little Fury upon her. And it was a point of pride for Kestrel now.

It would take a lot more than a few of Leighton's sweet and pleading words to erase the damage he had done now.

As the silence stretched on, Kestrel heard something from the other side of the door scrape along the ground. She looked down to find a small, blue circle appear from the crack beneath her door.

A ring.

"I—I meant to return that to you sooner, you just haven't given me the chance to—and that's entirely my fault. I know that. But, I know it belonged to your mother, so I wanted to make sure it made its way back to you. That is, if you still wanted it—I wasn't even sure if after everything you would—"

Kestrel bent to retrieve her mother's heirloom. "Is it safe?"

"Of course," he said, his tone hiking a little. "If you wear it, it will prevent you from using your magic, but it's safe to touch and hold onto. We could even get you a chain so that you could loop it around your neck if you'd rather not wear it on your skin and inhibit your magic —"

"I'd like that very much," she said hastily.

"Consider it done then."

She could hear the grateful smile in his voice, and it only served to irk her. As if he thought she'd let him off the hook that easily. And for what? For returning something to her that *he* had ripped away?

No.

But her stupid, naïve heart empathized with him. She understood his motive. All he had been thinking about was saving a father whom he hadn't seen in decades. Like he had told the queen, she had been an easy mark, a means to an end, a solution to a problem they'd been facing for years.

Kestrel liked to think she wouldn't have been so heartless if their roles were reversed, but she didn't know for certain. Already she was going to great lengths to try to save Thom. And if it had been her mother's fate on the line? If she'd had even a chance to see her again, would she not be willing to do just about anything?

Not that she was ready to openly forgive and forget. The pain was still too raw, too fresh.

But, while she was here, she would need to play nicely.

"I know why you did what you did," she told him, pressing her hand against the wooden door, as if she could feel him through it. And oh, how she still wanted to feel him. "It still doesn't make it hurt any less."

His voice sounded closer too, like he was pressed up against the door on the other side. "I know. And all I can say is... I was desperate and I am so terribly sorry. I should've listened to Micah and spoken to you about it. But I was scared. You are the daughter of one of the most deranged queens in history. I wasn't sure if I could trust you, and I was worried if I asked then you would just say no, and our only chance would be gone, and then I'd never get to—"

The last of his words cut off.

Kestrel heard him take a step back, as if he was walking away. Fear creeped into her chest. She wasn't ready for him to go yet. To be left alone again.

Kestrel flung the door open and found him pinching the bridge of his nose. He sniffled when he noticed her, his back straightening. He was so good at slipping back into the role he thought he needed to fill, and she wished she could find a way to convince him that he didn't need to. His tears were warranted. She understood.

Standing there, even decked in his armor and cape, Kestrel was starting to see him for who he really was. A scared little boy with the weight of duty and expectations upon his shoulders.

But he was more than that too. Someday soon, he would be the King of Irongate.

Leighton had power.

Power that she might need, if she had any hope at seeing Thom again.

"I know I don't deserve your forgiveness but—"

Kestrel cut him off. "Maybe you can earn it."

His expression slackened, eyes widening with shock and then eagerness. "Earn it how?"

Kestrel bit her lip. She couldn't remember a time she had been so bold to demand something from someone. But she was desperate. And so was he.

"My father. Thom—or Darius, as you call him. I want to speak to him."

Leighton exhaled deeply, dragging a hand through his flaxen locks. "I don't know if you can. We keep the dungeons locked tight for a reason. We can't just have anyone coming in and out."

"Then I want to know what's going on with him. When his trial is. What his sentence will be." Before he could deny her, she added, "Leighton, please. He is the only family I've ever known. I have to help him, and I know you understand what it's like to want to help your family."

If a protest had been readied in his throat, that more than anything else was what made him swallow it.

"I understand completely." Leighton gave a nervous glance down either side of the hallway before leaning closer, his voice a quiet whisper. "I will see what I can learn from the queen later, and let you know tomorrow after your studies. That is, if you're alright with us meeting like this again?"

Her immediate inclination was to say yes. But that felt wrong. Not wholly the truth.

"You know, my magic and what you planned to do with me isn't the only thing you lied to me about." She paused, letting him consider. But Leighton's brow only furrowed. "You're engaged?"

He didn't even look guilty about it, just weary. Maybe even a little annoyed. "Oh, that. It's not by choice, I can assure you."

Kestrel wanted to tell him she didn't think he could assure her of anything, but instead just nodded. Pretended like it hadn't stung to hear the words from someone else. Besides, this had been an easier truth to swallow; Kestrel knew from the books she read that arranged marriages were not uncommon among royalty. But she wanted to hear him explain it. Wanted him to try, anyway.

"Why are you marrying her then?"

"I have to. For the good of the kingdoms." When she didn't say anything, he added with a sigh, "It's complicated."

It wasn't the reply she wanted. It was hardly a reply at all. Another answer shrouded in vague detail that didn't tell her much of anything other than to let her know that Leighton was still hiding things from her, still unwilling to be open and honest. Of course the engagement was complicated, considering the two of them had interacted with one another the same passive way a cloud engages with the ground. Not to mention, the woman had been in *shackles.*

But Kestrel could tell Leighton didn't want to talk about Elora, so she changed her line of questioning.

"The queen, is she a good person? Someone I can trust?"

Finally, Leighton's glacial eyes meet hers again. "I don't know if I'm the right person to be asking."

"You're the only person I have to ask." When he didn't respond immediately, Kestrel stepped closer. She reached for him, desperate to pin him in place before he could retreat into his mind or wherever it was he kept drifting off to, but the idea of touching him lit a fuse of fear inside her and she couldn't bring herself to do it. Instead, her hands hovered in the space between them, upturned and pleading. "Please. I don't have the best luck with knowing who to trust. And if I'm going to be working with her, I'd like to know who she is."

Finally succumbing to one of her lines of questioning, Leighton shook his head and sighed.

"When my father was cursed, it was just Signe and us. For many years, I was resentful toward her. I was just a young boy, and I didn't understand why the curse had mangled our father into something so unrecognizable, while she had remained nearly unchanged. For a long time, I even blamed her—many of the Ironblood did. She came from Skogar, just like the Corrupt Queen, so many of our people thought she could've played a hand in the curse. I believed those rumors too, at first. And it only served to condemn her more that her version of the curse was just a mild inconvenience on her life, unlike all the other monarchs.

"I'm sure you can imagine, it caused a significant

amount of strife, both within our kingdom and between her and my brothers. No one believed her innocence."

"Do you still believe she played a part?"

"No," he said firmly. "But the damage is done. Back then, I hadn't thought about how much she had lost that day as well. Hadn't thought about her struggles and challenges. She'd already left her own lands to marry a king and start a new life, but that king wound up turning into a monster. Her sister was demonized for the damage caused by her magic, and Signe was too.

"I think she's done the best that she could, given the very difficult hand that she was dealt. She and I have no real relationship, but that doesn't mean things won't be different between the two of you. You get a fresh start with her. And who knows, perhaps each of you are the family you've always wanted."

Kestrel's insides warmed at the thought. For the first time since entering the Irongate castle, she felt hope. She wanted to give Queen Signe the benefit of the doubt. More than anything.

"Anyway, I ought to let you get some rest. And I'm expected to dine with my betrothed." Leighton bowed, prepared to leave.

Kestrel reached out, grabbing his shoulder. She had just one more question. "Why don't you like her? Princess Elora. She's...quite beautiful?"

It was the wrong thing to say.

At his sides, Leighton's fists wound so tightly, she thought for sure his fingers might snap.

"The Ashen are not people," he said, voice shaking.

"They are tainted, undead things that only bring death upon the realm."

Kestrel flinched at his ominous tone, releasing him immediately and staggering back.

Leighton blinked the rage away, but one look at Kestrel and he didn't even attempt to try to assuage her fear. Instead, he donned his regal mask again, and adjusted his tunic, standing taller. "But I'm sure you'll learn more about them with Barnabus soon enough. Rest well, Princess Kestrel. And good luck with the start of your studies tomorrow."

AN AWKWARD DINNER

ELORA

The candles on the table were beginning to drip. The steam that had been rising from the braised pot roast and stewed vegetables had already subsided. But Elora and Signe still sat, their plates empty as they waited for Prince Leighton to join them.

Neither of them were fools. They knew that it was taking him far longer than it should've.

Elora was just beginning to think the queen might call off the meal, when Leighton finally entered the room.

"Sorry I'm late. I forgot how many questions my brother has whenever he's instructed to start a new endeavor."

The queen's ire lifted ever so slightly at the mention of the plans she had set in motion. "But you spoke with him, yes? He understands his charge?"

"Yes, he'll begin with Princess Kestrel tomorrow. I arranged for her handmaiden to deliver her to him once she awakens for the day."

"Wonderful," said the queen, and she summoned over the servants without a hint of impatience left behind.

Leighton took a seat at the end of the long table, across from Queen Signe, while Elora sat somewhere near the middle. Three servants moved about them, grabbing their plates and ladling stew and meat and bread upon them. Elora didn't like eating meat. Like many of the people of Grimtol, she had been raised not to, considering the possibility that one could accidentally eat an animal that wasn't *just* an animal. But the people of Irongate didn't seem to care. And the creature on her plate was already slain. Since her only goal right now was to appease the two people in this room, Elora made no mention of the roast the servant served her with, and she began delicately poking at it.

The three of them ate in silence.

Elora couldn't think of a time when she felt more alone while she was in someone's company. She wondered if this would be what their marriage would look like: two strangers in a room together, barely acknowledging each other's presence. It sounded miserable. But also better than some of the alternatives, she supposed. She had heard horror stories about women being sent to distant lands, forced to wed men who were double—sometimes triple their age. Expected to perform certain sexual activities commonly shared between those who are married. Forced to bear heirs. It all sounded utterly barbaric to her, especially since the Ashen never shared any of these customs. They believed that the unionizing of two people occurred out of love.

But that wasn't the marriage Elora was preparing for, she knew that.

Did that mean it had to be one of misery though if it wasn't?

After a servant finished cutting up the meat on the queen's plate, they stepped back behind her into the shadows. Queen Signe speared a piece of slightly pink flesh onto her fork and let it hover before her thin lips.

"Well, now that you're here, we have much to discuss. Your wedding day. Your coronation—"

"My father's life celebration and burial?" Prince Leighton interjected, shoving a spoonful of roasted potatoes into his mouth. He stared across the table at Signe the entire time he chewed. Testing her. Daring her to tell him no.

Queen Signe seemed to pay him no mind though. Elora knew her strategic mind well enough to know that the queen had likely expected this from him, so she was unfazed. She finished her prepared bite before dabbing her mouth with a napkin.

"Of course. I have servants tending to him already, preparing his body for the display and public mourning period."

"Good. I would like to check on their work tomorrow then, after I've had some rest."

Elora was no stranger to death. She knew the many ways it made the heart ache, made the bones weary. Most of all, she knew how alone it could make someone feel.

Perhaps she and Leighton didn't need to fall in love, but she could still show him the kind of supportive wife she could be. Perhaps they could forge a friendship throughout all of this.

"I could join you, if you'd like," she offered.

Leighton's hand clenched his knife so tightly that Elora flinched. He kept his head down, the temper in his voice barely contained. "That won't be necessary. Preparing his body is a sacred thing and should only involve those closest to him."

"Leighton!" the queen chastised.

But Elora understood she had crossed a line, even if she did appreciate the queen trying to stick up for her. It would be no use though. Elora shrank back into her chair. She should've known better. Grief caused the heart to ache, and sometimes having support did help, but it also caused people to lash out. To isolate. To do all manner of strange things that they might not have done otherwise. She would have to tread carefully with him. Attune to his cues, wait for him to show a willingness to interact with her more personally. After all, Elora wasn't the only one being forced into this predicament.

But the queen didn't seem ready to let it go.

"Remember you are speaking to your future wife," she continued, her black eyes glaring him down. "And you should do so with respect and dignity—"

Leighton's fists slammed atop the table. "I owe her no such thing! You told me the time had come for me to wed. You insisted I marry her so that we could broach peace between Eynallore and Irongate. I told you I would first rather set my father free, and so that's what I set out to do. But he's dead now, so it's up to me. And as much as I wish you were wrong, I know the betrothal is what's best for

Irongate, so I will uphold my end of that vow. But I do not owe her or you anything else. This is a marriage based on political alliances, and nothing more. Understood?"

He glared between the two of them, and this time, Elora didn't shrink away. If she did, she worried she would be setting a precedent, one she was already trying to escape.

But the queen didn't back down either. Slowly, she rose from her seat.

"You will not speak to me that way, young prince."

Leighton jumped to his feet as well "I will speak to whomever however I see fit!"

Elora wished she could disappear. In a way, she supposed she had. Neither of them had eyes for her now.

Leighton continued to roar. "My father is dead! You can't expect me to go about these next few weeks with a smile on my face like everything is perfectly fine. I am grieving!"

"As am I," Queen Signe countered, every word enunciated with cool resolve. "And you will do so with the grace that is expected of a future king, not some petulant child. Do I make myself clear?"

Leighton's nostrils were flaring. It looked as though he might be considering chucking his steak knife at the queen. But Queen Signe's power rippled in the air. If Elora didn't know any better, she would've sworn the shadows were creeping in around them, filling the room and threatening to suffocate them all if they had to.

Neither of them were going to back down. They didn't have it in them.

And despite her botched attempt at kindness earlier,

and the promise she had made to herself to await his signal before attempting anything so forward again, Elora didn't want to leave him stranded. She wouldn't be the type of person to just sit by and let tensions build, anger roil.

In Eynallore, Elora had been raised to be a leader. She knew how much support it required to wear the title proudly and with justice. If she were to be Queen of Iron-gate someday, then she would be there for him, even if he wasn't ready for it.

Elora also rose from her chair then, careful to move slowly so as not to fuel the fire blazing in the room already. Both of their ire snapped to her, ready to lash out at anything. She remained calm and collected for all of them.

"Perhaps Prince Leighton is right. This is all a bit soon. He's only just returned from his mission, and as he mentioned, he has yet to rest. Might I suggest we table this conversation until tomorrow—" she said to the queen, but then turned her gentle gaze to the prince "—knowing that we cannot postpone it forever."

The heaving of Leighton's chest was beginning to slow.

"Wise words, Princess Elora," said the queen. "Leighton would do well to learn a thing or two from you about decorum."

No—the queen was doing it again. Twisting Elora's words for her own gain. Pitting them against each other.

Without another word, Leighton shoved away from the table.

As he stormed toward the door, Queen Signe cried out,

"We will reconvene this conversation tomorrow, whether you are ready for it or not."

The doors slammed shut. Queen Signe finally took her seat again, the rage lifting from her expression. She began spearing bites of her food as if nothing had happened. Since Elora didn't know what to do, she decided to sit and start eating as well.

"I see you're settling into the title of wife quite well," the queen said after a long moment.

Elora almost laughed. So far all she had managed to do was drive a bigger wedge between them, it would seem. Her socializing skills were rusty. How the queen expected her to befriend the princess was beyond her.

But she supposed, at the very least, she was staying on Queen Signe's good side. And that more than anything was how she would survive in a place like this.

CHAPTER 22

THE LIBRARY

ELORA

Elora could hardly sleep that night, not with the queen's direct orders barking in her skull. If she was to befriend Kestrel, then she needed to ensure their paths crossed, and currently the only thing she knew about the girl was that she would be studying with Barnabus in the library come the first-hours. And Elora would make sure she would beat her there.

Of course, as she marched down the breezy, stone hallways and approached the library doors, Elora realized a fatal mistake in her plan: she had no reason to be in the library.

Back in Eynallore, she had never been much of a reader. Not the way Dinian was, anyway. They were always more of the seeker of knowledge than she was. Whereas Dinian was content to lose themselves in a book or scroll or document for hours, consuming the text as if it were water, Elora was much more content living and appreciating her life.

Still, she had come this far.

Before doubt could usher her back to the safety of her room, Elora shoved the double doors open and entered the dusty library.

Stopping just on the other side of the door though, Elora marveled at the space around her. Walls of books towered over her from all sides. Some so tall, they stretched up to a second floor. Elora couldn't remember the last time she had even been surrounded by this many tomes, and her heart flared at the joy it would bring Dinian to be there with her.

Standing in the middle of the floor, she realized she should actually find something to browse through, otherwise when Kestrel arrived, she might wonder what Elora was even doing there.

Elora meandered to the nearest shelf when soft footsteps thudded near her.

"You're early—" a young man's voice, intelligent but whiny rang behind her. Elora spun around to face the prince she knew would be there. Upon seeing her grey skin, Prince Barnabus straightened. "Oh. I wasn't expecting you."

Elora felt herself retreating inward. She shouldn't have come here. She wasn't invited and therefore she was unwelcome, just like she was in almost every other space in the realm except home.

Her mouth flapped open, an instinctual apology on her tongue, but one she couldn't bring herself to utter. Because what was she apologizing for? Existing?

Instead, she spun on her heels, aiming for the door.

But Barnabus side-stepped in front of her, blocking her path and nearly making her trample into him.

"That was rude of me to say." He shook his head. "My apologies. I just meant, *you* weren't who I was told would be visiting today. Leighton told me it would be—"

"Kestrel," Elora finished for him. "I know."

"You do? Are you waiting for her too then?"

Elora didn't know how to answer that. She hardly knew this prince, and the queen had waited until the other three had left the room before giving Elora the task of befriending the new princess. Something told her that this was meant to be kept a secret. If so, then already Elora was failing at maintaining it because she had no other reason of being there other than the obvious.

This had been a mistake. An utter waste of time. She would need to get Kestrel alone perhaps. Or at the very least, try to run into her in a more organic way.

"No, I just—" Elora sighed, glancing at the shelves of books surrounding them. "I was just looking for something to pass my time. Now that I..." She allowed her voice to trail off, not wanting to finish that particular sentence. Everyone already knew that her freedom was new. She didn't need to tell him and remind him of that. But apparently Barnabus would do that for her.

"Now that you have the freedom to choose what you do with your time," he said simply, and dare she say, without a hint of judgement. "I bet that is a strange transition, to go from being a prisoner to being able to roam freely again."

Elora angled her head at him, unsure of what to make

of such an obvious but empathetic remark. She settled on a simple, "Yes."

"What sort of book were you hoping to find?"

"I'm not sure. I wasn't much of a reader before… Before."

Barnabus nodded as if he understood. But how could he? He was a prince. He'd grown up in this castle all his life, been sheltered from the horrors of the realm, and had likely never needed to fend for himself.

"Not much of a reader," he repeated, worrying his lips as he scanned the shelves. "Maybe what you need is a hobby then. Come along."

Barnabus motioned for her to follow. For a split moment, Elora considered running for the door instead. She didn't really want a book anyway and she wanted to be long gone before Kestrel arrived so her appearance wouldn't seem too suspicious. But leaving now without a book would likely be more so; she scurried after Barnabus instead.

He led her to the other side of the library, to a stack of dusty shelves that were tucked away in the back. "These books are all about learning and doing things—art, cooking, horseback riding."

Elora angled a brow at him.

His shoulders rounded with a brief, embarrassed laugh. "Right. Maybe not horseback riding then. But there is something here for everyone. Take your pick."

Not wanting to waste any more time, Elora stepped forward and began perusing the titles. Barnabus had been right, all the books here seemed useful or practical in some way. There were books on identifying plants and gemstones. Books on learning to sail and survive in the wilds.

Once she was about halfway down the shelf, she realized Barnabus was still there. Waiting. Not fleeing from her at the first chance he got. It was both comforting and unsettling. Elora wasn't used to such sustained company. She couldn't help but glance his way, curiously.

Barnabus shifted on the soles of his feet. "The books are organized in a specific way, so I'll just wait here until you pick one, that way I know what's being borrowed. Just standard procedure." Elora nodded. "But if you could hurry, Kestrel will be here any minute and I need to prepare for our study session today."

Elora had been prepared to grab the first book she saw after that, no matter what it was. But to her surprise and appreciation, one actually did catch her eye. A book on star-gazing, something she had always loved doing back in Eynallore, and she wondered if it would be as enjoyable here in Irongate.

"A good choice," Barnabus said as she plucked it from the shelves.

"Thank you," she said, a hand dragging down the leather cover.

"Anytime. Now, if you'll excuse me, I really must be getting ready."

Elora didn't have to be told twice, especially now that she had something to look forward to. Something of her own.

CHAPTER 23

A BRIEF LESSON IN HISTORY

KESTREL

Sleeping in a bed fit for a queen, Kestrel had one of the deepest nights of rest she'd ever. But with deep slumber came disturbing dreams—if they could even be called that. It was more like a stained-glass window of images. Snippets of scenes and moments.

A dark forest of dead trees.

Black feathers falling from the sky.

A glowing light that rippled as if it were surrounded by water.

A crack of thunder startled Kestrel from her slumber, and she woke with a racing heart. She felt...odd. Unsettled by the images that had played for her throughout the night, but unsure of how to make sense of them. Ultimately, she decided to ignore them. They were likely just the result of tireless journeying and the impossible reality of her parentage and royal bloodline that she was now trying to come to terms with.

Weird dreams were expected.

Today, however, was a new day. And Kestrel refused to start it on a sour note.

She climbed out of bed and tossed another log onto the dying fire before making her way over to one of the floor-to-ceiling windows. Outside, the sprawling lands were cast in a muted violet and pink sheen. The occasional burst of lightning made the kingdom flash bright for a moment, before resuming its usual cold gloom.

Judging from where the sun rested along the horizon, Kestrel couldn't tell if it was rising or setting, and she had no way of knowing when her handmaiden would return. So she spent the first-hours in languid relaxation, oscillating between her bed, the vanity, and the chair by the fireplace.

Just as Kestrel was beginning to lament about not having a book to snuggle up with by the fire, a knock sounded at the door.

Bored out of her mind and antsy to start the day, Kestrel raced across the room and opened the door. But on the other side, she was greeted by a pile of laundry.

"Good day, miss," came a muffled voice from around the clothes. "Excuse me while I get these garments settled for you, and then I can get your bath started."

Kestrel didn't know what to say. She didn't realize someone would be bringing her a change of clothes, but more importantly, the idea of a nice, warm bath made her melt in her skin.

"Thank you. That sounds amazing—" But the woman didn't wait for Kestrel to finish before blowing into the room like a gust off the coast.

Kestrel followed curiously behind her, watching her

every movement. From the back, all she could note was the grey, tight knot of hair bound at the nape of the woman's neck; it seemed to be the same style all the servants wore, a style that Kestrel couldn't fathom ever getting her hair into.

The woman hummed to herself as she carried the heap of laundry across the room and began stacking the individual garments into the armoire—from stockings, to skirts, to rigid looking materials that Kestrel had never laid eyes upon before.

"There we go," the woman said brightly as she stood back admiring her work. "Now, I'll be back in a few with that bath."

The woman was gone in a flurry, and reappeared not much longer with four other servants, a large wooden basin, and buckets full of steaming water. While most of the servants worked on filling the tub by the fire, the original servant marched back to Kestrel's side.

"Arms up, my lady," the woman said, tugging at the bottom of Kestrel's tunic.

Kestrel glanced to the others around the room. But if her disrobing in their presence was odd, none of them showed any indication of it. They merely focused on their tasks like diligent little birds building a nest. So Kestrel obliged the servant with the grey bun, sending her arms sprouting overhead like stiff saplings. The woman stripped her of her tunic, then her trousers, her undergarments. Fortunately, at the same time she was thoroughly naked, the other servants were done filling the basin and retreated from her quarters.

Kestrel all but dove into the steaming water, both

wanting a little concealment and also longing for the luxurious soak that awaited her. It had been weeks since her last bathing, since leaving her tower and adventuring across the arid desert, sleeping aboard dusty sand-gliders, and narrowly escaping the voracious king-beast. For most of that time, the dinginess hadn't bothered her; she had barely thought twice about it. But now that a bath was an option, she couldn't resist.

Her weary bones practically moaned as Kestrel sank into the scorching waters.

The mousy, grey-haired woman began scrubbing her with a brush, and Kestrel might've protested if the heat hadn't melted her into oblivion.

After she was finished, the woman helped her out of the tub and into a towel. She walked back over to the armoire, studied the items she'd placed inside before twisting back around to give Kestrel a quick up and down.

"Now, let's have a look at you. Oh, with hair like that, I bet browns suit you nicely. What do you think?"

"Browns?" Kestrel asked, her voice barely returning from its deep relaxation.

Instead of answering her, the woman exclaimed with a new epiphany. "Silly me. Green is definitely your color. I mean just look at those eyes. Blessed moon, they're positively radiant."

As the woman spun back around to the armoire, Kestrel glanced at herself in the mirror on her vanity. Nobody had ever called her eyes radiant before. It brought a tinge of pink to her freckled cheeks.

"Here we are," the woman said, dislodging a skirt the

color of a juniper bush. Draped over the servant's arms, the folds of fabric seemed heavier than her entire frame.

Kestrel staggered back a step the minute she saw it. She *hated* dresses. Skirts were just as bad. She found the swaths of fabric constricting, even when she was younger. Back then, the only thing she ever wanted to do was climb and lay upside down on the edge of her bed, or to perch on the ledge of their window, dangling one leg on either side. Skirts made all of those things difficult, if not impossible. And Thom had long-since stopped bringing them home to her as soon as she was able to express her distaste of them.

Kestrel preferred trousers to skirts, and long flowing tunics to whatever tight contraption the servant was holding up for her now.

But Kestrel was realizing she hadn't seen a single woman dressed in anything but gowns and petticoats since arriving to Irongate. Even the servant before her was swathed in thick folds of fabric that nearly dragged to the floor.

There was still so much Kestrel had yet to learn, and she didn't want to offend anyone or start off on the wrong foot, especially since she felt as though the game was already stacked against her due to her relationship to the Corrupt Queen. And this woman had come all the way up here with new garments just for her, probably nearly breaking her back in the process.

Kestrel forced a smile. "It's beautiful."

"Thank you." The woman beamed. "I dare say, I've got quite the keen eye, my lady. You're in good hands with me. Come, come."

She gestured for Kestrel to come closer, and she

obliged, already deciding that anything this woman wanted her to do, she would do it. There was an air of knowledge about her that Kestrel wanted to absorb. But more than that, she just seemed genuinely nice. Like the kind of person Kestrel would want to befriend. And she needed friends now.

"Arms up, my lady," the woman said, tugging at the bottom of Kestrel's tunic.

Kestrel obliged her.

"You can call me Kestrel," she stammered as the cold breezed across her bare skin. No one had dressed her since...well, she couldn't remember how long. It felt unnatural, too vulnerable, and the minute the last of her sleeves came off, Kestrel hugged her arms around her chest.

"Oh, that's nice of you, but it'll have to be *my lady* from me. You understand?"

She didn't, but Kestrel nodded all the same.

Since the woman was a good head shorter, she had to throw the new blouse up and over Kestrel's head just to get it on her. It looked as if she was ready to help her shimmy into the fabric, but Kestrel was too impatient. She wanted her body covered so she hastily stretched an arm into either side and tugged the blouse down. It was tighter than she usually wore, but bearable.

The woman raised an eyebrow at her behavior, but readied the skirts without so much as a word.

"And what do I call you?" Kestrel asked, feeling a little better now that her top half was clothed again.

"Oh my, where in the Hollows are my manners? My name's Marion."

"It's nice to meet you, Marion," Kestrel said as Marion held open a beige skirt, different from the green one she had originally shown her. Kestrel stepped inside and noted how light the fabric was as Marion buttoned the backside around her waist. A skirt like this, she could maybe still move around in without too much hassle. But then Marion grabbed the green one, and held it out to her as well. "Oh, I'll be wearing two skirts?"

A flicker of shock flashed behind Marion's eyes, there one second and then gone the next. "That's right. The queen instructed me to dress you like a proper lady."

"I...don't think I like being a proper lady," Kestrel muttered as Marion tied the heavy, green skirt around her waist.

The woman chuckled. "You'll get used to it. But maybe we'll skip your corset for now."

Kestrel nodded, grateful not to have to wear whatever additional item a corset was.

Marion guided her to the vanity, where she brushed and styled Kestrel's hair. She tried smoothing back the frizzy curls into a tight knot like all the other ladies, but what they were left with was a sort of disheveled nest fit for a bird and her hatchlings.

"I'll have to bring by some pomatum and powder tomorrow—fix you up right," Marion said, grunting as she finished wrestling Kestrel's hair into a sort of submission.

Kestrel wasn't sure what *pomatum and powder* were, but Marion seemed confident in their usefulness, so she didn't bother asking. Instead, she inched closer to the mirror to get a look at herself. It was a drastic change from the braids she usually tied every which way around her head, and surely it wasn't *neat* by any measures. But it framed her face in a way she'd never seen before, accentuating her square jawline. It made her look fiercer, more hardened, like someone not to be trifled with. Like some hewn from steel like the Ironbloods. And truthfully, Kestrel didn't think she much minded that. It made her feel like she belonged just a little more in the foreign kingdom.

"It's perfect." Kestrel angled her head this way and that. "Thank you."

In the reflection behind her, a sweet grin bloomed on Marion's face. The woman patted her shoulders. "If it pleases my lady, then it pleases me. Now, up we go. We have people to see and places to—cursed sky! I nearly forgot." Digging into her apron pocket, Marion retrieved a metal chain. "For you, my lady. From Prince Leighton. He said you needed it for something important."

Kestrel's heart galloped at the sight of it.

Already, she had forgotten about the promise he'd made to bring her a chain for her ring, and so it meant all the more that he had followed through on it.

Twisting around in her seat, Kestrel reached for the necklace and Marion let it pool into the palm of her hand. Not knowing what to do with the ring last night, Kestrel had set it in one of the drawers on the vanity. Hastily, she tore the drawer open now, grabbed the ring, and slipped the metal chain through it.

When she was finished, Kestrel held the completed necklace out in front of her.

"Let me help with that," Marion said, reaching around either side of her neck and fastening the necklace in place.

She gasped though, when she finally saw its reflection in the mirror. "Dragon's fire! Is that—that's Queen Aenwyn's ring."

Nodding, Kestrel twisted the ring around the chain, but she kept her eyes on Marion. She knew *this* was the reason the other servants and townsfolk had been treating her with such distance or distaste, and wanted to witness Marion's reaction in real-time to gauge how she could expect others to react as well.

But Marion blinked, and the shock was gone. She patted Kestrel's shoulders again. "Of course it is, she was your mother. Forgive me, I'm not used to seeing relics from that queen's past."

"You're afraid of her? Afraid of me?"

Marion's face softened, her crinkly eyes almost watering. "Fret not, my lady. You are not your mother, and you will not be blamed for her crimes. At least not by me."

"But some people do blame me for them?" she asked, and Marion's shoulders slumped.

"Some, perhaps. But pay no mind to them. They are only scared of what they do not understand, and you will soon have ample opportunities to show them who you really are."

Something clamped down on Kestrel's chest. It was an awful lot of pressure to put on someone who wasn't even sure she knew herself.

"Now, we must be off. We can't keep Prince Barnabus waiting or he might give us a lashing."

Kestrel's now worried gaze flitted to Marion's reflection in the mirror. But the woman was smiling so wide her eyes were nearly closed. It was enough to put Kestrel at ease, and she stood to follow Marion out of the bedchamber and into the dimly lit halls.

The path they took through the corridors was unfamiliar to Kestrel. Then again, she hadn't really been paying much attention the first time.

"I'll never be able to memorize this place."

Marion chuckled, a sound as bright as bells. "Oh, you'll figure it out in no time. Give yourself some grace, you've only been here a day."

As they meandered through the halls, still chilled from the lack of sunlight, Kestrel tried to mentally prepare for meeting yet another prince. The three she had encountered so far were all quite distinct from each other, and although she felt like she could maybe trust one of them—mostly Micah—the other two seemed too secretive to be relied upon. She wondered if Barnabus would be the same as Leighton, shrouded in deceptions that even hurt himself, and Kestrel vowed to keep her guard up this time.

There weren't many others out and about at this hour, or perhaps just not in this section of the castle.

However, as they turned down a new hallway, Kestrel spotted Elora striding down the opposite direction.

Upon seeing the two of them, Princess Elora instantly stiffened. Her pace quickened as if she had been caught red-handed doing something she wasn't meant to be doing. Then Kestrel noticed the book she pressed tightly to her chest.

The deep magenta of Elora's irises never met Kestrel's, although Kestrel desperately wished they would. She wanted to speak with the young woman. Wanted to hear her side of a story she was only starting to grasp. Instead,

Elora kept her neck stiff, her gaze fixed onward as she marched past them and down the other end of the hallway.

Kestrel couldn't let an opportunity like this pass her by though.

"Would you mind waiting here for a sec?" she said to Marion, and before the woman could even respond, Kestrel was racing after the princess. "Wait!"

The princess appeared to be doing no such thing, but when Kestrel finally caught up to her, she begrudgingly stopped.

"It's Elora, right?" Kestrel asked, panting.

Elora clutched her book tighter, her face a flawless canvas without any emotion. "Yes. We were introduced yesterday."

"Right. Of course. I just—" Kestrel suddenly felt awkward and didn't know what to say. Her gaze kept flitting to the book in Elora's arms. "What are you reading?"

Elora tucked the book under her arm. "What was it you wanted?"

"Nothing. I mean—" Sheepishly, Kestrel looked to the carpeted ground. Why did it feel like every interaction with this woman was wrong? Like no matter what, Kestrel couldn't say or do the right thing. She wanted to change that. "I get the sense that we got off on the wrong foot. I'm Kestrel." She thrust out a hand as a show of good faith, only to retract it. "Right. The no touching thing. Sorry."

If Elora was offended, there was no way of knowing. Her face remained unchanged. Unflinching.

"So," Kestrel tried changing subjects. "How long have you been at the castle?"

"Too many years to count."

"Right. Leighton mentioned—"

Elora's eyes flashed brighter, the only indication that something was boiling inside her. "And do you make it a habit of speaking with my future husband often?"

Kestrel flushed. "No! I just—him and I, we—"

Elora's scrutiny of her deepened. But at least now Kestrel thought she finally understood where the tension between them stemmed. This was about Leighton. Maybe she already knew about their kiss. Knew that Kestrel had thrown herself upon him in the alleyway and would've kept doing the same if it hadn't been for everything that happened at the Fortress of Thirst. But maybe Elora hadn't yet heard about that part.

The truth, Kestrel decided. The truth was the only way forward.

"Look, if this is about what happened in Mutiny Bay, I'm sorry. I didn't know he was a prince, let alone betrothed to you. Otherwise I wouldn't have ever kissed him."

One of Elora's brows shot up toward the silver crown embedded in her forehead. "You kissed him?"

Dragon's fire, she was making this worse.

"No! I mean, yes—but there is nothing between us now! I had never met anyone before, and he was cute, and he rescued me from a crowd that almost swept me away like the tide, and I just...I went for it. It was stupid though. And that was all before—before I knew who he was. Before he shoved me into that castle and left me to die. Before—"

The subtle shifts in Elora's expression were impossible

to decipher, especially for someone like Kestrel who had little to no experience reading other people's cues. Regardless, she still knew she was ruining everything.

Kestrel buried her face in the palms of her hands.

"I'm sorry. You are only like the fifth person I've ever met, and I don't want us to be on bad terms just because of...because of all that."

Silence stretched between them. It lasted so long that Kestrel had to peek from behind her hands just to confirm the princess had left her standing there alone in the hall. When she showed her face though, Kestrel was surprised to find Elora was still there, still watching her.

Finally, Elora pulled the book out from under her arm and showed it to Kestrel.

"It's a book on star-gazing. I figured I'd see if I recognize any of the constellations after all this time."

A triumphant smile began to bloom between Kestrel's cheeks and excitement bubbled within her to learn more about Elora's star-gazing. But before she could ask any more questions, the princess bowed her head.

"Now, if you'll excuse me, I hear you have some place to be."

And with that, Elora spun around on her heels and Kestrel watched as she disappeared down the hall.

There was more pep in her step as she made her way back toward Marion.

"Everything turn out alright?" Marion asked.

"Better than expected."

"I imagine so," Marion said. Then she motioned for Kestrel to follow. "This way. We're almost there now."

At the end of the hall, Marion stopped at two double doors.

"Here we are." She swung them ajar, and out wafted the familiar scent of parchment and ink. "You go on ahead inside. I'm sure Prince Barnabus is already in there somewhere, and we wouldn't want to keep him waiting. I'll return in a bit with some tea and pastries."

But Kestrel could hardly hear her as she breached the entrance, her wonderment overtaking her.

The library was expansive. Exhaustive, surely. Kestrel couldn't imagine there was a book in existence that wasn't upon these dusty shelves. Kestrel floated over to the closest bookshelf and dragged a finger along the vellum spines, barely hearing Marion as she shut the doors behind her. Reading the titles of a few of the books, Kestrel was quickly able to deduce that they were categorized. This section seemed to be about astronomy and science. There was another section on farming and livestock. Kestrel glided before each of the bookshelves on the first floor, eager for the moment she would find the staircase that would lead her up to the second level. That is, until the titles started to sound more familiar.

She came upon a section of stories, myths and legends and fictional tales, much like the ones she was used to reading.

Finding a title that sounded most intriguing, Kestrel pulled the book out and opened it to the first page.

"Please don't!" someone yipped behind her. "The books are organized very specifically."

Kestrel spun around, clutching the book to her chest. A scrawny but tidy young man was walking swiftly in her direction. He was holding a stack of books in one arm and pointing at her with the other.

"If you intend on borrowing a book, there is a loan system. However—" the young man snatched the book out of her clutches and eyed it suspiciously, as if he were looking for damages— "If you're who I believe you are, these aren't the books you're here to study. Is my assumption correct, Kestrel Highmore?"

"It's just Kestrel," she corrected, but the only confirmation he gave was a slight grunt as he nudged past her to put the book back in its place on the shelf. "And you must be Barnabus then?"

"The one and only—well, probably not *the only* one. That's just a thing people say."

"Right," she laughed a little, assuming it had been meant as a joke.

Barnabus' face remained stoic though, utterly unchanging. There was a scholarly yet youthful look about him that made him difficult to take seriously. But it was clear from how tidied his crimson tie was beneath the folds of his cyan vest that he took himself *quite* seriously. It would be all business with him, and she was okay with that. It left little room for shenanigans and deceit.

Kestrel nodded toward the stack of books he was still balancing. "Can I help with those?"

"No need. Follow me."

Barnabus spun on his heels without another word, and Kestrel scrambled to keep up with him. He led her over to a table closer to the window on the far end of the library. The sun was finally in the sky and shining down into the room, but he had already lit a lantern for them, just in case.

Thunder boomed outside, but Kestrel noted that she didn't hear any rainfall. The storms that blew in from the ocean where she grew almost always brought a downpour of rain with them, but she hadn't noticed a single speck yet in Irongate.

"There's been a lot of thunder here the last couple days," she said, attempting to make small talk.

"Not really," Barnabus replied matter-of-factly. "We've had more."

"Oh? Is that usual?"

As Barnabus scurried down a few steps and toward a table, he nodded. "Yes. Why else would we put it on our sigil?"

He gave a half-hearted bob of his head toward the window, and the two banners on either side of it that showcased the Irongate crest. Of course, Kestrel had seen it plenty already, but she still appreciated his thoroughness in assuring that she knew what he was talking about. It boded well for their study time together.

Barnabus stacked the books onto the table, one at a time, and Kestrel took it upon herself to take a seat in one of the chairs. He addressed her as he organized their readings.

"Leighton tells me that you don't know anything about the histories of Grimtol, but sometimes he exaggerates, so I wasn't sure what to grab, and just grabbed a bit of everything."

"In this case, he's probably not too far off from the

truth," she said, anticipating some sort of reaction. A guffaw. A joke. A challenge.

Barnabus merely frowned, considering the information. She realized then that his eyes matched his cyan vest perfectly, and she wondered if that was by mistake or if this young man was really that fastidious. She guessed it was the latter.

Barnabus moved the books around so that he could grab the second from the bottom of the stack. He handed it to Kestrel.

"We should start here then."

Kestrel read the title aloud, "The Day the Land, Sky, and Sea Shook?"

He shrugged, almost looking sheepish. "Is that too far back? I was told to cover only our most recent histories, but history isn't learned that way. Some things can only truly be understood once you delve deeper into what came before them. History builds upon itself. But if you're already familiar with—"

"I'm not," she interrupted, curiously excited to delve deeper into the unknown histories of Grimtol. "I mean, I've heard mention of that period of time, but I don't know the full story, and I'd be more than interested to learn it."

For the first time since meeting him, Kestrel saw Barnabus light up with excitement. "I was hoping you'd say that."

"And that's how the Maw of Death was created," Barnabus concluded, the book only halfway through.

Kestrel had so many questions, it was difficult to decide which one to ask first. She bit her lip as she considered her options.

"But if the Maw of Death was created by a meteor shower—"

"Technically it was just one meteor, not an entire shower of them," he corrected, but Kestrel continued as if he hadn't said anything.

"What's at the bottom of it? Or how did it get there because...there's definitely something sinister down there. But I don't think it's like the other cursed monsters, at least not like the ones I've met."

His cyan eyes glinted with intrigue, and something like skepticism. "You encountered the creature in the Maw?"

Kestrel nodded and he looked like his mind had just exploded. Hastily, he pulled a scroll of parchment from a pocket in his vest. There was already an ink well and pen on the table, so he dabbed the pen into it and began scribbling.

"If that's true, you might be the only person in history to have ever survived such an interaction."

"Really?"

Nodding, he blew on his scroll, trying to help the ink dry. With one hand holding the parchment open, Barnabus used the other flip to the next page in the book. He pointed at another passage. "At the time this book was written, it was still unknown what dangers lurked in the bottom of the Maw of Death. After facing so much tragedy, some people speculated that the place was cursed. Others believe that it is haunted by the very souls lost to the meteor on the Day the Land, Sky, and Sea Shook. However, in recent years, many Vallondeans have speculated there is something wicked in the air near the Maw, and they have been known to avoid wandering too near it, at all costs."

It wasn't surprising to hear. If Kestrel had known any better, she would've done the same, just to ensure that slippery voice wouldn't have slithered into her mind.

"What did you see there?"

The question immediately evoked memories that sent a shiver up Kestrel's spine. "Not much. These thick, oily tentacles reached out of the chasm for me. It spoke to me as if it was someone I knew, and...I think it lured me closer. I felt like I was under a spell, but only after I snapped out of it."

"Fascinating," Barnabus said as he continued scribbling on his scroll.

It wasn't the word she would use to describe it, but she supposed if she was the only person to have survived such an ordeal, any additional information they had about the creature would be intriguing, especially to someone like Barnabus who she was already beginning to understand was a devout scholar.

"How did you break its trance?"

"I didn't," she answered honestly. "A fox came and distracted it long enough for me to regain my composure. Then I ran."

Barnabus actually looked disappointed, as if he had been hoping the answer was more interesting. But Kestrel couldn't be offended, she was too busy thinking about that fox again, her savior. Every day since Micah had taken it away, she wondered how it was faring and whether it thought about her as well. She was certain it did, especially since the princes seemed to be convinced it was more than just a fox. An Animali, they had called it—whatever that was.

Perhaps now, in the midst of a mentor, was her chance to find out.

"I'm sorry if this is skipping around in Grimtol's history a bit, but what do you know about the Animali? Leighton mentioned that they couldn't be trusted, but I don't even know who or what they are."

Surprising her, Barnabus lit up. "Actually, that's a wonderful segue, because the next of the catastrophes from the Day the Land, Sky, and Sea Shook were the Xiran floods." Barnabus skipped ahead to the next chapter, skipping past a giant illustration of the Maw that chilled Kestrel to the bone, and landing on a new section titled *Flooding in Caelora*. Noticing her confusion, he supplied, "Xira used to be part of Caelora. They became sovereign after the Cursed Night, but we'll get to that. For now, the Animali you mentioned, they came from here."

Barnabus shifted the book toward her and Kestrel noted the illustration on the first page. It looked like a peaceful village, separated by numerous channels of water, and even though it separated parts of the village from others, it didn't seem to hinder the people. They used canoes and rafts to travel in between the floating islands, some carrying goods to sell, others offering to ferry one another around.

Then he flipped to the next page.

The center of the village was entirely flooded. Bodies

floated, face down, in the green waters, while others sank into the depths. The ones below the water's surface though were different than before. The people on the first page had just been that: people. But the ones here had grown gills. Others appeared to be growing fins or wings or scales.

"Yet another one of Grimtol's greatest mysteries: why some of the people caught in the floods miraculously gained the ability to shift into an animal," Barnabus said, sounding in awe himself.

"Those are the Animali then? People who can turn into animals?" Kestrel couldn't tear her eyes away from one of the illustrated figures in particular. He was the most animalistic, almost his entire human form replaced with the sleek body of some underwater creature. Some of the non-swimming animals clung to his giant fins, and he seemed to be carrying them up to the surface. Seemed to be saving them from their watery demise. "Why doesn't your brother trust them?"

Before answering, Barnabus glanced around the room, as if someone could be listening in, even though they'd been entirely alone for hours ever since Marion had brought them a mid-session snack.

"Not just Leighton," he whispered. "Many in Grimtol, but especially those in Irongate and Caelora, or anywhere that has a history of being anti-magic."

Kestrel's skin tingled. "Anti-magic? But..."

Maybe that was why so many of the people here seemed to disdain her so readily. Even if they hadn't seen her use magic, they knew she came from a powerful queen, and therefore likely assumed she was powerful as well.

"Don't worry. You're safe in the castle. And Queen Signe has been working hard to undo the preconceptions that the Ironblood people have about magic. Not everyone will fear you, but there are people who still do. They fear some magic more than others though. Like the Animali, because they can be difficult to spot."

"How do you mean?"

"This is skipping ahead a little, but the Cursed Night impacted them too. If an Animali was human when the curse pulsed across the lands, they could no longer transform into their animal selves."

Kestrel was already piecing together what he wasn't saying. "And if they were in their animal form when the curse happened?"

He was quiet for a long moment. Kestrel couldn't read the emotion behind those hollow eyes. Something like pain or fear?

"If they were an animal at the time of the curse, then they remained so. And have been ever since."

A heaviness plummeted to her stomach. Those people had been neighbors, friends, family. They had loved ones to return home to, and instead they'd been trapped as animals all this time, for nearly twenty years.

And for some reason, Kestrel felt as if it were her fault. It was her mother's magic, but wasn't that passed onto her? Not to mention, the Cursed Night had been the same day Kestrel had been born. The same day her mother had cursed the queens and kings of Grimtol, the Animali too, and then died.

She didn't want to consider the coincidences that implicated her as much as her own mother. More than that, she didn't want to consider that the same magic flowing in her veins could ever be capable of doing something so unforgiveable.

If those innocent people were victims of the curse as much as all the kings and queens were, then Leighton's distrust of them didn't make sense.

"Shouldn't we all feel pity toward them then? They lost a lot to the curse, much like many people, including all of you."

Barnabus shrugged, and Kestrel remembered that he was younger than Leighton, and therefore had only been a couple years old when the curse happened. It was likely he didn't even remember his father, and therefore didn't feel like he'd lost much.

"You would be right, except people are paranoid. They believe the Animali are spies. To be fair, their suspicions aren't exactly unwarranted. There *have* been an increase in animal sightings in strange places, appearing in rooms they shouldn't be able to get into, especially when confidential conversations are occurring. My brother is just protective of sensitive information getting into the wrong hands."

"The wrong hands? How? They're animals. They can't talk," she said with a fleeting burst of confidence. "Can they?"

"No, but some of them can write with their tails or talons. They're not inherently dangerous, but yes, many in Irongate treat them as such. Did you encounter an Animali on your way here?"

Kestrel reached for one of her braids to twirl around her finger, and felt naked when she couldn't grasp one. She started worrying at her lip instead, but Barnabus had already found his answer.

"The fox?"

Kestrel nodded.

"And my brother…disposed of it?"

Her wide eyes met his, brimming with tears. "Micah says it lives. But I don't know anymore. They both—"

She had been prepared to tell him everything, to launch into a litany of ways in which they'd shattered her trust and tried to mend it, and all the reasons why she was uncertain if she should allow them to. But then she remembered: this was their brother. Another Irongate prince. She couldn't trust any of them. She *needed* not to trust any of them.

But there had been something so alarmingly honest about him from the start, and it was different than it was with the others. With Leighton and Micah, she'd known they'd had their secrets—the subtle glances exchanged, the words unspoken and yet understood between them. Barnabus, however, had been an open book. It seemed every thought or emotion he had, he shared. And the only times she couldn't read him was because he was different from anyone she had ever met. Not guarded, necessarily, just less affective with his mannerisms and behaviors.

Regardless of whether she wanted to trust him or not, she already feared she did. More than that, she wanted to ask him a question, and hoped he would answer honestly.

"Do you think I can believe Micah when he says he didn't hurt that fox?"

Barnabus didn't even hesitate, nor did he look offended about her questioning his brother's integrity. "Definitely. Micah does what Micah wants, not what he's told to do. And Micah has always had a fondness for animals, especially the Animali." Seeing Kestrel's eyebrows shoot toward her hairline, Barnabus elaborated. "There was an Animali girl, her mother worked here so she was around a lot. Micah and her were close friends back then, and I think he still misses her. I think it's why he's cautious with all animals."

"All animals? He doesn't know what her animal form was?"

"No, he does. It's a principle thing, though. If you were going around killing humans, other humans might not want to continue being your friend. I think it's something like that."

The grim comparison both horrified and amused her. "What was she then? The animal?"

"I think a frog or a lizard. Something small. I don't know. He doesn't talk about her much and I was so young, I don't remember her." Abruptly changing topics, Barnabus slammed the book shut. "Well, it looks like we're done for the day."

"What? Done? Already?" Kestrel stammered, her mind suddenly reeling with all the things she still wanted to ask him. About the Ashen. About prisoners of war crimes and how they'd been dealt with in the past. Anything to help her better understand this place and the circumstances she'd been thrust into.

Instead, she'd let herself get swept away in the stories of their realm.

"Maybe we could do just a little bit more?"

Barnabus looked genuinely conflicted, but his eyes shifted to the door behind her. Kestrel turned around just in time to see Micah barging in.

"I've come to rescue you from boredom, fair maiden." He gave a sweeping bow.

Though Kestrel was endeared by his theatrics, her fingers still clenched the edge of the table. She wanted to insist on staying longer, wanted to devour the knowledge buried deep in these books, the information that had been kept from her for years.

She knew what they'd say though: better not to keep the queen waiting.

Kestrel forced herself to stand. When she did, Barnabus stood as well and he reached across the table to begin collecting his books. Before he could, Kestrel threw her arms around him.

"Thank you," she said into his shoulder, and felt him stiffen at her touch. "I am very grateful to you for leading my studies of the realm's history."

"Y-you are?" He softened just as Kestrel released him. "Most people don't find this sort of stuff that interesting."

"Well, most people haven't spent their entire lives shut away from everything, without any information about anything. And I'm discovering that I don't much like being left in the dark, especially when it seems like everyone else knows something I don't."

A sad smile tugged on his lips. "I know the feeling."

She wondered what he meant, but didn't think he'd answer if she asked. His eyes kept nervously flicking back toward Micah. Not out of fear it seemed, but just out of a general sense of wanting to be mindful of the schedule they had laid out for her.

As she was spinning away, he blurted, "I'm sorry for earlier. I know it's rude to snap at people, and I didn't do it because I was mad, I just—keeping the books organized is important to me."

Kestrel faced him again, settling a hand over her heart and feeling her mother's ring. "No apology necessary. I promise to keep the books organized. But maybe I could borrow one someday? I do love to read."

"So do I," he said. And then, looking back toward the bookshelf where they'd first met, he asked, "Are those the types of books you like? The ones you were looking at earlier?"

"Mhmm."

Barnabus nodded. "One will be waiting for you in your bedchamber by the time you're done with the queen then. I give you my word."

"Come on," Micah groaned from the entryway. "It's stuffy in here and I'm hungry."

As if her stomach heard him, it growled its agreement. She gave Barnabus a wave. "I suppose we shouldn't keep him waiting. You are coming, right?"

The suggestion made him look uncomfortable, like the very idea of leaving this library would turn him to ash. "No, I'll stay here. I need to prepare for tomorrow's studies anyway."

"If you insist. Tomorrow then?"

"Tomorrow."

Kestrel left him to it and made her way over to Micah who was leaning up against the doorframe.

"Finally! I was about to suffocate if I had to wait in that dusty old library any longer."

"Oh, it's not that bad." she said, as Micah shut the doors behind them.

Once they were a safe distance away, he eyed her suspiciously. "You're joking. That place smells like the butt-end of week-old bread stuffed inside my riding boots."

"Gross!" Kestrel laughed, and he did too.

After their laughter had faded and they were farther down the hall, he wriggled his reddish-brown eyebrows at her. "But really, now that ol' Barnacle is gone, you don't have to pretend to like it in there. No one does but him. He's odd like that. Likes to keep to himself. Doesn't much like people, unless they're in books."

The more he spoke poorly about his brother, the more Kestrel felt a heat in herself rising. Even though she knew Micah teased just about everyone, she still wasn't too keen on the idea that this was how people treated Barnabus. But she also knew humor was the only language Micah spoke.

"What's the matter, Micah? Worried someone might be more charmed by Barnabus than they are by you?"

His mouth fell open, a sly smirk quirking the edges. But then his lips closed and he gave her an approving nod. "You know what? You're going to fit in just fine here, *Princess.*"

"Don't call me that," she growled, giving him a playful nudge. But deep down, she was already starting to like the sound of it. Judging from the grin he flashed her, she knew he could tell as well.

CHAPTER 24

BY WEEK'S END

ELORA

Elora was the last to arrive.

To be perfectly honest, as she had made her way to the throne room, part of her wondered if Leighton would even come today. But by the time she arrived, he was already there. With his back turned toward her, she noticed how much taller he stood today. The rest he'd had appeared to do him well.

Since he was standing before the queen, Elora ventured to guess that was where she was expected to be as well, so she took her place beside him. He immediately shuffled a good step or two farther away. Elora tried to ignore the sting. By now, she was used to people giving her a wide berth.

The queen clapped her hands, ready to begin. "Now, we announced your betrothal weeks ago. And with the king's passing, the people will be expecting your coronation now, as well as your wedding."

"We should combine them," said Leighton, defeat

weighing down his voice, though his spine remained tall, his head held high.

The queen smirked. "I'm glad to find you're seeing reason today."

"Yeah, well, we might as well get everything done and over with." Tightness crept into Elora's chest. Not more than a day ago, she had thought the same thing, but now it felt like things were moving too quickly. "When were you thinking?"

"Well I see no reason to delay it much longer. I think the people would appreciate a little celebration. Perhaps by week's end."

Now it was Elora's turn to lose her composure. "That's only a few days away."

Queen Signe waved off her concerns. "That shouldn't be a problem. I've had the staff preparing already. Your dress is nearly finished. Leighton will likely wear the same garb that his father wore for all of his weddings. And the food is being prepared as we speak."

"But, what about my family? Have we heard word from them? Will they be able to attend on such short notice?"

Elora hated the way her heart ached for the answers. Especially since she knew Queen Signe couldn't really provide them. At least not to Elora's true questions, like if they *wanted* to come.

The queen looked down at her with pity. "Perhaps you forget, but the Hand of Death fell under the Corrupt Queen's curse like all the other monarchs did. And your— brother, was it? Dinian?"

"Sibling," Elora corrected. "But yes, Dinian."

"Well, I'm afraid intel of him hasn't been very promising. He's been spotted scouting the surrounding lands of Irongate. We suspect he's been trying to infiltrate the kingdom, maybe even lead an attack. I, for one, wouldn't feel comfortable with his attendance until after the marriage is final, and after a peace can be promised between our lands."

Elora bristled every time the wrong pronouns for her sibling were used, but that frustration was swiftly overshadowed by everything else the queen was saying about Dinian. Why would they be scouting the lands, trying to infiltrate the kingdom after all this time, now that Elora was finally free?

Even more devastating, was the fact that the queen was denying Elora's request to invite Dinian to the wedding.

Suddenly, Elora felt like she was drowning in an ocean of loneliness, but she managed to nod anyway. In her dejected state though, she thought about what the queen was suggesting. A peace treaty typically required people to convene and discuss the terms. Or at a bare minimum, for a spokesperson to be sent to negotiate between the lands involved.

Elora perked up, an idea forming. "Perhaps a royal visit to Eynallore then, after the wedding? To help broker a peace and introduce ourselves to the Ashen as the new reigning rulers of Irongate."

Leighton balked, jerking even farther away from her. "I wouldn't be caught dead in that place. Are you honestly suggesting we walk into a territory where every single tainted resident could kill me with a simple touch of their hand?"

The queen was frowning as well. "I must admit, Princess Elora, it does sound dubious. At least so shortly after the wedding. Maybe in time, after the alliance is stronger, the tensions lower."

Holding back tears, Elora nodded again. "Of course. My apologies. I wouldn't want to make anyone uncomfortable."

The queen's smile widened, but somehow made the room feel darker. "It's settled then. We'll have you two wed by the end of the week, and we'll announce you as King and Queen of Irongate."

Elora wanted to run from the room like Leighton had yesterday. Wanted to be alone and far away from these people who hated everything about her. But instead, she forced herself to leave gracefully. To gently close the throne room doors behind her. And to slowly shuffle out of the castle, politely nodding and smiling to every staff member she passed by, even though they all avoided eye contact like it would kill them where they stood.

And only once she was alone and in the comfort of the gardens, did Elora finally allow herself to cry.

THE QUEEN'S MAGIC

KESTREL

Micah led Kestrel into a dining hall so grand, so immense, that if they were to sit on opposite ends of the table, they'd have to shout just to hear one another. More impressive than the endless mahogany table in the center of the room though, was the extravagant display of food atop it. There were a variety of breads and cheeses, the golden platters crammed high with freshly picked fruits she'd never seen before, and steaming stews that made her mouth water.

However, in the center of the table, rested a roasted pig head that made Kestrel's stomach churn. She stopped walking around the table. Couldn't move. Couldn't tear her eyes away from the lifeless ones of the dead creature staring back at her.

Growing up, she and Thom didn't eat any animals— and now that she knew the history of the Animali, she understood why.

To have such a gruesome display here seemed so...so barbaric.

"Best if you just ignore it," Micah said, leaning into her ear. "That's what I do."

She heard the lump in his throat, but by the time he stepped around her to grab his own plate, if he had shown any other signs of distress, they were gone. Micah pranced around the room on the pads of his feet, grabbing rolls and fruit and anything that seemed to please him. Surprising her, when he was finished, he held the plate out to her.

"Try these. They're likely the least offensive of the cuisine prepared for us today."

Kestrel took the plate, examined it, and plucked a bundle of small, dark blue orbs up by a sickly, thin branch. "What are these?"

Filling his own plate now, he glanced over his shoulder. "You've never eaten blueberries? Well you're in for a treat!"

Ultimately, she set them back onto her plate. But Kestrel was still eyeing them suspiciously as she took a seat farthest away from the pig. She wanted to try new things, but the carcass on the table was distracting, and she wasn't sure if she could trust her stomach to be able to handle uncertainty quite yet.

So instead of starting with the blueberries, she began nibbling on a piece of white cheese.

"Will anyone else be joining us?" she asked him.

"You mean Leighton?" Micah threw his body into a chair beside her, one leg kicked up over the armrest. "Nah, not for lunch. The queen summoned him and Princess Elora to do some planning for his coronation or wedding or something. But I'm sure he'll be done by supper." He bit into a peach, juice dribbling down his chin as he talked around his bites. "Best not to get too attached to him though. He is engaged, after all."

"I'm not—that's not why—"

He raised an eyebrow that said he didn't believe her one bit. Which was fine. The fewer people who knew about Leighton digging into Thom's imprisonment for her, the better. She was only eager to find out what he'd learned, but maybe the wait would be worthwhile. Give him more time to dig into the queen's plans for him.

"And your other brother—well, one of your other brothers—Efrem, doesn't he eat?"

Micah shrugged. "Only when he remembers to. He takes his guard duties quite seriously, but I'm sure he'll join us at the end of his shift." Sinking his teeth into another bite, he crooked his eyebrows at her. "What's the matter? Am I not good enough company for you?"

Kestrel rolled her eyes at him, and they spent the rest of the meal playfully bantering with one another. They mostly talked about Irongate, how his favorite thing to do in the city was to sneak into festivals unnoticed and dance the late hours away as a commoner. Or how his favorite thing to do outside of the city was to cross the Hingsol Lake and sneak into the Skogar territories to watch the migration of the bighorn sheep. Or how when castle-life got really boring, he loved to sneak into the cellar and taste the finest wines from Skydust and Arebal Farms.

Mostly, it sounded to Kestrel like Micah simply enjoyed the sneaking around bits. He had a thrill for doing things he wasn't supposed to be doing.

"Don't you ever worry about getting caught?"

The grin that split his face was devious. "Little bird, a professional never gets caught."

By the time Marion entered the dining hall, Kestrel was entirely stuffed and had almost forgotten she was supposed to be joining the queen. Micah bid her farewell and told her he'd see her at supper. As she rose from the table to follow Marion out of the dining hall, Kestrel secretly looked forward to hearing all about the shenanigans he'd gotten himself into in the meantime. She had a feeling her next activities wouldn't be quite so enthralling.

Marion led Kestrel down a few quick corridors, walking past the throne room which gave Kestrel some semblance of her bearings, before stopping at a large bloodred door at the end of another hallway.

There were no windows down this way, and Kestrel knew before Marion could even open the door that it would be ominously dark inside. What she didn't expect was the eerie gust of wind that billowed from the room and wrapped around her like a noose.

Even Marion shuddered.

"The queen's waiting for you inside, my lady," Marion stammered, refusing to so much as glance inside.

Hesitation gnawed at her. Told Kestrel to run.

But this was the only way she knew how to appease the queen, and that was currently the only hope she had at earning Thom's freedom.

Kestrel had to kick the hems of her heavy skirts out of the way just to be able to step up the few stairs and enter. As she did, she folded her arms around herself, and before she could turn around and utter a thankful word to

Marion for leading her around all day, the woman had already closed the door shut behind her.

Kestrel swallowed hard and turned back to face the dark room.

It was just her and the queen now.

Her and *her aunt*, she reminded herself, hoping that would alleviate some of the stress she was feeling.

It didn't.

Something ominous hung in the air. It dangled around her like a tangle of cobwebs she had to push through. Or perhaps the ominousness was just because Kestrel wasn't used to seeing a room filled with a hundred lit candles. They cluttered every surface, some clustered on the floor beside each pillar, others mounted on the walls at every possible height, and even a few hanging from the ceiling in iron chandeliers.

But the most unsettling thing Kestrel noticed were the white sheets.

They were draped over various items—some with rounded tops that were as tall as she was, others were more square or rectangular, sitting closer to the ground.

And beneath their coverings, things stirred inside.

A rustling of feathers.

A low groan.

A scrape of claws.

The farther she crept into the long room, the more she wanted to run in the opposite direction. But the queen spotted her before she could think better of it. So Kestrel released the breath in her chest as she strode the rest of the way past the caged creatures.

"Welcome, my darling. Come come, don't be shy." The

queen ushered Kestrel closer, up more steps at the end of the long, dark room. When she placed a hand upon Kestrel's shoulder, it felt more like a talon. "I hope you had a productive time in the library?"

"I did," Kestrel managed to splutter before her eyes settled on the altar before them. Then her heart twisted.

Resting atop every inch of the stone slab in front of her was a different blade, each unique from the last. There were short ones, curved ones. Some with multiple sharp ends. Some that still had dried flecks of blood on them.

"And?" Queen Signe said, growing impatient in the silence. "What did today's lesson cover?"

It took Kestrel a moment to realize she was referring to her studies in the library and not the intimidating display of weaponry before them. She had to blink to force her gaze away, to try to conjure any memory other than the small arsenal at her hands.

When she did, Kestrel barely remembered that Barnabus told her he had been instructed to focus on recent events only, but that it was his personal belief that it would be better to start from the beginning.

Kestrel didn't want to get him in trouble. So she kept her response vague. "It's all a bit overwhelming, and I'm still trying to understand it all...especially how my mother's magic could've caused so much pain." There. That seemed like it would be an acceptable topic for them to have covered: Grimtol's most recent history with her mother's dark curse.

Considering the queen didn't press her further about her studies, it seemed to work.

"Yes, well, your mother was always quite powerful.

Did you know that she also released one of the dragons from its resting?" Kestrel's attention jerked to the queen, who nodded. "It's true. Her father gave her what he believed to be a magical item. It turned out the item was actually a dragon egg, dormant for who knows how many hundreds or thousands of years. And the moment Aenwyn beheld it, a dragon broke free."

The queen tsked at the memory, as if it tasted bitter on her tongue to reshare it.

"I didn't know that," Kestrel admitted, but this was precisely the kind of topics she hoped to discuss with the queen. "No one has really spoken to me about my mother, so I don't know much about her."

A quick, singular haughty laugh. "Yes, well, I suppose it's fitting that her magic released dragons upon us and terminated them as well." With a distant look in her eyes, Queen Signe's gaze drifted down to the altar. She dragged a slender finger along the sharp end of a dagger, but not hard enough to draw blood or so much as move the blade. It was almost lovingly. Longingly. "She had the sight as well, my sister. A talent of hers that our father prized above all others."

Sensing the bitterness in the queen's tone, Kestrel realized this conversation was getting her nowhere fast. She decided to change the topic to something perhaps more endearing to her aunt.

"And what about you? What types of magic do you wield?"

A grin as thin as a spider's leg curved her lips and she removed her finger from the dagger.

"The only magic the Skogarans know, my darling: blood magic."

Kestrel tried to conceal the dread from her face, but she could've guessed. Why else would the queen have brought her here? Beneath the weapons, Kestrel noted the hint of a deep rust color that stained the altar slab. Blood.

"Our magic is all about ritual. Intention. Sacrifice. It is a beseeching of power from the Sky-Blessed."

That caught Kestrel's attention. "The Sky-Blessed? As in…they're real?"

Queen Signe cocked her head and laughed. "Of course they're real. What in the Hollows has that man been teaching you?"

Ironically enough, Thom actually *did* believe in the Sky-Blessed. Kestrel would hear him praying to them every time before he left their tower, asking them to watch over the place and keep Kestrel safe. As she had grown up though, she'd become curious. Who were these Sky-Blessed, and what else could they do? As a young girl, Kestrel would test the lengths they would go to follow through on a request. Sure, their tower was always safe, but when she would ask for things like wildflowers to grow up the side of the tower, or for a new book to suddenly appear when she'd finished her last one, or for a gentle breeze on a scorching day, nothing would happen.

Soon Kestrel had drawn her own conclusions: the Sky-Blessed weren't real. They were either a weird idiosyncrasy of Thom's that she couldn't quite understand and presumed was from the old ways, before the curse had ended civilization.

Or—and this is where she had landed—or, it was just

a thing Thom would say to make her feel safer in his absence.

But she had given up the idea that there could've been any truth to their existence, let alone their power. So to hear Queen Signe suggest it now made Kestrel's head feel full and woozy.

"Nevermind the teachings of that insolent fool," Queen Signe said, waving the mere mention of him away like he was a cloud of pesky dust. "Yes, the Sky-Blessed are real. They are the source of your magic. You've felt them, right? Their presence around you?"

Kestrel's hand floated to her chest and she flinched when it met her ring. She wasn't sure if she was allowed to have it and suddenly found herself wishing she had left it hidden away in her bedchamber.

But if the queen was offended by it, she didn't say anything. Instead, she smiled lovingly down at her niece. "Exactly. That's where I feel it too. Everyone's connection to the Sky-Blessed is different though. Like I said, your mother possessed additional abilities that other Skogarans never had. It might be the same for you. Have you encountered any part of your magic yet?"

Kestrel shook her head.

The queen looked disappointed for a breath of a moment, but then curiosity overtook her. "And yet, you clutch your heart. Why?"

Kestrel averted her gaze, feeling as though she'd been caught in a lie she hadn't meant to give. The truth was, she had felt something awakening inside her when she was in the fortress. But it hadn't been in her chest. It felt more like it started from her belly and then twisted around her whole being. But she didn't know how to describe it. Had still only felt it a handful of times.

"Sorry, I guess I felt...something when I was in that place."

"The Fortress of Thirst?"

"Yes."

"What did you feel, exactly?"

Kestrel almost reached for a braid to gnaw on, but remembered her locks were still trapped in a knot at the base of her skull. She was beginning to hate not having them at her disposal. They left her feeling naked. Raw. Vulnerable to the world around her.

"I don't know," she answered at last. "It was just a... swirling feeling. Like something was spinning inside me and I could get swept up in it. Like a desert tornado."

When she met her aunt's gaze again, the woman had a knowing look about her. "It was the same way for your mother. And have you had any visions?"

"Visions?"

"Like flashes of scenes, people, and places, but they happen in your mind. Aenwyn would have them quite often, sometimes nightly, these graphic foretellings of what was to come."

"Like dreaming?" Kestrel asked, thinking back to the previous night and the strange dream she'd had about the forest of feathers.

"Oh no," Queen Signe said. "They are much different than mere dreams. Even Aenwyn would've told you that." Kestrel deflated a little, feeling like part of her mother had just been stripped away from her. "They were...quite vivid. The way she described them, she knew every detail of something that was about to occur. And after the vision ended, they would leave her drained and imprisoned in her own body for a time. She could not move. Not so much as whimper or cry out for help."

"That sounds awful."

Queen Signe nodded to herself, lost again somewhere deep in a nostalgia Kestrel wished she could follow her into. The queen shrugged that memory away as well. "No matter. Your power may grow still, or manifest in new ways, for you are not just made of her."

Lies, came Thom's voice, crashing into Kestrel's skull. *You are all Aenwyn; all Fury. That vulture had no part in making you.*

Kestrel had to resist the urge to slap her head and tell them both to stop. The way she was starting to see it, it didn't really matter who her father was, because she currently had no way of learning for certain. Her mother was dead. One of her possible fathers was in a dungeon. The other had been turned into a monster and likely wouldn't be able to talk about it, even if he wanted to.

But, if Kestrel's goal was to ingratiate herself to the queen, and the queen was now speaking of this man—this *king*—with a tone of respect, then Kestrel knew she needed to entertain the idea. At least for the sake of this conversation.

Kestrel inched closer, doing her best to muster a wounded but hopeful expression. "Can you tell me about him? King...was it, King Everard?"

At the sound of his name, Queen Signe glowed brighter than the candles surrounding them.

"He was a glorious man. A true king and hero to his

people. Aenwyn was very fortunate to wed someone so dutiful to his kingdom, so committed to his cause."

"And what was his cause?"

"To end the tyranny of dragons, of course." A subtle flash of ire winked behind Signe's black eyes. "Did Barnabus not cover this in your lesson earlier?"

Whoops.

Kestrel had to think on her toes, quickly. "We didn't quite make it to King Everard's plight yet. I had a lot of questions about the late King of Irongate. I felt bad that he died and I just...I wanted to know more about him."

Queen Signe flicked her wrist. "I encourage you not to waste another second of guilt or grief over that man."

Kestrel waited for her to say more, longing to know how she could possibly speak so chillingly about the man she had been betrothed to and supposedly waiting for all these years. But Queen Signe didn't say another word about him, and Kestrel didn't want that to be the end of the conversation.

"And now King Everard is cursed?"

"Unfortunately, yes."

"Is he locked away in a fortress somewhere as well?"

Queen Signe seemed shocked by the question, as if she couldn't believe Kestrel could ask something so obvious. But then she seemed to remember, and resumed her elegantly cold expression.

"No, King Everard could not be contained like King Ulfaskr could. You see, the curse turned your father into a giant serpent. Right where he stood, his body burst with scales as large as doors and claws as tall as houses. He erupted into a gargantuan monster, shattering the

Caeloran castle and rampaging all across the southern region of the kingdom. Not many were left alive in his wake. And then when he was done, he took to the sea, where he now guards his lands from the shallow depths.

"Which is why I am so elated to have you here, my dear niece. For years, I hoped your mother might still be alive to lift this curse. I've searched for her, all over the lands, even in portions of the realm that we are not meant to travel. But I've found no sign of her, and truthfully, I had given up hope. But you have rekindled it."

If Queen Signe's words had been meant to bolster Kestrel, they had the opposite effect. She never felt smaller, more incapable than when anyone started talking about how she was meant to save the realm from her mother's dark magic.

"And you really think I could end the curse?"

At the same time, something foolishly giddy flipped inside Kestrel's chest at the thought. In all her reading, she always admired the heroes but had never once allowed herself to believe that she could be one of them.

She *wanted* it to be true.

But she was a nobody who'd been locked away all her life and now was experiencing everything like a newborn doe.

Queen Signe stroked Kestrel's cheek with the back of her icy fingers.

"I believe you possess the magic to undo the damage your mother wrought. Which is why—" pinching Kestrel's chin, she adjusted her head so that she was looking down upon the arsenal of weapons again— "I would like you to choose."

Kestrel swallowed hard. "Choose?"

"Yes. Choose." The queen merely folded her hands, waiting.

Sensing she wouldn't get a further explanation on why she would need a weapon if they were here to practice magic, Kestrel stared down at the options on the altar. How could she choose? She didn't even know what they would be using the blade for, so how could she decide whether she would want something small and easy to conceal, or something with a longer reach, or perhaps something throwable.

Not to mention, she'd had *no* training with a blade—unless her trying to reenact scenes from her favorite books counted as training. She didn't think it did. If the queen expected her to be able to wield this weapon with any sort of expertise, she would be sorely—

Then Kestrel's eyes snagged on something that was more artwork than weapon.

It was a curved dagger, but it wasn't the blade that caught her attention. It was the decorative hilt. It gleamed with gold gilding and green lacquer. It seemed like the kind of blade that should be kept on display, not used in battle or in whatever magic ritual they were about to perform.

But it was the end of the hilt that cemented her choice.

Carved at the very top—perhaps in bone considering the white material it was made from—was the head of a fox.

Kestrel took the dagger into her hands.

"Ah, I suppose I shouldn't be surprised. That one belonged to your mother many, many years ago."

"Really?"

Kestrel clutched the weapon tighter, as if she was suddenly worried it would wink out of existence. There were so few remnants left of her mother, so few markings of her time in this realm aside from the dark curse that seemed to loom over people's lives. But her mother's ring and now this dagger? Those weren't part of the curse. They came from a time before, a time when her mother was more than a villain in this realm's history books.

"It's yours then," the queen said, and Kestrel's watery eyes flicked up to her, searching for any signs of deception or any strings attached, because surely she was lying. "Consider it a gift."

Kestrel had to swallow through a lifetime of pain to utter a weak, "Thank you."

"Of course, my darling," the queen said, and with a flick of that dainty yet powerful wrist, she announced, "And now, a demonstration."

Kestrel could still hardly see through her tears, hardly breathe through the pain cracking her chest as Queen Signe stepped around to the end of the altar. As Kestrel wiped at her eyes, vision clearing, she noticed the small cage in front of the queen with a rabbit inside. The creature's calm demeanor shifted as the queen unlatched its cage.

Kestrel was just starting to drag herself out of her pity and heartbreak as the queen grabbed the rabbit by its ears and held it out before her. The poor thing screeched and writhed.

"Wait, what are you doing?" Kestrel's voice shook. "You're hurting it! Stop it!"

Before Kestrel could so much as move, Queen Signe had a knife in her other hand, and she plunged it into the rabbit's chest.

Kestrel couldn't distinguish between her cries or the rabbit's. They twisted in the air with the stench of blood, wringing the contents in her stomach until they came burbling up.

Kestrel retched right there, all over the rest of the weapons, the top of the altar. She thought about the rest of the animals in the room with them—was the queen expecting her to kill them too? They didn't deserve this. They were just innocent—

And then with dread, a new realization settled over her.

The rabbit could've been an Animali.

A person.

It could've been Micah's long-lost childhood friend.

Or anyone, really. Someone with a whole life they had been waiting to return to after this curse had been lifted.

Her stomach bunched again, and Kestrel was ready to vomit what little remained left inside, when the queen began dragging the knife downward, the rabbit's flesh tearing as its cries intensified.

Kestrel could no longer watch. No longer listen.

She shielded her face with her empty hand, only to find her face wet and hot, but not with tears. She pulled her hand away. Blood streaked her fingers. The blood of an innocent. Of a life she had failed.

Horror-struck, Kestrel just stared at the blood coating her palm, almost not noticing Signe's mutterings.

"Sky-Blessed, I beseech you. Show this lost daughter

your power. Show her your might. Guide her so that she may save us all."

That's what this was for. For magic. For the so-called Sky-Blessed?

Kestrel had seen Thom pray to them dozens of times, and not once had he ever evoked such bloodshed, such unnecessary torture and pain.

Kestrel lowered her hand, taking in the full sight of her aunt, her only living family. She had never regretted leaving her tower more.

The queen still held the rabbit outward. The poor thing had stopped twitching, stopped breathing. Its tan fur was now stained red, its organs—Kestrel didn't look. She focused her fiery gaze past the creature and to its deranged murderer. The queen was smiling, grinning up at the ceiling as if the Sky-Blessed themselves were about to soar down and kiss her atop her head.

There was such fervent belief reflected in those black eyes, that Kestrel, too, glanced up toward the ceiling once or twice, just to check.

Nothing but the flickering candlelight danced upon the ceiling though.

And slowly, the queen's smile faded. If Kestrel didn't know any better, that was the glimmer of doubt replacing it.

It only served to fuel Kestrel's rage more. If the queen was doubting, that meant the magic hadn't worked, and this poor creature had died for nothing.

Kestrel's feet were moving before she was even aware. She stormed toward her aunt, an inferno brewing inside of her. She snatched the rabbit from her torturous grasp, not knowing why or what she was doing, only that she didn't want the queen anywhere near this poor creature. It deserved at least that much...

It deserved so much more.

It deserved the life that should've been before it. Frolicking through fields and nibbling on greens. Or returning to its family one day—human or otherwise.

As Kestrel marched down the long hallway, she began to sob, clutching the rabbit's soft fur against her chest. It wasn't fair. She hadn't had enough time to think. To act. She should've stopped Signe. She wished she could undo it all, reverse time so that the blade had never even pierced its flesh, and she would've taken the rabbit and run.

Kestrel heard a sound then. Something that could only be described as the reverse of tearing. Something growing. Re-knitting.

Halfway down the long hall, Kestrel stopped.

Blood was no longer dripping between her fingers.

Cautiously, Kestrel flipped the rabbit around in her hands so that it was facing upward. The fur was still stained red, but she gasped at the sight of its stomach. There, in the center of the creature's abdomen, the flesh was perfectly woven back together, as if there had never been a wound there to begin with.

Her wide eyes flew behind her, searching for answers from the only person available to give them.

Signe had already snuck up on her and was standing behind her, gazing at the rabbit over her shoulder.

"A healer," Queen Signe breathed, a hint of intrigue to her tone. Intrigue and vindication. "That is precisely what the cursed ones need."

Pride trickled in between the cracks left behind by the sorrow and rage. Kestrel looked back down at the rabbit, hopeful that maybe she had finally done something right. That she had finally saved someone instead of being the one who always needed saving. Maybe this magic could be used for good if it could do things like return life to the innocent. To heal such violent wounds.

But the rabbit's black eyes stared blankly up at the ceiling.

The creature did not breathe again.

As if sensing her disappointment, the queen tutted. "It's a start, my darling. You'll grow more powerful with time. You just need more practice—"

"Practice?"

Kestrel could see it now. All the animals in the cages around them, lined up and awaiting her blade. One by one, she was meant to kill them. To try to bring them back.

Only what if it didn't work? How many innocent lives was she expected to claim?

"Yes, well, no one masters magic the first time they—"

Kestrel's rageful scream cut the queen off, and she tore from the hallway like a cyclone, rabbit and dagger still in hand.

CHAPTER 26

WHAT HAPPENS BY THE FOUNTAIN...

ELORA

After meeting with the prince and the queen, Elora had needed some fresh air. What she craved was the scent of the mocking laceflowers of Eynallore. They were known more for their deadly beauty, their creamy white petals resembling the intricately sewn lace of a doily but with a surprisingly sharp cut should anyone dare graze them.

For that reason, most people avoided them.

Not Elora.

Before, back when she had been free, she would frequently sit along the outskirts of a field of mocking laceflowers and inhale their sweet, delicate aroma.

The closest thing Irongate had were the jasmine flowers out in their garden. Now that she was free from the dungeon, whenever Elora found herself heart-stricken and homesick, she would spend as much time as she could out there, near the jasmine and tulips.

She never felt more closer to home. And yet so far away.

Less than a week until the wedding.

Less than a week before she could never return to Eynallore again—at least, not as a revered leader. She would be an outsider, henceforth. A traitor, even.

The gardens were silent; the thunder that had been booming overhead had past and Elora relished the peaceful quiet as she paced down the white-pebble paths, a hand pressed thoughtfully to her mouth. She didn't know why she cared so much. It had been a long time since she'd been a revered anything. They had likely replaced her by now, probably hardly ever thought a second about her. She would fade into distant memory, the same way all their former leaders and rulers had.

And yet, Elora couldn't draw her thoughts anywhere else.

It felt like a puzzle that needed to be solved, only she knew she'd already solved it. This was the answer to her problems. Marry the most powerful prince—soon to be king—in all the lands and never again be someone's prisoner.

Prisoner.

That word though. It could mean so many different things. And although she had gained some of her freedoms back, although Queen Signe allowed her to roam the castle at her leisure unless she was called upon, Elora knew better than to presume herself a free woman. Despite Prince Leighton's insistence otherwise, she worried that a marriage to the King of Irongate wouldn't be much different. Already, he had his stipulations. The ultimatums that sounded like promises of freedom but were just more chains in disguise.

Elora wasn't sure how long she'd been out there. The cursed sky made it look as though it were the middle of the day, and yet she knew dinner would be announced shortly.

Soon, someone would come looking for her.

She didn't like when they found her out here. It felt like too personal of a detail for them to glean, something that could be ripped away, should they feel the need to punish her. Still, she didn't want to go back into the castle either. She wanted to wait outside until the moon rose in the sky, and she could gaze upon the stars and see what she could find.

But who knew how long that would take.

And the risk was too high to wait.

Elora began weaving her way back toward the castle, admiring the magnificent blooms around her, her hands plastered together at the crook of her waist. Even though she was shackled and her touch of death bound inside her, she wouldn't dare risk bringing decay upon this place, for those consequences would be dire.

As Elora approached one of the fountains nearest the castle's front entrance, the sun promptly fell. The moon rose high, casting the burbling waters into darkness. Were this the Ghostlight Gulf of Eynallore's shores, those waters would be glowing the brightest shade of blue now.

She halted, gazing longingly and imagining herself elsewhere for just a moment longer.

Then the front castle doors burst wide.

Elora's heart floundered. She pressed herself behind

the fountain, instincts telling her to hide from whoever had come out to retrieve her. They couldn't find her here. Couldn't be trusted to know this intimate truth about her, that despite the death magic in her blood, she found beauty and serenity in the calmness of plants. That there was nowhere she felt safer than surrounded by them.

But once the initial panic wore off, her sense returned. Hiding would serve no purpose but to condemn her. They'd think she was running. Or worse, perhaps trying to sabotage the gardens that the groundskeepers worked so hard to preserve. For what motive? It wouldn't matter. She was the villain in their eyes. Always would be.

Elora smoothed the creases on her silver gown and stepped around the fountain. A sobbing princess came running into view, her hands clutching something bloodied to her chest. Elora watched as the girl plopped down on the fountain's edge across from her. She didn't have to see the bloodied corpse to know what it was; that was the grim aftermath of the Skogaran magic.

They called Elora's magic dark, but she had seen the queen's sacrifices, she'd heard the countless arguments volleyed between Micah and her specifically, begging for her to stop. But Queen Signe heeded him none. Continued her gory display of power.

It made Elora sick.

Of course, she could never let on to that. Every time she'd been faced with it, she steeled herself with the cold resolve she had adapted during her time as a prisoner to the Caelorans.

She did the same now, ready to march past the weeping princess without a word and head to the safe confines of her bedchamber. What did it matter to her that the queen had slain another animal? There would be dozens if not hundreds more where that came from. It was better to shut it out now and save herself the misery, and the naïve princess would do well to do the same—not that she would be the one to advise it though.

But then Queen Signe's charge echoed in her mind: *Befriend the girl, make her feel welcomed, and encourage her to use her magic to bring an end to this forsaken curse.*

Cursed sky, Elora didn't want to do this. She didn't want to have to speak to a Caeloran and risk them spitting in her face. At least if she tried and the girl stormed away from her, she would be able to report back to the queen that it was of no use. Maybe then she'd be off the hook.

Rolling her eyes, Elora rounded the fountain and stood before the lost-and-found princess.

"Not how I expected to find a long-lost princess celebrating her first full day in a life of luxury." It was the best attempt Elora could do at friendly humor, but Princess Kestrel seemed unfazed by it. She merely sniffled, her face still angled down toward the mangled creature in her hands. There was a knife in Kestrel's grasp, but the blade was clean. Not a speck of blood on it. And Elora didn't need to ask to know who was responsible for the demise of this creature.

Elora cursed herself again. Of course this wasn't the time for humor, so she shifted tactics.

"I take it the queen showed you her perverse version of magic?"

That got Kestrel's head to snap up, but it also put Elora

on edge. That was precisely the sort of thought that could get her thrown back into the dungeons.

She pretended to examine the extravagant engagement ring she now wore on her finger, but angled her hand so that she could look down the pathway to see if anyone else was nearby. Only when she found them alone did her stomach stop clenching. Speaking so brazenly about the queen was a mistake she couldn't afford, nor one she would make again.

"She did," Kestrel said, pitifully.

And when Elora looked back toward the princess, she found herself fixed intensely beneath her hurt, green gaze. Like the girl was desperate to pull someone into her sorrows, to have them tell her that she was right to be so upset.

Perhaps the honesty had worked. So could the queen really condemn Elora for doing what she asked?

"And...you didn't like her magic?" Elora asked, unsure of what to say next but wanting to keep the conversation going, so she could explain to the queen she did her due diligence.

"Of course I didn't like it! Why would I? She killed this poor creature—" the rabbit's corpse shook in Kestrel's grasp and her sobs became ragged once more. "And I couldn't do anything to stop her."

It took everything in Elora not to roll her eyes. If she had a vial of tears for everything she couldn't stop these monsters from doing, she'd be drowning.

But the girl was still so naïve to the world, still learning about the harshness disguised in all the gowns and jewels. Part of Elora even envied her for it, for at least

Kestrel was still lucky enough to feel hope. She still had a strong sense of what was right and wrong, and there were no blurred lines in between for her. Which was why this was causing her so much strife. By her inaction, she felt culpable. Blamed herself for a death she had not caused.

Elora knew that pain. She remembered the first days that followed her and her people's resurrections, the countless lives they accidentally took just with a singular touch of their hands, not knowing that they had arisen to a new curse of their own.

But it hadn't been their fault. Not really.

And it wasn't Kestrel's either.

"Is that the only reason you're out here? Because someone else killed something?" Elora hadn't meant the question to come out so harsh. It turned out that being kind and friendly was a skill she had forgotten how to use.

But for whatever reason, it did the trick and kept Kestrel talking.

"I'm just...I'm worried."

That caught Elora by surprised. "Worried? About what?"

"About everything!" Those bloodshot eyes snapped up to meet hers again, and the green against the pink backdrop of flowers reminded Elora of the carnivorous shadevine of her lands. Beautiful but fierce. Deadly, even. "I'm worried about my dad and what will happen to him. About what I've gotten myself into. About who I'm becoming, what this magic will do to me. To others... I'm worried I made a terrible, *terrible* mistake and no matter what I do, everything keeps getting worse."

She had made a mistake, if her only options now were

to trust the people of Irongate. But Elora couldn't tell her as much. Sometimes you were dealt a horrible hand and just had to deal with it.

"Surely, it isn't all bad," Elora said stiffly, and tried mustering more warmth. "You're a princess now. That's got to count for something."

Neither of them believed her.

Kestrel let out a derisive laugh, petting the rabbit's unmoving head. "Yes, a princess born to the Corrupt Queen and either a traitor who kidnapped me at birth and kept me locked away in a tower because *the world is too dangerous and full of monsters* or a father who is now a serpent and destroyed the kingdom I was supposedly meant to rule one day. So I'm not sure it counts for anything. What am I, the princess of nothing? A princess of curses? Of loneliness and devastation? That's great."

This wasn't working.

Everything Elora said only seemed to fuel Kestrel's pain. If the queen found out she had inadvertently steered her toward a rebellion or departure, the whole engagement could be off. Elora could be deemed a traitor to the crown and thrust back into the dungeons.

She needed a new tactic.

Honesty had worked with Kestrel earlier, but it was perhaps Elora's least favorite method of interaction. Honesty meant vulnerability. And vulnerability meant she could set herself up for pain later.

The girl was reeling though. She seemed about three seconds away from bolting from the castle and never looking back.

There was no other option.

Cautious not to touch her, Elora sat down on the marble fountain ledge beside her. The girl was shivering, likely not used to the cooler, northern climate yet. If Elora was anyone else, she would be able to scoot closer, offering her the heat of her own body, but even with the hailstone manacles she knew better.

"Believe it or not, I do understand. I've had many years to think over my actions, the choices that led me here. I was once revered by my people. I was a leader, a battle-hardened warrior and someone who the Ashen admired. Then I was taken prisoner, and that's all I've been for more than twenty years now."

"Twenty years?" Kestrel looked up at her then. Those green eyes slid down the length of her. "You barely look twenty now."

Elora's eyebrow crooked. She hadn't expected such forwardness, but maybe she should have. Maybe that's why honesty was working so well on this girl, because she didn't know else to be.

"Sorry, was that rude of me to say? I don't know—" Princess Kestrel hung her head again.

"No, not at all. I'm just not used to people being so—"

"Unaware of basic common knowledge?"

Elora laughed. An honest, genuine *laugh*. "I was going to say so forthright with their thoughts."

Kestrel smirked up at her in thanks, and cursed sky if the responding twitch of Elora lips didn't deepen.

She cleared her throat and ripped her gaze forward. "The Ashen do not age. My first life ended shortly after I turned twenty. I died. I was reborn. And I haven't aged a day since. None of us have."

"How old are you now then?"

"Truthfully, I don't know. I haven't had much reason to keep track." Something cracked in Elora's chest, and she bit down on the warmth that rose in the back of her throat.

"Sorry," Kestrel said softly, and she sounded as if she genuinely meant it. As if she wasn't afraid of Elora for being seemingly immortal at all. Come to think of it, she hadn't even scooted away when Elora sat down. Kestrel looked a little sheepish as she added, "And here I am complaining about something that probably seems so trivial. Just doing what I always do, overthinking about the worst possible outcomes, even though I know it does me no good."

"Worrying is only natural," Elora said once she had composed herself.

"Sure, but to what end? All worrying does is make me feel frantic and weak. It doesn't fix anything. It doesn't *do* anything. I just sit and stew, like a coward, instead of being brave like my—" She cut herself off, but Elora already knew what she had been about to say.

"Like your father?" Ire bubbled inside her like a festering wound.

Kestrel nodded, a single tear dripping down her cheek and landing on the rabbit's blood-tinged fur.

This was a subject they could not discuss, not without Elora spewing like the churning volcanoes of Galorfin. Telling this weeping girl how much the traitor deserved the pain that was coming to him would not be the sort of thing that would ingratiate her toward her.

All mention of *Darius Graeme* aside though, Elora was

surprised to find herself actually relating to this young woman—the daughter of the people who had caused her suffering for years. She had lost count of the times she had fallen into a dark pit of grief and guilt over her own actions, what she could've done differently, if there was still anything left to do to change her own circumstances. It was a dangerous cycle of thought to be trapped inside.

"I have days like those," she confided. "Blessed moon, I have entire weeks and months like those."

"You do?"

"Of course. You spend enough time away from your homeland, from the ones who truly understand you, who see *you*, and you start to believe that...maybe you are different. Wrong in some innate way." How many times had she wished to be someone other than herself? For her magic to cease. To be *normal*. But Elora had since learned that normal was a lie, a falsehood that people told themselves to justify the pain they were causing others. Defiantly, she smiled to herself, almost forgetting Kestrel was even there. "But if you're lucky, you remember that the very same reasons these strangers make you think you are weak and wrong are the same reasons in which you are strong and great."

It had been that truth, that mantra, which had kept Elora from breaking all these years.

"I don't really have anyone who truly understands me. I thought my father—" she shook her head, a red curl springing from the place where it was tightly pulled back. "But it turns out most of what he taught me wasn't true. He told me there was no one left out here, and yet I have met so many people now...but the first one I met lied to me as well. And now I'm having a hard time trusting anything." Kestrel's eyes were still wet as she looked up at Elora. "How do you convince yourself of something like that, that you're strong when you feel nothing like it and so much evidence is pointing to the contrary?"

Elora had to think a long while before she could answer.

"I suppose it helps that, where I come from, my people are proud of our magic. Everyone else claims it to be evil. But in Eynallore, we use our power to disrupt invasive species so that we can preserve the unique flora of our forests. We put injured creatures out of their misery, so they don't have to suffer—a long time ago, we offered the same to terminally ill humans. Because to us, death is an honor. A privilege. Something to be celebrated, not something to be feared."

Kestrel's voice was shaking between rage and sorrow. "Even unwarranted deaths? Brutal ones that didn't need to happen?"

Elora couldn't answer.

The truth was she had always found the queen's methods far too insidious, the magic unnecessarily ruthless, and quite honestly, a bit suspect. If the Sky-Blessed were by some chance bestowing miracles upon the Skogarans, it seemed unlikely they would require such bloody sacrifices.

But saying any of that wouldn't steer Kestrel closer to the queen or her magic.

She was toeing a fine line between honesty and outright duplicity.

"Maybe some deaths we don't understand or have a

hard time accepting, but they are still warranted, yes." She didn't sound convincing, even to her own ears.

"Yeah?" Kestrel laughed bitterly. "And what about those shackles they have you wear? Are those warranted to?"

The brutal words hit Elora like an unsuspecting blow.

Self-consciously, her hands lifted to the cold collar around her neck and the chafed skin beneath it. She had always hated it, not only for the message it gave everyone who saw her—an overt symbol of her continued captivity—but because of how it made her feel: completely shut off from the thing that made her who she was, an Ashen.

Without the collar, however, the people of Irongate would find her too dangerous to let her go walking around. It was the only reason she'd been permitted to leave her hailstone-imbued prison cell. So as much as she hated it, she was more grateful to be allowed to roam the castle, to feel the sun on her skin, to smell the flowers.

Kestrel stared down at the rabbit. "I'm sorry. That wasn't what I—I shouldn't have said that."

"It's fine. You're fine." Elora straightened where she sat, the silken fabric of her silver gown lifting from her spine and allowing air to cool her back. "To answer your question, yes. My shackles are a necessary key to my freedom. They are the only reason I am permitted to walk the grounds and live a relatively normal existence again."

That was the truth.

At least, it was the truth Elora had told herself and would continue telling herself, otherwise she feared she would go mad.

She felt Kestrel's gaze burning into the side of her face

for the duration of the long silence that followed. When the lost princess finally withdrew her attention, it was to tend to the rabbit in her lap. She picked it up and gently placed it on the fountain's ledge beside her. Now that Elora had a better view of the dagger, she noted the ornate hilt with the head of an animal carved into it—a wolf or a fox maybe. Kestrel shoved the dagger into a corded belt around her waist before plunging her bloodstained hands into the crystal-clear waters and washing away the red.

"And are you?"

The question caught Elora off guard. "Am I what?"

Kestrel continued rinsing, splashing the water up her forearms, careless of how drenched her tunic was becoming. "Are you free?"

It was not a question anyone would've ever asked outright. It was an unspoken rule to pretend. To turn a blind eye. And everyone within the Irongate walls had been happy to oblige. Even Elora played her part and pretended that the small amount of freedom she'd been granted was anything but another version of a cage.

For just three simple words, they were earth-shattering. Already, they were unraveling the very small amount of certainty she had about her miserable existence.

And if it were anyone else, Elora would tell them what she was supposed to say: that she was grateful to the queen for the opportunities she had been provided. She would claim the queen had saved her. She would lie and tell her how excited she was to soon become a bride and a future queen to a powerful throne.

But here they were. Two forsaken princesses. Alone together in an enemy territory.

"No," Elora said, surprised by her own honesty. "I am not yet free. But I hope someday I will be."

A heady quiet surrounded them before Kestrel finally said, "I hope you will be too. You deserve that much. Everyone does."

Elora wasn't foolish enough to believe that Kestrel was only talking about her. Surely, she was referring to Darius Graeme, how he deserved freedom as well. Elora couldn't stomach having him brought into such a space where she had just been so brutally vulnerable. It made her bristle. Made her question everything, every word that had come out of the princess' mouth.

Here, Elora thought she was the one manipulating the princess. Perhaps she was wrong. Perhaps it was Kestrel manipulating Elora the entire time. Making her believe that she was some innocent, trustworthy doe-eyed girl who couldn't do anything as conniving as use people for her own gains.

Who had Elora been fooling? Someone spends enough time around manipulative royals, and they can adapt quite quickly. She knew she had.

Finishing with her washing, Kestrel slumped back onto the edge of the fountain, facing the castle.

Elora had been about to excuse herself, to retreat to the safety of her room where no one could play their dubious mind tricks on her anymore, but Kestrel stopped her with a sigh.

"I don't know what to do."

It wasn't the sort of question the queen would want Elora to leave lingering. "About what?"

"About the magic. I want to learn how to use it, but I

can't just—" She gestured to the rabbit beside her. "I can't do *this*."

And just like that, Elora wondered again if she had been wrong. If Kestrel truly was a girl without a single malicious bone in her body. If this was the outcome of someone being kept away from all the tyranny and bloodshed and manipulations for all their lives, if that meant they got to grow up not knowing how to play mind games. How to lie. How to sense when they were being played.

It would be Kestrel's greatest blessing, but also her gravest mistake.

It left her vulnerable.

And once again, Elora felt herself relating to the young woman in ways she never thought possible. Because long ago, Elora had been vulnerable too. It's how she had been caught. Out on a mission to attempt to spread peace and kindness, to assure the people of Grimtol that they had no reason to fear the Ashen. And King Everard had acted like he wanted to hear her out, like he had any interest in peace.

"Then don't," Elora heard herself saying, words that the queen would reprimand her for later. But in this moment, she didn't care. "Don't trust anyone you're not ready to. Don't *do* anything that feels wrong. Forge your own way. Figure out a different path. There are many types of magic in this world—mine for example requires no sacrifice."

Kestrel leveled her with a dubious grin. "Your touch is lethal though, isn't it?"

Bad example.

"Fair point. But it's not malicious. It's—it doesn't

matter what it is, because there are other types of magic too. The Animali, for one. They can shift into their animal form at will—at least, before the curse impeded their ability to do so. But there are magical items all across the lands, some that grant wishes, others that block magic. There is magic all around us, Kestrel. You are only just discovering it, but you will start to see its signs more and more now that you are becoming aware, and I'm sure you will find that most of it is not nearly as violent as *that*."

The longer she spoke, the more she watched Kestrel perk up, and there was something so beautiful about the hope that was igniting in her eyes. Beautiful as well as fearless. There was a fire inside this woman, one that Elora hoped the queen, nor anyone, would ever extinguish.

"You're right," Kestrel said, bouncing to her feet. "I felt it before, when the prince shoved me in that fortress. I swear I felt something awakening inside me. No sacrifice needed. It was just...there. Like it had been waiting. Like it was ready for me to call upon it, but I didn't know how."

Elora nodded, rising to stand beside her. "Well, sounds to me like you have additional study material for tomorrow then."

Kestrel beamed. "Thank you. Thank you! I can't thank you enough!"

Her arms went wide. Elora barely had time to brace herself for what was coming.

She tried stepping back, an impulse meant to keep distance between the two of them. But there was nowhere to go.

Elora's heels bumped against the edge of the fountain.

Her balance lost. But Kestrel was right there, ready to save her.

Her arms looped around Elora's waist. Suddenly she found herself floating, caught between the mercy of gravity and the surprising strength of the Caeloran princess.

Kestrel was holding her. Touching *her*. An Ashen. And there was not an inkling of fear or doubt within those dazzling green eyes.

Kestrel smirked, her freckles disappearing behind the red tinge of her cheeks. "That was close. You almost went for a swim."

Elora was grateful for the dark shade of her skin, for it hid her own blushing.

She squirmed in Kestrel's grasp. Fuming. "Yes, well, if I had known I was going to be mauled, perhaps I would've kept my distance."

Finally, she broke free, Kestrel righting her away from the fountain before letting her go.

"Right," the lost princess said, tucking a loose, untamed curl behind her ear—and cursed sky, if the pained look on her face didn't make Elora regret her sharp tongue. "The no touching thing. Sorry to have overstepped —" But then Kestrel paused, her face twisting with consternation before blurting— "Actually, no. I'm not sorry."

"What?"

"You didn't have to comfort me tonight. Or listen to my complaining. But you did. And I'm grateful you did. But I won't apologize for wanting to express my gratitude —I mean, unless being touched is something you really don't like. But I was under the impression it was more of a rule forced upon you, yet another shackle, another way for them to make you feel like a monster among humans."

Everything Kestrel was saying made Elora feel on the brink of shattering. Like the contents of her heart would spill all over the garden like a weeping maiden.

Because Kestrel was right. It had never been what the Ashen wanted, to be treated like vile, untouchable monsters. It had just become the way things were. And after so many years, Elora no longer questioned it.

"I don't understand it," Kestrel confessed, chancing a step closer. This time Elora fought the urge to step away. "You're wearing hailstone anyway; your magic is blocked. So why can't I touch you?"

Eyes as verdant as the Eynallore forests crept up to meet hers. They locked Elora in place as Kestrel's hands floated closer. Hoping. Asking.

Elora had a choice: she could continue the way things were, the way things always had been, with her maintaining a status quo that was never meant to serve her, only sever her.

Or...

She could take a chance.

Leap into the unknown.

Her fingers twitched at her sides. The pull between them was palpable. Intoxicating.

One hand shook as it drifted up to meet Kestrel's, hovering but a breath away—

When the castle front doors burst open.

"There you are, little—" Micah glanced between them. "Elora. Hey."

Elora tore away from Kestrel in the least inconspicuous way possible. But they had been too close. It would've raised questions; it still might. But at least this way, the evidence was gone. Because, much like she didn't want the Erickson family knowing the gardens brought her joy, it turned out she also didn't want them knowing she was actually enjoying connecting with the lost princess.

Kestrel noted the distance between them and her jaw tightened. But whatever emotion had blown through her, she snuffed it out as she addressed Micah.

"Micah! I was just going for a stroll. Want to join?"

"Not a chance," he drawled, leaning against the stone banister. "I'm still recovering from all the strolling we did the past few weeks. Besides, there's food inside, and my belly's grumbling. I was just coming to see if you would be joining us for dinner. But if you're busy with something else—"

"No!" both princesses cried in unison.

"Right." Micah's smirk was all too knowing. "Well then, you coming?"

"Of course," Kestrel hollered to Micah. Then, her voice lowered, becoming as chilled as the evening air. "What about you?"

She didn't even look at her. And Elora couldn't even blame her, but it stung, nonetheless.

"Not this time."

Nodding, Kestrel made for the garden exit. Stopped.

"Dragon's fire, I almost forgot." She spun around, her hollow gaze fixing on the rabbit's corpse. "I can't just leave it there."

"I'll take care of it," Elora said. It was the least she could do.

Kestrel's head cocked to one side. "Oh. You don't have to—"

"I don't mind. Dead things don't bother me, and you've had to deal with a lot tonight."

"Oh," the lost princess said again. "I mean, thank you. For everything."

Elora bowed at the waist, and by the time she came back up, the princess was gone. That was for the best. Something about the presence of that girl seemed to make Elora behave erratically, making senseless decisions that would only serve to condemn them both.

Because the truth was: she *couldn't* touch Kestrel.

Or at least, she shouldn't.

The truth remained that, without the hailstone, her touch was lethal. And if Kestrel didn't perform to the queen's liking, then Elora had already been instructed to kill her.

Yet, as Elora cradled the dead rabbit in her arms, she was conflicted. Under normal circumstances, she would take the carcass to the cooks, like Queen Signe did with all of her sacrifices. But the thought of them serving rabbit stew to Kestrel for dinner or lunch made something twist and ache somewhere long forgotten in her chest.

If Elora could use her magic, she would simply make the animal wither and decay until it was nothing but bones. But only a key could free her locks, one forbidden to be in her possession.

Instead, she carried the frail creature to a nearby flowerbed and began to dig.

And as her fingers dug into the soft soil, Elora had felt *something*.

Warmth bloomed in her chest like a rosebud in spring.

Someone had *wanted* to touch her—to *embrace* her. To treat her as an equal.

And for the first time in years, Elora had dared to allow herself to want the same.

CHAPTER 27

SONGS, DANCES, AND VISIONS OF THE DEAD

KESTREL

As they entered the castle, Micah was rambling, telling her something about how they should go to the soaking pools sometime so he could teach her how to swim.

But Kestrel could hardly hear him.

All her thoughts—all of her being—was back at the fountain.

Back with Elora.

It was her delicate scent that lingered most of all. Even as they passed by torchlit sconces and burning oil, all she could smell was Elora. Like a lone, white petal flower kissed with dew, blooming in a moonlit meadow. There was nothing that smelled so enchanting back home. And Kestrel was certain if she scoured the farthest reaches of Grimtol, explored every inch of land, she would never find a scent that rivalled its elegance or allure.

But every time she started to smile at the thought of

being so close to her, the feeling was soured by the cold stab of the abrupt rejection that had followed.

Micah had come outside, and Elora had wrenched away.

Just like Leighton had.

Like they were both embarrassed by the thought of being seen with her.

Kestrel wrapped her arms around herself.

"Are you even listening to me?" Micah asked, bumping against her with his shoulder. "Did you hear a word I just said?"

"Hmm?" Kestrel's ears twitched and she wrenched herself to the present, leaving all memories of Elora at the fountain where they belonged. "Oh, sorry. What were you saying?"

He rolled his steel blue eyes but answered anyway. "I said, I don't think I've ever seen Princess Elora speak to anyone like that. Not willingly anyway."

"Oh."

When that was her only response, he added, "Come on. What's your secret? Were you holding her hostage or something?"

Kestrel's arms squeezed tighter, the chill of the night air still piercing. "Something like that."

Micah groaned. "Okay, little miss mopey. I know what you need. A good meal, some exquisite company—as well as the mediocre company of my brothers; sorry, this can't be helped—and perhaps a jaunty tune."

"What's a tune?" she asked, just as they reached the dining hall, and he threw the doors wide.

Kestrel was pulled in by the hearty waft of vegetable

stew that seemed to wrap around her. Yet again, the meal displayed on the table was unlike anything she could've even dreamed, more food than she had seen in an entire month, or more.

But this time, before her stomach could guide her into grabbing a number of tasty baked treats, something else tantalized her senses. A rhythmic, pleasant sound that she knew immediately but had never had the pleasure of experiencing before.

Music.

At the end of the long table, a young man perched one leg upon a chair as he strummed a wooden instrument with strings. Leighton, Efrem, and the young man were singing, chanting so jubilantly, none of them even noticed Micah and Kestrel's entrance at first.

Micah abandoned her at the door to run over to Efrem. He grabbed him around the thighs and hoisted him into the air, all while joining in on the upbeat song.

Kestrel grabbed one of the pastries—a flaky crust that had some sort of fruit or jam atop it—and found Barnabus at the opposite end of the table, his fingers crammed into his ears.

"Is that your other brother? Nic, I think Micah called him?" she asked, pointing with her tartlet before taking a seat in the chair beside him.

Barnabus took his fingers out of his ears. "What?"

"I said: is that Nic?"

Upon hearing his name screamed from across the room, the young man jerked his neck toward her. When he grinned, he was all Micah—minus the bravado. His smile was a shy one, the smile of someone who still had yet to grow into themselves the way Micah had. Given his musical talent and charming good looks though, Kestrel didn't think it would take him too long.

"Oh, yeah," Barnabus answered. "Niculas, but I guess most people call him that."

And without another word, he promptly crammed his fingers back into his earholes. He didn't seem perturbed by the music, necessarily. In fact, he bobbed along with the beat in between spoonfuls of soup. For someone so accustomed to the quiet peace of the library, she could see how his ears could be sensitive to a place as boisterous as this. If anything though, Barnabus just seemed glad to be a part of the festivities, even if he needed them muted some.

Nic struck a chord, and the brothers all belted out the same drawn out note before the melody picked up again. Quickening. Chasing itself.

It reminded her of a game she and Thom used to play when she was little. He would start with his eyes closed and Kestrel would try to hide somewhere in the tower without him finding her. Whenever he'd get too close, she'd move somewhere else. But each time he heard her giggle, he got to open his eyes a little more and hasten his step. Soon he'd be chasing her around every corner of the tower, and she'd be laughing so hard his eyes were wide open and she could hardly breathe.

Kestrel watched Leighton throw an arm around Efrem and Micah. She wanted desperately to ask him what he had learned. It had been plaguing her all day.

But seeing him so happy, so carefree and joyful, she

decided she didn't want to interrupt. Her questions could wait.

The song slowed and sped up and slowed again, and the next time the melody hastened, Micah and Efrem were up on the table. They tapped their shoes and clanged the silverware. Kestrel's heart lurched, worried that they might knock over every dish in their path and waste so much delicious food that she hadn't even had a chance to try yet. But to her amazement, they danced around the table, dodging every platter and bowl with precision.

Singing the entire way, Micah pranced to the end of the table where Barnabus and Kestrel were sitting.

"Please go away!" Barnabus yelled, leaning forward to clutch his bowl and spoon to keep them from rattling. "It's unsanitary what you're doing."

"I'll leave as soon as the lady agrees to dance."

Blinking and mid-chew, Kestrel looked up to find Micah's hand outstretched toward her.

"Oh, I couldn't. I don't know how—"

"Nonsense!"

She had held her hand out in protest, but Micah seemed to take it as an invitation. He yanked her up onto the table. Her tart fell from her other hand, lost to the ground.

"Dancing comes from the heart, so everyone can do it."

Kestrel grinned, feeling the music trill inside her as if it was its own source of magic.

At Micah's encouraging smiles and nonverbal coaching, Kestrel bobbed and swayed along in time with the beat. But her cumbersome skirts made maneuvering around the food much more challenging than either of the twins made it seem. She made a mental note to talk to Marion tomorrow about procuring different attire, if at all possible. Something more similar to what the princes were wearing, except maybe Leighton who always seemed a bit more extravagant than the others.

Eventually the song ended, but the merriment had only just begun.

"This next one is a song I wrote about my brothers and the time I had to drag them out of a moat."

Efrem groaned, pointing an accusatory finger at Micah. "If you had just let me handle them, I wouldn't have spent that night pulling seaweed from my arse."

Micah bellowed with laughter and skipped back to the other side of the table to throw an arm around his twin. Nic started playing and singing again, the twins dancing together, one arm over each other's shoulders.

But Kestrel had been left standing there, unsure of what to do from atop this high table.

"Need a hand?"

When she glanced down, two sky-blue eyes stared up at her as if they were gemstones dazzling among the stars.

Her traitorous heart fluttered, but she was starting to realize her attraction toward Leighton wasn't as real as she had once believed it to be. That maybe she had only fallen for him because his was the first charming face she had ever seen.

Still, Kestrel was trapped on a table, with a dozen trays of food surrounding her. And the gown she was wearing made her feel like a walking, bumbling tumbleweed. She didn't know how to get down.

Kestrel accepted his hand. "Thank you."

His other cradled her waist, and before she could ask him what he was doing, he lifted her up and lowered her back down to flat ground.

"Better?" he asked, gazing down at her.

"Yes," she said, tucking a nonexistent strand of hair behind her ear just to try to conceal her blush. "Believe it or not, that was my first time dancing on a table."

"Could've fooled me," he laughed, and then changing his tone to something more sober, he tugged on the hand that he still hadn't let go of. "Come on. Let's find somewhere quieter to talk. I believe I have some news to give you."

Nothing else could've made her heart stammer more.

Kestrel let Leighton guide her out of the dining hall and into one of the empty chambers nearby. It seemed this castle had hundreds of them, a room for every occasion. The narrow room they scurried into seemed to be used for storage. On one wall was a series of shelves stocked fully with various canned goods, herbs, and barrels of perhaps wine or mead.

Leighton kept his voice low even though they were clearly alone.

"I don't know how to put this gently, so I'm just going to come out and say it: I don't have any new information for you—" Kestrel opened her mouth to ask him why in the Hollows he dragged her here and pretended like he did then, when he held up his hands. "Wait, I mean I don't have anything concrete. But I have a theory."

"Tell me your theory then." Kestrel folded her arms and leaned against the wall.

"I think the queen is stalling. Most prisoners are

sentenced within a week of capture, but the really bad ones—sorry, the ones who are suspected of committing crimes like treason, they are dealt with swiftly. Sentenced almost immediately."

"Okay, so what does this mean?"

"I don't know what it means, exactly. But I think the queen is maybe...conflicted about his sentencing. Just, given your relationship with him, and all."

Chewing her lip, Kestrel thought for a moment. "You think she hasn't sentenced him yet because she's worried it will upset me?"

"Perhaps."

Well that wasn't such bad news, Kestrel thought. If the queen cared so much about what Kestrel thought of her, she could use this to her advantage. It meant she had a chance at bargaining for his safe release after all.

But the look on Leighton's face was anything but victorious or hopeful.

"You think this is a bad thing?"

He started tapping his mouth with a finger. "I don't know if it's a bad thing. But it's definitely out of character for her."

"How do you mean?"

"Queen Signe is...swift in her judgements. She never teeters when it comes to exacting justice. And to be honest, she has been awaiting Darius Graeme's capture for as long as anyone."

Kestrel tried not to prickle at his words and reminded herself he was only talking that way about him because he hadn't had a chance to know Thom yet. None of them had. Not the Thom *she* knew anyway.

"I don't know," Leighton said, pacing up and down the narrow closet. His slate blue cape tried billowing behind him, but the confined space left it with nowhere to swell. "But I worry she's either conflicted about his punishment and wants to appease you, or she's waiting for an opportunity when you won't notice or care as much."

"I'll always care," Kestrel snapped, the blood in her veins boiling with the heat of the sun.

Leighton held up his hands in surrender again. "I'm not saying there will be a time when you won't, I just—I don't know what she's up to. But typically, traitors are dealt with publicly. A spectacle is made of their deaths in order to keep the people in line, to prevent anyone else from doing the same. And the townsfolk are talking. They know he's here. They'll be demanding his retribution soon—"

"And what? They just get whatever they want? Even when they have no idea of the man he truly is?"

"No, but the more outspoken and outraged they become, the more pressure it puts on her to act. And in my experience, when people are under pressure, they often don't make rash decisions."

Kestrel's eyes were tearing up, and she cursed herself for it. This was by far the worst news that he could've given her. He could've pulled her in here to say that Thom's execution had already passed, that he was gone forever. This should give her hope. Or at the very least, time.

"I'll talk to her about him. Make her see that he's no threat to anyone."

Inhaling deeply, Leighton dragged a hand through his

flaxen hair. He thought about his choice of words for a long time before settling on, "You're welcome to try."

When they left, he offered to walk her back to the dining hall, but Kestrel was no longer hungry. No longer in the mood for celebrating and dancing. Thom was sitting in his cell, alone and probably hungry, and what had she been doing? Living the life of a princess, flirting with one royal or another.

She needed to refocus. All of her efforts moving forward had to have one goal in mind: figuring out how to appease the queen.

Kestrel instead excused herself to her room, not entirely sure of the exact location, but certain she could figure it out. It only took a half dozen wrong turns before she finally found it. Kestrel heaved the door opened then closed behind her before she slumped against it.

Everything felt so heavy.

Her heart.

Her head.

Her stupid gown.

She couldn't stand it. Kestrel began tearing the fabric off of her, each layer of silk and cotton and lace and everything else until she was standing in her undergarments panting.

When her vision went black.

Kestrel froze.

At first, she thought maybe the fire in the hearth had blown out. Even then, her room had large enough windows and was up high enough that the moon would surely be offering some illumination.

She had no sense of her body though. Not her bare

flesh, nor her heaving chest as it rose and fell with each panting breath.

It was as if she wasn't herself. Adrift somewhere that didn't exist.

Then through the darkness, faint slivers of light began to emerge. They carved jagged pieces out of the blackness, leaving behind different shades of grey. Shapes began to form. Tree branches. Hundreds of them. Weaving in and around each other like a net of loose threads.

She was standing in the Hollows. The same place she'd been in her dreams, she realized.

Much like in the dream, Kestrel noticed the black feathers that were falling from the sky as if hundreds of birds were molting overhead. Large chunks of stone sprang from the earth like fingers, smooth along the curved tops, as if they had been carved and planted there.

Kestrel turned around, finding the still lake behind her. A blue glow emanated from within its depths.

Before she could walk closer, before she could even think to blink, Kestrel felt the water lapping at her ankles and found herself suddenly standing in the water. In the next breath of a moment, the water came up to her knees. Then her hips. Her chest.

Soon, Kestrel was completely submerged, following that bright blue orb into the depths. But she couldn't swim. Couldn't breathe.

Suddenly, Kestrel woke up gasping, completely shrouded and tangled in the lace curtains that were hanging over her windows. She clawed for freedom, barely managing to escape. When she did, she realized that dark shadows were oozing from her fingertips like thick tendrils of black smoke. Slowly, they receded, and Kestrel felt herself expanding, a sense of comfort and wholeness returning to her.

Then her bedchamber door creaked opened.

"Evening, my lady. I thought you might—oh my!" Marion gasped at the sight of her, and Kestrel wasn't sure if it was because she was almost entirely nude or if she looked as wild and disoriented as she felt. Marion's eyes scanned her head to toe before falling to the discarded garments by the door. "Well, I see you managed to undress yourself. Might I suggest putting on a nightgown before traipsing in front of your windows and displaying yourself for the entire kingdom, my lady?"

Kestrel twisted around, glaring outside. She didn't much care if the people saw her like this, not that she thought they could from how far away the denizens of the city resided from the castle.

Besides, she had problems farther away than the Iron-bloods to worry about.

Why was the Hollows calling to her?

What lurked below those waters and why was it showing itself to her?

With a tut and long sigh, Marion collected the garments off the floor, tossed them on the bed, and came behind Kestrel to throw a nightgown over her. Kestrel shimmied into it without a word, much less an awareness of what she was doing.

"Will that be all then, my lady?"

Half dazed, Kestrel nodded and bid her handmaiden a goodnight. But before the door could shut behind her, she remembered one other thing.

"Marion? Actually, would you be able to bring me less formal clothing tomorrow? Maybe something with trousers?"

Marion's smile was warm and knowing. "I'll see what I can muster."

CHAPTER 28

A LESSON IN THE BALLROOM

KESTREL

Kestrel was still sound asleep, her face pressed in the center of a book when Marion blew into the room.

"Rise and shine, my lady. You have a busy day ahead of you."

Blearily, Kestrel blinked her eyes open, some of the pages sticking to her cheek. Gently, she peeled the pages from her face and closed the book. Barnabus had sent it up for her, and she had only seen it on her nightstand after Marion had dismissed herself the previous night. Kestrel had tried to read it but apparently had fallen asleep.

Still dazed and groggy, Kestrel watched Marion whiz by the bed, a new stack of clothes slung over one arm and a pastry in the other hand. She tossed the sugary bread to Kestrel before striding across the room where she heaved the clothes onto the armchair by the fire.

"Don't mind the mess. I'll swap out the old garments for the new ones while you're studying with Barnabus."

The mention of his name was the cold bucket of water Kestrel needed to awaken fully.

Studying with Barnabus meant learning more about the kingdoms. About magic.

Kestrel grabbed the pastry, flung her heavy blankets aside, and nibbled on her breakfast while she waited for her handmaiden to dress her. She was thrilled when Marion grabbed a pair of tan trousers and a slate grey doublet from the pile. She layered the doublet over a long-sleeved, cream-colored tunic, and when Kestrel finally got to look at herself in the mirror, her freckled cheeks hurt from grinning so broadly.

"Oh, you hate it," Marion jested.

"It's perfect. Thank you."

Marion ushered her over to the vanity and grabbed the hairbrush. Yesterday, Kestrel had been happy to accept the woman's help with everything, if not just to experience the culture of Irongate and better understand the people here. Today, however, Kestrel felt the need to reclaim part of herself.

Setting her pastry down, she gently reached for the brush in Marion's hand.

"That's alright. Today, I'll do my own hair."

Marion looked reluctant, but stepped aside and waited as Kestrel finished tying her hair into the braids she was accustomed to. Today she had a thick, loose one down the center of her scalp, with a few smaller ones accenting the sides. The rest of her hair, she asked Marion to twist into the tight bun she'd given her the day prior, in an effort to attempt some form of blending in with the customs.

The last thing Kestrel grabbed was her dagger. Marion

gave her a questioning glance, the first sign of doubt the woman had ever directed toward her, but it was swiftly appeased by a quick explanation.

"It belonged to my mother."

Warmth creased the edges of Marion's eyes. "Very well, my lady."

When Kestrel was finished getting ready, she and Marion made their way to the library; Kestrel devoured the rest of her pastry along the way. Marion bid her a farewell at the door and told her she'd be back to fetch her around lunch.

It wasn't until then that Kestrel remembered what awaited her after her time in the library; she would have to face Queen Signe. Maybe even apologize for fleeing from their training so abruptly. The thought made her stomach clench. If anyone owed an apology, it was the queen. Not that Kestrel could tell her as much, especially not with Thom's life on the line. From this point forward, her sole mission was staying in the queen's good graces. Even if it meant practicing her gruesome magic...

But that could be fretted about later, she decided, entering the library.

Kestrel greeted Barnabus with a cheerful, "Hello."

He lifted his nose from the book it had been buried in. "Oh, you're early."

"Am I? Marion made it seem like I was keeping you waiting."

He glanced at the books strewn about the table and seemed to think more on it. "Maybe you were. I get caught up in reading and lose track of time sometimes." When he looked up, his eyes caught on her hair, making Kestrel touch her braids self-consciously. "I like your hair. It's different. But a good different. Was the book I sent up for you to your liking?"

Embarrassed by her own rudeness, Kestrel flushed. She had started to read the book, but once she'd laid down for bed, sleep had overcome her.

The last thing she wanted was to disappoint him.

"It was perfect. I'm still only at the beginning though, I was too tired to read much before bed."

He nodded, and then seeming self-conscious added, "I haven't read that one, but it seemed like something you'd enjoy. It was actually inspired by some of the Sky-Blessed history—but it's still fiction, so some of the events aren't historically accurate."

"Well now I'm even more excited to read it," she said, earning her one of those rare Barnabus grins. "Speaking of historically accurate events, what did you have in mind for us today?"

Once again, the hours flew by as Barnabus led her through the daring trials and tribulations of the realm and the various kingdoms within it. They covered everything from the War of Destruction where thousands of Sky-Blessed were slain, to the rise of dragons, to the recent sovereignty of Xira, the largest home of Animali in all the realm.

Kestrel soaked in every word. Every detail.

It seemed like no matter what era in history they covered, there was bloodshed, heartache, and betrayal. But there was also freedom and resilience, and she clung onto that the most. Even though the realm was cursed now, it seemed like there would always be a light at the end of every dark tunnel.

When they reached the point in history when the Ashen rose from the dead, Kestrel was struck with an even more fervent hunger to learn.

"They floated up from the Ghostlight Gulf and claimed to be the fallen Sky-Blessed from the War of Destruction some thousands of years prior."

"But that means—" Kestrel tried doing the math, but it was too much. "Elora mentioned her resurrection, but I hadn't realized how long she'd been dead before then. That must've been so disorienting, to wake up—or come back around, or whatever—so many years later."

"Probably not as much as you think."

"What do you mean?"

"Well, they don't remember much from their lives before. Just their deaths."

"That's horrible," Kestrel said, the end of her braid dropping from her aghast mouth. "And that's all they remember? Nothing about their lives before or anything?"

Barnabus nodded. "At least as far as we know."

Kestrel tried to imagine what it would be like to be dying one second and then to suddenly appear in a lake the other, to swim to the surface among people who looked like you but whom you didn't recognize. And then to be forced to learn about your own history from books written by the very people who killed you—the very people who would then turn around and decide *you* were the unsafe ones. The ones too deadly to trust.

"It sounds so...disorienting. So frustrating."

Barnabus nodded his agreement, as he dragged his

finger along the book in search of anything else he might want to share. But Kestrel was stuck on something else he had said.

"What did you mean by, *as far as we know*?"

He lifted his head, auburn curls shifting by his ears. "Well, the thing about history is that it's told from one viewpoint. These books were written by Ironblood and Caeloran scholars mostly, maybe a few by Vallondeans. But there have been centuries of strife and distrust between many of the kingdoms, as I'm sure you've gleaned from everything we've covered so far. And that means that our access to certain perspectives in history has been limited. Take for example the Skogaran's rebellion from Irongate—everything we've read is about the devastating impact their rebellion had on our kingdom, and not the brave and tumultuous fight for freedom that your people endured."

The words *your people* made her stomach flutter. She had been so removed from the realm, from any of it for so long now that it was easy to forget her connections to these stories. Her own mother had been Skogaran. According to the history Barnabus had shared, this rebellion—or rather, their *uprising*—could've happened during her mother's lifetime.

What Kestrel wouldn't give to talk to her about it, to hear her side of the story.

Barnabus closed the book, and they sat in silence for a long moment.

Kestrel's mind was anything but silent though. Her thoughts were a churning mess, ricocheting from Elora and her tragic life, to her mother's, then to Thom, all the while stewing on what history had taught her could happen to prisoners of war, or anyone caught on the losing side.

The more she thought about Thom and the violent history surrounding Grimtol, the more she worried about her training with Queen Signe.

Kestrel didn't want to be part of the dark history that surrounded this place, and she feared if she practiced this dark magic, she would be. But she was conflicted because currently it seemed like her only chance at saving Thom, the only leverage she could offer the queen. Giving up on that seemed unbearable; a world without Thom was unbearable.

But was that how so many people throughout history had excused their own violent choices? Had it all been to save their loved ones?

By the time Marion returned, Kestrel's stomach was a tight knot. All she wanted to do was retire to her bedchamber and curl up by the fire for hours. Not that she could though. The queen would be waiting.

But to Kestrel's great relief, once they bid Prince Barnabus farewell and were heading down the hall, Marion informed her that Queen Signe had given her the day off.

"Not feeling well, I'm afraid." And if by way of explanation, she added, "The curse, and all that." Kestrel wanted to know what she meant exactly, but was too relieved to ask. They were just coming upon the dining hall doors. "So, it looks like you'll have the afternoon to yourself. Would you like me to come fetch you once you've finished your lunch?"

"No, I'll be alright," Kestrel said, confident that Micah or the others would have plenty ideas of how they could spend the afternoon. Maybe she could convince him to try to teach her how to swim, like he'd promised on their march up here.

Marion bid Kestrel farewell and left her to it.

Kestrel burst into the dining hall, eager to see her friends. But the room was empty. Well, empty of the princes she had hoped to find inside. The table, however, was yet again stacked high with a variety of pastries and potatoes and stews.

Maybe the princes would be coming by shortly, Kestrel reasoned. After all, according to Barnabus, they had gotten an untimely start to their day, so maybe she was just early for lunch.

Kestrel sat quietly in one of the chairs and began picking at a small plate of food. She wasn't very hungry considering she had spent most of the first-hours worrying about what her time with Queen Signe would entail. But she also wasn't one to let good food go to waste.

Kestrel forced a few bites of bread and cheese down while she waited.

And waited.

By the time a regular meal would've ended, still none of the princes showed.

Eventually, Kestrel decided that she would try finding them on her own. At the very least, some exploration of the castle would do her some good, help her get her bearings more.

When she was ready to leave, Kestrel grabbed a lit

candlestick from the table, worried she might accidentally stumble upon one of the queen's numerous darkened corridors. Fortunately, she never did, likely because she hadn't needed to go very far at all before finding the first signs of other people.

Only a few rooms down from the dining hall, Kestrel heard a faint humming. She followed the dreamy sound all the way to a lavish ballroom with tall arched windows covered in lead strip designs. Outside, the sun abruptly set, the moon launching into the sky and casting the gothic ballroom in a faint, blue light.

And dancing in the center of the ballroom floor was Princess Elora.

Elora wore a crimson, floor-length ballroom gown with white gloves that came all the way up to her elbows. She twirled about the room with more grace than a flower being blown by the wind. She made it look so effortless, so easy to twist and pose, despite the heaviness of the robust skirt that was surely weighing down her every flawless movement. In fact, as Kestrel watched her, she couldn't think of ever seeing someone more natural in their element. The only thing odd about it was the way Elora was holding her arms out, as if someone else should've been nestled inside them.

It filled Kestrel with an overwhelmingly amount of sadness, especially following everything she had just learned about the Ashen and the way they had been treated.

The somber nature of the song Elora was humming wasn't helping either.

On her next twirl around the open floor, Elora's eyes finally fell upon Kestrel and her flickering candle.

The princess halted abruptly. Her arms fell to her sides.

"What are you doing here?" she snapped.

"Oh," Kestrel said, nervously glancing about the room and fidgeting with her hair. She hadn't meant to stare; Elora's spell of elegance had just been too captivating and she had forgotten what she'd been doing. "I was just looking for the princes."

Elora frowned, a hint of worry edging her expression. "Why? Was Prince Leighton supposed to be here? Did the queen send him?"

"I don't know. I just—" Kestrel sensed Elora's hostility, but didn't understand it. She hadn't even mentioned Leighton by name. Then, with sinking dread, it dawned on her. "Why would the queen send him here?"

"To practice for our wedding, obviously." Princess Elora pulled her gloves higher, adjusting them to make sure every inch of her skin was still covered.

The truth stung even more than Kestrel was prepared for. And it shouldn't. Prince Leighton was no longer of interest to her. He had betrayed her and lied to her in too many ways to ever recover from, at least romantically.

But of course, Kestrel was lying to herself. Trying to convince herself that *he* was the reason for this newfound twinge of jealousy. When in reality, it had everything to do with the alluring princess before her.

Before she could think better of it, before the idea had even fully formed in her foolish skull, Kestrel heard herself blurt out, "Well if you need a dance partner, I could help."

Elora stilled. And Kestrel regretted the suggestion instantly. She had only wanted to help—and perhaps be near to the strange girl again, the one who had haunted her thoughts ever since she left the gardens.

The princess huffed.

"Fine," was not the answer Kestrel had expected Elora to utter, but it was one that she gladly—if not a little nervously—accepted.

CHAPTER 29

THE DANCE OF TWO PRINCESSES

ELORA

The queen's command still rang in Elora's ears: *Befriend the girl, make her feel welcomed, and encourage her to use her magic to bring an end to this forsaken curse.* She told herself it was for that reason—and that reason alone—that she was accepting the offer.

This was a means to an end.

A way to ensure her wedding day would go as smoothly as possible.

This meant nothing more than that, regardless of whatever had occurred between Elora and Kestrel in the gardens the night before.

But even after Elora accepted the offer, Kestrel started at her, dumbfounded for a moment.

It made heat rise to Elora's cheeks, much the same way it had when she'd found the lost princess watching her dance from the ballroom doorway.

"Well don't look so shocked," Elora snapped, chin

pointing high. The longer the girl watched her, the more difficult it was becoming to convince herself her reasonings had been innocent. She gestured to Kestrel's clothes in an attempt to keep things nonchalant. "I mean, you are wearing boy's clothes, so it should be easy to pretend."

But Elora's words came out sharper than intended, that tongue of hers always more of a blade than a caress. It was far from the compliment Kestrel deserved. She softened her tone and tried again.

"You do look rather...dashing in them, though."

It was a swing too far in the opposite direction. Too vulnerable. Too...honest. It made her feel as if she were caught in a blaze, worsened only by the radiant smile Kestrel flashed her in response.

"Why thank you, my lady. And you look rather..." she thought for a long moment, seeming to struggle to find anything nice to say. It hurt more than Elora expected. Until the lost princess leaned in closer and whispered, "What would be a proper way to compliment the future Queen of Irongate?"

Elora battled her blushing and lost. "You could call me ravishing."

Kestrel bowed at the waist. "In that case, you look positively ravishing. Now, may I have this dance?"

Elora's heart trilled at the sight of Kestrel's offered hand. It should be such a mundane gesture, two hands meeting. It was the sort of motion even strangers went through on a daily basis whenever they greeted one another.

But for Elora, there was a lifetime of hurt and pain behind the simple act.

And now, here Kestrel was, threatening to unravel it. To wash it away like the gentle tide lapping upon the shore.

Everything inside her felt like it was shattering. But Elora kept her tone as sour as she could muster. "Yes, yes, let's get this over with." It was her only defense against a girl who seemed so keen on breaking all of her walls down.

Bounding across the room as spry as a spring chicken, Kestrel set her candlestick in an empty sconce, dusted what Elora suspected was crumbs from lunch onto her trousers, and returned to Elora in the center of the ball-room. Elora watched her the entire time, admiring the way the new bluish-grey doublet hugged Kestrel's frame, and the slight curve the trousers gave to her hips. It was more of a subtle femininity compared to the lavish gowns she was accustomed to seeing royalty wear, herself included, but it suited Kestrel nicely. Made her look like the distinctive and daring woman that she really was.

When Kestrel was barely more than a few steps away from her, she stopped. "So, how do I do it?"

Elora frowned. "What do you mean how do you do it? Have you never danced before?"

"Of course I have!" Kestrel spluttered and fidgeted on her toes. "I just—every dance is different. There are different customs and all that. Right?"

Rolling her eyes at the semi-valid point, Elora pointed to one side of her hip.

Kestrel's eyes followed and she swallowed hard before her hand closed around Elora's waist. Even through the fabric of the gown, Elora felt Kestrel's warmth. It pulsed across her hip and abdomen, threatening to bloom else-where as well.

Elora cleared her throat and fixed her attention on the next step. She placed one hand on Kestrel's shoulder and held the other one up in a readied position. Kestrel raised her hand, but stopped again.

"You sure it's okay? I wouldn't want to break the no-touching rule and all that—"

"Oh shut up and take my hand."

Laughing to herself, Kestrel obliged, cupping Elora's hand into her own as if they had done this a thousand times. It fit there better than it fit in the gloves she was wearing. Like Kestrel's hand was the perfect contour of her own. The Sky-Blessed or whoever designed them would be cruel for that, considering no matter how Elora felt for her, they would never be able to touch skin-to-skin, not without grave consequences.

But oh, how Elora wouldn't be daydreaming about it for days to come...wondering what Kestrel's touch might feel like. Whether it would be velvety smooth or ruggedly tough. Something told her it was the latter, and the thought of those rough hands against hers made her stomach dip.

Elora shook the thought from her mind.

She couldn't afford such frivolous fantasies.

She was getting married.

She refocused her attention on the dance and began humming a common, upbeat tune she'd heard at a few weddings prior to her imprisonment. A dance that would start as just the two of them, the bride and groom, before others would be invited to join in. A crowd of couples would circle around them, mimicking the same one-two-three rhythmic steps, only at the top of the third count, they would swap partners, while the bride and groom would remain together for the duration of the song.

But as soon as Elora and Kestrel began the dance, the other princess was already stumbling over herself. At first Elora thought maybe it was just her own gown, the bulbous material making it difficult for Kestrel to maneuver with, considering she likely hadn't danced with anyone in such a garment before.

But then Elora realized she was tripping over her own feet as much as she was Elora's skirt.

"Ow," the Ashen princess grumbled when Kestrel somehow managed to step on her toe through the thick layers of fabric. "You're terrible at this."

Kestrel's smile was crooked, uncertain. "I said I'd help, I never said I was any good."

"Usually when people offer help, it's because they have expertise."

Kestrel feigned looking thoughtful. "Huh. I'll try to remember that next time. You, on the other hand, seem to be great at this."

Curse this girl, and curse Elora, for the way her heart seemed to flutter at the ever-beaming smile Kestrel flashed her.

"When is the wedding?"

That question cooled her down a bit.

"A few days' time," she said stiffly.

"By the Hollows, that's soon." She bit her lip before

mustering another sheepish grin. "Well, I guess it's lucky for you then that you're better at this than I am."

Elora barked a haughty laugh.

It made Kestrel's smile grow, as if she was imbued with sunshine. "Well, at least I got you to laugh. I don't think I've ever heard you do that before."

The unfortunate truth was that she was almost right. Elora couldn't remember the last time she'd laughed genuinely, at least before having met the princess.

Doing her best to deflect the comment, Elora rolled her eyes. "This is utterly useless. I thought you said you'd danced before." She waited for Kestrel's reply. When she didn't, she started to become concerned. "You have danced before, right?"

Kestrel groaned. "Alright, fine. I may have overstated the truth a little."

"How much is a little?"

The lost princess winced, still trying to keep up with Elora's footwork. "Like...one time?"

"One time!" Now it was Elora's footing that faltered. "When was this? And what dance, because I'm not convinced you know the footwork for any."

Kestrel still wore a pathetic but playful grimace as she looked down at Elora with her emerald green eyes. "Last night? And I'm not sure what the dance was—to be honest, I didn't know there were different types."

Something tightened around Elora's chest then, a twinge she tried ignoring. Had this dance happened before the gardens, or after? Not that it mattered to her, any.

Elora straightened her back and continued the dance, leading Kestrel along the way as best as she could. But it was like dancing with a newborn calf. The poor girl was all gangly limbs and too-slow toes.

"With whom?" Elora asked, trying and failing to keep the tightness from her words.

"Oh, just Micah. Their brother Nic was playing music on some instrument, and the twins were dancing up on the table. Micah pulled me up to join them. But to be honest, it was nothing really like this."

Relief washed over her. At least it wasn't with Leighton. For multiple reasons, that made her feel better.

Elora was much more relaxed when she said, "That's not how a princess is expected to behave. You can't just go dancing up on tables whenever you're beckoned."

"Why not?"

Elora guffawed. "What do you mean why not? Because! It's—you—that's just not how things are done."

Kestrel shrugged, a coy tilt to her smile. "Maybe it should be."

Elora's mouth fell agape. She was too stunned—no, too flabbergasted to have a retort.

"What?" Kestrel laughed. "I'm just saying, I had fun. I see nothing wrong with that."

Releasing her hand, Kestrel used her fingertips to tap Elora's jaw closed. Then she grabbed her hand again and leaned to the side, as if she was trying to resume their dancing. But Elora was frozen in place. Not only by the gentle but calloused touch of Kestrel's fingers upon her chin, but also by the reality of their conversation.

These two girls, they came from different worlds. One, a place that had taught the Ashen princess that life was a brutal game of deceit and strategy, with both a winning side and losing side—and Elora had been born to the losing team. While the other had come from a place that had sheltered her, allowed her space to follow her whims, to make her own rules, and helped her develop the belief that life could be filled with joy if she just believed it so.

One of those worlds was reality. The other, a falsehood that could get someone killed.

They had both been prisoners, it's just that one of them didn't realize it.

Abruptly, Elora released Kestrel's hand and shoulder, the dance done.

"Life isn't all about fun and merriment. You would already know that if you hadn't spent your entire life in captivity."

Kestrel looked taken aback, a frown deepening between her eyes. "I wasn't a prisoner. Thom took care of me."

Another haughty laugh as Elora rolled her eyes. "How can you still defend him? After everything you've seen. You've said it yourself; he *lied* to you."

"He didn't—I mean, he did lie to me, I know that. But I also know he had his reasons. I just haven't been able to ask him for an explanation yet."

"What's there to ask? Blessed moon, he stole you from your own parents and then lied to you about the state of the realm, told you that there was no one living out here anymore, told you the kingdoms were festering with monsters, all to ensure you never tried to escape. I mean, he may not have locked you away, but a cage is a cage—"

"You're wrong!" Kestrel's voice was shattered glass, fragile but sharp. Elora could hear the way her words shredded her throat, fighting through a lump of tears just to burst free. But it was the rage that simmered behind her green eyes that gave Elora pause, like she would set the world ablaze if she could. Just like her mother had. "You don't know him like I do. He was a good father."

"A good father?" But Elora, too, could wield anger. Hers had been building for nearly half a century. And no longer could she contain it. "He was my torturer!"

The last word shot across the ballroom with the precision of an arrow.

Elora stood tall, proud in her conviction to speak her truth.

That is, until the arrow found its mark, and penetrated Kestrel's last thread of strength. Her rage snuffed out. All that was left was a lifetime of questions, of doubt, of horror. And Elora watched it all unravel around her.

"Kestrel, wait. I—"

Kestrel's eyes glistened like lakes that were ready to overflow.

Elora reached for her, but the princess was already fleeing.

Then she was gone.

And Elora stood in the empty ballroom utterly alone.

Which should've been fine—she had spent decades with no one and nothing to keep her company. The loneliness had become a comfort. A reprieve from the pain. One she told herself she welcomed.

Except this time, the loneliness felt unbearable. Weighted down by pity and guilt.

And it infuriated her. She had done nothing wrong. She'd only spoken the truth.

But what she had forgotten in her anger and pain was a crucial truth she and most of the Ashen had wished others had learnt years and years ago: that there were always two sides to every story, and no one was ever just a villain, no matter how much someone claimed them to be.

CHAPTER 30

A VISION, A CURE

KESTREL

With her fists clenched at her sides, Kestrel stormed down the castle halls. She could feel the steam seeping from her nose. Her enraged huffs echoed down the empty chambers.

Elora didn't know what she was talking about. She didn't know Thom. She didn't know anything about Kestrel and her upbringing, let alone why Thom had done what he'd done. They were all assuming the worst intentions from him without so much as hearing his side of the story—but not Kestrel. She *would* hear him out. If it was the last thing she did.

No more waiting and biding her time.

If the queen was too ill to train her today, then Kestrel would take her training into her own hands. And if the Sky-Blessed needed blood to invoke her magic, she'd give it to them. All Kestrel needed was a knife.

She blustered back to the dining hall, the only room where she was certain she could find one. At least a dozen knives rested on the dining table. Most were just butter knives with blades too dull to cut skin, but there were a few sharper knives placed next to various roasts and meats. Those blades were serrated, perfect for cutting through flesh.

Then Kestrel remembered the dagger Queen Signe had given her. The one that belonged to her mother. Kestrel retrieved it from her belt. She admired the fox carving on the hilt before her eyes dragged along the sharp edge of the blade.

This would hurt.

Before she could talk herself out of it, Kestrel slid the sharp end of the dagger across her palm. She hissed at the sting of flesh tearing and resisted the urge to clutch the wound tight. But she needed the blood. Needed to give a sacrifice to the Sky-Blessed so that they might do her bidding.

The ruby red liquid gushed onto the table.

Realizing she was making a mess, Kestrel grabbed an empty goblet and let it pool into the chalice instead. As her blood continued to pour from the hot wound, she called to the mighty idols the way she'd heard Thom and Signe beseech them, although she felt foolish doing so.

"Oh great and powerful Sky-Blessed, hear my plea! Accept my offering and guide my path. Tell me what I need to do to save Thom from his imprisonment and possible execution!"

She wasn't sure if the shouting was necessary, but it seemed fitting. The Sky-Blessed needed to hear her, wherever they were. Her plea needed to reach them.

With the goblet held high, Kestrel waited.

And waited.

At the first breath of wind that blew through the room, she nearly cried.

It worked. The Sky-Blessed had heard her call. They were sending her an answer!

Kestrel set the goblet down on the table and inhaled the magic that danced around her. It smelled of charcoal, rain, and salt. A fiery spark that felt like fate. And Kestrel wanted to bathe in it.

And then, her vision clouded with darkness.

Panic overcame her.

No, not now.

The dining room faded. The burning in her hand disappeared much like every other sense of her being. She wasn't used to these visions yet. Wasn't sure she ever would be. Only once the darkness was complete, did light begin to shine through the cracks.

Kestrel recognized the bare limbs of the tree branches in the Hollows quicker this time. The same scene played around her. A rainstorm of black feathers. A lake with a blue light seeping from the depths.

Only this time, Kestrel wasn't alone.

Beside her stood Princess Elora, as striking as ever. The chains around her neck and wrists were gone. The crown that was embedded or tattooed in her forehead was dazzling, the silver ink shining as she reached up toward the sky and gathered a collection of feathers into her arms. And she was smiling. Grinning, completely unburdened by the cold and hardened exterior Kestrel had come to associate with her.

She was radiant, but not radiant like the shining of the

sun. Her radiance was darker, like the voidless gleam of a black gemstone, or the velvety petals of a midnight flower.

She was beauty. She was darkness. She was a Queen of Death.

Kestrel wouldn't have been able to turn away from her, if it hadn't been for the splashing she heard from her other side.

Twisting around, Kestrel found Signe trudging into the lake, the water like ink around her. When she reached the center, the queen sunk her hands into the black fluid, all the way up to her shoulders, until she could grab the blue light from below. She brought it up to her face, a star held in her grasp. The light shone so brightly, Kestrel had to cover her eyes, but she could still make out the shadow of the queen, a light and dark version of her splitting in two from the radiant blue glow. The light version of her almost seemed juvenile, like there was a touch of innocence about her that belonged to a younger version of herself. While the darker side of her became mangled and beastly, a monster ready to prowl.

All the while, the blue light kept shining until all Kestrel could see was blinding brightness.

Her head swam. Ears ringing. And Kestrel didn't realize she was screaming until she came to in Efrem's arms. The rafters of the castle ceiling whizzed by in a blur. With shaking breaths, Kestrel managed to lift her head up and find Micah jogging beside them as the three of them bounded down one of the castle hallways.

"What's happening?" she asked, voice hoarse. "Where are you taking me?"

Micah startled at the sound of her. Jerking around, he

rushed in closer. "Thank the sun. Are you alright?" She started to nod her head, but stopped when the slightest movement made her dizzy. "We came in for a quick bite before training, and you were passed out on the floor, blood all over your hand. And your eyes! They were... gone!"

"Gone?"

"They were white," Efrem corrected. "Rolled all the way back like you were under some trance." He said it like a question, and Kestrel felt compelled to answer.

"I think I was. I think...I think I'm having visions like my mother used to."

"Visions?" Micah asked, still seeming dubious of her well-being. "Like...magic?"

This time when she nodded, the world wasn't quite as wobbly. Thinking she had regained at least some composure, and feeling a little ridiculous in Efrem's hulking arms, she beckoned him to put her down and he did. She noticed the haphazard wrap around her aching palm and the tear in the sleeve of his uniform and thanked him.

"So what does this mean? Are you, like, able to use your magic now?" Micah was still swarming her, watching her every move to make sure she was alright.

Although she felt utterly exhausted, Kestrel managed a small grin and confirmed his suspicions. "It would appear so."

Without missing a beat, Micah punched her in the arm, all signs of worry evaporating.

"Well good on ya! Although maybe next time don't attempt to bleed out on your own. If we hadn't come when we had, you could've died."

Kestrel staggered on the impact, but managed to hold herself up. "Over a cut to the hand? That's unlikely."

"It's true." His chest puffed up with mocked bravado. "We saved your life just now."

"My heroes," Kestrel said, her voice dripping with sarcasm.

Only Efrem didn't laugh, too focused on what really mattered. "What was the vision about?"

In her disoriented state, Kestrel had almost forgotten about it. The eerie black forest flooded her thoughts now though. "I think I was in the Hollows."

Micah shuddered. "Sounds more like a nightmare."

"It wasn't though. I don't know how to explain it, but it's like something has been calling me there. The queen she—we found something in a lake, and I think it might've been meant to cure her."

Micah and Efrem exchanged a look, Efrem's seeming more skeptical than his brother's.

"Should I...tell her? I mean, I don't want to get her hopes up. I'm still new to this, so I'm not sure what it meant exactly but—I *saw* her change. Whatever was in the Hollows, it's like when she touched it, it leeched the curse out of her, leaving her former self behind."

Looping his arm around Kestrel's shoulder, Micah's grin was conspiratorial. "Not gonna lie, I don't understand this magic stuff either. But if anyone does, it's the queen. And trust me, she'll want to hear about this. In fact, she'll have our heads if we don't tell her, right, Efrem?"

His brother grunted.

"Should we summon her then?" asked Kestrel.

"Now?" Micah's eyes bulged out of his skull. "Dragon's

fire, no! She'd also have our heads for disturbing her on a day like today."

The curiosity was finally too much for Kestrel to bear. "What's wrong with her? I mean, I'm guessing it has something to do with the curse, but I thought her curse was under control as long as she stayed inside the castle, out of sunlight."

"Your guess is as good as mine," replied Micah, folding his arms behind his head. "Every couple of months though, there's a day when she refuses to leave her room, and we are forbidden from seeing her. Not sure if it's because of the curse or something else."

Kestrel worried her lip, wishing she were close enough to the queen to ask, but knowing if she did it would be another one of those she'll-have-your-head type of things.

"But—" continued Micah— "first thing tomorrow, we'll send word for her, tell her you'd like to speak with her immediately."

He started walking back the way they'd came, presumably to return to the quick bite he had left back in the dining hall. Despite herself, Kestrel stopped him.

"Wait, we'll need to summon the princess too."

He looked over his shoulder. "Oh yeah? You want your new best friend there?"

Kestrel cheeks burned. "She's not my—no. But she was in the vision. I think she has to come there with us."

Shrugging, Micah continued down the hall. "We can try, but don't get your hopes up. The queen hasn't allowed Princess Elora to leave the grounds. Not until her wedding is final."

It made Kestrel's stomach sour to think about it, both

the wedding and Elora's continued captivity. Despite their disagreement earlier, nobody deserved to be kept locked away.

Even if it wasn't a matter of morality though, the vision had been quite clear: Elora had been with them. More than that, she had been unbound. Free.

And come tomorrow, Kestrel would have to insist they allow her to join them in the same way, because somehow, she knew that was the only way they would be able to see her vision to fruition.

That was what the Sky-Blessed had shown her.

That was how she would save Thom.

CHAPTER 31
A DECREE FROM THE ORACLE PRINCESS
ELORA

Elora was brushing her long, silver hair at her vanity when a gust of wind rattled the windows. It had been blustery of late, the kingdom starting to settle into its autumn, which meant that Elora's skin was beginning to crack. It happened in any climate, really, except Eynallore's.

But for the first time in years, Elora had access to oils and creams to help moisten her skin and ease her discomfort.

She dragged a finger over the handful of vials the queen had procured for her—well, not personally, but she had asked a servant to purchase some from the market in preparation for the wedding. The queen was difficult to read like that. Detached and menacing one minute, but caring and considerate another. Of course, Elora knew that her kind gestures always came at a cost. A bribe. Or as a reward for a job well done.

These were clearly a thank you for how well she had been doing with Kestrel.

They also served as a threat. A reminder of the queen's power and the numerous luxuries she could take away from Elora should she falter.

But today, Elora didn't want to ruminate on the malicious message behind each vial, and instead relished the soothing caress as she spread the first cream onto her forearm. It smelled of raindrops with a floral undertone that immediately had Elora drifting away into memories. She had expected to fall into Eynallore's forests, the place she frequented whenever struck by nostalgic feelings and stimulations.

This time, however, it was Irongate's gardens that she envisioned, and a certain unsophisticated yet bubbly princess beside her.

Kestrel's arms were around Elora's waist, leaning her backward. A strand of her fiery hair streamed down from behind her ear, and tickled Elora's cheek. She wanted to reach up and coil it around her finger. Wanted to tap each and every one of Kestrel's delicate freckles.

Elora's eyes fluttered open and she shook the daydream out of her mind. To the furthest depths where it couldn't bother her again.

It would only serve to torment her more, for in a few short days, her fate would be sealed. Elora would be a married woman, never to be touched by another—unless her and Prince Leighton came to some sort of arrangement—

Elora set the jar of hand cream down so roughly she was surprised the jar didn't shatter.

Frivolous; that's what these imaginings were. Even if he would agree to something like that, it wouldn't be extended to Kestrel, not when his conflicting feelings for the princess were already so clear.

There would be no happiness for her at the culmination of this union. At best, she could hope for quiet contentment. And the sooner she accepted that, the easier it would be.

And yet...

Her thoughts drifted back to Kestrel, to their last conversation—if she could call it that. It ended more like a confrontation, but Elora hadn't meant for it to. Her words hadn't come out right, or at least not as delicately as she would've liked them to. But she hadn't lied either, so she shouldn't feel so torn about it. But the hurt on Kestrel's face as she stormed out of the ballroom was enough to make her second guess everything. Maybe if she talked to her—

Just then, a quiet knock rattled on her bedroom door. Elora startled at the sound, still re-adapting to the notion that having a visitor didn't mean that her torture was about to begin again.

Elora stood from her vanity, answered the door, and found a servant outside with her head bowed.

"Beautiful day to you, Princess Elora."

Elora returned the gesture, although she was still not accustomed to that either. She wondered how long it would take for her to get used to being greeted by title and with signs of respect again.

"Beautiful day to you as well," she parroted, a little stunted.

The woman thrust a piece of parchment out toward her, the writing unmistakable, even at first glance. "You've been summoned to the throne room by the queen."

"I'll be there," she said, voice shaking as she accepted the summons. "Thank you."

The servant left and Elora scoured the parchment for any indication of what this might be about. Another last-minute wedding meeting? It seemed unlikely, considering typically a servant would simply come and inform her of those; they had never delivered an official summons.

But the note in her hand was simple, vague.

Dread pooled in Elora's belly like poison. Had the queen found out about her argument with Kestrel yesterday? If she had, there was no telling how displeased she would be. Elora had very clear instructions: befriend the girl, not make her cry and storm out of rooms. What if she had barricaded herself away, refusing to come out and participate in the queen's lessons?

If given the chance, Elora would apologize—not only because she knew that's what Queen Signe would want, but because it was what she wanted as well.

Hopefully the queen would give her the chance to set things right.

Elora was already dressed for the day, wearing a silver, long-sleeve gown that fell all the way down to the floor like moonlight draped over her body. She took a few moments to tie back the top half of her hair before venturing down to the throne room to face the queen.

When she finally arrived though, she was stunned by who she found inside.

Kestrel stood in the middle of the candlelit room, wearing another outfit that seemed more suitable for a young man than a princess. Not that Elora minded. In fact, she admired her all the more for it. Here was a girl who didn't care what the queen's expectations were of her. If she wanted to wear a doublet and trousers, and braid her hair like the wild Skogarans, then that's exactly what she would do.

Kestrel startled at Elora's entrance. Not in the way that it suggested she was surprised to see her, not like Elora had been. It was more of a general jumpiness, like she was on edge about something. Perhaps she'd been standing in a dark and quiet room alone for too long.

But what were they both doing there? Had the queen summoned her as well?

As Elora entered the room, Kestrel looked anywhere but at her. Okay, so she was still upset. Rightfully so. But Elora could fix that. Especially since it was just the two of them, giving them time to speak alone.

Instead of taking her spot beside the throne, she walked to the center of the candelabras next to Kestrel. She forced her to look upon her. "I owe you an apology."

"It's fine," Kestrel said, her mouth drawn tight. "We both have our truths."

Elora winced. "Truth isn't always one thing though. And Darius and I we...we have history. My judgement of him is clearly biased because of it, and it is unfair of me to project my truth—my pain—upon you."

With a shrug, Kestrel told her it was fine again, but Elora sensed it was anything but. She wasn't reaching her. Not fully. Because she wasn't being vulnerable enough yet.

So Elora would force herself to go deeper. To share more of the heartache that she hated to revisit.

"I did the same thing everyone did to me. I villainized him because...that's what he was to me, Kestrel. I can't change that for him, and I can't lie to you and tell you I forgive him for all the pain he caused me. But I have been the villain before. My loved ones have been villains too. All of my people. And so, although Darius did unthinkable things to me, I also know that there is always another side to the story, and that means he likely has good in him as well."

When Kestrel's eyes finally met hers, they glistened like dew-kissed leaves.

"Please, forgive me for succumbing to such simple-minded ways," Elora added, falling into her gaze.

Kestrel gave her a subtle nod and it almost broke Elora's heart all over. Kestrel reached for her as if she wanted to give her a hug again, and this time Elora wasn't sure if she would back away. She had her shackles on, the hailstone bracelets and necklace. Kestrel would be safe.

But before either of them could lean any closer, the main door leading into the throne room opened, and Prince Leighton strode inside.

The girls jumped back from one another. Elora used the momentum to take her place at the side of the queen's throne, while Kestrel seemed to become suddenly trans-fixed by the dancing flames in the nearest candelabra. If they were hoping for discreet, Leighton's suspicious gaze as it shifted between the two of them was a good indica-tion that they had failed.

He cleared his throat as he approached Kestrel, took

her hand, and planted a gentle kiss atop it. Elora didn't know what shocked her more, that her betrothed was so blatantly bestowing affection upon another woman in front of her, or that he was doing it so casually with Kestrel in particular.

From where she stood, she couldn't hear the quiet words he said to her before he took his spot on the opposite side of the throne, but she noted the guilty angle of Kestrel's gaze as he walked away.

Something had clearly happened between the two of them. Kestrel had mentioned the Fortress of Thirst and his betrayal of her there, and Elora hadn't thought to ask more about it. She wasn't sure if she should. Wasn't sure if she wanted to know.

Soon after Leighton's emergence, the twins entered the throne room as well, the queen following shortly after.

Everyone waited patiently as Queen Signe claimed her spot on the throne and fanned her sleek silken dress out over her legs.

"Thank you all for joining us today. I'm told we have some rather exciting news."

Elora frowned as the queen spoke. If she wasn't the one with news, then who was?

Sucking in a deep breath, Kestrel stepped forward. "Queen Signe, you told me the other day that my mother's magic gave her the sight, and I believe it's happening to me as well."

The queen clapped her hands together. "Well that's wonderful news indeed. Please, tell me, these visions of yours, when did they happen?"

"I had one yesterday," Kestrel continued, and gestured

to the twins. "Micah and Efrem found me in the dining hall in the midst of one."

"Her eyes were completely rolled back," Micah interjected. "I thought she was dying or something. We threw her in Efrem's arms and started carrying her to the—"

The queen gave a swift swat of her hand, silencing him. Her focus was trained on Kestrel.

"Tell us about the vision, my darling niece," Queen Signe said, in that cool and graceful tone of hers that Elora had come to fear. "That must be why you've summoned us."

Perhaps *that* was the source of the queen's nearly imperceptible irritation; she didn't like that Kestrel had been the one to call them to court. The queen was not one for sharing power.

Kestrel, likely oblivious to it, continued toeing the line of danger.

"It is. It seemed important. In the vision, I was in the Hollows—well, the three of us were." She gestured to herself, the queen, and then—to Elora's surprise—to her as well. "There were black feathers falling down from the sky—all over. Hundreds of them. Princess Elora was gathering them up in her arms..."

Kestrel's words faded as Elora's heart became a solid stone in her chest.

Visions could mean anything. It was foolish to attempt to interpret them. But feathers were of great importance to the Ashen, for before they were slain, their wings had been eviscerated from their backs. Even after death, their rebirths did not regenerate them. And yet, they still felt the absence of them, despite forgetting the majority of their lives before their re-awakenings, most of the Ashen still grieved the gruesome scars on their shoulders where their glorious wings had once been.

The feathers in Kestrel's vision, what if they were showing her the way her people could reclaim their wings?

She shook the impossible hope from her mind, if only to glean more details from Kestrel's recounting.

"That's when you, my queen, saw a blue hue in a lake beside us. You waded into the depths, following the light until you were standing right above it. And when you gathered it into your arms, I saw—you were—" Kestrel struggled to put words to what she had seen, leaving the queen hanging on the edge of her throne.

"What happened to me? Spit it out!"

Flinching at the hostility she likely hadn't yet seen from the queen, Kestrel spluttered, "It changed you. It was like it sucked the cursed parts out of you, and only your pure former self remained."

Hope hollowed Elora out like a dark and ominous tunnel. Hope was dangerous. It meant the possibility for disappointment. For grief. And yet it consumed her and everyone else in the throne room all the same.

If this was true, if Kestrel had really foreseen the answer to the curse that plagued the kingdoms, then this changed everything. It would mean they could save every-one. All the monarchs. Unfortunately, it would mean curing King Everard. But it would also mean curing Aethic. Her people and the pain they had endured these past decades, whatever it may have been, it could end. They could be at peace. All the kingdoms could be.

And their wings—maybe they would be restored somehow as well by the power possessed within this blue light? Or maybe they would learn how to reclaim them— Elora wasn't sure. Visions were often difficult to interpret. But this was the closest her people had ever come to having that answer, and for that, she was grateful.

"Is what you speak the truth?" The queen spoke deliberately, each word swift and lethal.

"Yes," answered Kestrel. "I know magic and the curse and all of this is new to me, but I have never understood something more clearly than I did during that vision. We are meant to go into the Hollows. It is where we'll find the cure, and how we'll save the kingdoms."

Slowly, Queen Signe slid back into her chair. She tapped her long nails, thinking, making them all wait. "If there is one thing I've come to understand, it's that one must always heed a seer's visions."

Kestrel's eyes illuminated. "So we'll go? Now?"

The queen let out a haughty laugh. "Not so hastily. I will consult with our scholars first. And, Efrem, I will need you to prepare our men; we can't go wandering into the Hollows unarmed."

"Of course, my queen," said Efrem emphatically, causing Micah to roll his eyes. Elora wasn't sure anyone but her saw, which was probably for the best.

"We'll set out after lunch," the queen said. "That should give everyone a few hours to prepare, both mentally and physically for what lies ahead." She raised her hand to excuse everyone, but Kestrel interjected.

"Queen Signe?"

"Hmm?"

"There was one more detail in the vision. Something that I think was too specific to be ignored."

The queen twirled her fingers in the air. "Well then, go on. Tell us."

Kestrel swallowed hard, and Elora had never seen her look more nervous.

"It's about Princess Elora. In my vision, she wasn't wearing her hailstone chains. She was unbound."

The queen became so unnaturally still that Elora felt herself inching away on instinct.

But Kestrel continued. "I know her touch is lethal to us all, but if she was unchained in the vision, then—"

"Then she shall be unchained for the real thing."

Elora's neck almost snapped off her shoulders to stare at the queen. Leighton's and Micah's as well, although Efrem seemed to be resisting the urge to show any signs of questioning her.

But Elora couldn't believe her ears. Freedom. Kestrel had just earned Elora her freedom. Whether it would be for an hour or a day, it didn't matter. It meant more than the sun and moon and all the oceans combined.

When Elora slowly shifted her gaze toward Kestrel, she found the lost princess beaming, like a complete fool. Like she didn't care if anyone saw how much something like that meant to her as well. As if she was unaware of how easy it was for others to twist your joys against you like knives.

Yet again, Elora admired and pitied her all the more for it.

"We'll meet in the courtyard after lunch. And we'll wait until we're at the Hollow's edge before removing

Princess Elora's collar, but she shall be unbound—as you put it—while we are within the Hollow's boundaries. Is there anything else of importance you need to relay to us?"

Kestrel shook her head, her smile falling away with it.

"Very well."

At the queen's dismissal, Kestrel was the first to leave the throne room, practically skipping as the door shut behind her. None of the brothers moved though, and neither did Elora. They all sensed the queen was not yet done with them.

"Efrem, I'll need you to assign guards to watch Princess Elora's every move while we're in the Hollows. They have permission to strike her down and re-chain her if she so much as breathes the wrong way." Her last words were uttered through clenched teeth, and although she was looking at the twin when she said them, it was clear they were meant for Elora's ears. Another threat. Another warning.

"Of course, my queen." Efrem bowed and also exited the throne room, already acting on his mission.

Having guards on her would be fine. Elora had no plans of misbehaving or stepping out of line. That side of her had been squashed a long time ago. And with the wedding just a handful of days away now, with a less stringent type of freedom so close, there was no way she would jeopardize it.

"That will be all then," Queen Signe said.

Elora didn't wait around to see if she'd change her mind. She took the closest exit, even if it was farther away from the one Kestrel took. She wanted to find her and thank her for what she had done.

But as Elora left the throne room, Leighton inched out of the door behind her.

"Princess Elora, can I speak with you a moment?"

Every vertebra in her spine stiffened at the sound of her future husband's churlish voice. It was rare that he sought her out of his own accord, if he ever had. The two of them tended to avoid each other unless absolutely necessary, so Elora knew that whatever he wanted to speak about, it was either important or awful. Perhaps both.

But she did what was expected of her, and turned around to acknowledge him.

"Of course, Prince Leighton. What brings me the pleasure?"

His face was more scrunched than usual, his eyes distrusting. "Should anything happen to Kestrel or to my family by your hand while we are in the Hollows, know that will be the end of all hope for you. This wedding, this truce between our people, it will be called off, and I will personally drag you down into the dungeons where you will never see the light of day again."

Always a monster in their eyes. No matter how much wickedness they bore in themselves. After all, wasn't it him who shoved Kestrel into the Fortress of Thirst? Hadn't he been the one to risk her life?

Not that she could say that to the future King of Irongate.

Not that she could say anything to make them see what she saw.

So, once again, she did as was expected of her: Elora

gave the prince a polite but stiff bow. "Of course, your majesty. I understand. No harm shall pass to anyone."

He stormed off before she could even rise.

And as she stood there, hinged at the hips and listening to him briskly walk away, Elora wondered what Kestrel would've done in her place. There was no doubt in her mind, Kestrel would've given him a piece of hers.

Elora imagined it then, a version of her life where expectations and years of obedience hadn't weighed her down into submission, if she would've had the nerve to tell the prince that it was him who needed to watch himself. For if he ever harmed Kestrel again, if he so much as laid a finger upon her that was not invited or to her liking, Elora would not hesitate to be his demise.

CHAPTER 32
THE DUNGEON
KESTREL

With the queen meeting with Barnabus, Kestrel found herself suddenly without either of her studies and with some extra time on her hands. Knowing that they were about to venture into a dark and tormented forest where Micah said the tree roots liked to grab people and suck them below the earth, Kestrel readied herself with her dagger, and then decided that she would spend the time trying to relax.

She returned to her bedchamber to find the fire in the hearth was nearly out. Fortunately, she had plenty of experience reigniting one. Before no time at all, the flames were reaching up into the chimney, the heat emanating as far into the room as her vanity. Kestrel grabbed the book Barnabus had sent up for her, plopped down in the armchair closest to the fire, and read.

The story consumed her. Chapters flew by as she read about a brave young woman searching for a magical cure to her sister's ailment. The farther into the pages Kestrel went, the more she thought about the task ahead of them. When they ventured into the Hollows, they'd be searching for a cure as well, although one that no one seemed to even know existed. Stranger still was the fact that it was even in the Hollows to begin with. Micah had told her that the Hollows were created long before the Cursed Night, so it struck Kestrel as odd that the cure to the queen's curse had been in the bottom of a lake there all along.

Unless it also served another purpose.

Maybe it wouldn't just reverse the curse in its victims. Maybe there was something else it had been designed to do.

A soft knock tapped at her door, pulling Kestrel out of her thoughts and out of the book in her hands. If it had been Marion's knock, she might've ignored it—she was already halfway through the story and honestly was curious to see how it ended, just in case some of the story might be useful to them during their time in the Hollows.

But this knock had less gusto behind it than Marion's powerful raps. And if it were the queen, or someone else coming to tell Kestrel they were ready to leave, she didn't want to miss it.

Leaping from her chair, Kestrel kept a finger wedged in the middle of her book as she answered the door.

Elora stood on the other side of the door, one arm crossed over her chest self-consciously. It was the most un-elegant Kestrel had ever seen her.

"Oh!" Kestrel shoved the book behind her back. "Princess Elora. What are you—are the others ready to go?" She wasn't sure why she hid the book, but it felt like the best way to show that the princess had her full attention.

Regardless, Elora hardly seemed to notice. She looked deep in thought, and like she couldn't decide between certain choices that Kestrel wasn't privy to—though she wanted to be. Sometimes it felt as if Elora's mind was as fortified as these castle walls, and Kestrel was stuck outside trying to figure out what lay within them.

Finally, Elora sucked in a breath and blurted, "Why did you do that for me?"

"Sorry?"

"In the throne room. You told the queen that I should be unbound when we entered the Hollows and I—I don't understand why."

Suddenly Kestrel didn't understand either. She thought the princess would be relieved. "Is that not what you wanted?"

"No—I mean yes!" The silver ink of her crown scrunched in time with her face. "Of course it's what I wanted. But...nobody has ever advocated on my behalf like that before. No one has ever suggested the hailstone be removed, not even temporarily."

Kestrel shrugged. "Well, as much as I'd like to take credit for being so heroic in your eyes, it was also just what the vision showed me. It's what needed to happen."

But Elora was shaking her head. "Vision or not, it would've been easy to leave that part out of your retelling. For your own safety, as well as everyone else's."

"Please," Kestrel said, blowing air between her lips, and waving the book in Elora's direction. "I don't believe you'd hurt me for a moment. Or anyone else for that matter."

A sad smile returned to Elora's lips. "Well, you might just be the only one." Kestrel watched as Elora's eyes deepened to the darkest shade of magenta she'd ever seen. So dark it almost reminded her of blood. It wasn't the only thing to change. Elora's entire expression collapsed, her chin wobbling. "Besides, you shouldn't be so certain. My touch is death. It *could* kill you, whether I mean for it to or not. The hailstone is for everyone's safety."

If she was trying to convince Kestrel to change her mind, it wouldn't work. They hadn't known each other for very long, but Kestrel already knew that this woman was not as terrifying as everyone else made her seem. She was fragile and tender. She had a kind heart and a respect for life. Not to mention her resilience and strategic mind for survival. But nowhere in that mix was she dangerous.

"That's just how they justify it," Kestrel reminded her. "It's how Thom justified keeping me in the dark and locked away as well, I think: out of fear." With Thom though, she wasn't sure if he had been afraid for her safety, or afraid that her magic might turn out just like her mother's. She may never know... Kestrel shook the somber thought from her mind. "There was no way I would've ever omitted that part of the vision, not just because it was the truth, but because it honestly should've been said sooner. And I'm sorry I didn't think to."

"That's not something you need to apologize for. You have done more than enough, and I am truly grateful."

"Is it though? You've been granted, what? A few hours of freedom and then they'll return you to chains again?"

Kestrel shook her head. "No one deserves to be a prisoner…"

But as the words left her mouth, she regretted them immediately. Not because they weren't true, but she couldn't help but think back to one of their last conversations, how heated this topic had become for them. Elora wasn't the only prisoner. And even though they had made amends after their argument about Thom, it still felt like dangerous territory to embark upon again.

Besides, Kestrel didn't want to argue with her. Especially not now, right before they were supposed to set off into the Hollows.

To her relief though, Elora didn't seem to be thinking about all of that. Once again, she had retreated into the fortress of her mind, a place shut off to Kestrel. Thankfully, she didn't make her wait long to share what was inside this time.

"Are you busy right now?" Elora asked.

Kestrel, still clutching the spot where she'd left off in her book, tossed the thing onto her bed. "Not anymore. Why?"

Elora's eyes flashed a metallic shade of magenta as one of her rare smiles slowly ticked into place. "I'd like to take you somewhere then."

Kestrel's stomach dipped, a giddiness making her want to prance. "Lead the way."

"Are you planning on telling me where we're headed, or am I supposed to guess?"

"Guess?" Elora's rich laughter bathed the dreary hallway in much needed warmth. "That would take ages in a place like this."

"That's what I hoped you'd say. So tell me! Where are you taking me?" Kestrel was practically bouncing on her heels.

"What are you, part hummingbird?" Elora eyed her up and down as if she was disturbed by Kestrel's display of enthusiasm, but Kestrel could tell by the glow of her eyes that she kind of liked it.

"Not a hummingbird," Kestrel said, matter-of-fact. She stopped hopping around long enough to adjust her evergreen jerkin. "I am a *princess*, I'll have you know."

"The strangest princess I've ever met," muttered Elora.

"You like it," Kestrel said, bumping her hip into Elora's before she could think better of it. To remember that this was a girl who stiffened at touch, who shirked away and caused fights any time they got too close.

But to Kestrel's astonishment, the princess bumped her right back. "Maybe I do."

Kestrel's pulse skipped. Her wide eyes pierced the side of Elora's face, but she refused to look at her. As if it hadn't even happened, though the slight tinge of her cheeks confirmed otherwise.

As much as she wanted to beg Elora to expand upon what exactly she meant by *maybe I do*, she also didn't want to push her luck. Instead, Kestrel decided she would change the conversation. But to what? Every topic that came to mind—the Hollows, the wedding, the last couple decades of Elora's life—none of them were exactly happy topics of discussion. The more time Kestrel spent with Elora though, the more she wanted to get to know her.

"Do you like to read?" she finally asked, hoping it wasn't a stupid or offensive question.

"Sometimes I suppose. If I'm being honest, it's been a long while since I've read a book though. They didn't exactly provide reading material while I was in the dungeons."

Dragon's fire! Kestrel had done it anyway. She'd soured the conversation, even when she'd been trying her best to avoid dangerous topics of conversation. She hoped maybe she could salvage it though.

"What *did* you like to do then? Before...everything?"

Elora faltered a step, but recovered so quickly Kestrel almost could've missed it. She might've, if she hadn't been watching her so intently, listening so fiercely.

A long stretch of silence followed.

"I suppose I enjoyed star-gazing. Dancing. But most of all, my favorite thing to do was tend to the flowers around Eynallore."

Now they were getting somewhere.

"Ah, hence your fondness for the gardens."

"Mhmm."

"Describe it to me. Eynallore, I mean. What's it like there?"

A dreamy haze muted Elora's eyes. "You've never seen anything like it, especially if all you have to compare it to is Vallonde—that's not to say that Vallonde isn't breath-taking in its own right. But Eynallore is like—it's like a dream. In the summer, our meadows fill with amethyst beetles, and whenever the dark hours shadow the lands, the moonlight reflects off their crystalline shells, illuminating everything in a deep, purple glow.

"Since Eynallore is in the northern region, winters hit us harder than they probably hit you in the south—depending on how long you stay up here, you might catch a glimpse. But even winters in Irongate don't compare to winters in Eynallore. Our lands become a snowy wonderland. Ice builds on the tall spires, and our lakes frost over. Our lives slow down, and almost every Ashen can be found outside, ice skating or playing in the snow."

"Snow?"

Elora gawked at her for a moment. But then she blinked the shock away. "Right, of course you wouldn't know. I don't imagine Vallonde gets any. Snow is like sand, I guess. But softer. Colder. More whimsical."

Kestrel tried imagining it, but she was afraid her experiences were too limited to bring it fully to life. Hopefully, Elora was right, and she'd get to experience it here. With her.

"It sounds wonderful."

"It is," Elora said sadly. "But my favorite time of year in Eynallore is spring. That's when all the flowers bloom. It's when Eynallore is truly at its most beautiful. I wish everyone could see it. Maybe then they'd feel differently about us." Kestrel was about to offer her what little words of comfort she had, when Elora interjected, "Anyway, we're almost there. Maybe now you know where we're headed?"

Kestrel had been so thoroughly consumed by Elora's story, that she hadn't realized they were approaching the front doors to the castle. They were leaving. Perhaps Elora was taking her back out to the gardens—it seemed like a place she admired, and Kestrel did as well, considering the heart-skipping memory she had of the two of them by the fountain. It was the first time they had really spoken, truly and deeply, anyway. The first time Kestrel had held her. Felt the curve of her lower back and hips as she kept her from falling.

But as they exited the castle, Elora guided them around the gardens, not into them.

It was only once the grey, gloomy building on the outskirts of the courtyard came into view that Kestrel finally pieced it together.

"The dungeon?" Kestrel peered over at Elora, not wanting to allow her heart to hope. "But why?"

"I have a favor to repay," she said simply, before greeting the guard on duty. "Hello. We've come to see a prisoner."

He bowed, shakily. "P-Princess Elora. I wasn't expected you."

"It is an unexpected visit for me as well. As you may know, my former captor is inside. I wasn't able to face him the other day, but I am ready now."

The guard glanced nervously from side to side. "The queen never said anything about you coming to visit him."

"The queen has had a lot on her mind, as of late. Her niece arrived unexpectedly, she had a bout of illness, and now she's preparing to venture beyond the castle walls for the first time since the Cursed Night."

Kestrel noticed that even the guard seemed surprised to hear that the queen was willingly leaving the castle. But he regained his focus swiftly. "I'm sorry, but without royal approval, I can't let you in."

"*I* give royal approval, as the Ashen Princess. As your future queen." Power rippled off Elora in waves, making Kestrel's stomach dance in strange ways. The guard still looked uncertain, and Kestrel was beginning to doubt this was going to work. She appreciated the effort regardless, and was about to tell Elora that it was alright and not worth the trouble, when the princess steeled her voice even more. "Or I can go tell my betrothed that you have chosen to treat me like some common peasant instead of your Royal Highness, and we shall see how much longer you're permitted to be among his guard then."

Elora spun on her heels so quickly, Kestrel didn't know whether to follow. Before she could decide, the guard spluttered, "Please don't do that. I need this job. It's how I feed my family."

Elora spun back around to face him. "Then we have an agreement."

The guard was already fumbling for his keys. "Make it quick then. Shift change is any minute now, and I'd prefer this to stay between the three of us. Yeah?"

"Of course," Elora said, and flashing Kestrel a quick, private smirk, gestured for her to enter. "After you."

Kestrel slipped by, Elora following after her, and then the door closed behind them with a thud.

"If I had known it would be that easy, I would've asked you to do that days ago."

In the darkness, Kestrel couldn't see Elora's expression clearly, but she heard the pride in her voice all the same.

"There are benefits to having a title. You just have to know how to wield them."

"Well that's one trick I wouldn't mind learning," admitted Kestrel as she stared into the dimly lit room, her eyes still acclimating. "Where do we go from here?"

Elora stepped around her, motioning her forward. "This way. Follow me."

The farther into the darkness they descended, the more detail Kestrel was able to discern. None of it surprised her. Stone walls. Stone flooring. Everything was cold and grey—except for a few cells that had bright blue bars that Kestrel recognized immediately as hailstone. Cells, that she realized, were reserved for their magically inclined prisoners.

Her blood hummed as they walked past them.

"Was one of these cells yours?" Kestrel asked, the dread of a new understanding sinking in.

Ahead of her, Kestrel could just make out the back of Elora's silver-haired head slowly bob once. She didn't think it would be considerate to ask which one, certain that all of them brought up too painful of memories for the princess to share. Instead, she tried keeping them focused on the task at hand, hoping that maybe that would help prevent Elora from sinking too far into her past harrowing experiences of this place.

"Thom wasn't here then, but you know where they're keeping him?"

"I don't." When Elora spoke, her voice was cold. Distant. It sounded as if it was taking a tremendous amount of effort for her to bring herself back, but she did it. "But I'm sure you'll recognize each other when we find him."

Sure enough, eyeballs peeped from within every cell they passed by, and Kestrel searched them all for Thom's familiar nightfall gaze. There must've been dozens of people down here. Upwards of fifty, maybe more. Kestrel tried not to worry her tender heart about their sentences, their need for justice, their plights. Only Thom's could matter to her. His she could change, or so she had to believe.

Most of the eyes that watched them were dull, exhausted things. Others, filled with untamable rage. But few shone quite as bright as Thom's or Elora's. In fact, Kestrel realized that since leaving Vallonde, she'd seen fewer and fewer people with the same sort of striking hues. She filed the thought away as something to ask Barnabus about during their next study session.

Finally, two black eyes blinked from a cell near the end of the dungeon. They would've blended in with the darkness, if not for the starlight glow that Kestrel always said reminded her of the midnight sky on a calm night.

Recognition sparked in them. Then fear. Then outrage.

Kestrel flung herself at the cell door, elation bubbling through her at the sight of him, at the same time Thom stormed forward from the other side.

"What are you still doing here?" he chided, his voice gruffer than usual. His obsidian irises flicked to Elora, and some other emotion washed over him. Not quite fear, but something like it that Kestrel couldn't place.

Behind her, she heard Elora's diaphanous gown rustle as she folded her arms.

Kestrel shifted to block their view of each other. "I don't know how much time we have, but I needed to see you."

Thom's attention shifted back to her. "You need to leave. These people are not your friends. You can't trust them. You can't trust anyone."

And for the first time in all of Kestrel's nineteen years, she thought she was finally seeing him for who he really was. Not the fearless hero of her childhood, the one who had vanquished the cinders and carried her in his arms all the way back to the safety of their tower. Here was a frightened, paranoid man with a lifetime of distress and suffering that she would likely never know, let alone come to understand.

She tried lacing her fingers around his where they gripped the bars. "I'm not leaving until they let you out of here."

Thom's head hung, forehead pressing against the iron. "They won't release me. I am a traitor in their eyes. They're claiming I—I—" When he couldn't bring himself to say it, Kestrel did.

"I know. They're saying you caused the curse—or that you made my mother use her magic to cause it." His gaze met hers briefly, assessing, uncertain about the ground they were walking on. For years, these topics had been secret. Kestrel hoped he wouldn't retreat from them now, not when they had such little time. She wouldn't let him. "That's why I'm going to cure it."

"Cure it? There is no cure. Only Aenwyn—" he swallowed her name like it was a brick, one of the many he had carefully stacked to construct the wall of lies that surrounded their lives. Thom tried speaking again, the new word sounding foreign and unfamiliar on his tongue. "Only your *mother* can undo her magic."

"That's not what I've seen."

Concern crumpled Thom's brow. He leaned in ever so slowly. "What do you mean, *what you've seen*?"

Kestrel hadn't anticipated sharing this much with him, afraid of how he might react, that he might try to stop her. But they were on a streak of truth, and she wanted it to continue.

"I had a vision. Like the ones my mother used to have." Watching the tidal wave of emotions that overcame him only confirmed what she already knew: he had expected this. He had known all along who's blood ran through her veins. "Why didn't you tell me about her? About my magic?"

This time, he didn't fight the truth. "I swore to your mother I would keep you protected. Keep you safe. I didn't want them finding you and blaming you for her mistakes. So I...I kept you hidden away. Your magic, too, in case there was some way they could trace it back to you. But I only ever did any of that to keep you safe, to honor the promise I made to her."

Kestrel's chest felt like molten rock, cracking and shifting with surges of heat that threatened to consume her. How could she hold any of it against him, when he had only been obeying her mother's wishes?

With tears brimming in her eyes, she asked the question she'd been terrified to hear the answer to for days now. "And you're not my father then?"

His mouth opened, then shut again. "Not by blood, no."

"Then what about him, my father? Why would my mother take me away from King Everard? Wouldn't he have protected me—if she hadn't cursed him?"

Thom slammed his fists against the iron bars. Kestrel jumped, her back colliding against Elora.

"That man is not your father."

The initial shock and fear wore off quickly.

"He's not?" Kestrel asked, curiosity pulling her forward again. "Then who is?"

But Thom was merely shaking his head. "I don't know. I don't even know how to answer that."

Kestrel looked behind her to Elora, wondering if she had heard anything about any of this. But the princess just shrugged, then said, "We should probably be going soon."

Kestrel nodded, twisting around again to face—her father? The man who raised her? She didn't know what he was to her anymore. Not a father by blood, but he had been her only guardian. He'd taken care of her. Taught her how to read and climb and laugh. He was the only parent she'd ever known. And the other one...

"So, it's true then? Queen Aenwyn, my mother, is the reason for the curse?"

"Yes—but you have to understand, she isn't who the stories say she is. Your mother was fierce and loyal to her people, to *all* the people of Grimtol. The entire reason she left Caelora was to slay the dragon and protect the people."

"Then what happened?" Kestrel asked, as memories of the king-beast thrashed in her skull. She watched him die again. Saw the princes collapse in grief around his lifeless body. Then she thought of all the other monarchs who'd been ruined by her mother's dark magic. "How did she go from trying to save the people to condemning them all?"

Thom dragged a hand through his greasy hair. "They betrayed her…"

"So she turned innocent people into monsters? Left them to wreak havoc on their kingdoms? On their own families?"

"I'm not saying she was in the right. I'm just saying she had her reasons, and in that moment, in her eyes, the ones she cursed weren't innocents. They were the culprits and puppeteers who orchestrated years of her suffering." Suffering? Kestrel hadn't heard about that part of the story yet. She wanted to ask him more about it, but he was already spiraling deeper into painful memories of their past. "You weren't there to witness her heartache when she realized how everyone had betrayed her—her father, her sister, her own husband. To see how much they took from her. How much of her pain and misery was carefully designed.

"I don't believe for one second that what she did was right, but I don't think she did it on purpose. Her magic—*your* magic—it's powerful. It has a mind of its own, if you're not careful with it."

"So she just lost control? Is that going to happen to me?" Kestrel's mind was reeling. She stared down at her hands. They were small; they looked the same as they always had, like they were incapable of hurting so much as a mouse.

"Of course not, Little Fury," Thom said, trying to be

reassuring. "No one is going to hurt you like they hurt her."

It was an empty promise though, Kestrel knew. One he had no control over. For she had already experienced hurt, betrayal, deceit. So far, it seemed like everyone she'd met had crossed that line between friend and foe, including him.

Everyone except Elora.

How much more heartbreak would it take before she snapped just like her mother did?

Elora's voice leaned over her shoulder. "We should get going before the guards change."

Kestrel nodded again, even though leaving was the last thing she wanted to do. Truth be told, she could've spent hours down there with him. But that wasn't possible yet. And the two of them would soon be needed for their journey into the Hollows. This was meant to be a quick visit. Just to make sure he was alright. And to ask him...

"I just need to know one more thing."

His tired eyes met hers. "Anything."

"What's your real name?" Maybe it was a stupid thing to waste a final question on, but it was something that had been tormenting her. And if they were to go on to maintain any sort of relationship after this, she needed to know.

A sad smile creeped up one side of his face, crinkling the scar across his cheek and eye.

"I've been Thom now for nearly twenty years. Part of me always will be. But before you were born, I was called Darius."

"And you changed your name so that we could go into hiding?"

"Correct."

Kestrel nodded, thinking. She wasn't sure what that meant for what she should call him, but she could figure that out later. "We have to go now, but I wanted you to know I am going to end this curse. And when I do, I'll demand your freedom. You just have to wait a little longer."

Despite the gloom around them, Darius actually smiled. "You are so much like her, you know that?"

Kestrel didn't, but she felt something warm bloom inside her all the same.

Saying goodbye, she turned around to join Elora on their walk back out of the dungeon, when Darius called out one more time.

"Princess Elora? Might I have a word?"

CHAPTER 33

FORGIVENESS IS A TEARING OF THE HEART

ELORA

Elora had been listening to the two of them, watching their interactions like a guarded owl in a tree. Darius looked like the same person, if only a bit more weathered and weary. His hair was longer, the scar on his cheek a little more profound with the aging and sagging of his skin. But he *sounded* different. Ages apart from the cold and stoic guard who had overseen most of her torture in Caelora.

In his soothing and hushed words to Kestrel, Elora could hear the father in his voice. The protector. Sometimes, it was so at odds with the monster she remembered him to be, that she felt herself dizzying, one hand needing to brace herself on a beam nearby as they discussed a lifetime of secrets between them.

By the time they were ready to go, Elora was eager for fresh air.

She needed distance between them—both the

memory of the man and this new version she couldn't quite reconcile with.

And then, he called her name.

"Princess Elora?" Truth be told, she wasn't even sure he'd known who she was. After all, he had likely tortured hundreds of Caeloran prisoners in his time as a guardsman. Then again, she supposed an Ashen stood out—and one of their nobles, at that. "Might I have a word?"

Elora had never wanted to disappear into darkness more than she did in that moment.

She couldn't face him. Wasn't ready to. Not after everything he'd done. Not when she was just starting to feel like a form of herself again.

Beside her, Kestrel was watching though. Hopeful and expectant. Elora couldn't bring herself to let her down.

Elora fixed her expression with ice and faced her former torturer. "Darius?"

He winced at the bite in her tone but nodded as if to say he accepted it. Deserved it. She wanted to scream that he deserved that and so much more, but she would try to be civil for Kestrel's sake.

"I know it can't mean much, given all I've done to you, but I wanted you to know that I've spent the last twenty years regretting it." He struggled to maintain eye contact, those liquid night pupils of his dodging this way and that. But he kept forcing himself to return to her gaze. To try to face her. "Back then, I didn't question things. I didn't use my own head. That's not to try to excuse my actions, I know I hurt you in ways that are unspeakable...and I just wanted to say I'm sorry."

The last words struck her like dragon's fire. Burning. Warming. Threatening to both comfort and consume her.

She didn't know—hadn't realized—how much she had needed to hear it. Words that she still wasn't ready to accept openly, but ones that she could feel chipping away at the icy shards around her heart.

Hanging his head, Darius continued. "I wish I had half the backbone that Kestrel has, that her mother had. Half the sense of justice and human decency, so that I would've recognized what I was doing was wrong, and I would've stopped it sooner. Set you free, perhaps. Or...I don't know. Done something." He shook his head, caught in an internal argument with himself. "I don't know, maybe that's not the full truth. Because I did know what I was doing was wrong. It's why I tried to make your suffering quick. Why I always volunteered to be the one in charge because I knew the others were so much more ruthless with you because of who you were, what you represented."

It was all flooding back to her.

The endless beatings.

The stabbings.

The strangulation.

So much pain, and yet death would never come for her, only a loss of consciousness. And when she would come back to, she would still be trapped in that dark cell, hailstone chains around her wrists much like they still were now.

She hated him for it.

Hated every single Caeloran who had ever lived.

But something about what he was saying reigned true

for her as well. Even then, she recognized how much harder he would strike her, how quickly she would succumb to incapacitation at his hands. At the time though, she had always assumed it was because he was the most brutal. The deadliest. But could what he was saying be true? Had it been a mercy? The other torturers certainly had drawn out her suffering, sometimes making her scream and beg for days for them to stop.

"Not that I'm trying to say I was a saint or anything," he continued. "I didn't stop them. I blindly obeyed my orders because I was too much of a coward back then."

Sometimes she felt the same. Had Queen Signe not instructed her to connive a way into Princess Kestrel's good graces? Had Elora not blindly, willingly obliged, simply for fear of what refusing would mean for her own freedom?

But this was years of torment they were talking about. Not a few days.

Yet...part of her could see where he was coming from. Part of her wanted to see him in a different light. It felt like a gentle hand over her heart, something that had the power to heal what had long-since been shattered.

The whole conversation left her skin itchy and aching. She wasn't ready to heal. Wasn't ready to forgive. That would make her weak and pathetic, vulnerable to future pain—because who in their right mind would believe the sappy apology flowing from their former torturer's lips?

His next words shook her even more thoroughly. "I don't deserve your forgiveness, or any ounce of kindness from you, so I won't ask for it. But I know you helped Kestrel come and see me, and for that I am grateful. And that must mean the two of you are friends. And so, although you don't owe me a thing, I'll ask this anyway: please look after her."

That was all he wanted to ask of her? An Ashen Princess. The future Queen of Irongate.

He could've begged for his freedom. For a swift execution—since they both knew it was coming to that, regardless of Kestrel's hopes to save him.

Not a ploy for his own life. Not a trick to lure her into trusting and releasing him.

All he wanted was for his daughter to be safe.

That, more than anything, melted the icy walls surrounding Elora's heart.

He cleared his throat, this time addressing Kestrel one last time. "I kept you sheltered. And I worry I didn't do the best to prepare you for how this cruel world works."

Kestrel's voice was thick with tears. "You did fine—I'm doing fine. I'm figuring things out."

But he seemed unconvinced. He fixed his gaze on Elora again, a silent question hanging in the air between them.

And Elora found herself standing at the edge of a crossroads. One where she could hold on to her sense of vengeance, of justice, where she could let the anger and pain of her past fuel her every action and fester within her until she became as broken as they had wanted her to become.

Or she could accept this olive branch. Find a way to make peace—or at least, something close to it.

"In the short time I have known her, Kestrel has shown me that she doesn't need me to look after her. But I can promise you, I will be by her side for as long as I am able. As long as she will have me."

When Elora glanced to Kestrel, she found her soft lifts tilted upwards, as if to say that she felt the same. It sent shivers skittering up Elora's spine. But she had already felt too vulnerable for one day, so she shook the feeling off.

"We really must be going now."

Kestrel nodded.

Darius said, "Of course. Thank you again. And, Kestrel, if things get hairy, I want you to leave me. Don't put your-self in danger for my life. I've done and lived plenty, and it's time for you to do the same. So if anything does happen...leave these parts. Keep searching for your mother. I know she's out there somewhere...she has to be."

Elora's ears perked at that. It seemed to have the same effect on Kestrel, which meant she was likely hearing this for the first time as well.

Sure, there were many throughout Grimtol who believed the Corrupt Queen survived her own curse. But after two decades of searching for her, Elora assumed that rumor was nothing but false hope for those seeking justice. Magic that powerful tended to have a high cost, so it made sense to Elora that it had claimed the queen's life in the process.

But Darius had been there. He had seen the queen unleash her power. And now it sounded as if he was suggesting that he had seen her survive it as well.

Elora had a dozen questions. So did Kestrel, she guessed. But they really were running out of time, and they didn't need Queen Signe to know they had come down here.

"Come on," Elora forced herself to say. "Let's go."

At first, she wasn't certain Kestrel would allow herself to be pulled away, but she seemed to remember they had other important matters to attend to.

"I will make this right, Darius. You'll see. Give it another day or two, and you'll be walking out of this place a free man." Kestrel's reassuring smile was illuminating in a grim place like this. And Darius tried to muster one in return.

But Elora couldn't do it. She shielded her face from both of them and started walking back the way they had come, for she knew how unlikely it was for the queen to release him.

CHAPTER 34

AN ARMY

KESTREL

They exited the dungeon in silence, each deep in thought for their own reasons.

Nodding to the guard, Kestrel only barely realized it was the same one who had permitted them to enter. Her mind was elsewhere. Reeling from everything she and Thom had talked about—or, she supposed she should call him Darius now. The moniker of Thom had served its purpose. They no longer needed to hide.

This time, Darius had been honest with her. Now that all of his secrets had been exposed, Kestrel supposed he had nothing left to hide.

If he had just been willing to speak so freely last time, she wondered where they would be now. Certainly not in Irongate, not with him trapped behind bars and her preparing to blunder headfirst into one of the most frightening places she had ever heard about.

But it was news of her mother that set her mind ablaze. Darius believed she was still alive, after all this time. His frequent disappearances made much more sense now; he'd been out searching for her, for the woman he loved. For her mother. She could hardly fault him for that, even if she wished he had just told her from the beginning.

But that didn't matter now.

After they returned from the Hollows, after Kestrel dismantled the curse, she would convince the queen to set Darius free so that the two of them could continue his search, together.

Or at least, that's what Kestrel had wanted a week ago.

Now, the thought of leaving Irongate, and more importantly Elora, made her stomach tighten. They were just starting to get to know each other. Kestrel didn't want to give up on that so soon.

Then again, perhaps that would be for the best. Elora was going to marry Leighton in a matter of days. Soon she would become queen. And what role would Kestrel play in her life then?

As the two of them crossed the open field and headed toward the gardens, Kestrel snuck a glance at the quiet princess marching beside of her. There had been revelations for her back in that dungeon as well, and although Kestrel wanted so desperately to hear every thought that was now tumbling through that pensive skull of Elora's, she knew better than to prod just yet.

The silence, however, was killing her.

"Thank you for that," Kestrel said, jarring Elora from her thoughts.

"I didn't do anything that you couldn't," she replied, the distant glaze to her eyes fading. "Now that you're a princess, you have power here. You just need to learn how to use it."

"It's more than that, and you know it. Going down there, seeing him, I know that wasn't easy for you. But it meant the world to me. I needed that. So, thank you."

Stiffly, Elora gave her a nod. There was something more distant about her, like they were just meeting again for the first time, and Kestrel hated it. She wanted to throw her arms around her and force Elora back into the more relaxed state she had displayed with her earlier, but that would only serve to make the princess prickle more.

The idea sparked something in Kestrel though. A memory—well, not a memory, but something from the vision.

"Have you ever...been able to touch someone? Like without, you know." Kestrel pantomimed dying, her tongue lolling out the side of her mouth. Elora's face finally illuminated with a crooked smile—one that seemed to suggest Kestrel was the most ridiculous person in the realm, but that was a title she would accept with pride if it was the reason for Elora's smiles.

"You mean without killing anyone?" Elora asked, the curve of her lips drooping. "I'm afraid not. At least, not in this lifetime."

Kestrel waited, expecting her to question why she was asking. Maybe she would've, if the clanging of metal hadn't interrupted them. Nearby, they could hear it rustling, a shifting of metal plates upon plates.

Kestrel and Elora cast questioning glances at each other before emerging from the gardens and finding the queen and a small army waiting in the courtyard.

Kestrel was rendered speechless by what the queen had pulled together for their adventure. It was nothing like her vision. For starters, she had only ever seen the three of them in the Hollows, and for a moment she worried what bringing anyone else would mean. At the same time, it would be reckless to wander into those woods without backup, she supposed. And these knights were trained to handle the monsters that awaited them inside, surely.

While Kestrel marveled at the sight of the knights she would be marching with, Elora leaned closer to whisper in her ear. "If anyone asks, we were strolling through the gardens so I could tell you about the flowers that are native to these areas, and some of their medicinal and useful properties, in case you need that knowledge in the Hollows."

That made sense to Kestrel. For some reason, she didn't think it would go over well with anyone to find out that they had gone into the dungeons to speak with someone wanted for treason.

"Sounds good to me," Kestrel replied. Then, taking a deep breath added, "Well, let's not keep them waiting."

Scanning the militia, all clad in iron and blue, it was easy to spot the queen like a smudge of shadow at the center among their ranks. Doused in black from head to toe, she sat atop a warhorse with her legs crossed to one side and an awning stretching above her, keeping her shielded from the high-noon sun and subsequently from the effects of her curse. She was wearing one of her signature black gowns, a delicate piece that clung to her every curve. At first glance, Kestrel thought it was ill-fitting since they were meant to trudge into the Hollows, a place full of monsters. She would think the queen would want something more protective—then again, neither Kestrel nor Elora were really dressed for such an occasion either. Besides, as Kestrel drew nearer, she noticed the chest plating stitched beneath the fabric of Queen Signe's dress, the additional padding added to her shoulders and protecting her arms. The queen might be regal and poised, but she originally came from Skogar, just like Aenwyn, so she knew how to ready herself for battle, Kestrel figured.

When the queen spotted Kestrel and Elora parting the ranks as they approached, she waved with her long now-red fingernails in their direction.

"There you two are. We were beginning to worry you had forgotten your own decree." Her crimson lips were so taut, they barely managed a thin smile. "What kept the two of you?"

"Just preparing," replied Kestrel, hastily. "Elora was telling me about some of the native plants here, and how some of them might be useful in the Hollows."

The queen arched a slender brow. "Oh? Which ones?"

Cursed sky! Kestrel hadn't expected the queen to challenge her—but of course, she should have. This clever, scheming aunt of hers always seemed to be one step ahead of everything. Kestrel tried wrangling her tongue, but it was a heavy, untamed beast.

"Umm, well, there was this white flower. I think? Or maybe it was yellow. But it—"

"She's not the best understudy," Elora huffed, swooping in to save her from herself.

But just when Kestrel thought they were in the clear,

the queen snapped at the princess. "Or perhaps you're not the best teacher." Then she smiled down upon Kestrel. "No matter. We have our guards to ensure our safety. You won't need the aid of useless plants, especially ones that have long-since died within the boundary of the Hollows."

Kestrel shot Elora a nervous glance, worried that their ruse was about to be called out and unsure of what to say next. But the queen had already moved on, redirecting her attention to the larger army surrounding them.

"Prior to our convening, I held counsel with the scholars of Irongate's libraries."

Kestrel realized she was talking about Barnabus as the knights huddled nearer. Amongst their ranks, she spotted three of the Erickson brothers nudging their way forward—Efrem, Micah, and Leighton.

Elora let out a quiet grumble. "What are the three idiots doing here?"

Kestrel, on the other hand, was partially relieved to see their familiar faces. Although she did have to wonder what Leighton was doing. Efrem and Micah made sense—Efrem seemed to hold a position within the Thunder-sworn Brigade, and Micah of course did what he pleased, chasing the thrill of adventure wherever it took him.

But Leighton was the future king. Surely, a mission like this was too dangerous for the heir to the throne to attend.

If the queen was perturbed by their presence, she didn't let it show as she continued belting her speech for all to hear.

"According to our records, the blight within the Hollows started near the center and spread. For years, no one has been skilled enough to enter and return unscathed, no matter how deep they venture. Unfortunately for us, we must reach the center of the Hollows, the place where it all began." She swept a hand toward Kestrel. "Our seer, Princess Kestrel of Caelora, reports there is magic within a lake there, the same place where our scholars believe to be the original site of the desecration of those lands. So we will need to venture deep within the Hollows, reclaim the magic that resides there, and return unharmed. I am putting my utmost faith in all of you to keep the royal family safe throughout this endeavor, and in return, your families shall be rewarded greatly."

Kestrel took note of the wary but brave faces around her. She wished she could reassure them. Tell them that her vision had suggested no harm would befall anyone. But the Thundersworn Brigade hadn't been in the vision. And telling them that much would only demoralize them more.

The queen announced that they were ready to embark on their mission, and the masses began to march forward.

"Stay within the middle of the ranks," Queen Signe said down to Kestrel. "Do not fall behind. Do not leave yourself vulnerable to an attack. Understood?"

Kestrel nodded, feeling more afraid than she anticipated.

Her vision had been peaceful. Victorious. But being surrounded by so many armed guardsmen made her feel as if they were marching into battle.

All Kestrel could do was trust in her vision's accuracy. Believe no harm would come to them.

As the queen began her march, the three brothers

finally caught up to them. Efrem immediately branched off, blending in with the other knights, but Micah and Leighton joined the two princesses.

"What in the Hollows are you two doing here?" Elora asked.

Micah slanted her a grin. "What? You thought we'd leave all the fun to you ladies?"

"It's not meant to be fun," snapped the princess.

Micah merely shrugged. "Better than being couped up all day."

"And you?" she asked Leighton next, but the bite in her tone had already lessened. Kestrel wondered if that was simply because she knew it was futile, or if it had anything to do with their betrothal.

Leighton smoothed his golden locks back and out of his eyes. "What would the people say if they saw my bride marching into battle and their future king nowhere in sight?"

The terse yet intimate conversation made Kestrel's stomach queasy again, so she turned from the three of them and focused her attention forward. On the path that stretched ahead of them. On the Hollows, and whatever magic lay inside. Elora's fate was to marry a prince, but Kestrel's fate still lied ahead, somewhere in the unknown.

CHAPTER 35
INTO THE HOLLOWS

KESTREL

Marching through the town of Irongate, Kestrel should've known they'd draw the attention of onlookers. Everyone stared. Whispers followed. And the townspeople crowded around them, as curious and judgmental as they were the day Kestrel first arrived.

"You alright, little bird?" asked Micah from behind her.

As much as she wanted to tell him no, to insist he hold onto her to keep her from spinning out of control again, she wanted to master this feeling more...whatever it was. Something akin to fear, but different. Being around so many people made her heart quicken. It shortened her breaths. It made her feel as if she were trapped in the Fortress of Thirst again with no way out and no one to save her.

Which was preposterous, because these were just curious onlookers. Not deranged beasts.

Not that her insides would listen, nor her ears that

seemed so keen to attune to every single malicious remark spewed at them like venom.

"*There were already too many Skogarans in Irongate, if you ask me.*"

"*The whole crown's gone to the Maw these days.*"

"*If we're lucky, maybe they'll all die, wherever it is they're headed.*"

Elora was right beside her, the perfect image of stoic grace. "Ignore them. Their beliefs about you are uninformed and inaccurate."

Kestrel summoned a grateful smile. "How do you do it? Ignore them and not let all their anger bother you?"

"It gets easier the longer it goes on. Easier still when you're surrounded by those who understand and believe in you." It was Elora's turn to flash Kestrel a smile now, and oh, if it didn't flood her traitorous body with warmth. "Of course, there will always be good and bad days. But today, you can feel proud knowing what you're doing is right by them. You aim to save them. To undo a curse that no one else has been able to combat. That can help."

Elora was right. Kestrel hadn't even thought of it that way yet.

"You'd think they'd be a little more grateful for what we're about to do then," Kestrel grumbled, making sure that only Elora could hear her. The last thing any of them needed was to insult a grumpy mob and turn them into an aggressive one. "Don't they want the curse to end?"

Elora remained facing forward, her chin held high so that the silver crown of stars reflected in the sunlight. "I'm sure they do. But as far as I'm aware, they have no idea what we're up to."

"They weren't informed?" Kestrel glanced around the scowling faces, some smudged with grime and dirt.

"The queen will likely wait until we know for certain what we're dealing with. There's no point in getting their hopes up if we are unsuccessful, or have misinterpreted your vision."

That made sense, Kestrel supposed. Even if in her heart she knew this was the answer they had all been waiting for.

It was only then that Kestrel realized her nerves were calming. The conversation, or perhaps the distraction it provided, was working. Reminding her that she was in no immediate danger.

The longer they marched and the more voices she overheard, she also realized that many of the insults weren't even directed at her. Many were aimed at Queen Signe. Atop her steed, the awning mostly did its job at protecting her from the sun's wrath. But every few steps it shifted, allowing a sliver of light to pierce her.

From where Kestrel marched behind the queen, she couldn't see what the light did to her, but she heard the crowd hissing and gasping every time her curse was illuminated.

Like Elora though, the queen continued to hold her head high.

Kestrel was beginning to wonder if that was what it took to be royalty, to silence your reactions and emotions. There was something both admirable and tragic about it. Kestrel didn't envy either of them, but she also found herself in awe of the strength and fortitude they both possessed.

She supposed she would need to learn the skill too someday. Perhaps even soon. Once the curse was lifted, her life would change forever…again. The king of Caelora would be free. Kestrel didn't know what that meant for her, considering according to Darius, King Everard was not her father. But Kestrel still had some claim to that throne at least, thanks to her mother—whether or not she would be expected to reign there, she wasn't sure. Hopefully, that would be something she and Darius could figure out together, perhaps even with her mother at their side… if they ever found her.

Of course, none of that was certain, and that made her belly pool with dread.

As they approached the blackened trees of the Hollows, everything quieted.

Not so much as a bird flitted overhead, nor did the wind rustle any leaves.

Everything was silent, except for the horses. They whinnied and stamped their hooves, none of them wanting to draw any nearer to a place so dead and ominous.

And then a crack of thunder boomed so loudly overhead it made nearly everyone jump.

"Great, just what we need, a storm," Micah mumbled over his shoulder at Kestrel.

Elora didn't look at him as she said, "It could be a good thing. Maybe a storm will conceal our footfall."

Micah frowned in a way that said he was both impressed and in agreement with her.

Somewhere amid the troops, Efrem shouted his orders. "We go on foot from here."

It only applied to a few guardsmen, as most of them were already on foot, but a couple closest to the queen began helping her down from her steed as well. And during the momentary lapse of cover provided by her awning and the umbrella another knight thrusted over her head, Kestrel finally caught a glimpse of the curse that marred her aunt.

Queen Signe's slender features became sickeningly worse, her rounded chin and nose becoming a jutting bone as sharp as a knife. It appeared as though her eyes had concaved, the dark circles beneath them so cavernous, they made her look like death incarnate. But it was her mouth, or rather the teeth inside it that made Kestrel's breath catch. Serrated fangs, sharp enough to tear through flesh. She put the late King Ulfaskr's ghastly appearance to shame.

"Avert your gaze," Elora whispered.

Kestrel did as she was advised. Not only because she couldn't bring herself to watch any longer, but because she knew just how much the queen disdained being seen in that form—and Kestrel couldn't blame her. She was monstruous. Horrifying. It was no wonder she hid herself away from the townspeople; none of them would ever accept her like this.

Hopefully, Kestrel's vision would soon change everything for her though. As much as she didn't fully understand her aunt, she still believed she deserved a life of peace. One where she wasn't cowering in the cold Irongate castle for the rest of her days.

Once the queen was down on her feet, umbrella in hand, she gestured toward Elora.

The guards marched over to them, and Kestrel's stomach tightened like a fist. She felt the urge to leap between them and the princess, for fear of what they were about to do. But then she saw the key in their hand and remembered.

They eyed Elora warily, examining her collar and manacles, before finally tossing her a bluish-silver key.

Elora's wide eyes stared at it for a moment, blinking. She muttered an awkward, "Th-thank you." But even then, she just continued staring, as if she couldn't believe it was real.

"Would you like some help?" Kestrel asked.

"Don't!" Elora's horror-stricken gaze snapped up so swiftly, Kestrel jumped. "I mean—my apologies, but I must do this myself, and you must keep your distance after the hailstone is off."

Kestrel had never seen her look more serious, more afraid.

Nodding, she took a step back, and it felt as if she were severing something inside her. But she gave the princess enough room so that she would feel comfortable to remove her own bejeweled shackles, to claim her own freedom for the first time in who knew how many years.

Elora unlatched the chain around her neck first, a subtle gasp blowing past her lips as the fresh air grazed her raw skin. Kestrel tried not to wince at the purple bruising beneath it. This was supposed to be a happy moment for Elora. She wouldn't ruin it. Then Elora removed each of the shackles around her wrists, rubbing the bare skin there once it was freed.

She looked up at Kestrel, her magenta eyes aglow with disbelief and joy.

"Step back," one of the guards barked. "I need to collect those."

Kestrel and Elora looked to the ground where he was pointing at her discarded chains.

Elora did as she was told, and the guard retrieved her manacles before shoving them into a satchel. Kestrel noted how he was one of the few who hovered near the princess at all times, clearly charged with her punishment, should she step out of line. It boiled her insides to know just how much they all distrusted Elora. Disdained her, really. Even though she had never wronged any of them, at least not that Kestrel was aware.

"Wonderful," the queen announced with a jovial clap of her hands. "Now that that's settled, Kestrel, would you mind coming this way and telling our men exactly where you spotted this lake?"

Kestrel didn't want to leave Elora alone, but she was also eager to embark on this voyage, to be useful for once. So she did as she was told and came at the queen's beckoning.

Her aunt slid her free arm around her shoulders and guided her to the men at the front of the line.

"Now, spare no detail. Give them as much direction and description as you can recall."

Kestrel opened her mouth, wanting to get this over with as soon as possible so the queen would stop holding onto her, but then she stopped. Everything would change once they entered the Hollows, once they collected that blue light. And Kestrel needed security. Reassurances that her role in all of this would be well-compensated—and not in terms of wealth.

"I will," Kestrel said softly. But like Elora said, she had power by title and blood now; she just needed to learn how to use it. So she steeled herself the way she had seen the queen and princess do dozens of times. "But I have one condition."

"Oh?" the queen asked, and despite her fragile smile, Kestrel heard the impatience simmering beneath it.

"I want Darius freed after this. Please," she added, just so her aunt wouldn't feel like this was a threat. "He's the closest thing to a father I have, and we can leave Irongate if you'd like—or stay. I don't care. I just need to know he won't be—that nothing bad will happen to him."

Queen Signe's expression softened, as if she had been expecting this and was relieved that Kestrel wasn't demanding something more. "It will entirely depend on what we find, I'm afraid. If this endeavor winds up being for nothing—"

"It won't be. I promise you," Kestrel blurted, cutting the queen off. But she didn't care. She didn't want to hear about the what ifs. Kestrel knew this was going to work. It had to. "So if we find magic or the answer to the curse inside the Hollows, you will release him and drop his charges?"

"Certainly. It would be the least I could do to thank you for ending such a terrible time in our collective history."

Kestrel beamed and began sharing every little detail she could think of with the knights who were going to be leading them into the Hollows. It wasn't much, unfortunately, just the same vague landmarks that had already been shared. But they appeared earnest as they listened, and conversed quietly amongst themselves afterward, strategizing their path forward.

And when they were finally ready, they motioned everyone to follow as they began their trek into the ominous forest.

The minute they set foot on the other side of the boundary, the silence that had surrounded the Hollows was replaced with skittering. Kestrel could hear them, the monsters Micah had warned her about when they'd passed by this place on their way to Irongate. If she hadn't known any better, she might've mistaken the unnerving creaking of limbs for the mundane sounds that trees made as they swayed.

But underneath the creaking, she heard them.

The clawing.

The scratching.

Creatures climbing up from the earth and thrashing about the forest as they stalked their prey.

The roaring clouds overhead only served to add to the frightful tension. Every blast of lightning illuminated the path but somehow darkened the forest's shadows.

Micah had told her about two kinds of monsters here: the gravemoors and the rootless. And Kestrel wasn't sure which she feared more, the ones who would grab them from the ground and pull them under, or the ones who were able to roam freely and snatch them away to do who knew what.

The knights who were clustered nearby shook in their armor. Everyone did. The royal party huddled closer.

Elora kept her distance from them all though. She stepped into the Hollows, her periwinkle gown like a beacon of hope amidst so much gloom. She was forging a path near the front, Kestrel realized, whether intentionally or by default of the knights who parted in her wake. It made Kestrel's throat tighten, thinking about her without the protection of the army to surround her, so Kestrel started to push forward too.

"Kestrel," the queen hissed in warning.

But Kestrel pretended not to hear her. She would not let Elora sacrifice herself for this. It was too dangerous. Kestrel had misunderstood the vision, clearly. They needed to turn back before the monsters descended upon them.

But it was already too late.

Near the back of the party, someone screamed, a gurgling sound that coiled around Kestrel's spine. She heard a heavy thump, then something being dragged away through the dried, dead leaves. Murmuring and panicked chatter rose like a tidal wave from the back of their militia. Not that it mattered if they were quiet, it seemed these creatures knew about their presence the moment they had entered into their domain. And now they were cutting off their means of escape, attacking from behind.

Another scream filled the air.

"Stand your ground!" yelled Efrem to his troops. "Remember your training and protect your queen!"

The queen shouted Kestrel's name again, this time more insistent.

Still, Kestrel pushed onward. Elora was just ahead. Just

barely out of reach—not that she could grab her, she reminded herself. But she would talk to her, tell her they needed to turn back before it was too late. To stop trudging forward without protection to surround her.

Glancing at the trees nearby, Kestrel saw the monsters ambling about. Some were rapid, darting from one tree trunk to another so swiftly, she almost couldn't see their branch-like features. But there were more languid ones too. They slowly inched closer, one painstaking limp after another, as if their limbs were weighed down by swamp water, clogged and putrid. It was those ones that Kestrel could finally see more clearly. The gnarled twigs that coiled up and around their bodies for legs, arms, even their torsos. A few of them even had something resembling a face, a screaming carving that was embedded in their wood. Others just had broken stumps and splinters for hair. But all of them seemed hungry, intent on grabbing their prey and dragging it off into the trees, never to be seen again.

Kestrel finally caught up to Elora.

"Finally," she breathed. "We have to go. We can't keep pushing forward like this, or they're going to..." Her voice trailed off when she noticed the look of awe upon Elora's face.

Elora was staring down at the ground, at a tree root that was encroaching upon their path.

Micah had cautioned Kestrel about the tree roots, calling them gravemoors and saying that they would grab unsuspecting travelers and wrench them underground. So Kestrel knew to be vigilant. She had expected the same from everyone else. But instead of watching the roots with horror, Elora watched them with curiosity. With something close to playfulness. Almost like she wanted to tempt them. But to do what?

She tilted her head and took a tentative step toward the root.

Before Kestrel could open her mouth to scream out in warning, they both watched as the tree root recoiled.

The girls exchanged a quick look before Elora tried again. This time, it retreated farther, slithering away from her foot until it had nowhere else to go but back into the tree.

Kestrel peered into the woods and noticed that the monsters lurking between the trees were also retreating. With every step Elora took toward them, they mimicked one in return by backing that much farther away.

"Did you know—" Kestrel started to ask, but Elora was already shaking her head.

"Dragon's fire, are the rootless actually afraid of you?" This time it was Micah who had apparently maneuvered his way to the front of the party to see what the two of them were up to. "The gravemoors too?"

"It would appear so," Elora said, still sounding utterly mesmerized.

"Well thank the sun for that." Micah raised his hand as if to give her a hearty pat on the shoulder, but then thought better of it. Instead, he called out to Efrem. "Looks like we don't need the Thundersworn Brigade, we just needed an Ashen!"

"What?"

Micah beckoned his twin closer, likely not wanting to get too far away from Elora and the protection her presence apparently supplied them. Kestrel only halfway listened as the two of them discussed sending the majority of their troops back for their own safety; she was too preoccupied with the princess who was still gazing down at where the tree root had been. There was something like sadness pinching the place beneath Elora's silver crown.

"Are you alright?" Kestrel leaned in closer so that only she could hear.

Elora's smile didn't light up her eyes. "Who knew that there was a benefit like this to my power."

Kestrel wasn't falling for her cheerful tone though. She heard the unspoken and shattering truth beneath it: even the monsters were afraid of her. This was just one more thing retreating from Elora in fear. Even if it did benefit them, she could only imagine how lonely such a life must be. She wished she could take Elora's hand into her own, squeeze it until she knew that Kestrel would always be there for her. Instead, all she could do was offer her company, and continue being one of the few people who didn't flinch at the princess' presence.

Kestrel turned around just as the guard who had been responsible for carrying Elora's chains handed them off to Efrem and then began retreating to the Hollows' entrance with most of the small army. Only the royal family and a handful of guards remained.

"I guess it's you two leading now," Micah said after catching them up on the new plan. Then he flashed that crooked grin of his at Kestrel. "Think you can handle it, little bird?"

"With this one at my side?" Kestrel nodded to the

princess, hoping some levity might cheer her up. "I feel practically invincible now."

It wasn't quite a smirk than it was an amused scoff that escaped Elora's lips, but it was close enough.

"I'm afraid I disagree," said the queen, closing in on them. Her eyes shifted nervously from one side of the forest to the other. "We don't know the limits of the princess'—" she struggled to find the word "—repellent magic. I think it best if she remains centered in the group as we travel, while Kestrel leads us the rest of the way."

"I agree," Leighton chimed in, broadsword gleaming in his grasp. Towering at least a head taller than the rest of the party, he didn't have to project his voice to make sure everyone could hear him. "I'll be at the front as well, ensuring Kestrel's safety."

"Yes. Good." The queen waved him off. "Now, let's keep moving. I doubt any of us would like to be here longer than is necessary."

Kestrel wanted to insist she and Elora stay together, but based on what logic? What the queen was saying made sense. Elora was the only protection they had in here. They needed to keep her close. Besides, maybe it would do them all some good to finally view her in a light other than destructive. Maybe this would give them an opportunity to see that thanks to her magic or ancestry or whatever it may be, *she* was protecting them. Not harming.

Kestrel flashed the princess a look that she hoped conveyed that she was sorry to leave her side no matter how momentary, and then marched to the front of the small convoy with Leighton in tow.

As they continued to infiltrate the Hollows, they kept watchful eyes on the forest around them.

The rootless still lurked there, stalking them like the wild coyotes of Vallonde. But they kept their distance behind the treeline. And for that, Kestrel and the others were able to walk freer, less rattled with fear.

Although they still had to be mindful of every step, careful not to wander out of Elora's magical reach—which was difficult to do since none of them knew exactly how far it extended. On one occasion, Kestrel and Leighton were a little too far ahead of the group, and the rooted arms of the gravemoors didn't shrivel back in time.

They lunged for them, vine-like claws reaching and nearly snagging Kestrel by the ankles.

Leighton had his sword ready though. In one clean strike, the branch was hacked in two, the remnants sent crumbling back to the tainted earth where they decayed in seconds.

"We should slow down," advised the prince.

The suggestion was so obvious that Kestrel was tempted to mock him. As if after nearly being snatched and dragged away that wasn't her first thought as well. But their dire surroundings and her still-racing heart had drained her sense of humor, so she merely agreed.

Once they resumed at a steady pace, Leighton turned to Kestrel and asked, "Is any of this looking familiar to you?"

Kestrel peered out at the blackened trees, each branch bare and identical to the last. "Yes and no. This whole place is like a mirrored version of itself. It all looks the same; tree after tree, lurking monster after lurking monster."

"I won't let them harm you."

"That's not what I—" Kestrel sighed, frustrated by his chivalrous intentions. She had never wanted to be the damsel in distress. Had always admired the heroes for their bravery, loyalty, and their commitment to putting everyone else above themselves. There was a time when she had admired Leighton for the same, when his gallant nature had heated the very depths of her belly with desire.

But that was before everything. Before he had betrayed her trust. Before she'd learned he was engaged. Before she'd met Elora.

Kestrel had moved on. But Leighton was still pining over her, or at least that's how it seemed.

That wouldn't do. Elora deserved better. And Kestrel would make this right.

It wasn't exactly the best place for this conversation, but they needed to have it.

"I don't need you to protect me. Besides, I'm not the one you should be protecting." When he looked at her with genuine confusion, she clarified. "Princess Elora? Your betrothed?"

Leighton flinched at the title. "She doesn't need my protection; if anything it's the other way around."

"You're wrong," Kestrel snapped, perhaps a bit too fiercely considering the way his eyes burst wide. He stared at her, assessing, as if he was starting to understand something she didn't want him to. There could be nothing between her and Elora; this was about them. Kestrel shoved the outrage down somewhere deep so that it wouldn't bother her again. "You know how people view her. What they say about her. The snide comments, the kingdom-wide loathing—it's hurtful. And after your wedding, she'll have to live in a kingdom where she has been hated for years. It will wear on her, and she will need someone by her side. Someone to support her. Someone... like her husband to take care of her?"

Leighton scoffed. "I'll have to. She'll be my queen."

"No, not because you have to. Because it's the right thing to do!" Kestrel stamped her foot, barely containing the growl in her voice. "Cursed sky, Leighton. I thought you were better than that."

The prince just shook his head, a look of disgust etched in his features. "I guess not."

Kestrel wanted to scream. She wanted to smack him upside the head the way she would with Darius whenever he was being an idiot. But princess or not, something told her if she struck the future king, there would be consequences.

"You haven't seen what her power can do. How deadly she can be," he continued, his voice a hollow, haunted thing as he kept scanning the perimeter. "Did she tell you she killed thirteen of our troops while she was transported over here? *Thirteen.* Men and women with families, with full lives ahead of them. And she snuffed all that out, ruined all those lives with a single touch."

No, she hadn't known. And now that she did, Kestrel's heart ached for those families. But it ached for Elora more. She wouldn't have slain those men on purpose, nor would she have taken any joy in it. Her power was uncontrollable, innate. Just like Kestrel's mother's had been.

"And what about me?" she asked. "Why be kind to me when you know my lineage? The dark history of my past. Dragon's fire, my mother cursed your father and now he's dead. Doesn't that make you hate me?"

His jaw was a taut cord ready to snap. "No, I could never hate you."

"Then why hate her?"

"Because I'm not in love with her!" he hissed, a little too loudly.

Behind them, Micah cleared his throat, and when Kestrel looked back she found him trying to look anywhere but ahead at the two of them. Elora, however, was staring right at her, with a look that seemed to say *what are you doing and please stop*—minus the *please*, perhaps.

"That's enough," snapped the queen, whose gaze was also like daggers at their backs. "We need the two of you focused."

"Yes, my queen," Leighton said through gritted teeth.

It was the last peep Kestrel heard from him, from anyone really. Until she finally saw it.

"There! I think I see it!"

As they rounded a crooked bend in the path, just beyond a collection of mangled trees, Kestrel spotted it. A stagnant body of water the color of soot.

Together, they hastened their pace until they were standing over the motionless lake at the center of the Hollows. Staring down into the grey mirk, it seemed so undisturbed, so untouched, so unlike the rest of the tainted forest. No monsters lurked below. In fact, the ones who had been stalking them all this way, kept an even farther distance now, as if they were afraid of this place.

Perhaps, they couldn't swim either, Kestrel thought to herself.

Or perhaps there was something here. Something unseen keeping them at bay. The magic she and the others had come for.

No matter how long they gazed into the waters though, no blue light emitted from them.

"This is it? You're sure of it?" snapped the queen once she grew tired of bobbing on her toes to see past the knights standing guard around her.

"Yes," Kestrel answered. "This is it. This is the same place I saw in my vision."

Although now that she was thinking of it, the blue light wasn't the only thing amiss. Feathers weren't raining down upon them either, and therefore Elora wasn't gathering them into her arms until it looked as if she was holding a flock of crows.

But this *was* the place.

Kestrel was certain of it.

She recognized the lake, the slabs of stone that jutted from the earth. Even the way that moss had grown on them, obscuring the inscriptions beneath. This was where they were meant to be.

"Wonderful." Queen Signe's voice was a noxious singsong. "Where is it then?"

Slowly, Kestrel said, "I don't know," as she glanced around the perimeter. "Maybe there's something we're supposed to do, like a way to trigger it."

"Like a trap?" Elora asked, incredulous.

"No, not like a trap. More like a—" Before Kestrel could think of the word, the queen provided one for her.

"An offering. A way to activate the magic here."

Images of the queen's altar and that poor rabbit flashed red in Kestrel's mind. Her stomach tied itself in knots. She didn't like the way the queen said the word *offering*, but the general idea of doing something to set off the magic was one she had considered as well. But it was difficult to think of what that might be, now that all she could imagine was that rabbit's entrails...the warmth and slickness of blood as it dripped from her hands.

"We're not killing anything." The growl that came from Micah's throat was more menacing than any of the creatures they'd encountered thus far.

Unbothered by the declaration, Queen Signe tapped the shoulder of one of the guards in front of her so that she could step around him and into the clearing. Kestrel realized then that she was no longer holding her umbrella—perhaps she dropped it during the attack earlier. Without it, the trees could only provide so much protection from the sunlight, her curse uninhibited.

As Queen Signe approached, fractals of light filtered down between the tree branches. The ghastly breaks in the shadows cast her in an everchanging marring of flesh and pallor. Wherever the sun grazed, Signe's flesh became as mottled as rotten fruit. Those sharp teeth of hers gleaming through the cracks.

Kestrel could not avert her gaze this time.

"Whoever said anything about killing?" the queen said, either oblivious that the veil had been pulled, or pretending to no longer care. "I'm merely suggesting that the magic here needs some...arousing."

Micah's eyebrows waggled.

But it was Leighton who asked, "Arousing? How?"

When the queen responded, she wasn't looking at him. The black pools of her eyes were fixed on Kestrel. "Like calls to likeness. Your visions summoned you here, my dear niece. And you saw yourself in the lake, correct?" Kestrel didn't like where this was headed, but she nodded, eyeing the murky waters warily. The first time, it had been her in those waters. Although in one of the visions, she'd seen Signe reaching down into them, a discrepancy she hadn't realized until now. Before she could say as much though, the queen continued on. "I think *that* is the missing piece. The thing we need to awakening the light."

Kestrel swallowed hard. Bodies of water were not her friend.

But the queen was right. In at least one of the visions, Kestrel had been in the water, so it was worth trying. After all, they'd already come all the way here.

Kestrel took an intrepid step toward the stagnant waters, reminding herself that this would be different than the time with the cinder. This lake at least appeared shallow. Even from where she stood at the edge of the bank, she thought she could see the bottom of the lake all the way across, and it looked no deeper than her hips.

If anything went awry, she reminded herself that there were multiple people nearby to help her.

With her shoes still on, Kestrel stepped into the shallow waters.

If her heart hadn't been racing, the sound of the water

lapping at her ankles as she waded in deeper might've been peaceful. Relaxing. But the distant growling of the gravemoors all around them was too familiar to the snarling cinder who'd chased her into that oasis all those years ago.

Kestrel forced herself to take one step after another. Forced a haggard breath into her lungs with each and every one.

When the water was barely halfway up her shins, she stopped. The last ripples rolled past her. And once the lake was calm again, she scanned the grey water for the blue orb they were searching for.

Nothing.

No light emanated from the murky depths.

Kestrel twisted around, her gaze inquiring as it fell to the queen.

"Well?"

"Nothing's happening," answered Kestrel.

Queen Signe stared down at the ground, thought for a moment. "Your ring. It could be blocking your magic still."

Protectively, Kestrel's hand floated to the ring on her necklace. It seemed unlikely that it would be blocking anything, since she'd been wearing it around her neck for days now, and still she was able to receive visions. She had even been wearing it in the queen's sacrificial chamber, and she had summoned enough magic to be able to repair the rabbit's wound.

But to rule it out, Kestrel supposed she might as well try.

She unclasped the necklace and tossed it to the bank, careful to watch where it landed so she could retrieve it later. Micah seemed compelled to retrieve it for her and keep it safe, but the only part of him that budged were his eyes that darted toward the queen and then seemed to think better of it. That was alright. The necklace would be safe. Kestrel just needed to get this over with.

As she turned back to face the waters, something was already glowing from the center of the pond. It seemed deeper now though, like the center of the lake had dropped and was now a bottomless thing.

The queen gasped. "What are you waiting for? Retrieve it!"

Kestrel couldn't budge. "I—I can't swim."

She wasn't sure if her eyes were just playing a trick on her, if she could wade to the center and just bend over to retrieve it. But even if she did, her head might need to go under water, and the thought of that made her lungs hurt as if she was drowning again already.

Besides, in the vision, it had been the queen who retrieved the orb.

"I'm not telling you to go for a swim," Signe hissed. "Kick the thing over here, if you have to—"

"She doesn't want to do it!"

Kestrel hadn't expected Elora to defend her, not with her position among the royal family still so precarious. Standing up to the queen might cost her. And Kestrel didn't want Elora to suffer just because she couldn't muster enough courage to do the very thing they had come here to do.

Before she could announce she would try though, it was Leighton who offered an alternative.

"Queen Signe, maybe it should be you to retrieve it.

After all, you were in Kestrel's vision, were you not? Didn't the glow intensify in your grasp? What if Kestrel is the key to awakening it, but it's you who is meant to claim such a power?"

Kestrel's heart swelled. Whether his intention had been to protect Elora or not, she didn't know, but she hoped that their conversation earlier had at least left its mark. Maybe Elora would be well taken care of after all. That was all Kestrel wanted for her.

Queen Signe considered his suggestion for only a moment before hiking up her skirts and trudging into the pond. As the queen had suggested, instead of submerging herself to reach into the depths, she toed the bluish light with her foot until it was in shallower waters. She was standing beside Kestrel when she finally bent down to retrieve it, and once it was lifted from the waters, the blue glow was even more luminous. It made the queen's dark eyes flash like storm clouds, bolts of lightning bursting from their centers.

"Yes," the queen said dreamily, gazing deep into the blue orb. Kestrel couldn't tear her gaze away from it either, the bright hue both blinding and mesmerizing. "I suppose you were right, Leighton. Apparently, I was meant to claim this power, and honestly, the last thing this realm needs are two saviors anyway."

Without further warning, the queen shoved Kestrel.

Her hand struck Kestrel so hard, it felt as if those bolts of lightning that had been reflected in Signe's eyes had struck her instead.

Kestrel's body was sent hurtling into the muck, into too many painful memories.

She was back at the Fortress of Thirst, Leighton pushing her inside and cementing his horrifying betrayal. Then she was falling into the oasis again, the water folding around her, dragging her down.

Distantly Kestrel heard people yelling, but with her head underwater, she couldn't make out what anyone was saying, let alone who they were. The water splashed into her mouth and the panic began to swell. She flailed her arms and legs, seeking purchase, convinced that she had nothing to kick off from, no ground to touch, just like in the oasis.

But the water around her was still shallow enough that once it settled, she realized her head was just barely above the surface.

Kestrel could breathe.

Everything was alright—mostly.

As the voices continued to roar and blur, the last few moments replayed in her mind. She struggled to make sense of them. This was her *aunt*—her kin. What reason did she have to push her like that? Unless it had been an accident? But no matter how much Kestrel wanted to believe that, she couldn't. There had been blazing intent behind the queen's eyes, scathing hatred in her tone.

"The last thing this realm needs are two saviors..."

Was that what this was about? Queen Signe was worried that Kestrel would be credited with saving everyone from the curse while she wasn't? Had this been her plan all along? For Kestrel to lead her to the answer, just so she could steal it away from her and claim her own glory? She wished the queen had just asked; Kestrel didn't need the glory. All she wanted was Darius' release—

And then with sinking dread, she realized that likely was no longer an option, if it ever had been.

Blinking the murky water out of her eyes, Kestrel stared up at the queen.

With an indifferent flick of her wrist, Queen Signe said to Elora, "Finish her like we discussed, and your freedom is yours."

Kestrel felt her heart sinking even lower into the depths. Felt her world crumbling around her. Especially when she searched Elora's face for signs that the queen was lying. They hadn't talked about anything. Surely Elora had never planned to lay a finger upon her.

But the dull hue of her hollow eyes said it all.

Elora *had* planned on killing her. That was what the queen had instructed her to do. It was likely why they had been spending so much time together, Elora trying to get close to her, to befriend her, just so...what? So it would hurt more? So that if she had to come pounding on Kestrel's door in the middle of the night, Kestrel wouldn't hesitate to welcome her inside?

Kestrel's eyes were welling with tears and a heaviness pressed on her chest. She almost wanted to sink. Almost wanted the waters to carry her away—anywhere but here.

"What is this?" Leighton's growl was low and ominous. "This was never part of the deal!"

"That was always part of the deal, young prince," said the queen with detached grace. "You think I want my sister's daughter roaming around the realms, free to unleash another curse upon us all?"

And for whatever reason, that was the part that finally shattered her.

Kestrel quietly sobbed. Sobbed for her mother and that magic she had lost control of. Sobbed for Darius, the man who raised her and who would now be condemned to death. Sobbed for herself. For her foolish heart for always trusting the wrong people. Always being lied to and betrayed.

Except...Elora wasn't moving, she realized.

If she intended to kill Kestrel, now would be the time. Kestrel was vulnerable. Blubbering like a fool. Meanwhile, the princess and her dark magic were untethered by hailstone. Power was at her command. All she would have to do was take the few steps toward Kestrel and press one finger upon her skin.

But she was standing firm.

The dull hue of her magenta eyes had started to glow, to burn like gemstones caught between embers. And Kestrel wanted to believe the hope fracturing her heart, wanted to trust that Elora had never—would never intend to harm her. But her trust had been broken one too many times. She could no longer dole it out freely.

From where Leighton stood between the queen and princess, he drew his sword and raised it at Elora's chest.

Kestrel screamed for him to stop.

But the moment her mouth cracked open, the sludge of the pond floor gave way beneath her.

Something cold and boney wrapped around Kestrel's ankle, and she was lurched into the depths.

Arms spiraling, Kestrel thrashed against the hold upon her. She flailed and grasped, searching for anything to hold onto and fight against the tug taking her under. The light above was dimming too rapidly, the pond too deep. She was losing.

Finally, slowly, Kestrel turned her head and faced whatever was dragging her downwards.

Two yellow eyes met her gaze. Kestrel was not alone in the lake.

CHAPTER 36

THE TOUCH OF DEATH

ELORA

All Elora could do was stare at Kestrel who was watching her with such a wounded expression she wished she could tear her own heart out. If only she could explain—Elora never wanted to kill her, had already decided she wouldn't. But what could she say, especially now with the audience they had around them? The truth was, when the queen had first approached her with the offer, she *had* considered it. A few days ago, there was no price she wouldn't have paid. But that had all changed once she'd come to know Kestrel. Come to care for her.

If she admitted to that now though, her freedom would be lost forever.

She couldn't go back to those dungeons. To a life of torture and fear.

But she couldn't kill Kestrel either.

Leighton raised his sword to Elora's chest, pulling her from her thoughts.

The steel glinted as lightning struck overhead, and Elora thought that maybe this would be for the best. He would strike her through the heart, and she would die— for a brief time. And when she came back to, all of this would be over. She wouldn't have to confess to the queen that their deal was off, and she wouldn't have to kill Kestrel.

But if she was incapacitated, there was no telling what would happen. The queen still had at least a half dozen guards at her bidding; if Elora wasn't able to fulfill her wishes, surely one of them would.

The thought of rising from death again, only this time to a world without Kestrel in it, was enough to set Elora's blood on fire.

No one would lay a finger upon her princess.

She needed a plan.

But before Elora could concoct one, Kestrel screamed, the sound cut off abruptly by a gurgling of water as her head disappeared below.

For one fraction of a moment, it was like the realm had stilled. Like time had stopped and no longer held any meaning.

Everyone gaped at the spot where Kestrel had been, at the bubbles floating to the surface. The water looked darker now, somehow deeper.

It was Micah who called out for her first, his voice sounding as disbelieving as Elora felt. "Kestrel?" He waited a moment. Tilted his head to get a better look. When Kestrel didn't emerge, he barged forward.

"Ah-ah-ah!" Queen Signe snapped her fingers, and

three of her guards closed in around the prince, their lances and swords aimed to kill.

"Leave him alone!" Leighton snarled, twisting around as he heaved his sword, leveling it at the queen. "What did you do to Kestrel?"

"I've done nothing to the girl," the queen replied cooly. "But if the fool can't swim, then this is a fate far better than any I could've schemed." A small, bite of a laugh escaped her. "To think, her own vision lead her here to her demise. It's splendidly cruel."

"Let her go!"

But the queen didn't respond. Already, her gaze was becoming hazy, her focus intent on the glowing prize in her hands.

Growling, Leighton reared back. He started to sprint for the pond and Elora had never been more grateful for his stubborn heroism. But before he could make it more than a bounding stride, Efrem stepped in front of him. In a flurry of blows, the young guardsman managed to disarm Leighton, and sent him buckling to his knees.

"What are you doing? We have to save her!" bellowed Leighton, straining to break free.

"The queen's orders are to—"

"Curse the queen! I'm your brother. The future king! Let me go or I swear I'll—" His frantic gaze kept cutting to the water, the rage in him waning, replaced by something far more panicked and desperate. "Please, brother. I can't let her die."

If there had ever been a doubt in Elora's mind that the prince had cared deeply for Kestrel, the sound of him cracking diminished it entirely.

Efrem didn't say a word. Leighton muttered something about never being able to forgive him for this, but Elora could hardly hear him. She could hardly hear the queen beginning her chants to the Sky-Blessed, trying to access the power of the orb that she had claimed. Elora was too busy staring into the grey waters, horror-struck and frozen. The air bubbles were slowing. Kestrel still hadn't resurfaced; she was nowhere to be seen. She couldn't swim and Elora didn't know how long she could hold her breath—maybe a minute? A few? If she couldn't help herself, then she needed someone to do it for her.

But there was no one left.

No one but Elora.

Except if she went into those waters, if she so much as grazed Kestrel with the slightest touch, the young woman she was coming to admire would be dead. Without any hailstone to block her Ashen magic, Elora was useless—

Only then it struck her.

There was hailstone here.

Kestrel's ring.

Elora had almost forgotten. But there it was, sitting on the bank, looped around her discarded necklace.

It was just a stride away. But it would cost Elora everything.

There would be no going back if she did this.

Across from her, she heard Queen Signe curse at the orb. "Why isn't it working? Sky-Blessed hear me, grant my pleas and bestow upon me this ancient power! Do as I command you!"

Out of the corner of her eye, Elora noticed the orb changing colors. The blue light dimmed, engulfed by a dark red hue that now emanated from the center like an ominous warning.

The queen began to gasp and cry, juggling the orb from one hand to another. The guards who weren't monitoring the princes and Elora rushed to her side to try to aid her, but the queen refused them.

"Don't you dare! Keep your hands off it! It's mine!" Her cries penetrated each command as the orb seemed to grow angrier, hotter.

This was Elora's chance. While most of the guardsmen were distracted.

Elora spun around to the knight behind her first. He was so preoccupied watching in horror as the queen's hands burned that he almost didn't notice her lifting hers toward his face. With one outstretched, slate-grey finger, Elora pressed against his forehead just before he could cry out. Power surged from her. His eyes went cross. Then they blanched white. His cheeks became gaunt as her magic tore through him and siphoned every last day of life he had left in him.

She didn't allow herself to think about the family he'd be leaving at home. Nor the unaccomplished hopes and dreams he had left to achieve. The guilt would consume her later. For now, all that she knew was that he had to die.

As the last vestiges of vivacity were drained, before his body could fall, Elora was already turning toward the guard in front of her. The thump of the first man's body hitting the ground made the other guard jump. He likely thought it was just the rootless traipsing in the forest around them. But he would never find out.

Before he could spin around to investigate, Elora's

hand was upon his flesh as well. In an instant, the life drained out of him, leaving behind a sickly husk of the man he had been.

His body collapsed and Elora bolted around him. She tripped over her skirts, slamming into the dirt as she reached the ring. Someone shouted, but she didn't hear what they were saying. Couldn't focus on anything but the ring.

She fumbled with the chain of the necklace, cumbersome and tangled, but finally she managed to slip the ring around her finger.

Without her magic keeping them at bay, the monsters of the Hollows descended upon them.

Gravemoors lurched from the ground, ensnaring the guardsmen and dragging them below the earth. The rootless who had been patiently stalking suddenly charged through the trees from all directions. Their vines and branches whipped and snatched anyone they could. They eviscerated knights, crippled their limbs.

As chaos ensued, the Thundersworn Brigade turned their attention to the monsters.

No one seemed to notice Elora.

No one except Prince Micah.

His eyes were wide. He watched her in a way she'd never seen him look at her before. Like he believed in her. Like he was counting on her.

Elora dove into the water without another thought about the carnage happening behind her or the dangers lurking below. All she could think about was Kestrel. Save Kestrel. Get Kestrel out of here.

But the pond was even murkier beneath the surface.

The waters grainy and difficult to see through. Her eyes burned against the debris, but she swam onward. Deeper. Farther down than a pond like this should be. There was something both ominous and magical about this place, and she didn't like it. It reminded her of the Ghostlight Gulf, when she and all of her Ashen brethren had swum to the surface, reborn. Those waters had seemed endless too, like a cold void they would never escape. Only, they did. So she had to believe she and Kestrel would escape this too.

Finally, Elora thought she saw something, buried deep down at the bottom of the suddenly vast lake. It floated in the water like a strip of crimson rope, but she would recognize that intricate braid anywhere.

As fast as her arms would allow, Elora plunged deeper into the dark waters.

Even from this distance, she could tell Kestrel wasn't really moving. Floating, her arms spread wide, her head upright—but if she were drowning, if she were panicked, she'd be flailing. It made Elora's stomach twist and writhe. Maybe she was already too late.

As she swam closer, she realized they were not alone.

A creature floated before Kestrel, one that looked just a sickly as the dead bodies Elora had left up on the bank above. If it had been human, most of those parts were gone now, its flesh dripping from bone and barely hanging on. But most of its head and face were still intact, if not addled with water-rot and age.

It almost resembled a woman.

Thin strands of hair drifted around her like a crown of seaweed. But the eyes were bulbous and yellow, like some horrific deep-sea monster that survived by feasting upon shipwrecked sailors.

Kestrel and the water-horror were staring right at each other. And as Elora cautiously drifted closer, she saw Kestrel's eyes were entirely white. They shone like pearls down here in the bottom of the lake. Like she was lost in a trance of this monster's making.

Elora didn't know what to do. Trances were not a form of magic she was familiar with, let alone whatever this creature was. To interrupt it could cause Kestrel immense harm, for all she knew. But leaving her down here much longer would as well.

The water-horror tapped her own chest, and something hollow began to form there. A red light filled the empty space, blooming and growing so bright that Elora had a difficult time looking at it.

Kestrel, however, seemed to be drawn to it. She couldn't look away. In fact, she drifted closer, one arm outstretched for the strange light.

The glint of red light caught on the dagger in Kestrel's belt.

Elora didn't waste another second.

She jerked the dagger free and swiped the sharp blade at the water-horror.

But then, it was gone. The red light disappearing with it too. So was the deep chasm, as Elora realized the darkness had lessened around them, the surface just within reach overhead.

With the creature gone, Kestrel's eyes blinked. The white pearls disappeared, fearing flooding her green eyes instead. Kestrel's arms flailed to find purchase and Elora nearly let out a breath of relief as she wrapped her arms around the girl's waist and kicked off the bottom of the pond.

They resurfaced with gasping, gagging breaths. Elora didn't stop dragging her to safety until they were out of the pond, the terrifying, mysterious water lapping at their heels but no longer surrounding them.

Cries filled the air. Distantly Elora heard commands being shouted. The queen shrieking. Someone sobbing. Bellows of rage and despair.

As much as she wanted to let Kestrel catch her breath, they couldn't stay here. This was their chance to run.

She turned to Kestrel to say as much, when she realized the young woman was already standing. Kestrel's eyes had changed again. This time they were pools of black, like bottomless wells of ink. It was a menacing enough sight alone, but it was the furrow in her brow that really caused Elora alarm. She had never seen Kestrel so enraged, so thirsty for blood.

And for the first time since holding onto Kestrel and swimming to the surface, Elora considered that maybe the water-horror hadn't really disappeared. Maybe she had just mistakenly brought something else up from the depths.

CHAPTER 37

DAUGHTER OF DAYBREAK

KESTREL

In those yellow eyes, Kestrel had seen so much. More than she should have.

Daughter of Daybreak.

She witnessed the calamity. Watched the Maw crack the earth in two. Saw the wings torn from the Sky-Blessed. Watched as Elora's people swam to the surface of the Ghostlight Gulf.

She saw bargains struck. Alliances forged and broken. Everything.

But mostly, she saw her mother.

Daughter of Daybreak.

Aenwyn's entire life unfurled before Kestrel like a tapestry of tangled threads. A peaceful childhood among a gatherer community. A rambunctious adolescence of three untamed sisters and their powerful clan. A gift. A dragon egg hatching. Regret powerful enough that she had sacrificed her own happiness to serve her people and all the kingdoms.

Queen Aenwyn had not been a vicious sorceress.

She had been a caring sister. A doting daughter. A dutiful queen.

She had been caught between vows and temptation, betrayal and duty.

Daughter of Daybreak.

Kestrel had seen her mother the day of the Cursed Night. That magic had been no accident, though Aenwyn hadn't known it was within her either. She had just felt pain. The discovery of her family's betrayal—her own father and sister and husband plotting and construing her entire life without any regard for her well-being—it had pushed her over the edge. Darkness and rage had filled her to the core. And only Darius had been there for her.

When King Everard's men had landed the killing blow on the dragon—the same creature who had shown Aenwyn everything—Kestrel had watched as black magic had surged from her mother in one dreadful thought: make them suffer for what they have done, let them be the monsters they truly are.

Queen Aenwyn's magic had done her bidding. Not the Sky-Blessed. *Her* magic. Ancient and powerful. A magic that spanned lifetimes.

The same magic that was inside Kestrel.

Daughter of Daybreak.

All the king's men were burned by eternal flames. The rulers of Grimtol were punished for their conniving and scheming—even though Aenwyn was only certain about the complicity of a few, she knew political corruption ran deep in Grimtol, and she wasn't about to risk letting any of them go unscathed.

And now, back on dry land, facing the same people who had betrayed her mother, the same bloodlines who had lied repeatedly and tricked her as well, now Kestrel would do the same.

She was the new Daughter of Daybreak. A source of power as magnificent as the sun. Like her mother, she could heal life. Or she could take it.

Kestrel channeled all of that heartbreak—two lifetimes worth—and summoned the black magic that dwelled within her.

They would know suffering again. They would rue the day they ever crossed the Daughters of Daybreak.

CHAPTER 38
THE CURSED BEAST
ELORA

The clouds flashed, cracks of light that illuminated the deadly scene below. Black smoke rose up from the earth around Kestrel, like sprouting trees—thick ones, hundreds of years old. They writhed below where Kestrel hovered, these dark columns of power, like a shield moving with languid but deadly intent.

Whatever they were, Elora knew no one would survive them.

She staggered back, but she was too close to get far enough away.

Magic erupted from Kestrel like a star bursting in the night sky. The might of it alone knocked Elora back onto her rear. But as she squinted through the power, she realized it wasn't actually reaching her. It rolled over her like a grey stream of water, like she was guarded by some impenetrable shield. Never in her life had she seen such a thing. Was this the hailstone protecting her? Preventing the magic from reaching her? Or something else entirely?

Through the black haze of magic surrounding everything, Elora peered up at Kestrel and wondered at her sheer power.

This wasn't the work of the water-horror—how ridiculous she could have been to have ever thought as much. This magic was familiar, even though she herself had not seen it. But she had heard of its descriptions. This was curse magic. The same that Queen Aenwyn had wielded, all those years ago.

Everyone else near the blast was sent flying.

Leighton surged across the meadow, his body flung like a ragdoll into a mound of stickerbushes with thorns as long as fingers. Even through the smoky magic, Elora could see the blood trickling from his face. Hear his guttural cries as he pawed at the thorns that pierced his eyes.

Efrem's body was sent careening through the air as well, until his spine smacked against a massive tree. The crack of his bones was sickening. His body fell limp, but no one could rush to see if he was alright, for the gravemoors at the tree's base clambered for him, dragging him below the moment he landed.

Micah had already been low to the ground, so the blast mostly just held him in place. But seeing his brothers flung, hearing their cries of pain, he couldn't stay put. Slowly, with immense effort, Micah fought to drag himself across the earth, through the dense and heavy magic, toward the sounds of his brothers. He screamed too, for he watched as Efrem's body disappeared beneath the earth. Still, he kept crawling, kept calling out for his lost twin.

Elora watched in horror as the gravemoors reached out for him next. Not the same tree, but one he had crawled past and hadn't even been paying attention to how close he had become. It wrapped its gnarled fingers around his ankles. Two of the rootless were nearing Leighton, hunger in their eyeless faces that made Elora actually want to defend him.

Remembering the power at her own fingertips, she realized she could.

Elora tore the ring off her hand. Instantly, the Hollows stilled.

The gravemoors whined, retreating back into the soil. The rootless shrieked and scurried back toward the trees. Elora only hoped that perhaps she had just helped spare some of the carnage, and some of the guilt that Kestrel would surely feel later.

All the terrors of the forest had gone back to where they belonged.

All except for Signe.

Kestrel's magic was still writhing around the queen like a tornado. It carried her into the sky, leaving only the orb behind where her feet had been, the magical item returning to the same shade of light blue it had been to start with.

With a surge of power, the magic encasing the queen expelled itself in a gust. In its wake, only a monster remained, the same one the queen had been trying to conceal for years. A winged beast of gnarled bones and mottled flesh, she shrieked her rage into the sky. With a flap of her black wings, the rest of the magic spooling out of Kestrel dissipated.

Kestrel collapsed to the ground, utterly spent. Magic like this would do that to a person, Elora presumed. Magic like the queen's. And this was precisely the same magic. The same curse that now took root fully in Signe who was not pleased.

The queen-turned-beast dove for the crumpled princess, wicked claws outstretched. She plummeted atop Kestrel before Elora could so much as move. By the time she was bolting toward them, the winged queen was already slashing into Kestrel's chest and face. Ruby bursts of blood splattered Elora's as she dove for the queen, prepared to barrel into the creature and let her lethal touch do the rest.

But as Elora lunged, the queen twisted around, sensing her coming.

With a gust of her mighty wings, she launched herself into the sky.

Elora scrambled to a halt before she could fall atop Kestrel and accidentally kill her instead. She stopped just in time, though as she gazed down upon her, she noticed her dire wounds. Her chest was torn to ribbons and bleeding profusely. But with the threat still at hand, Elora couldn't do anything for her yet.

Instead, she shielded her eyes and stared up into the sky. Her heart pounded as she prepared for another attack. This time it would be her those claws would tear into, and she could take it. At least a few strikes, if she needed to. Anything to let the queen get close enough for her to touch her. And if that didn't work, there was always

Kestrel's dagger that Elora was still clinging to. She almost hoped the cursed monsters would be immune to her touch of death. There was something satisfying about the thought of plunging the blade deep into the queen's flesh and wrenching it downward, letting her suffer the way all of her sacrifices had.

But instead of another attack, the queen-turned-beast shrieked. A cry of rage so high-pitched and horrible that it sent ripples across the pond and nearly shattered Elora's ears.

Then, the winged creature tore off through the sky, heading west. Maybe back to Irongate.

Elora only feared for the Ironblood people for half of a thought before her concern barreled back toward Kestrel. She was starting to blink her eyes open. That was a good sign, she hoped. And they were once again the same emerald eyes Elora had come to adore. Like peaceful meadows untouched by corruption or death— only, there was a darkness to them now. A shadowing that hadn't been there before. And Elora couldn't help but wonder if the woman she had been falling for would be different now. Changed. Darkened like the rest of Grimtol.

It didn't matter though.

Life had a way of leaving its mark on everyone.

And regardless of who Kestrel was becoming, what this magic was doing to her, Elora knew there was nothing that would keep her from being by her side throughout every moment of it.

Behind her, Elora heard Leighton shuffling about, still blind to his surroundings, his eyes oozing blood. A few of the guards hobbled back from the forest, their arms bound by vines, their bodies scratched and lacerated.

Micah was still half-buried in the ground, screaming for someone to come help—but not for his sake. He was still digging in the dirt, trying to reach his twin, whom Elora knew was already long gone.

Everyone was distracted by the chaos. It would only be a matter of time before they turned their ire toward the person responsible for so much of it.

They would imprison Kestrel for this. Perhaps even kill her.

And for what? All because the queen betrayed her, had shoved her into that lake and plotted the demise of her own niece.

Elora knew the real story. Perhaps in time, the princes would come to understand the truth as well. But for now, amidst so much grief and anguish, there would be rage. They would demand justice for the loss of their brother, for the perceived attack upon the crown prince.

The two of them couldn't stay. They needed to run. But Elora wasn't sure Kestrel could.

As quietly but as swiftly as she could, Elora crouched over her prone body.

Kestrel was already trying to lean up on her forearms, inspecting herself. That was a good sign too, Elora thought, until she saw the damage up close.

It wasn't good. Blood was spurting from some of the claw marks. Some of the wounds were so deep, that there was no way Kestrel would be able to run with them.

Elora wanted to cradle her in her arms, but the ring still dangled on the necklace in her grasp. She couldn't put it on yet. Couldn't condemn them all, at least not if she didn't have to.

She folded one arm over herself instead and gawked down at the horror of it all. She didn't know what to do. How to save them. Never before had she felt more worthless.

CHAPTER 39
AWAKENED

KESTREL

Blearily, Kestrel opened her eyes. Through the trees, she thought she could see large, leathery wings just before they flew out of sight. Her head was throbbing. One of her eyes was swollen shut, that entire half of her face alit with fiery pain, but it was nothing compared to the agony in her chest and torso.

Kestrel felt air in places where it didn't belong.

Carefully and wincing with each inch of progress, Kestrel raised herself up onto her elbows. She peered down at her body. Her chest laid bare, the tunic ripped to shreds, and beneath it all she could see was bloody scraps of flesh and bone.

She was in so much pain. Unbearable and blazing.

But pain, as it turned out, was the primary source of her magic. So was blood. And Kestrel had ample of both.

Without time to explain, Kestrel ignored the worried way Elora was watching her and acted on instinct. On new knowledge. Thanks to the vision, or whatever had happened to her when she was underwater, Kestrel now understood the power inside her so much better. Had seen her mother grow into it, spending a lifetime adapting and learning how to wield it. Like Signe, she too had once believed that they needed to invoke the Sky-Blessed to access such a power.

But the day of the Cursed Night, Aenwyn had learned otherwise.

Power had always been inside her. Just like it had always been inside Kestrel.

Aenwyn's healing magic was different than the magic she used to curse all the rulers of Grimtol. For that magic, she had only needed a site of pain, and the more blood she could see, the easier it was to command it. It was why Kestrel had been able to heal that rabbit so easily.

Kestrel stared down at her tattered chest. She focused the light and airy magic inside herself, willed it to her bidding. The charge built in time with the raucous booming of thunder above them.

Just like with the rabbit, her skin began to knit itself back together, burying the bone back where it belonged, and leaving fresh, pink flesh behind.

But then she grew winded. With gasping breaths, Kestrel's magic stopped before it could heal her fully. She was too exhausted to do anything more, but at least it was better than nothing.

Elora gasped, watching her with awe. "How did you —"

"I'll explain later," Kestrel said, each word dragging with effort. "Can you help me up?"

But Elora flinched away. "I can't. I have to keep the ring off, otherwise..."

Elora glanced behind them, and for the first time since surfacing from the pond, Kestrel heard the chaos around them.

Screams and retching.

Labored breaths and mournful cries.

Unassisted, Kestrel hobbled to her feet and peered around the meadow. She spotted Leighton first, a trail of thorny vines dragging behind one of his heels. But his face? She had never seen anything more horrific. Waterfalls of crimson trailed down his cheeks. A thick thorn jutted from one of his eyes. Judging from the gaping hole where his other eye had been, she guessed it had met a similar fate until he had plucked the obtrusive bramble out, his eye along with it.

Kestrel could fix this though. With her new magic, she could heal him.

Leighton was staggering. Stumbling. Feeling around with one hand while the other raged wildly, sword choked to the hilt. And all the while he was shouting.

At first, she couldn't make out what he was saying, only that there was a menace in his tone that she had only caught glimpses of before.

Then the words became clearer. It was her name on his tongue.

"Kestrel!" Another wild swing of his sword. "You'll pay for this!"

Shaking her head, she stumbled toward him, unaware that she was doing so. "Leighton, I'm so sorry. I can help you. I can—"

"Kestrel!" he roared louder, as if her voice were bellows to the fire of his wrath. "I'll kill you for this! You hear me?"

There was no reaching him.

He wouldn't even listen to her. Wouldn't even let her try to help him.

If she dared any closer, he would hack her to pieces before she could even attempt to summon her magic. She wasn't even certain she had any left in her just yet. She was already spent. But she would've tried. She would've done anything to right this wrong, if only he would've let her...

Kestrel clutched the spot where her ring was usually dangling around her neck, forgetting that the space would still be empty. But oh, how she wished it wasn't. She wanted Aenwyn there. Wanted the comfort clutching her ring would provide. After all, she was the only person in all of Grimtol who could know how Kestrel was feeling.

Close to Leighton but half-buried in the earth lay Micah. Or at least, who she thought was Micah. It was difficult to tell without his usual crooked grin or the way his eyes always looked like they were scheming. There was no joy about him now though. No teasing shenanigans brewing in his skull. His face, slick with tears and splotched red, was the grimmest sight she thought she'd ever known. And even before she could scan their surroundings for Efrem, she knew—somehow she *knew*—what the reason was.

"No," she muttered, hand clutching her breastbone tighter. The scars were still tender there, her fingernails making her wince.

Micah's eyes crawled up to hers. Hatred burned in their depths.

Kestrel staggered back, one foot resoaking as it slipped into the pond.

Her magic had done this. The same darkness that had been within her mother, and now she had released it as well.

But she couldn't take all the blame, could she? She hadn't fully meant to. She had just been filled with so much hurt and anger that she'd lost control. Just like her mother had. Kestrel had been provoked. It was an accident. A mistake.

That wasn't how the people would see it though. Rumors would abound now, the Corrupt Daughter to the Corrupt Queen.

This would be her legacy.

Blamed for Efrem's death.

For Signe's gruesome transformation.

For Leighton's maiming.

A gentle voice eased in behind her. "Come on."

Kestrel's wet eyes met Elora's. There was nothing she wanted more than to throw herself into her arms. But then she remembered what the queen had said. They had plotted to kill her. The queen had demanded it. But the princess was a prisoner, Kestrel reminded herself. Would she have really had much of a choice in what the queen told her to do? Besides, when the moment had come, Elora *hadn't* done the queen's bidding. She'd been the only one to come and save her.

And maybe Kestrel was foolish to trust her now, but there was a tenderness in her gaze that she couldn't ignore. An unspoken plea for forgiveness, and Kestrel wanted to give that to her, with all of her heart. Wanted to have someone by her side after all of...this.

For now, she told herself as she started to walk toward the princess. They could talk more about everything later, but for now she would choose to trust her.

"Wait," Kestrel said, something from her original vision tugging at her. "What about the feathers? Your people's wings, we never found them."

"Stop them!" bellowed Leighton, thrashing more wildly at the sound of Kestrel's voice.

Elora shook her head, white hair sopping wet and clinging to her shoulders. "It's not important. We have to go."

Before Kestrel could reach her, she noticed the blue orb on the forest ground. She remembered then that the underwater vision had shown her the power of the orb as well—it had opened the creature up, a doorway to some place that few ever returned from. She now knew what that orb could do. The power it contained. And she certainly didn't want it to fall into the wrong hands.

Scurrying as fast as her healing wounds would allow, Kestrel limped over to the orb, grabbed it, and fled.

"Guards!" Leighton kept shouting, spit spewing from his lips like molten lava. "By order of your king, I command you! Apprehend her!"

Tears were streaming down Kestrel's face when she reached Elora again. "Put the ring on."

"Are you...are you sure? Micah, he's still—"

Kestrel felt the strength she possessed shatter. She stared at the half-buried prince, horrified. He had been her first friend. When Leighton had betrayed her at the Fortress of Thirst, it had been Micah who'd returned to save her. Micah who held her hand as they marched through Irongate. Micah who had made her laugh and feel welcome in his home.

Her first friend.

And how had she repaid him?

The guards were gaining on them.

Kestrel wiped the tears that were streaming down her face. "I don't think we have a choice."

Elora didn't wait for another request. She simply slipped the ring onto her finger and let the Hollows come back to life.

"You can't catch us and save your princes!" Kestrel shouted behind her as Micah's screams tore through the woods again. All she could do was hope they would choose to save him instead of chasing after her.

Then, she and Elora ran.

And this time, Kestrel didn't look back.

CHAPTER 40

THE ROAD AHEAD

KESTREL

As healed as Kestrel was, it still wasn't enough. Dodging and jumping over sentient tree roots while also trying desperately to outrun the guards she was certain were gaining on them, Kestrel was having a hard time keeping up their hastened pace.

Elora eventually offered to let her lean on her shoulder, so that she could help carry some of her weight. But it only slowed them down more.

The rootless were ravenous around them.

The gravemoors clawed at their feet.

They wouldn't make it out of the Hollows alive. Not like this.

"Take off the ring," Kestrel huffed, narrowly leaping over one of the gravemoors that was reaching up for them from the dirt.

"What?" Elora balked. "I won't be able to help you if I—"

"You will," she said, remembering another part of her underwater vision.

Fractal splices of that vision kept splicing through her mind. Kestrel didn't know how long she'd been down there, but it had felt like an eternity—the vision *had covered* an eternity. Years and years, centuries of events, millennia of history, some of which Kestrel couldn't help but wonder had previously been lost to time. She had seen so much of Grimtol's past that it was difficult to sort out the important parts, the ones that still made sense.

Elora cast her a dubious glance. She didn't know everything Kestrel now knew. Didn't understand how much knowledge she now possessed about...everything.

But in that vision, Kestrel had witnessed her own birth. Heard the promise the dragon had made to her mother to *"give back what had been taken."* Not even Aenwyn had understood the implications then, not until her belly had swollen with a new bundle of joy.

Kestrel. Her only daughter. Her only heir.

Kestrel was still making sense of the tangled tapestry of history that had been splayed before her, but she had understood this: Aenwyn had been infertile. The eggs in her womb, dead. And the dragon had brought one of them back to life. It had chosen Kestrel and raised her from the dead.

Elora and Kestrel were more alike than they had ever known. And Kestrel would prove it to her.

Before Elora could pull away, Kestrel reached for her hand and tore the ring from her finger.

"Don't! You don't know what will—"

Elora flung herself from Kestrel—or at least she tried

to. But the Daughter of Daybreak was holding tight. It was just a hunch, but if she was right, it could change everything.

And Kestrel *was* right.

Clutching onto Elora's hand, nothing happened to her. The death magic that everyone feared—it had no effect on Kestrel, a princess who had also been brought back to life.

Elora's eyes slammed shut, a terrified shriek ripping from her lungs.

"It's alright," Kestrel said, a touch of wonder to her tone for even she couldn't believe her eyes. "You can't hurt me."

Peeling one eye open, Elora peered down at their entwined fingers. Her magenta eyes had never blazed brighter. She looked up at Kestrel then, a heady concoction of fear and hope and longing reflected in those glimmering eyes.

"That's...impossible," Elora breathed, but her fingers tightened around Kestrel's, testing their hold. "How are you still alive?"

A smirk inched up one side of Kestrel's face. "I promise I'll tell you all about it, once we're somewhere a little safer."

With the ring now in her possession, Kestrel looped the necklace back around her neck as the gravemoors and rootless jerked away, begrudgingly retreating back into the crevices of the earth and trees from whence they came.

With their snarling gone, Kestrel could better hear the guards shouting, somewhere farther in the distance than she had previously feared. Leighton was still barking orders, commanding his guards to locate and bring back the two runaway princesses, dead or alive. Distantly, she thought she heard Micah trying to plead with him to have mercy, but she was certain she'd misheard him. A trick of the mind trying to ease the heartache of guilt that was already threatening to consume her.

"Come on, we've got to find the exit."

As they sped off into the forest, Kestrel kept her gaze fixed forward, toward an uncertain future, one without any promise of safety and refuge. They had lost everything —Irongate, their friends, Kestrel's family—and now they were being spat back out into the Wilds like rabid animals. Like fugitives.

She supposed that's what they were now, and she couldn't pretend to know the full weight of what that meant yet.

Eventually, the two princesses emerged near the south end of the Hollows from what Kestrel could tell, judging by the familiar drier lands of Vallonde.

"Cursed sky!" Elora exclaimed, glancing across the expanse and likely noting the sparse foliage. "We're too out in the open here. There's nowhere to take cover and lay low so you can rest."

She was right. Vallonde always had been a desolate place. It was jarring coming face to face with it again, even though Kestrel had only been in the lush kingdom of Irongate for a short while.

But a thought struck her.

"When the princes and I came up this way, we had sand-gliders. They were too big or maybe just not well-equipped for the terrain of Irongate, so we left them just outside the mountain pass. Maybe they're still there?"

"If they're Irongate property, I'm sure they're well-guarded."

Elora was probably right. Not to mention, they'd still have to travel around the Hollows to reach them. Kestrel cursed, knowing they were running out of options and time.

"Then I guess we just start walking and hope no one else makes it through the Hollows until we're too far away to see."

Tightening her arm around Kestrel's waist, Elora nodded and tugged her along.

A lot had gone wrong in the Hollows. Things had happened that Kestrel knew hadn't fully sank in yet, and when they did, they would make her ache in ways she had likely never imagined. There was still a lot left for her to figure out. But at least for now, leaving with the Princess of Eynallore at her side, Kestrel felt like they would be alright. Like as long as they had each other, it wasn't a mistake that she had left her tower. It couldn't be. Because if Kestrel had stayed in her tower, Elora would still be a prisoner. And Kestrel would likely still be in her tower, waiting for Thom's arrival, and it would never come. She wouldn't know anything about her mother. About her own lineage and power.

Even with everything that had gone wrong, Kestrel knew—believed beyond a doubt—that she and Elora were somehow exactly where they were meant to be.

As the Hollows began to fade behind them, the uncertainty grew in Elora's expression until she could bear it no longer.

"What are we going to do now?"

Kestrel laughed, a bitterness to it as she considered everything storming through her mind. There were so many answers to that question, and Kestrel was still parsing through them all. She still wanted to save Darius—only, that would be near-impossible now. And her mother? She didn't even know where to begin to look, but Darius had suspected she was alive and Kestrel now knew he was right. She had seen it. That power had not destroyed Aenwyn, just like Kestrel's power had not destroyed her. The only question was: where had she gone then?

And none of that took into account the likely numerous things Elora wanted to do now that she was free.

But they could do none of it until they were rested, and Kestrel healed.

"For now? We find somewhere to rest. For a day, maybe two. But I think we're going to need it for everything that lies ahead of us."

"Us?" Elora tried guarding the edge of hope in her voice, but it was to no avail.

And honestly, Kestrel was glad. They deserved hope between the two of them, after everything they had endured. They deserved to forge a life for themselves, to make their own choices, and to have each other by their sides. They still had much to discuss. Much to discover about each other. But Kestrel was looking forward to the freedom they both had now, and what it might do for their budding relationship.

Kestrel stopped walking. She turned toward Elora, taking her hands into her own.

Elora flinched, but hopefully in time, she would learn that her touch could not harm Kestrel. That they were meant for each other.

"Yes *us*," Kestrel said, her thumb stroking the top of Elora's hand. "That is, if you're willing to go on this journey with me?"

Elora's grey cheeks flushed pink. She sucked in a deep breath, but fell silent for a long moment, like the words she wanted to say were too difficult to muster. But this was the Ashen Princess. A wielder of death. And Kestrel's savior. There was nothing she could not do. Nothing Elora could not face with strength and grace.

Finally, Elora held her chin high, all reservation gone as she met Kestrel's eyes. "You have been a star in my night sky, Kestrel. A beacon of hope in an otherwise grim existence. I would follow you to the depths of the Maw and back if you asked me. I would—"

Unable to stop herself any longer, Kestrel grabbed Elora by the neck and dragged her nearer.

There was no tenderness when her lips crashed into Elora's. Only a desperate promise. A plea.

For a brief moment, hesitation tightened to Elora's lips. Uncertainty and perhaps fear made her close herself to Kestrel. But then Elora sucked in a deep breath and dove into the unknown.

She melted beneath Kestrel's touch and pressed her soft lips to hers in return. Their mouths parted, and Kestrel knew how Elora would taste even before their tongues caressed each other. Like honeysuckle and lilac. Sweet and delicate and blissful.

The desert sun had already done wonders for drying

out their sodden clothes, but there was still a dampness to them as Kestrel slid an arm around Elora's lower back and pulled her in tighter. This was where she belonged. In Elora's arms. Cherishing where their bodies met. The warmth of Elora's stomach and breasts pressed against hers.

Hesitant at first, Elora slowly crawled her hands up and around Kestrel's neck. The closer they became, the deeper her tongue explored the vast unknown of Kestrel's mouth, and Kestrel savored every stroke and dance. She relished that with each explorative plunge, Elora became hungrier. More eager for the taste of her. As if she couldn't get enough.

Neither could Kestrel.

She could've lapped up this woman for hours. And would have if it weren't for a deliciously ravenous but unfortunate maneuvering of their faces that caused Elora's nose to press into the unhealed wound on Kestrel's cheek.

The hiss it elicited from her was entirely involuntary.

Elora shoved herself back. "Dragon's fire! I'm so sorry!"

"It's alright," Kestrel said, the pain already forgotten. She was reaching back out for Elora, determined to extend this moment, this kiss that she had wanted for so long. "I'm fine. It was just one of the scratches."

But Elora swatted her extended arms away. "They're not scratches. Your face is gouged. It might even be infected."

Kestrel smirked. "I don't think infections work that fast."

"You know what I mean," Elora huffed.

Kestrel did, and she appreciated the caring thought toward her wellbeing more than she could describe.

"I can just heal it. I'll be fine, I promise," she said, trying to reassure her. Trying to resume the tender, delicious moment they were having before everything had been ruined. But before Kestrel could wrap her arms around the princess again, Elora was already pacing away, scanning the desert in all directions.

"You're right. You can heal yourself. But first, you need to rest. And we shouldn't be standing out here in the open anyway."

Kestrel wanted to protest, but how could she argue when Elora was right. Not to mention, the longer they stood there in the blistering heat, the woozier Kestrel was beginning to feel.

There would be time for more kisses soon—and hopefully even more activities that she had yet to discover with another body. Now that they were free, they had all the time in the world.

So with a groan, Kestrel kicked a lose rock and followed after her.

"Fine. We'll find somewhere to rest. Figure out our plan. And then more kissing?"

Elora smiled shyly, but there was a wicked glint in her eyes. "Oh, there definitely will be."

And Kestrel knew no matter where they went, as long as they were together, nothing else mattered. Not Leighton. Not Signe. Not any of the monsters in all the realm.

Because together, they were stronger.

Together, they would change the realm forever.

Thank you for reading
A Crown of Deceit & Ruin!

To be continued in:

A Crown of Ashes & Death

<u>Leave a Review</u>
Help other readers find this dark saga by leaving a review on Amazon, Goodreads, Bookbub, or any other reading website. Even a simple "I loved it!" can really help!

<u>ARC Team</u>
If you're someone who loves leaving reviews and you're excited by the idea of having early access to all of my books, check out my website for more information on how to join my ARC Team: www.jessacawillis.com/ARC

<u>Social Media</u>
And last but not least, if you'd like to stay connected, you can find my social media links here:
https://linktr.ee/jessaca_with_an_a

Check out the Primordials of Shadowthorn series—the prelude to Blood & Magic Eternal—on Amazon

504

But when the Prince discovers his sister is in danger, he flees the palace with her, leaving Sinisa with only two options: journey through the mortal realm to find and slay her mark, or face the consequences of returning to the underrealm empty-handed.

It's no choice at all. She has come too far to stop now.

Besides, no one can outrun a Reaper... Or can they?

~Check out the Reapers of Veltuur Trilogy on Amazon~

Jessaca is a fantasy writer with an inclination toward the dark, epic, and romantic sub-genres. She draws inspiration from books like Nevernight & ACOTAR, videogames like Dark Souls III, and television shows like Game of Thrones and The Witcher. She is a self-proclaimed nerd who loves cosplay, video games, and comics, and if you live in the PNW, you just might see her at one of the local comic conventions dressed in one of her favorite RWBY cosplays!

www.ingramcontent.com/pod-product-compliance
Lightning Source LLC
Chambersburg PA
CBHW070540310726

48982CB00010B/1420/J